Brides of
IDAHO

Brides of
IDAHO

3-in-1 Historical Romance Collection

LINDA FORD

BARBOUR BOOKS
An Imprint of Barbour Publishing, Inc.

Contents

Glory and the Rawhide Preacher

Chapter 1

His name was Levi. Levi Powers. Twenty-six years of age. A man intent on fulfilling his vow. He pulled to a halt in front of the saloon, tugged his worn cowboy hat low on his head, and swung from the back of his mount, landing neatly on his feet. This was where he intended to start.

His boots thudded on the wooden sidewalk in front of the swinging doors. He strode inside, grabbed a chair, stood on it, and called, "Would you care to put away your whiskey and cards for a few minutes and hear from God's Word?"

The place grew quiet. Deadly quiet. Then several tipped chairs dropped to all fours with the crack of a rifle shot.

He studied each and every face. The hardened men, the eager boys who probably shaved once a week, the anxious greenhorns, and—

He stared. A woman. A young woman. A very pretty young woman who flashed him a bold grin. Not the sort of woman who frequented saloons. No tight, revealing bodice. No rouged cheeks. From what he could see as she sat behind a table, she wore a tanned leather vest. A battered cowboy hat hung down her back. Her sorrel-colored hair was bound in a braid as thick as a woman's wrist.

He jerked his gaze away, but three faces away it returned to her. She leaned her elbows on the table and regarded him as steadily as he did her. Not the least bit ladylike at all. And yet. . .yet. . .he felt trapped by her insolent beauty.

What was she doing in here? What sort of town opened its saloon to women? Apart from the usual crude types? Right then and there he knew he had his job cut out for him.

He forced his attention away from her, angled his body so he wasn't able to look directly at her, and opened the Bible. He had long thought about the words he would say when he found the place where he would start his work. And yet he paused, momentarily forgetting his plan.

Thankfully, the pages fell open at the chosen place. "I'm reading from the Gospel of John, chapter ten, verse ten, where Jesus says, 'I am come that they might have life, and that they might have it more abundantly.' My name is Levi Powers, and I am here to tell you about this abundant life Jesus offers. I'll be available anytime, day or night, if you want to talk. Otherwise, I will be walking the streets, stopping where I see people and telling them the good news. And Sundays, I'll hold services."

One bleary-eyed patron raised a hand. "Mister Preacher, where you gonna hold these here services? Ain't no church." He gave what Levi expected was supposed to be a laugh, but it sounded more like a choked sigh.

"I'll preach in a field until I find suitable quarters for a church." He closed his Bible, signifying he was done.

The room was quiet. Someone coughed. Slowly the noise grew, though not to the deafening level it had been when he stepped inside. He understood his presence made some of them uncomfortable, and he strode toward the door, allowing his gaze to slide to the woman, rest there only a second before he schooled it away. Not the sort of woman a preacher man should be admiring.

She nodded briefly as if acknowledging his thoughts then pushed her chair back and rose.

He hurried out. Heard her booted feet following and waited for her on the rough-board walk.

She dragged a half-drunk man at her side who staggered wildly when she drew up to give Levi an insolent stare.

"Ma'am." He suddenly didn't know what to say, but he hadn't come here to run from challenges of any kind. "Sort of surprised to see a lady in the saloon." He was even more surprised she wore form-fitting, faded brown britches. He shifted his gaze upward, crashed into her gaze. Her eyes impaled him. Light brown, almost golden. Hard to look at. Impossible to pull away from.

She leaned back on her heels and hooked her thumbs through her belt loops. "Did you?"

"Did I what?"

"See a lady." She didn't wait for his reply. "I don't claim to be a lady. I do what suits me without regard for silly rules."

"I see." Though in truth he didn't. What rules did she consider silly? Her words had the same ringing tone Matthew's voice carried as he rode away from their grandparents' farm and straight into trouble. He perceived she was another rebel. This was confirmation of his calling to this town. This woman needed redemption for sure.

"Mr. Powers. . .or Preacher Powers, or whatever you've a hankering to be called. . .I got no objection to hearing a sermon now and then. Certainly no objection to you reading the scriptures to us, but don't be thinking you can make rules for everyone to follow. Might be some will gladly do so. But I won't be one of them." She grabbed the elbow of the swaying wide-eyed man she'd dragged from the saloon, paused to give his horse the once-over. "Yours?"

"Mine."

Something flickered through her eyes before she dragged her friend down the street.

"Glory, you sure are a sharp-tongued woman," the drunk muttered. "But I don't mind." He threw an arm across the woman's shoulders, almost upsetting them both.

Levi took a step forward, thinking to extricate her from the man.

The squeak of the swinging doors signaled another person's arrival. "I wouldn't interfere if I was you."

Levi ground to a halt, though it took a great deal of effort.

"That girl could chew up a man like you and spit him out without a thought."

"Like me?" He turned to face the speaker. A man like so many he'd seen—his face work hardened and full of weary discouragement.

"Allow me to introduce myself. Claud Wagoner." They shook hands. "You really going to start Sunday services?"

"I am." And so much more. He'd made a bargain with God and intended to keep it. *God, You work on Matt, and I'll work for You out here.*

Claud shook his head. "You're lucky Bull Johnson is away. He owns this saloon and wouldn't take kindly to you disrupting his business. If ya know what I mean."

"I expect I do."

"Bull would not make a good enemy."

Levi snorted. "Never known of a good enemy." His gaze had shifted back down the street where the girl and the drunk turned the corner and disappeared from view. "What's her name?"

"Who?" The man followed the direction of Levi's stare. "Oh her.

11

That's Glory Hamilton."

Glory. An unusual name for an unusual woman.

"Best you stay away from her. She's not the sort a preacher man should spend time with."

He had no intention of spending time with any woman except for the sake of turning her feet to the right path, but he wondered why Claud should have such an opinion and asked.

"She is wild as the winter wind. Why, she's a horse trader."

This Glory just got more and more interesting. No, that wasn't the word he meant. It was only that he saw clearly she was part of the reason the Lord had directed him to this place.

Levi tipped the brim of his hat in a good-bye gesture and gathered up the reins of his horse. He didn't bother to swing into the saddle but led the horse down the street giving each building careful study.

A mercantile that appeared to be doing a brisk business, a freight office, likewise busy, a barber shop also offering baths. He considered the two bits it would cost and decided he would save his money and take a dip in some quiet place in the river. There was a lawyer office and a hardware store with an array of shovels, picks, and buckets displayed in the window. The sign to his left read HOTEL, but it was like no hotel he'd ever seen. A rough building. The two windows on the front were missing panes. The door hung crookedly. Flies buzzed around a bucket, and even across the street he could smell the contents. A glance as he passed revealed rotting piles of garbage to the side of the building and he shuddered. He guessed the rooms would be no more appealing. And knowing the sort of person who would stay there rather than outdoors in the clean air, he knew it wasn't a place where a man could expect to wake up with his belongings still in his possession.

He thought of the business close to the ferry. Bonners Ferry Stopping House offering home-cooked meals. That place looked a lot more appealing as temporary quarters. He'd also noticed a small shop offering to shoe a horse. He'd make his way back there first chance he got and ask to borrow the man's tools so he could do a little work on his mount's hooves.

He came to the end of the businesses with modest houses tucked behind them and continued on, passing scattered shacks farther along the road.

A hunched figure trudged toward him. A shriveled woman struggling under the weight of an armload of wood.

He trotted toward her and dismounted as he reached her side. "Ma'am. Let me help."

She resisted his offer to carry the wood. "It's mine. Leave me alone."

"I only want to help. Let me carry it for you."

Reluctantly she released it and gave him serious study up and down his length. "You new here?"

"Yes ma'am." He gave his name and lifted his hat. "Where to?"

She pointed to a shack that looked like it would leave in a good wind.

He shortened his stride to match her slow shuffle and wondered if each step hurt. She was bent forward forty degrees.

They reached the front of the hovel and she stopped. "Here's good enough. Just put it down. I'll take it the rest of the way."

"I'll take it to your kitchen."

The sound grating from her throat was neither disgust nor amusement yet somehow both. Then she shouldered open the door. It scratched against the rough wood floor.

He stepped inside to see four bare walls he could touch with his fingers without moving. It was nothing more than a primitive entryway. He stepped through the second doorway to a room not much larger. In it stood a stove made out of an old barrel. A rough piece of lumber nailed to the wall served as table; sawed-off logs provided seating. A battered wooden bucket and two old tin cans made up the rest of the items. "You live here?" He managed to keep the shock from his voice. Barely. The place was hardly big enough to shelter a horse in a bad storm. He could see light through the cracks between the boards forming the walls, and he suspected from the damp smell that the roof leaked.

"So long as no one objects."

He couldn't imagine why anyone would, but here was another being needing his help. Levi prayed for wisdom on how to deal with this without offending the woman. As he considered his options, he arranged the wood near the stove. Far as he could tell, the woman had no food. He didn't need to glance out the window to see if she had a garden. It was too early in the season for anything but a few greens. His job finished, he brushed his hands. "Ma'am, I'm here to preach the Gospel. Would you like me to read from the Bible?"

She sat cross-legged on the floor.

He did the same, facing her.

"Name's Ina Kish—the widow Kish. I used to be a churchgoing

woman. But there's no church here."

"I aim to change that."

"Don't know if there's many Christian people around here. I've seen no evidence of it."

He hadn't either but refrained from saying so. "Then I guess my work is cut out for me." He always carried a small New Testament in his vest pocket. He pulled it out and read several verses, noting the tears glistening in the woman's eyes. A few minutes later, after a prayer with her, he departed.

But he didn't head back to Bonners Ferry. He rode along the valley until he found and shot some prairie grouse. He dressed them and took them back to the widow Kish.

Tears again sprang to her eyes. "You are a godsend."

"Thank you."

"It is me should be thanking you."

He touched the brim of his hat as he backed away. Her words of thanks were affirmation for his task. Already he'd found two people to help—both women. One who welcomed his help. The other, he sensed, would not.

Where did the horse-trading Glory hang her hat? She looked like she could provide her own game probably better than many men. But he felt her rebellion like a canker sore under his tongue.

He would make it a priority to locate her and find a way to break through that rebellious spirit.

Glory didn't slow her steps until she rounded the corner out of sight of the preacher. She wanted nothing to do with a cowboy intent on reforming others. No man would ever tell her what to do. No woman either, for that matter, unless it was one of her sisters.

She realized she held Toby by the elbow and practically dragged him after her, although half the time he dragged her to the right as he lost his balance.

"Glory, what's the hurry?" He struggled for breath. "Whatcha running from?"

She stopped and gave him a chance to right himself. "I never run from anything. You ought to know that."

Toby nodded. "You're pretty tough. Especially for a girl."

She let it pass.

He shifted his gaze to their back trail. "I thought I heard him say he was a preacher."

He didn't expect an answer, and Glory didn't provide one.

"Sure never seen a preacher like him before."

"That's a fact." She made a movement suggesting they should continue on their way, and Toby started again. Steady enough now to walk on his own. That meant she had found him before he got seriously drunk.

"Did you see his vest?"

Of course she'd seen his vest. Hand-tooled leather with Concho-style front leather ties and a fringed yoke. She'd seen a whole lot more. The thickness of his fawn-colored hair that couldn't be disguised or hidden by his hat. His square jaw that said better than words he meant business. The way his blue eyes slanted in hard assessment when he studied Glory. "I don't care what the man thinks."

"But his vest. No preacher wears a vest like that. Nor a hat like that either." Toby ground to a halt and struggled to retain his balance. "Say, I bet he ain't even a preacher. Seems I saw a poster once about a crook who wore a fancy vest. They call him the Rawhide Kid. I heard he pretends to be a nice guy then steals everything but the ground beneath your feet."

Rawhide Kid. Suited him better than preacher. Toby might have something in his rambling observations. What better disguise than posing as a preacher? It would fool a lot of people, especially when he read from the Bible in that deep ringing voice.

But she wasn't one to be fooled by well-spoken words or a rumbling voice that no doubt made others think of thunder rolling from heaven, the very voice of God even. Nope. Not Glory Hamilton. If she had learned one thing in her nineteen years it was to trust only what she could build and hold in her own two hands. Figuratively speaking.

She'd be keeping a close eye on the rawhide preacher. "Come on, Toby. You need to get some wood for Joanna."

"Aw."

"That's the agreement. Remember? You help Joanna around the stopping house in exchange for meals." Glory and her sisters, Joanna and Mandy, ran the stopping house. Joanna was the cook. Mandy, the hunter. Glory. . .well, Glory did whatever was needed unless she could get Toby to do it.

"I can work for Bull, and he gives me cash."

"Which you promptly give back to him in the saloon. Good deal for

Bull. Not such a good deal for you."

Toby muttered something about it feeling good right now.

Glory chose to ignore the comment. If Toby didn't do the agreed-upon work, Joanna would be after Glory to do it, and Glory had other things to do with her time. She managed to steer Toby to the stopping house and turned him over to Joanna, who issued instructions to get firewood and water, take out ashes, and empty the slop pail.

Toby explained to Joanna about the man in the saloon. "Said he was a preacher."

"Bonners Ferry could use a preacher and a church, too," Joanna said, slanting a pointed look at Glory.

"He can preach his heart out. Won't change me."

Joanna sighed. "You're always so defensive. No one said anything about changing you. But comes a time in all of our lives when we have to stop running from life and simply learn to trust God with it."

"I trust God."

"Trusting covers a lot of things."

"I hate it when you get all philosophical. You got something to say, come right out and say it."

Joanna handed the bucket of vegetable peelings to Toby and waved him away. "All I'm saying is. . ." She shrugged. "I don't know. Never mind. I suppose I mean for myself more than anyone else. Where are you off to?"

Glory laughed. "Who said I am."

Joanna lifted one eyebrow in mocking amusement. "Let's see. Could it be because you keep shifting from one foot to the other and glancing toward the door? Or maybe because I know you well enough I just know?"

"Probably both. I want to check on those horses I have up the hill."

"You'll be back for supper?"

"Of course. And I'll wash the dishes and sweep the floor and whatever else needs doing."

"Good. Then go see to your horses."

Glory reached for the door.

"Glory."

Her sister's voice stopped her.

"Be careful. Some of those horses you rescue are mean."

"They have reason to be." She too often saw horses neglected and abused. When she did, she tried to buy them from the owners and nurse them back to health, train them to be good mounts, and sell them to men who would treat them right. She'd keep them all if she could, but it wasn't practical, and selling them provided her with funds to buy more to help.

"I'm not saying they don't. But you are up there alone. I worry."

"No need. I never take chances. You know that."

Another quirk of Joanna's telltale eyebrow. "I certainly do."

Glory shook her head in bewilderment. Joanna seemed set on talking in riddles or raising questions she didn't intend to answer. And Glory had no time for such nonsense. She left the stopping house, crossed to the shop where she ran a small farrier business and kept her current mount.

The beautiful palomino was nothing but a bag of bones when she rescued him. The gelding now glistened with health and had turned out to be a smooth ride. It was one of the times she thought seriously of keeping an animal. Indeed, unless she was offered a good price, she wouldn't let him go.

She threw on a saddle and swung to the animal's back. "Come on, Pal. Let's go visit your friends."

In order to reach the place, she had to ride back through town. Past the saloon where the rawhide preacher had hitched his black horse. A beautiful horse. But the horse no longer waited patiently. The pair must have moved on. She tried to put them from her mind. But instead, the piercing gaze of the man seemed to glaze her thoughts to the exclusion of all else.

Rawhide Kid.

A desperado. A criminal. A confidence man.

Not above using the Bible as a means of portraying the picture he wanted to create.

Yet. . .

She jerked her thoughts away from how he'd boldly walked into the saloon and opened the Holy Word. *Course if Bull had been there, he might have gone out on his ear.*

As if her thoughts didn't have enough trouble erasing him, she glimpsed a big black horse in the woods. Had to be the rawhide preacher man. What subversive thing was he up to? Perhaps he had partners in crime hiding, awaiting the chance to steal from the good citizens of Bonners Ferry.

She pulled her own horse off the path and dismounted, hiding as best she could behind a patch of trees to watch.

In a minute, he broke from the trees and sauntered up the trail.

She let him pass, then, keeping to the leaf-protected ground at the edge of the trail, followed at a safe distance behind him.

He turned in at the shack where Widow Kish lived, swung off the horse without touching the saddle horn, and landed neatly on his feet. He reached behind him and lifted off two dressed birds and carried them inside.

She squatted in the dappled shadows and waited. If he had harmed the widow and taken possession of her shack. . .well, he would have to answer to her. The smell of woodsmoke drew her attention to the battered piece of stovepipe poking through the roof. Smoke billowed upward. She waited.

Then the door sqawked open and he stepped out into the sun. Bareheaded, his hat in his hand, the sun glistening in his hair.

"I can't thank you enough." The widow patted his hand.

"My pleasure." He jammed his hat on, swung into the saddle in one swift movement, and reined toward town.

Glory remained where she was, watching until he rode down the hill and out of sight. Still she didn't move. What was he doing? Was he playing some kind of game intended to make everyone trust him?

He'd soon learn Glory Hamilton didn't trust so easily.

She pushed to her feet, pulled Pal back to the path, and got on his back with a lot less grace and ease than the preacher did. The fact did nothing to ease her suspicions.

A few minutes later she arrived at the temporary corrals she'd built for her horses, and her mood immediately improved. Animals were so uncomplicated. Treat them right and they rewarded with loyalty. Most wanted to please, and those that didn't learned the joys of obeying given enough patience and kindness. She knew how to give plenty of both.

One big gray gelding snorted and reared away as soon as she approached. He would take a long time to realize she meant him no harm. But at least his wounds had healed nicely.

"Don't worry, big guy. I'm not going to rush you." She threw handfuls of oats from her saddlebag to each of the horses. Big Gray wouldn't go near his treat until she backed away, but every day she gained ground. "Won't be long until you're eating out of my hand." He didn't snort and act up at her voice anymore.

She spent the better part of the afternoon with the animals. This place was perfect. Close enough to town she could tend the horses each day. High enough to not suffer from the spring floods. There were lots of trees, a stream that ran throughout the summer, open sunny patches of grass, and a view that filled her with pleasure. Too bad she didn't own it. But no one had objected to her using it, and until someone did. . . She hoped when the time came she would be able to buy this bit of land.

It was time to leave unless she wanted Joanna to send some young buck in search of her. Joanna had done it before. She'd do it again. She took her role as eldest sister seriously.

Glory caught up to Pal, threw the saddle on again, and rode back to the stopping house. Basins of water and towels were set out in the lean-to entryway, and Glory stopped to wash off the smell of horse as best she could.

A rumble of voices came from the long dining room. Sounded like a full house. They usually served about twenty travelers and a handful of regulars. Which meant lots of dishes to wash. There'd be no getting out of it today. She'd already promised Joanna. Besides, it was the least Glory could do. Joanna did the bulk of the work, never complaining. Mandy spent long hours out in the woods keeping the place supplied with fresh meat. Glory had to contribute in some way, even if it was drudge work like washing dishes and cleaning floors.

She dried her hands and swiped them over her hair making sure it was relatively free of grass then stepped into the noisy room, giving a quick glance around to see who was in attendance. Her gaze skidded to a halt at the man sitting at the far corner of the table. Levi Powers.

His eyes met hers across the distance, and at the way they narrowed, she knew he was as surprised to see her as she was to see him. And she felt a silent challenge as his gaze swept over her dungarees and back to her face, checking her hair.

She clenched her fists at her sides to keep from brushing her hands over her hair again. Nothing he did would make her ashamed or embarassed about who she was and how she chose to dress. Nothing he did or said would make her change.

Nothing.

She spun away and marched into the kitchen, her boots ringing with more force than normal. She grabbed two heaping bowls from the service table. "What's he doing here?" Her voice was harsh, accusing, as if it was Joanna's fault.

Joanna chuckled. "You'll have to be more specific. At my count there are twenty-one men in there."

"The preacher. Why is he here?"

Joanna lifted one shoulder dismissively. "Because he paid me to eat here. Isn't that what we do? Feed people who pay?"

Glory choked back her protest. Yes, it was what they did. The few dollars that were her share of the profit filled a tin can. Slowly. Someday it would be enough to buy her precious piece of land. "Of course it's what we do."

She carried the bowls into the dining room, put them down, and chose a spot on the long bench at the far corner of the room from Mr. Powers. She spared him the briefest glare. Let him think what he wanted of her. If he even thought of her.

Joanna took her place at the end of the table, close to Powers. Mandy found room on a crowded bench next to Toby. Joanna signaled quiet. "We are a Christian family and always say a blessing before the meal."

Glory allowed herself a flicker of her eyes toward Powers and was pleased to see his surprise. *Just goes to show you can't judge people,* she silently crowed.

Joanna continued. "Today we have a special guest at the table. Mr. Powers. Preacher Powers. He's going to start services here in Bonners Ferry. Now I know most of you won't be here past the night, but for those of you who are, I'm sure you're as happy as I that we're going to have a church."

Glory kept her gaze glued to the tin plate in front of her. She wasn't pleased at all. Besides, who—other than himself—said he was a preacher? Rawhide Kid for all they knew.

Joanna was still speaking. "Mr. Powers, we'd be pleased if you'd ask the blessing tonight." She lifted a hand toward him in invitation.

Powers pushed to his feet and looked at each one around the table.

Glory refused to meet his glance. She demanded a whole lot more than his say-so to believe he was a preacher and nothing more, nothing less.

Chapter 2

L evi struggled to his feet. The heavy bench, held in place by so many bodies, pressed against his calves. He half welcomed the discomfort, nailing him to reality as it did.

He'd been some surprised to learn the Bonners Ferry Stopping House was run by three sisters. But the smell of supper convinced him to stay. He'd met Miss Joanna when he paid for his meal, noted she wore a split skirt under her big white apron. He'd met Miss Mandy as she skittered away when he went to wash up. Miss Mandy carried a dozen prairie grouse and hung them on a nail. She wore baggy pants and a big slouch hat. So he shouldn't have been surprised when Miss Glory slid to an empty spot at the table.

Except he was. Somehow he thought she'd be hunkered down by a campfire someplace deep in the woods. Exactly why he thought such a thing baffled him. Sure, she looked a little rough around the edges, and her gaze, as she glared at him, suggested she didn't much care what people thought. Him in particular. But just the same, his assumptions were foolish. Of course she had family. Likely friends. The young man she'd dragged from the saloon sat further along the bench. Finding her in a saloon, befriending a man who had been partaking, he supposed his mistaken idea came from evidence she herself had provided.

He shepherded his thoughts back to his purpose. "Folks, I'm here to bring God's Word into this area. I'm available if you want to hear it read, or talk about His love, or pray. Feel free to come to me at any time. I'm looking for a suitable place to hold Sunday services. I expect we'll meet outdoors for a few weeks. Now let us pray." He bowed his head and asked God's blessing on the food, thanking God for His many mercies.

For several minutes after he sat down, the food was passed, plates loaded, and people put their attention to eating before they began talking. Much of the conversation centered on the trail ahead. Most of those present were headed for the Kootenais to look for gold. Hope and desperation hung like flags over the table.

Levi listened to the man on his right tell how he'd sold everything and left his wife and children with her parents. "I aim to make enough to buy myself a piece of land and build a big house."

"And if you don't?" It always bothered him that pursuing dreams without considering reality so often led to desperate actions.

The man shuddered. "I don't think I could continue to face life."

Levi had let his gaze and attention wander to Glory, who was in animated conversation with the man next to her. What had her so enthused? But his attention returned to the man at his side, and he dismissed all other distractions in his concern for the confession from the man's lips. "If you find yourself in such a situation, I urge you to pray and ask God to provide direction to something productive. There are always alternatives to desperation." Just as there were always alternatives to crime, though he didn't voice the thought.

Suddenly everyone pushed back as if given a signal. He hadn't been watching. Perhaps Miss Joanna had indicated the meal was over.

She spoke now. "For those planning to spend the night, the room will be ready by eight. Feel free to return then and claim a spot. In the meantime, you are welcome to make yourself comfortable outside and enjoy the sunshine."

Levi had noticed benches outside against the walls of the stopping house and guessed she meant those.

Joanna continued. "Ladies"—she referred to the four female guests— "you're welcome to stay indoors if you prefer."

Mandy strode outside, lifted the birds from the nail where she'd left them, and disappeared behind a shed in the far corner. Levi suspected she meant to dress them ready to cook.

He barely got his feet under him when Glory started to gather up the tin plates with a good deal of racket. She carried them into the kitchen and dropped them into a basin of water.

He made his way to the door.

A great amount of clattering came from the kitchen.

He emerged into the slanted evening sun and leaned against the warm wall.

The young man he'd seen with Glory sidled up to him. "Hi, I'm Toby."

He shook hands with the younger man.

"You really a preacher?"

"I am."

"Where all you preached?"

"Several places." He named two towns in the Dakotas where he'd done what he could and moved on, ever wanting to do more.

"So whatcha doing here? This here is a tight ship, as my pa would say."

Levi didn't know if he meant the town or the stopping house and didn't care to discuss it. He had his work cut out for him whether a kid who got drunk in the middle of the afternoon thought so or not. "Where's your pa?" Seemed Toby ought to be with a parent still.

"Back home in Indiana."

From the open door came more clattering. Washing tin plates seemed to be a noisy affair.

Joanna, working in the dining room, called out, "Glory, could you keep the noise down a mite? My ears are hurting."

Levi grinned deep inside. Seems something was annoying Miss Glory to the point of taking it out on innocent dishes. Could be one of the reasons the stopping house used tin plates.

Toby leaned back against the wall, shoulder to shoulder with Levi, by all looks, intent on a long chin-wag. Well, it was what Levi had invited. Part of what he'd vowed to do. The words he'd said to God on his knees guided his every decision. *Lord, You work on Matt where he is, and I'll work for You out here.*

"I was headed for the Kootenai gold fields. Sort of ran out of steam about here."

Levi read between the lines. Ran out of money. Ran into a saloon.

"The buffalo gals sort of helped me out, if you know what I mean."

Levi did. "Buffalo gals?"

Toby tipped his head toward the door. "That's what they call them three."

"How so?"

Toby shrugged. "Can't say. Never asked anyone. It just is."

It just is. Seems a lot of life was like that. No reason for why things were. No reason for parents dying and leaving two boys orphaned. No reason for one choosing to follow God, the other choosing to run wild. Except—Levi's teeth clenched of their own accord—he believed things could be different. If someone would show kindness to the hurting, reach out a hand to those in need. . .

It was what his task was. He'd do it to the best of his ability and trust

God to do His share where Levi couldn't.

Another man, dressed in a suit better fitted for sitting behind a desk, edged toward Levi. He waited for a break in the conversation. "Can I talk to you?"

"Certainly."

"It's kind of private."

"Of course." He unwound himself from the wall and followed the man away from the crowd toward a place where they appeared to be alone.

The man looked around to be sure before he spoke. "Preacher, would you pray for me?"

"By all means. What shall I pray?" He listened to the man's story, read some encouraging scriptures, and prayed.

By then the sun was setting, sending flares of red, orange, and pink across the Kootenai River. He'd planned to set up camp in a quiet spot among the trees, but now it was too late to find a decent spot. And it seemed he could best live up to his purpose if he stayed closer to town and hung around the stopping house, which practically burst with people.

Besides, if he stayed, perhaps he could talk to Glory and find out what made her eyes glint like sun off a rifle barrel every time he glanced at her. Seemed the gal had a mighty big grudge fueling her audaciousness.

Levi had left his saddle and bedroll in the lean-to, which served as luggage area for all those at the stopping house. He gathered up his bedding and headed inside. He dropped the necessary coins in Joanna's palm and looked about the dining room. The table had been pushed against the wall, the benches tucked underneath, leaving plenty of floor space. The ladies had disappeared into the far room where two big beds allowed them a measure of comfort and privacy.

"Help yourself." Joanna waved about the room. Where had the other two Hamilton girls disappeared to?

Already several places had been claimed by way of unrolled bedding and sometimes a carpetbag. He chose a spot close to the kitchen door with his back to the wall and sank to the floor. He opened his Bible and began to read. That's when he heard voices from the kitchen and recognized Miss Glory and Miss Mandy.

"I still think we should be trying to find Pa." He knew immediately it was Miss Mandy, whose voice was softer, gentler than Glory's.

"Don't see why. We got a nice situation here."

"He's our pa."

"I know. And how many times have we caught up to him, think we're part of his life, when he up and disappears?"

"Glory, he's just trying to make a living."

"Mandy, you can dream things are the way you wish they were, but they aren't. Truth is, Pa is restless. More concerned with scratching his restless itch than worrying about three daughters. Besides, aren't we big enough to take care of ourselves now?"

Levi listened shamelessly, hearing the harshness in Glory's voice but hearing so much more beneath—a history of pain.

Glory reminded him so strongly of Matt, whose disappointment and frustration had led to his recklessness. If someone had reached out to Matt before it was too late. . .

Thank You, God, for this glimpse, this insight into what makes her tick.

Suddenly Glory stood in the doorway. "You're staying here?"

"Paid my money to your sister." He knew that wasn't what she meant. She simply objected to his presence, but he wouldn't give her the satisfaction of acknowledging it.

She made a protesting noise deep in her throat but didn't voice her disapproval in words. Perhaps because Joanna watched them. Instead, she marched toward the door. "I'm going to check on Pal."

"It's late. Almost dark," Joanna protested.

"I'll go with her," Mandy said.

Glory stopped and planted her hands on her hips, glaring from one sister to the other. "I do not need a nanny. Or a mother. Or a guard. Or. . .or. . ."

Joanna waved her away. "I expect the two of you back soon so I can close the doors."

Exasperation burst from Glory's mouth in an explosive sound, and she tossed her hands in the air in a gesture Levi took as defeat.

He grinned.

She slanted him a glare with the power to straighten his mouth and make him sit up straighter. "I need no one and nothing," she muttered before she strode out the door.

Levi's grin returned as soon as the door closed behind her.

Joanna stepped past him into the kitchen area and settled at the table, entering figures into a big ledger and likely waiting for her younger sisters to return. She left the door between open partway so she could keep an eye on the outer door for more overnight guests.

Many of the men had tucked into their bedrolls already. Several snored loudly.

But Levi sat up, continuing to read by the faint lantern light from the kitchen. He wouldn't settle down until he knew Glory and her sisters were safely in their beds.

∞

Glory steamed after Mandy, hot air burning from her lungs. Why had that man chosen to spend the night at the stopping house? Seems a real preacher would have found a quiet place to sleep.

Like a hundred miles away straight up the tallest mountain.

They reached Glory's shop, and she made a great show of filling Pal's water trough, checking the gate, and examining the inside of her shop. As if someone might have moved in and taken over.

Just like Levi had taken over every spare thought in her head. Oh, how she hated that she couldn't stop thinking of him. "I think I'll go check on the other horses." They didn't need it any more than Pal did, but returning to the stopping house, knowing that man was there made her skin feel too small.

"You can't do that. It's nearly dark already."

"I can do it if I want." She sounded petty and childish but couldn't seem to help it.

"Why are you so angry? It's because of Mr. Powers, isn't it? I saw the way you kept looking at him."

She ignored her sister's questions. They didn't deserve acknowledgment.

"Why does he bother you? He's here to start a church. Seems you should be glad for such a thing."

Glory snorted. "Who says he's a preacher? Besides him. And why should we believe him? He could say he was anything, and we'd have no way of knowing. Does he have papers to prove it?"

"Glory, listen to yourself. We didn't ask Mr. Murray to prove he was a lawyer. No one asked us for proof we could run a stopping house."

"Proof is in the product, I'd say. We run a good clean establishment with satisfying meals and rules about conduct."

"Then I guess Mr. Powers deserves the same consideration. A chance to prove himself."

Glory stared at her sister. Should she tell her of the suspicions? Mention that Toby thought Powers looked like a robber on a wanted poster? "Did you see his vest?"

Mandy grinned. "Sure did. You think he'd sell it?"

Glory rolled her eyes. "Who cares?"

Mandy got a faraway look on her face. "I suppose you noticed how handsome he is."

"Is not."

Mandy's gaze jerked to Glory, disbelief written in every line. "Is too."

Not prepared to argue with her younger sister, Glory simply rolled her head back and forth.

Mandy suddenly crowed and slapped her thighs. "You think he's too good-looking to be a preacher."

Glory favored her sister with a scalding look but utterly failed to curb Mandy's amusement. Finally, unable to stand still for the mockery, she placed a playful punch on Mandy's shoulder.

Mandy immediately turned and cuffed Glory on the side of the head.

This was a familiar game they played, throwing pretend punches, dancing back and forth in mock attack. As usual they ended locked in each other's arms, squirming and laughing.

"I give," Glory called.

It didn't matter who said it first. It was all in fun. They broke apart, grinning at each other.

"Give the man a chance, even if he is too handsome for his own good," Mandy said, throwing her arm across Glory's shoulders as they headed for home.

"Best I can do is try and stay away from him." Though she intended to watch him carefully and wondered how she could do both at the same time.

They quieted as they reached the stopping house, knowing some of their guests would already be asleep, and tiptoed inside to the kitchen.

Joanna sat at the table and closed the ledger as they entered. The three headed toward their quarters beyond—a small bedroom on the far side of the kitchen from the room where their guests slept. Glory brought up the rear, and as they crossed the floor, Levi murmured, "Good night. Sleep well."

Glory broke her stride, struggled to control her annoyance. Then sucked in air and hurried along. How was she to ignore him if he wouldn't let her?

Chapter 3

L evi left after breakfast—a meal eaten in haste as if people were anxious to be on their way.

Glory had pointedly ignored him all through the meal then hurried to the kitchen and disappeared.

What did it matter? He planned to be around a long time. . .or at least as long as it took to accomplish his purpose.

He rode over to the shop to see about trimming Billy Bob's hooves. A sign tacked to the door said OPEN 9 TO NOON. COME BACK THEN. That would be another hour. Time enough to check on the widow Kish.

He detoured into the mercantile and purchased a few supplies then stopped at the hardware store for a new bucket, which he filled at the town pump and carried carefully to the shack on the edge of town. At the door, he saw a basket covered with a bit of rag and folded it back to see four eggs, a loaf of bread, and six potatoes. He covered the basket again and grinned up at the sky, silently thanking God someone else cared about the widow's dire circumstances. Somehow it made him feel he shared the task with a person of like mind.

His knock brought the widow shuffling to the door. He tipped his head to indicate the basket, and she scooped it up and peeked under the cover.

"The Lord provides," she murmured. "Blessed be His name. About once a week I find a basket like this on the step. And now you bring me water from the well. The good Lord says a cup of cold water given in His name is rewarded. I'm sure you'll receive an even greater reward for a whole bucketful."

"It's nice to see you feeling better. Yesterday you looked about ready to lie down and die."

"That's about how I felt, but my faith is renewed."

He spent a few minutes with her. "I'll be back tomorrow." He left feeling she had given him far more than he gave her.

She waved him away. "If you're so all-fired set on helping people, why don't you check on Mr. Phelps? I've not seen him for several days." She led him to the door and pointed out a modest house several yards down the trail toward town.

"I'll do that." He rode to the house, dismounted, and hung the reins over the hitching post. His boots echoed on the wooden steps as he approached the entrance. His knock rattled the door and rang through the house.

No one answered.

He knocked again and called out, "Mr. Phelps? Are you in there?" Still no sound apart from his own voice. He tried the door. It opened and swung inward. The place had a sour, sick smell to it. "Mr. Phelps? Is anyone here?" Did he hear a faint sound through the door to his left? "I'm coming in."

He stepped into a kitchen. A half-eaten meal remained on the table, but the stove was cold, the room slightly dampish from being unheated. If he had to guess, he'd say it had been more than a day or two since the stove had been lit.

A door stood past the stove, and he crossed to it and pushed it open. The sour smell practically knocked him back on his heels. An untidy soiled cot stood in one corner, the covers tossed to the floor in disarray. A wardrobe, a chiffonier, and a wooden rocker completed the furnishings. He half turned away when he noticed the pile of blankets on the floor move. Someone or something was in that mess. He crossed the room in two strides and eased the fabric aside.

A man lay there, as white as death, soiled from head to bottom.

"Mr. Phelps, I assume?"

The man flickered a look of acknowledgment.

"You've been sick." Levi wondered how long the poor man had lain in his own filth. He threw aside the soiled blankets, scooped the man into his arms, and gently laid him on the cot. "You're safe now." He found a clean blanket and covered the man. "I'll clean you up and take care of you."

First thing Mr. Phelps needed was water. Levi hoofed it back to the kitchen, found two empty buckets, and dashed outside to see if the man had a well. He hated the idea of leaving the man to go into town for water, though it wasn't far. But he'd need lots of it.

He looked about, saw no pump, and wished for an alternative to trotting back to town. *God, perhaps You could send help.* He heard the clop of a horse and raced around the house, back to the trail.

Glory headed toward him on a beautiful palomino horse. He'd seen the horse yesterday, standing contentedly in a small pen next to the farrier's shop.

He waved and called.

She reined in. "What are you doing in the middle of the road yelling like a madman?"

"I only—" He didn't have time to argue though he wanted badly to say he only called out for her to stop. "I need help with Mr. Phelps."

"What's wrong? Is he hurt?" Her expression shifted so suddenly it startled him.

"He's ill. I need water and lots of it, but I don't see a pump on his place."

"No, he gets water from the town supply."

"Do you think—?" He held the buckets toward her.

She yanked them from his hands, almost taking his arms off at the shoulders. "Be right back." And she kicked the horse into a run.

Levi stared after her. Talk about mercurial. But he didn't have time to worry about how Glory chose to act. Mr. Phelps needed attention.

Levi found a wood supply, carried an armload to the house, and built a fire. They'd need a barrel of hot water to clean Mr. Phelps and his bedding.

He explained to the man he would have water in a few minutes then gathered up the soiled laundry and hauled it outside. He located a washtub hanging on the side of the house and dumped the bedding into it. As soon as he had water, he would put it to soak.

While he was out, Glory returned. By the time he got to the house, she had filled a pitcher with water, dumped some in the reservoir to heat, and headed back for more water.

Levi shook his head. The woman was as unpredictable as the weather.

He took a glass of water to Mr. Phelps then filled a kettle and set it to boil. He was in the bedroom, sponging Mr. Phelps, when Glory returned, her boots ringing across the floor as she carried water to the reservoir and filled it. "Miss Glory," he called, but she was gone. She returned twice more while Levi cared for Mr. Phelps, found clean bedding and a clean nightshirt, and made the man comfortable.

"Powers," Glory called from the kitchen.

Levi went to the door.

"There's water soaking the bedding. I filled every container in the house. What else do you need?"

Levi stared at her. Water soaked her britches to the knees, and her hat hung down her back as if she had ridden furiously back and forth. Sometimes her wild behavior had a bonus to it. She'd brought more water in less time than any other woman, and many a man, could have done.

"Powers?"

He shook himself back to the task at hand. "The man is weak. He needs something gentle to eat. Don't suppose you know where I could get some chicken soup for him?"

She spared him a look rife with disbelief. "I don't know of anyone with chickens to butcher, and no one around here would kill a laying hen." Then she brightened. "But Joanna had venison stewing on the stove. That'll do." And she was gone so fast Levi could do nothing but stare after her.

One more task to be done. There was no avoiding it. He removed his vest and hung it over the back of a chair, rolled up his sleeves, and went outside to take care of the laundry.

He heard Glory return, but he was up to his elbows in hot sudsy water.

She poked her head out the door, saw what he was doing, and grimaced. "I'll see if Mr. Phelps will take some broth." She closed the door firmly after her.

Levi laughed aloud. "Trade you," he called.

Her muffled voice came from the other side of the door. "Not this time."

He laughed again. She might be wild as an unbroken horse, rebellious and headed for trouble like his brother, but he certainly appreciated her help.

He rinsed the sheets and strung them over the clothesline, dumped out the water, and returned the tub to the nail where he'd found it. As he headed back inside, he heard Glory ride away and stopped to stare out the window, wondering why she hadn't stayed. Was she that anxious to avoid contact with him? Never mind. They would spend time together somehow, somewhere. He'd see to it.

After he checked again on Mr. Phelps, promising to return later in the day, he returned to Widow Kish and reported on her neighbor.

"I'll maybe go on over and check on him myself. Poor man."

Levi thought it might do her a world of good to have something to do. Time now to return to town and attend to Billy Bob's hooves.

Glory's palomino was in the pen again. Must be where she kept her horse. The door to the shop was open, and he stepped inside.

Glory looked up from a book she read. "Yes?" When she saw it was him, her welcome faded. She seemed to struggle a moment with her re-action and schooled it away. "Mr. Phelps okay now?"

"He was resting. Widow Kish said she'd go check on him. Thanks for your help this morning."

"He's one of us, and you're a stranger. Why wouldn't I help him?"

Words of protest raced to his tongue, but he bit them back. Soon enough she'd see he meant to be one of them, too.

"What can I do for you?" Right words, begrudgingly spoken.

"My horse needs his hooves trimmed."

"Great. Put him in the corral, and I'll tend to it."

"Uh." She was a farrier? Not that it surprised him all that much. He had about figured out Glory could do anything she set her mind to, no matter how unconventional. "I was hoping you'd lend me the tools so I can do it myself."

She shook her head. "Don't lend my tools." She stuck a rasp in her back pocket, lifted the nippers in one hand and the hoof knife in the other, and headed for the side door opening to the pen. "Bring him here, and I'll do it."

"'Fraid not. You see, my horse is particular about who gets close to him."

She strode past him to stand looking at Billy Bob. "Nice-looking horse."

"Yup. Many have admired him. Few have ridden him."

She turned, her eyes flaring with interest. "How's that?"

"He's a one-man horse."

Her gaze shifted from Levi to the horse then back to Levi. "Really?" Her voice rang with doubt.

"Take my word for it."

She reached out for Billy Bob's reins and headed for the gate. "He's coming along fine." She closed the gate after the horse and put her tools on a stump obviously used for that purpose. "Now let's get at this job."

"Glory, listen to me." He rushed forward and took the reins before she could do anything more. "He won't let you touch him."

"I never met a horse I couldn't handle." She positioned herself in front of Billy Bob.

Knowing what would happen, Levi pushed the horse away.

Glory turned and glared at him. "Let me do my job."

"Lend me your tools, and I'll do it. If it's the money you're worried about, I'll pay the same as if you did it."

Her chin jutted out. "I don't lend my tools. Now hold his head so I can look at his foot." She again stood, her back to Billy Bob, and leaned over to touch his leg.

Levi moved as fast as he could, but Billy Bob was faster and got a chunk of Glory's rump between his teeth.

Glory yelped and jumped away.

Levi pulled at Billy Bob's head. "Stop it, you blockhead." He kept a firm hold on the animal as he glanced over his shoulder at Glory. "Are you okay?"

The surprise in her face shifted to defiance. "I'm fine. Why didn't you tell me he bites?"

"Glory Hamilton, you have got to be the most cantankerous woman alive. I warned you he wouldn't let you touch him. But you wouldn't listen. Now all of a sudden it's my fault? Just stay away from my horse and give me the hoof pick."

Still she hesitated. All kinds of names came to mind. Foolish. Ornery. Stubborn. Headstrong. "I'll pay. Just let me deal with this."

Reluctantly she handed him the pick.

He bent over and took a hoof and set to cleaning it.

"I see lots of horses who have bad attitudes. Usually there's a reason. What's the story behind Billy Bob's behavior?"

"Bought him off a farmer a few years ago. He was in pretty bad shape. The farmer shouldn't have been allowed to have animals the way he treated them. Hand me the nippers, would you?"

She seemed reluctant to put the tools where he could reach them himself but at least handed him what he needed without further argument, for which he was grateful.

"I tended his wounds and gave him lots of good feed. In return he is as loyal as one could ever ask. Just won't let anyone else touch him. The rasp, please."

She handed it to him and took the nippers in exchange.

Seemed she meant to hang about and watch his every move. He meant to take advantage of it. "Where's your pa?"

"Guess you heard my ma is dead. My pa is off looking for gold in the Kootenais."

He had Billy Bob stand so he could check the hoof was level then took up the next foot. "Why do they call you the Buffalo Gals?"

"Why do you ask? You planning to write a book or something?"

"Don't get all prickly. I'm just making polite conversation."

"No. Polite conversation is, 'How are you? Nice weather we're having, don't you think? Did you enjoy the sunshine yesterday? Suppose we might get rain?'"

He laughed, earning him a scowl. "Do you?"

"Do I what?"

He straightened and grinned at her, undeterred by her annoyance. "Suppose we might get rain?"

She lifted her hands in mock frustration. "Mud just dried up from the spring runoff. I would like to enjoy a few days mud free."

"What about the sunshine? You enjoy it yesterday?"

A smile lifted the corners of her mouth. "Sure did."

Curiosity about how she spent her days crowded all else from his mind. "What did you do?"

"Let's see. I had a race with two men off the ferry who thought they could ride better'n a girl. I proved them wrong." She laughed. "I took care of three horses a man had neglected to trim hooves on for some time." A teasing light flashed across her eyes. "And of course, I spent time in the saloon."

He knew a challenging tone and expression when he saw it. For a moment they did silent battle with their eyes. He decided to let it pass. After all, he had lots of time to find what drove her to defy all sense of what was right as if she resented being a woman. "So why do they call you the Buffalo Gals?"

She blinked, and he knew she'd been expecting him to say something about her being in the saloon. "Because of Pa." She scowled as if she'd said more than she meant to. "Pa was a buffalo hunter, among other things." Before he could ask what other things, she guessed his question and provided an answer. "Gold prospector, Indian hunter, guide, railroad worker—" She drew in a deep breath. "There isn't much he hasn't tried."

He heard a "but" in her voice and waited, but she seemed inclined to say no more and fiddled with the nail nippers. Levi turned his attention back to Billy Bob's feet, but his mind twirled her words about, trying to find the "but" in them. "Sounds like he's a wanderer."

"Suppose so."

"He take you girls with him?"

"When Ma was alive, she followed him, and after she died, we just continued to follow him like she'd taught us."

Again he mulled over her words, looking for the meaning beneath them. "When did your ma die?"

"Eight years ago, when I was eleven."

He put Billy Bob's foot down, done with the hoof trimming, and studied Glory. She stared off into the distance, and Levi wondered if she even remembered he was there. Was this the pain she tried to kill with her outrageous behavior?

He shifted his gaze to the end of her shop, saw a FOR RENT sign. Saw the flicker of red gingham at a window next to the sign, caught a glimpse of a table and stove. Let his gaze go further, to the blue sky, the distant purple mountains.

But what he saw was inside his heart. The way Matt had run from the pain of their parents' deaths. His refusal to follow any rules—those laid out by their grandparents who took them in and gave them a home or those made by man. And look where it had led him.

Levi felt the same angry desperation in Glory as if she, like Matt, didn't know how to deal with the way life had turned out. He feared her path would take her perilously close to the same destination it had for Matt—a prison sentence. *God, I'm here to do Your work in Bonners Ferry, and I trust You to do Your work in Matt's prison cell.* "Glory, you can't fix your disappointment in life by defying all the rules."

Her gaze hit him with the blast of a blacksmith's fire. "Who appointed you judge and jury of me? Besides, I am not disappointed with life." Her laugh was bitter. "Shows what you know." She spun on her heels. "Pal, come." The horse trotted over to her. She swung up on his bare back and guided him toward the gate where she leaned over to unhook it and throw it open. "Put the tools away. Leave your money on the table." And she kicked her horse into a gallop, clinging to his back without saddle or bridle, like some kind of wild Indian.

Levi stared after her, his throat tight. It was dangerous to ride in such a fashion. But he understood she cared nothing for the dangers involved. Whether or not she knew it, she was trying to outrun some kind of pain. But he'd pushed too hard, too soon, and now he'd lost ground that would take precious time to regain.

∽

Glory didn't allow Pal to slacken his pace until they reached the spot where her other horses munched on grass.

Three of them whinnied at her approach and ran toward the fence to greet her. Big Gray headed for the far side of the pen. The other two only lifted their heads to watch her.

She'd left in such a huff she'd neglected to bring oats for them. "I'll bring your treat next time, for sure." She enjoyed talking to all of the horses and giving them attention. Big Gray wouldn't let her near without oats.

She sank down in the warm grass and leaned her back to a tree. Powers was so annoying. Unsettling. She'd been surprised twice by his willingness to help those in need. Of course, what better way to give people the impression he was a preacher. But shouldn't he preach, maybe try and close down the saloon, instead of rolling up his sleeves and washing laundry?

She allowed herself a grin at the thought of his laboring over the washtub. For a moment, she'd almost liked him. Or at least, respected him. And then he got all. . .all. . . Well shoot, she didn't even know how to describe it. Preachy. Judgmental. And none of his business in the first place. Or the last.

She would do what she wanted so long as she broke no laws. And not because, as he seemed to think, she was disappointed with life. She loved life. She raised her arms to the sky and whooped. Life was good. Made for enjoyment. And she intended to enjoy it as never before.

Joanna had once taken them all to a circus with coins handed to her by their pa. They'd watched a man in tights do trick riding. It looked like so much fun. Joanna had noted her excitement, and the moment Glory opened her mouth to say she was going to do that, Joanna had grabbed her by the arm. "Pa holds me responsible for you and Mandy. If either of you gets hurt, it will be on my head. Promise you won't try such foolishness."

At first Glory had refused and tried to squirm away, but Joanna had a grip like a vise and wouldn't let her go until she promised.

But that was when Glory was a child. Joanna was no longer responsible for Glory. She answered to no one but herself and God.

She'd learned several of the riding tricks. Pal had turned out to be such a trustworthy mount, she had a great deal of fun standing on his back while they raced down the trail. It always made her heart beat fast. It was exhilarating. She had done the death drag several times. At first, it frightened her to see the ground so close to her head as she hung from the saddle by one leg, but conquering her fear, gaining confidence, was worth every risk.

An idea burst into full bloom. One of her horses was proving to be gentle and easy to train. She'd stood on his back and ridden around the corral. If she worked with him and Pal together, she might be able to have some real fun riding them both side by side, standing with one foot on each back. No time like the present.

She caught up the horse she had in mind—a beautiful blue roan that should have been treated as the special animal it was. She'd decided to call him Blue Boy. When she got through with him, anyone would be able to touch him. Not like that stupid horse of Preacher Powers. If he was a preacher. She sure wasn't convinced of it.

A glance at the sky later revealed she'd been out there for hours. Joanna would be wondering if she meant to help with the chores, and likely Toby needed dragging from the saloon before he could get falling-down liquored up.

She rode back to town, satisfied with the afternoon, and jumped from Pal's back in front of the saloon, glancing to the right and the left and over her shoulder. No sign of Powers. Annoyed with herself that she'd let him make her feel guilty, she pushed the swinging doors open and strode in.

Toby nursed a bottle.

She wondered if it was his first. But it was definitely his last. "Come on, Tobe. Time to leave."

He drained the bottle and wiped his mouth on his sleeve and gave her a bleary-eyed look bordering on defiance.

"Toby, I need your help." She'd long ago learned to make him think he did her a favor by leaving. She grabbed his hand and urged him to his feet.

He staggered, but she steadied him. It was her fault he was so far gone. She'd stayed with the horses too long.

Gently, she guided him to the door, swung the panels open with her hip, and half dragged Toby through them. Her attention on keeping him going in a straight line, she wasn't watching where she went and bumped into someone holding the door ajar. "Sorry." She spared the man a glance and instantly her apology died. Powers. Could she never escape his challenging stare?

She gave him silent defiance for a full ten seconds then turned back to Toby and navigated him toward the stopping house, Pal in their wake. She had done nothing wrong. No reason she should feel guilty just because a man who called himself a preacher commented about the presence of a lady in the saloon. Like she'd told him, she was no lady. Following Pa from one frontier place to the next wild town had taught her to be otherwise.

Besides, who wanted to dress frilly and silly? Pretend to be weak and helpless so a man could run to her rescue? Not Glory Hamilton, that's for sure. She needed no man to rescue her or take care of her.

Somewhere in the back of her mind she remembered how Ma had tried to maintain a real home wherever they went. Joanna had taken over after Ma's death and did a fine job of being a mother. If she and Toby didn't get home and attend to their share of the chores mighty quick, Glory would be reminded in a very firm way that Joanna could reduce her to feeling like a child. "Hurry up, Toby. We're late."

He sucked in air. It seemed to clear his head or perhaps made him burn off some of the alcohol.

They reached the stopping house. Because they were late, Glory helped Toby carry in firewood. She intended to fill the box and get back outdoors before her sister could comment, but Joanna stopped her before she made her escape. "Glory, I need your help to run this place. But you know that."

"I'm sorry. I got busy with the horses."

Joanna sighed. "I figured as much, but it's a lot of work cleaning the place and cooking for a crew."

Glory nodded. "I'm sorry. I'll not do it again." She really didn't mean to leave Joanna with her share of the work, and she regretted she had. Life could be so complicated, and all because she'd taken time to do what she enjoyed most.

She grabbed up the ash bucket and dashed back outside. Joanna had set a sack of potatoes outside with knives and a big pot. Glory sat down on a rough stool, Toby at her side, and they quickly began to peel the potatoes.

"I saw you talking to Powers last night. You learn anything about the Rawhide Preacher?"

"Rawhide Kid," he corrected then paused and chortled, his foggy brain connecting his thoughts. "Oh, I get it. You mean because. . .

Rawhide Preacher. I like it."

Glory guided his brain back to her question. "Did you learn anything?"

"He said he worked in a few towns as a preacher." He named them.

Glory had never heard of them, but that didn't mean anything. Towns sprang up in a matter of days where there had once been nothing but grass and trees. And she had no way of keeping up. Never had time to read a newspaper. And even if she had, the ones they got were old news.

Toby stopped peeling to explore his thoughts. "Course he could be lying. I've met many a good liar in my time."

"Me, too. Doesn't pay to believe everything a person says."

"Ain't that a fact?"

"What makes him think he can boss people around when you can't even trust what he says?" She whacked off a slice of potato and then, feeling guilty at the waste, popped it into her mouth.

"Uh-huh." Toby looked uncertain, as if not knowing what he had agreed to. "Course he did pray with some folk. Said grace real nice, too." Toby nodded vigorously. "And I heard him reading the Bible to some man."

Glory stifled an urge to roll her eyes. Toby made no sense, but then what did she expect from someone she'd dragged from the saloon less than an hour ago?

But her own thoughts echoed Toby's arguments. She'd watched him care for Mr. Phelps, seen him washing out soiled laundry, spied on him taking things to Widow Kish. Glory had secreted away a few things each week for the woman, but it wasn't enough. Maybe with Powers helping, the woman would do better. Nice to know she had an ally in helping the widow. "Well, shoot!" She threw the peeled potato into the pot so hard she splashed Toby.

"What's wrong with you?"

"Nothing." How could she explain that one minute she tried to believe Powers was a fraud and the next rejoiced he was a saint? Her mind must be affected by hanging upside down as she practiced her trick riding. But her horses were the safest company she could find right now, and she'd be spending a lot more time there and a lot less around town.

Except she needed to help Joanna. When did life get so complicated?

When the Rawhide Preacher rode into town. That's when. What would it take to get him to ride back out?

Chapter 4

Levi would have thought it impossible for Glory to avoid him, but she'd certainly done her best. Although they shared the same table, so did twenty others, making it out of the question to have a private conversation with her.

He wasn't sure what he'd say if he had the chance. He thought of apologizing for suggesting she was disappointed with life. Except he was almost certain it was the truth. The outward signs might be different from Matt's—though not all that different—but he suspected they both felt the same way. Glory's mother had died. Her father left them to fend on their own. It was almost as bad as losing both parents. Perhaps even worse.

He'd watched for an opportunity to speak to her, prayed for one, knowing without a shadow of doubt she was one reason he was in Bonners Ferry. He'd even hung about the farrier shop waiting for a chance, but she dragged young Toby with her. He liked to think it was to keep Toby out of the saloon, but deep down he suspected it was to make sure she wasn't alone with Levi.

In a way, he didn't mind. Toby was welcoming enough, and he liked the younger man. Right now they played a game of checkers, which seemed to be one of Toby's favorite pastimes.

Levi's gaze wandered back and forth to the open door, which gave him a good view of the little pen and Glory trimming hooves on the two horses brought to her.

"Now do a good job," the impatient man ordered. "I'm off to the gold fields and can't afford a lame horse."

Glory didn't even glance up from her task. "Most foot problems can be prevented. You might try cleaning their hooves at night. They deserve that much after toting you around all day."

Levi held a bubble of amusement in his chest. Trust Glory to tell a man exactly what she thought.

Toby jumped Levi's kings. "I won."

Levi brought his attention back to the game. "So you did. You're pretty sharp for a young fella."

The boy bristled. "I'm not that young."

"Didn't mean to suggest you were."

Glory finished the horses and pocketed the money she'd earned. She let the man and his animals out the gate and then turned and began grooming her palomino.

Levi could see her lips moving but couldn't hear what she said to the horse. No doubt secrets she didn't share with others. He leaned toward the door, hoping to discover what they were.

"How old are you?" Toby asked.

Holding back his frustration, knowing Toby deserved his full attention, he answered. "Twenty-six. How about you?"

"I'm eighteen." He hung his head and mumbled. "Almost."

"I expect your folks are worried about you."

Toby bristled. "I can take care of myself."

"Don't stop your parents from wondering if you're okay. That's what folks do when they care about each other."

Glory suddenly stood in the doorway. "I suppose you know all about it? Folks caring and all."

He hadn't noticed her approach and startled, faced her. Their gazes met and held. And he saw one of her secrets. Though he already knew it. She had been disappointed by events in her life—likely her pa's regular disappearance and her mother's death. "My folks died when I was thirteen. My brother and I went to live with my grandparents. They cared for us in their own way." Trouble was, Matt didn't accept their way.

"What's that mean, 'their own way'?"

"They were strict but only because they feared we might get into trouble if we were allowed to follow our own inclination." They proved to be correct.

"So you think everyone should obey rules."

He hadn't meant for her to apply his words in such a fashion. "I only meant they showed their caring that way. The only way they knew how."

Her eyes blared like the sun had peeked around the corner and pooled in her irises. "Seems to me a man who calls himself a preacher would know love has certain requirements laid out in the scriptures. Perhaps you recall First Corinthians chapter thirteen, where it describes love as charity. Says it is long-suffering, kind, and never fails." Her words came fast and furious.

"Strange you pick those virtues when it also says charity vaunteth not itself, rejoiceth in the truth, and hopes all things." Stranger still she knew the passage. Yet perhaps not. Joanna made certain grace was offered at each meal, so the girls had been exposed to godly teaching at some point in their lives.

She tried to stare him down, but he wasn't backing up, physically or mentally. When she realized he wouldn't budge, she made a noise of exasperation, grabbed the saddle and saddle blanket, and stomped outside. A few minutes later she rode down the trail at a gallop.

"She shouldn't ride so fast through town," Toby observed quietly. "Joanna is always telling her. But Glory doesn't listen."

No, Glory doesn't listen. That about summed it up.

∞

Sunday dawned clear and promising. *Thank You, Lord, for a nice day.*

One thing Levi had no control over was the weather, and meeting outdoors required good weather. He'd scoured the town looking for a suitable building to rent and had come up empty. All the buildings were in use.

He'd posted notices about town that he would hold services on the hillside south of the ferry. He'd announced it again at the supper table. Still he wondered how many would show up. Would Glory?

He took extra time with his grooming, aware of young Toby watching him.

"You really gonna have church outside?"

"Yup. Jesus held open-air services, you know." Levi finished his shave and wiped his face on the towel. As he finished and hung the towel, he caught a glimpse of Glory as she passed the open dining room door. "Are you coming?" He directed the question to Toby but hoped Glory heard it as well.

"Guess so. Glory says it might do me some good." The younger man hung his head and scuffled his feet. "She says maybe it will help me quit drinking." Suddenly he gave Levi a hard, demanding look. "You think it would?"

Levi gave the man his undivided attention. "Toby, going to church won't help you so much as listening to God will. God can give your life new purpose. He will forgive your sins and let you start over. Come to

42

the service and hear what I have to say, and if you have other questions, I'm always willing to talk."

Toby brightened. "I'll be there."

Levi caught up his black suit jacket and donned it over his vest. Some might think it was an odd combination, but he didn't mind. Maybe they needed to see the preacher was more than a suit jacket. He was also a man. Did Glory see it?

Why did his thoughts always circle back to Miss Glory? Even at night, he recalled images of her—racing through town, scolding the man with horses, glaring at him across the table. Whether she smiled or glared, he derived a great deal of enjoyment out of picturing her.

He pushed the thought away. Today was not about him. Or her.

He picked up his Bible and headed for the field where the service was to be held. No one was there when he arrived. Nor did he expect it. It was a full hour before time to start. He'd come to pray and mentally prepare and welcome any early arrivals.

Half an hour later, people started to trickle in. Levi greeted each one. Claud Wagoner, whom he met the first day. Mr. Murray, the lawyer, and his wife. Widow Kish leaning on Mr. Phelps's arm.

Levi strode over and shook Mr. Phelps's hand and squeezed the widow's shoulder. "Glad to see you both. You're looking much better," he said to Mr. Phelps.

"Doing much better, thanks to you." He squeezed Levi's hand hard then released it and found a place for them to sit.

Others arrived. People he'd not yet met. A dozen people from the stopping house who decided to delay further travel until after the service. It was almost time to start. He swallowed back his disappointment. He'd hoped Glory and her sisters would come.

He took his place at the front and prepared to start the service.

At that moment, the three sisters strode down the path. Each wore her usual outfit—Mandy in loose pants and baggy shirt, Joanna in a split skirt and dark brown blouse, and Glory in tight britches, form-fitting shirt, and worn brown vest. But he had never seen anything he thought looked finer.

He smiled at them, his gaze skimming the older and younger sister and resting on Glory.

But she didn't return his smile. She scowled.

He turned away to face the gathered people, his smile widening. Her frown perhaps said more than a smile. It revealed the same uncertainty about her feelings for him as he had for her. He let the satisfaction of such knowledge fill his heart. Better to be frowned at than to be ignored.

"Welcome. We'll begin with a song." He didn't have hymnals but chose hymns familiar to most and led them in singing, pleased to hear some strong voices from the congregation. Mr. Phelps had a deep voice that carried the others along.

Then Levi began his sermon. He'd wanted to preach on rebellion being as the sin of witchcraft, or whatsoever a man soweth that shall he also reap. But he had no peace about such passages and instead chose others.

"Today, I want to remind each of you about God's everlasting love. In Jeremiah thirty-one, verse three, God says, 'I have loved thee with an everlasting love: therefore with lovingkindness have I drawn thee.'" He went on to give illustrations from the scripture of God loving people even when they failed and sinned.

He tried not to speak directly to Glory though his heart strayed there on its own. She watched steadily. But her expression revealed nothing, giving him no idea whether the words spoke to her or not. But that was not his responsibility. God would use His Word in His way. Levi's task was to speak it.

Toward the end of the service, a large man sauntered to the edge of the clearing and leaned against a tree, his arms crossed over his chest. He plainly, silently said he wasn't there to hear from God.

Levi continued. "I want to remind you of the assurance in Numbers chapter twenty-three, verse nineteen. 'God is not a man, that he should lie; neither the son of man, that he should repent: hath he said, and shall he not do it?' and again in Joshua twenty-three, verse fourteen, 'Not one thing hath failed of all the good things which the Lord your God spake concerning you. . .not one thing hath failed therof.' God keeps His promises. I challenge you, read your Bible, find God's promises, trust them. 'O taste and see that the Lord is good: blessed is the man that trusteth in him.' Psalm thirty-four, verse eight."

He closed in prayer then moved to join the others, thanking them for attending and letting them know he was available for spiritual counsel or whatever they might need from him.

Many thanked him.

He sought Glory's eyes, wondering what she thought. More than once he felt he spoke directly to her, praying God would use his words to heal her hurt and disappointment. But she scrambled to her feet and seemed in a great hurry to get Joanna and Mandy to leave. However, they seemed more interested in speaking to their neighbors.

The late arrival still leaned against the nearby tree, a mocking expression on his face.

Levi strode over and introduced himself.

The man didn't unbend an inch. "I'm Bull Johnson."

"The saloon owner. I've been hoping to talk to you. I need a building for church services and thought you might be willing to let me use the saloon on Sunday."

Bull pushed away from the tree. He was big and brawny and used his body in a way meant to intimidate Levi.

Levi didn't budge an inch nor did he flinch. He'd met bigger, meaner men in his day. They didn't scare him. Big didn't make right.

Bull pushed his face to within an inch of Levi's. "Preacher, you stay away from my saloon on Sunday and every other day of the week. I won't have you interferring with my business."

Levi felt the silent watchfulness of his congregation. They waited to see how he'd react to this bully. He slowly drew himself to his full height, holding the Bible at chest level like a shield or perhaps a sword. "I will go where the Lord directs, when the Lord directs, and to whom the Lord directs. I will not fear any man when it comes to serving my Lord."

Bull edged closer, but Levi refused to move, forcing the man to teeter on the balls of his feet. He stepped back, a nasty look on his face. "Stay away from the saloon." He strode off, thunder in every footstep.

Levi turned away. Caught Glory's watchful look but could not read her expression. Admiration? He welcomed such. But perhaps it was only warning. Did she think him foolish for standing up to Bull? Or perhaps he only wanted to see something he could rejoice in. Could be she was only curious as any observer.

∞

Glory tried to hurry Joanna and Mandy away from the church service. Levi tangled her thoughts with his words and actions. She'd come to the meeting fully expecting a fire-and-brimstone sermon. Warning about repentance and sackcloth. Instead, he preached love and trust. Neither of which she had any faith in.

Who was this Levi Powers? Seeing him help Mr. Phelps and Widow Kish, observing his fatherly way with Toby, and now hearing his words of welcome. . .well, it left her struggling for balance. Who was he?

Who was she? Did God really love her? She'd once believed. When Ma was alive. But it was so long ago she could barely recall, and she was but a child then, trusting her parents to take care of her.

That had changed, and she was no longer a child.

"I'm ready to go," Joanna said.

"Finally." Glory didn't bother to disguise her impatience.

Mandy nudged Glory in the ribs. "Still think he's too good-looking to be a preacher?"

Joanna shot them a startled look. "What's looks got to do with whether or not he's a preacher?"

Glory pinched Mandy's elbow, warning her not to josh with Joanna about it. Glory didn't much care to have another sister mocking her.

Mandy gave a naughty grin but said no more about the subject. She fell in on one side of Joanna and Glory on the other as they trooped toward home. The stopping house served only two meals a day—breakfast and supper—so the girls had the rest of the afternoon to themselves. No need to hurry back to the kitchen.

As they walked, Glory mulled over Levi's words. *"Read your Bible. Find God's promises."* Her voice careless, she asked, "Didn't Ma used to have a Bible? I wonder what happened to it."

"I've got it," Joanna said. "I think it's time I put it out so we can read it. I know Ma would have wanted us to." She sighed like she carried a heavy pack on her back. "Ma would be disappointed with me for not living up to her expectations."

"No, she wouldn't," Mandy and Glory said at once. Glory fell back half a step and cast a protesting look at Mandy. They'd seen Joanna get all worried and overly caring about how her younger sisters were turning out. She knew from Mandy's expression she didn't welcome such a mood any more than Glory did.

"We're grown-up now," Glory said. "You don't have to worry about us so much." She vowed she would be more careful about how she acted and—she knew Joanna hated her going in the saloon even if it was to get Toby—where she went.

Joanna shrugged. "I will always feel responsible as the oldest."

"You've been the best big sister we could ask for. Isn't that right, Mandy?"

"Sure is." Both girls hugged Joanna, who started to laugh.

"Still. I don't think it would hurt us any to read the Bible just as Levi said. Ma would want us to."

Glory didn't need to promise Joanna she would. Something deep in her soul wanted to know more about God's promises. Could He be trusted wholly and completely as Levi said? She sure hadn't found it easy to trust people. But then God was God. A different matter.

As soon as they got home, Joanna went to their room and lifted a box from the top shelf of the wardrobe. She opened it to reveal an old photo album and a tiny bonnet. "It was Mandy's. I've never been able to give it away." She set the album and bonnet aside. "Here's the Bible." Joanna stroked the worn leather cover gently. "Do either of you remember Ma reading to us from it?"

Glory nodded. "I remember her sitting in a rocking chair while we sprawled on the floor at her feet."

"I don't remember clearly," Mandy said. "I can never seem to remember Ma." She looked longingly at the photo album. Glory figured with Ma being sick so much when Mandy was little, her sister had learned to depend on Joanna for much of her care, and Ma kind of faded into the background for her.

Joanna sat on the edge of the bed, took the album on her lap, and patted the covers on either side of her. Glory and Mandy crowded close. It had been some time since they had shared a moment like this.

Glory knew what the pictures were. Grandparents she'd never met. Aunts and uncles she couldn't remember. Cousins no one could remember the names of. And Ma with Joanna as a toddler. Then Pa and Ma and the three girls, Mandy just a baby.

Joanna lingered over that page. "We were a good family."

Glory bristled. "We're still a good family. Just the three of us."

"What about Pa?" Mandy sounded mournful.

Glory didn't wait for Joanna to answer. She knew her sister would say Pa missed Ma. Never got over her dying. They had to understand that. But they had lost their ma, too. "We don't need Pa. Let him chase after his dreams. We manage just fine without him, don't we?"

Joanna stared into the distance as if seeing and wanting things she couldn't have.

Mandy sighed—a sound as sad as the wind off the river on a dark night.

Glory sprang to her feet. "I'm going to check on my horses." She sped from the house as fast as she could. But she couldn't outrun her thoughts. Pa would show up someday with the same empty promise of staying and providing a home for the girls. But they no longer needed him. Or wanted him and his promises—forgotten as quickly as they were given.

Promises. The word made her think of Powers's sermon. Maybe she needed to consider God's promises. Might be something there.

She spent the rest of the day with her horses, pleased at how well Blue Boy and Pal worked together.

Later that evening, she sneaked into the bedroom, lifted Ma's Bible from the dresser where it now held center stage, ducked out the back door, avoiding her sisters and Powers, and found a secluded spot to read from its pages. There were promises galore. Surprised her some to see all the good things God promised to give. And it seemed they were meant for her, too.

Her back to a tree, the setting sun painting the river water violet, she tried to sort out her feelings. What if Powers was only a confidence man, with enough skill to convince them all he was a preacher?

Would that change God's promises?

No, it wouldn't. But it would change how she looked at the scriptures. Because, she reluctantly admitted, she heard the words in Levi's voice. And if he proved false, that wouldn't work.

Her instinct, her experience warned her to be cautious.

Her heart, her longing wished he could be all he said he was.

She closed the Bible and returned it to the dresser.

∽

Two days later, she left the horses early and headed back to town to get Toby and attend to their chores. She strode boldly into the saloon and looked about. No Toby. For the second day in a row. Yesterday she'd found him already at his chores, no smell of liquor on his breath. He explained he'd been too busy with other things to go to the saloon. But he refused to say what the other things were.

She rode slowly down the street, checking each corner and alley for a glimpse of Toby, fearing he had passed out somewhere. Not a sign of him. She neared the stopping house and saw nothing of him scurrying about the yard or perched under the overhang peeling vegetables.

It was early yet. Perhaps she'd missed him. She reined about and made another pass through town. Still not a sign of him. She rode on.

She neared Mr. Phelps's place and saw Levi's horse in front of the house and turned in there. Perhaps he'd seen Toby. She dismounted and led Pal toward the hitching post.

That was when she heard the murmur of voices and thought she recognized one as Toby's.

She edged around the corner of the house and stared. Levi Powers and Toby sat side by side, an open Bible between them. Mr. Phelps faced them. All three wore intent expressions.

Levi spoke. "It doesn't matter what we think or feel. It's what God's Word says that matters."

The other two nodded.

"And we just read where God says as far as the east is from the west He has removed our sins from us."

More nodding.

"If God says it, that settles it for me," Mr. Phelps said.

"Me, too," Toby echoed.

Glory backed away. So this was what kept Toby from the saloon. That was a good thing. So why did it feel like he'd betrayed her?

She returned to Pal and led him from the yard. Only someone selfish and petty would resent that her friend was being helped. And yet she did. In fact, her throat was tight. As if she wanted to cry.

She. . .Glory Hamilton. . .did not cry. Not when Pa rode away without a backward look. Not when Toby found what he needed from Levi. And not because she ached to be able to believe Levi was who he said he was. . .that she could trust his words.

Chomping down on her teeth until they hurt, she pushed away her foolish thoughts. She was glad for Toby.

And if she wanted to trust anyone, it would be God.

Chapter 5

From the doorway where Glory stood drying the heavy pot Joanna used to cook porridge in, she could see the comings and goings on the ferry. Another busy day of people flocking to the gold fields of the British territories, to some mysterious place called the Kootenais.

She and her sisters had planned to find Pa and join him there until they saw the opportunity to make a good living by running a stopping house. Mandy had wanted to push on and join Pa. But Joanna and Glory outvoted her.

Glory liked it here. Perhaps they would stay for a long time. She thought of the land she hoped to purchase.

A big black horse riding toward the ferry caught her attention. Levi's horse. She'd recognize it anywhere. Just as she'd recognize the man riding it. The relaxed yet watchful way he sat his horse. His proud posture. The fringed leather vest so out of place for a preacher. Rawhide Kid seemed a more fitting title.

He rode his horse to the ferry and crossed the river.

Toby appeared at her side.

"Where is he going?" she asked.

"Didn't say."

"Just rode off without a word?"

Toby continued to look at Levi. "Said he felt an urge to cross the river and see if anyone needed his help."

They watched until Levi rode out of sight on the far side of the river.

Glory shifted her gaze to Toby and for some inexplicable reason was annoyed. "I wonder if he's off looking for people to help. More likely to help himself to their things. Have you forgotten the Rawhide Kid? He could be a fake. Remember?"

Toby took his time turning to face her. "He knows about God."

Glory's eyes narrowed, and her heart squeezed hard. Toby was her friend. Yet he was choosing to believe Levi over Glory. "You believe him?"

Toby gave the merest shrug.

Glory's insides tightened until she wondered something didn't snap. "I thought you were my friend."

"I am. What does believing Levi have to do with being your friend?"

She couldn't answer because nothing made sense. "Forget it." She spun away and headed for her shop.

In minutes she had saddled Pal and rode out of town to her horses. At least horses were loyal to anyone who treated them right.

Recognizing she was too upset to work with the animals at the moment, she plunked down in her favorite spot, her back to a tree, and looked out at the wide, green valley below. She never grew tired of the view, and slowly her thoughts calmed.

Why had she gotten so upset? It wasn't like she needed Toby's friendship. She had learned many years ago not to get too attached to friends.

Nor did she resent the time he spent with Levi. She was glad his association with the man kept him out of the saloon.

Deep inside the truth sought acceptance. She was—

No. She didn't ache for Levi to show her the same kindness and attention. She didn't long for friendship from him. No way. That was silly nonsense. Why would she pin her hopes on a man? Any man. She'd learned the folly of such at a young age.

She sprang to her feet and returned to her horses. As she fed them and petted them, her good humor returned. This was who she was and where she belonged. Nothing else mattered. Silly to let other things upset her for even a moment.

Pal and Blue Boy worked perfectly together. They were ready and there was no time like the present. She'd do it today. Excitement filled her insides with rolling whitecaps like those blown up on the river by a strong westerly wind.

She rode Pal and led Blue Boy until she reached the beginning of the street running down to the ferry. "This is it, boys." She pulled them to a halt, clambered from the saddle, and put one foot on the back of each horse, finding perfect balance before she flicked the reins for them to go forward.

She was in complete control. The feeling was powerful, pulsing through her veins in sweet victory. She held the reins in one hand and punched the air with her free hand. "Whaahoo," she called.

Several men crossing the street stopped to stare, the surprise on their faces fueling her excitement. Two more men crowded through the door of the hardware store at the same time, anxious to see.

"Look, Ma," a young boy called. His mother stared, one hand holding her son firmly at her side.

Glory rode down the street, grinning so widely her cheeks hurt. She reined in before she reached the stopping house, preferring not to have Joanna see her, then turned and rode back through town.

A familiar figure stood in front of the general store. Joanna. Glory's heart thudded against her chest. Wasn't Joanna supposed to be home cooking up something? Instead, she gave Glory a look full of reproach.

Glory faltered. The horses felt it and broke their pace, setting her off balance. She struggled to hold her footing. "Pal, Blue Boy, it's okay."

Suddenly Levi stood directly in front of the horses and grabbed each by the bridle.

"Let them go." Glory stood atop motionless horses, feeling slightly foolish. She was supposed to ride from town without a hitch.

"Get down." His eyes blazed brittle blue. His words, though low, had the power of a gunshot.

"No. Release my horses."

"Glory, get down before you hurt yourself."

Anger flared through her, burning away every rational thought. She dropped to the ground in one swift motion and flung to his side. "You ought to mind your own business."

"And you ought to behave yourself." His voice dropped even lower. "Did you see the look on your sister's face? You scared her. She cares about you. Do you think it's fair to worry her like this?"

She did silent, vicious battle with her eyes. He had no right to interfere. But then she hadn't intended for Joanna to see. Yes, she would hear about it eventually, but after it was over and done and Glory could laugh and say there'd been no risk involved.

Out of the corner of her eye, she saw Joanna striding toward her. She yanked Pal's bridle from Levi's hand, but he refused to release Blue Boy. Knowing if she didn't make tracks she'd have to face Joanna, she headed down the street. Like a shamed dog with her tail between her legs.

He kept stride with her, bringing Blue Boy along.

"You humiliated me in public. I'll never forgive you for that."

∞

Levi held his tongue because the words wanting to burst from his mouth would not be God-honoring. He wanted to tear her apart for such a foolish act. When the horses had faltered and it looked like she would fall, he'd stopped thinking and acted on sheer instinct. All he wanted was to keep her from getting hurt.

And for that she vowed she would never forgive him.

A whirlwind of emotions swept through him. Relief she was on the ground walking on two sound legs. Though he wasn't sure his legs were so sound. His knees were strangely wobbly. He recognized it as the aftereffects of his scare. "Are you crazy or something? You could have been killed."

She made a most unladylike sound. "I was in complete control."

"Of everything, I suppose. People who might inadvertently step into the street and startle the horses, or some sudden noise. Sure you were in control. I suppose you were in control of the shock it gave Joanna, too."

She glared at him. "She wasn't supposed to be there."

"That makes no sense. How would it worry her less if she hadn't seen it?"

"What she doesn't know won't hurt her."

"Your shenanigans only give her cause to worry all the more when she can't see what you're up to. Don't you stop to give a thought to those who care about you? Don't you care about yourself?" He dropped back, too upset to continue walking with her. "I'm going to check on Mr. Phelps."

She pulled to a halt in front of the man's yard facing him, anger and defiance wreathing her face.

He stared at her as truth surfaced. He'd worried she might do something lawless like Matt had. But that was not the risk she faced. Her defiance would lead her to put herself in danger with no regard for the consequences. "Why are you so determined to prove nothing matters to you?"

She glared at him, her eyes flashing. "Because it doesn't." She blinked as if realizing what she'd said. "I am not foolish."

He grabbed her by the shoulders and gave a little shake. "You are indeed foolish if you think you don't matter to anyone. Or nothing you do matters to them."

Her gaze bored into his, probing, testing, wanting. Then she scowled.

"What do you know about it?"

"I know this. I care what happens to you. I care about you."

Disbelief filled her eyes.

He saw an argument about to start. He didn't care to have his confession debated and pulled her close, tipped her chin up, and silenced her with a good, solid kiss. Her lips siffened with what he presumed was shock. He knew he should stop, back away, behave like a gentleman, but he allowed himself a moment more of sweet tasting then pulled away. "Never argue with a man when he says he cares about you."

She stared.

He turned away to hide his smile. If he had to guess, he'd say it was the first time in her life Glory had been rendered speechless.

Levi hummed as he waved good-bye to Mr. Phelps. He'd spent a pleasant half hour visiting and now headed back to town.

When he saw the ferry, he remembered what he'd found on the other side. . .what had bothered him since he returned.

Two children, a boy and a girl, sitting by the side of the road.

"Waitin' for our pa," the boy said. "He said he'd be back for us."

Levi had hunkered down beside the pair. "How long have you been waiting?" He thought they'd say an hour, maybe most of the day. But what they said shot through him like a bullet.

"Been three days now," the boy said, and the little girl sobbed quietly.

"Maybe you should wait back in town. I could take care of you until he gets back."

The little girl's eyes widened with hope, but her brother shook his head. "I promised Pa I'd stay here."

He gave them the biscuits and jerky he had with him and refilled their water canteens then headed back to town. "The offer is open if you change your mind." It troubled him to leave them there, but he didn't want to forceably remove them. How would he explain dragging two screaming children into town?

Perhaps their father had returned by now. *God, keep them safe. Bring their father back to them. Guide me as to what I should do.*

He spent the day visiting various people. But his thoughts returned over and over to Glory and the kiss he'd stolen. He went back to the stopping house more eagerly than usual. He could hardly wait to see her at the evening meal. See if her cheeks flushed when she saw him.

She clattered into the dining room and crowded in next to Mandy. "Sorry I'm late," she murmured.

Levi had seen her earlier peeling potatoes and doing the other chores that seemed to be her responsibility, Toby assisting her. The boy had stopped going to the saloon. Not something Bull appreciated, but Levi was pleased.

He stood to say the blessing as had become his habit then sat and waited for Glory to glance his way. She made a great show of being busy with passing the food. He grinned. Avoiding him proved more than an angry glare would have, and he turned his attention to the man on his right to answer a number of questions.

"Could you please pass me the salt?" the man on his left asked.

As Levi turned to do so, he looked toward Glory and caught her watching him, her expression serious, guarded. Yet the hunger in her eyes made him forget what he was doing until the man spoke again.

"The salt, please."

He passed the salt and directed his attention to his plate. Suddenly the impact of what he'd done hit him. What was he thinking? He had no business telling Glory he cared. His task required all his time and attention. And he silently repeated the vow he had made to God. *I'll devote myself to working for You while You work on Matt in prison. Keep him safe. Bring him to repentance.*

After the meal, he joined the others outside, but he listened to Glory cleaning up the meal inside. She usually left the house after the chores and disappeared until dark. He'd watched her. Saw she carried a Bible. Guessed she found a quiet place to read it, and he rejoiced in the fact. He didn't like to interrupt her reading, but tonight he would follow her and apologize for kissing her. Not that he was sorry. But he had no business.

He knew the moment she slipped from the house even though he didn't hear her or see her. His heart tracked her as she crossed the yard and ducked into a thicket of trees. Giving her a moment to settle, Levi excused himself from the knot of men visiting and sauntered away, choosing an indirect route. As he neared the trees, he called softly, "Glory, I need to speak to you." Then he hastened forward before she could escape.

She sat with her back against a tree, the dappled light making it difficult to read her expression. "Can't a person enjoy some peace and quiet without you interrupting?" And she turned her attention to the Bible in her lap, pointedly ignoring him.

There wasn't room to lean against the same tree, and she made it clear she didn't welcome closeness, so he chose the next tree over and sat down, his legs sprawled out in front of him. He took in a deep, satisfying breath. "I won't keep you. I only want to apologize. I shouldn't have kissed you. Or said those things."

"You're taking it all back?"

He considered his answer a moment and could find nothing better to say than, "Seems the best thing to do."

"Not surprised." She spoke so quietly he wondered if he'd misunderstood her.

"What do you mean? It isn't like I've done this before."

She shrugged, looked as if she didn't intend to answer then sighed. "Not you. Others have though."

"Others?" He didn't want to think other men had stolen kisses. Or worse, been given them. "How many beaus are we talking about?"

She gave him a scowl fit to dry up the river. "Not beaus. I got no use for that nonsense."

"Then who?"

"My pa. Not that it's any of your business, but he's a great one for saying something then changing his mind."

Levi digested the information. It appears it was her father who disappointed her. "What did he do?"

A heavy sigh pushed past her lips. "It was what he didn't do."

"All right. What didn't he do?"

She slowly turned and fixed him with a look full of defiance but also laced with regret and longing.

He ached to be able to comfort her, but he didn't have the right. Would never have the right.

"He couldn't be bothered to be a father. It interfered with his plans."

He held her gaze, reading past the anger to the pain. "I'm sorry. However, I am not your pa. Nor do I wish to hurt you. I care about you, but I don't have the right." He gathered his feet beneath him and stood. "I will never have the right." He strode away, not daring a backward glance. He had set his face to the plow and would not look back.

The next day he would again cross the river on the ferry and ride to where he'd last seen the children, hoping they were gone—safely with their father. Hoping they had not been bothered by someone with less than noble intentions.

The morning couldn't come too soon for him.

Chapter 6

Glory forced herself not to toss and turn, knowing it would bring questions from Joanna and Mandy. Instead, she curled on the far side of the bed she shared with her younger sister and stared into the darkness.

Of course Levi didn't mean what he said. Why had she expected he would? She was no more than twelve when she realized words were easily given and just as easily taken back.

Her Pa had taught her well. Every year—sometimes several times in a year—he'd promised he'd stay with the girls this time. And every time he rode out of their lives, most times without warning or good-bye.

She'd lost track of the number of times they'd been thrust upon the care of others until they rebelled. Joanna was sixteen, almost seventeen, when they'd convinced her they could manage on their own. As a trio, they'd tried to keep up with Pa, depending on him to give them a home. But they got tired of that real quick. Seems the more he saw of them, the more he wanted to move on. Still, they tried to stay close. After all, he was their pa. They learned to manage on their own, hunting, fishing, cooking, cleaning, tending children. . .whatever it took to survive.

She firmly pushed regrets to the back of her mind. That was the past and there was no benefit in moaning about what might have been. They now had their own successful business. It should have been enough for all of them and it was, but besides helping run the stopping house, Glory wanted to take care of abused or neglected horses, nursing them back to health.

She thought of the tin can under her side of the bed where she kept her earnings. How long would it take before she had enough to buy that piece of land?

By the time morning dawned, she could hardly wait to be up and about her chores. She hurried through them, barely taking time to stop for breakfast.

Somehow she managed to keep her gaze from roving toward Levi. Kiss her and regret it would he? Well, she didn't need the likes of him. She was drying the last dish when she saw him on the ferry, again crossing the river, and her suspicions mounted. He said he would never be free to care for her. That wasn't quite the word he'd used. The right. He'd never have the right. Whatever that meant. But if he was part of a gang, involved in robbery or other illegal activity, wouldn't it mean he didn't have the right?

Was he the Rawhide Kid posing as a preacher? She didn't like to think so, but it made perfect sense.

She wished it didn't.

As soon as she recognized the thought, she wanted to boot herself across the yard. What difference did it make to her? None. None whatsoever. She was only thinking of how many people would be disillusioned when they discovered the truth. She was above and beyond disappointment. That was one good thing her pa had taught her.

As soon as she'd done her share of chores, she returned to the horses. A pleased grin curved her mouth. She'd ridden the horses in tandem. It gave her a great deal of satisfaction.

Simply for the sheer fun of it, she stood on the backs of the pair and rode them around the pasture. She did the death drag from Pal's back. The thrill of the trick blew away all her troubles.

After she had enough, she turned her attention to the big gray gelding. Today she was determined to get him to let her touch him. She shook some oats into her hat and slowly approached the animal. He quivered but didn't snort and race away. He liked his oats too much.

She laughed softly as he allowed her to close the distance between them. His nostrils quivering, he reached for the oats, but she kept them close to her body. "If you want them, you'll have to forget your fear of me."

The big animal shook his head, but his gaze returned to the oats and he jerked forward, almost reaching them, but he shivered away without so much as a taste.

"Take it easy, big fella. I won't hurt you. In fact, you might find you like having me touch you." She shook the hat, reminding him of the waiting treat. "Oats. See? You know how much you like them."

Slower, but still cautious, he stretched out his neck and managed to lick up a few grains.

"Not enough to satisfy you, is it? Come on, forget about the past and people who have hurt you. I'm different. I won't hurt you. You can trust me."

The horse eased forward and suddenly buried his nose in the hat, forcing Glory to hang on with both hands. She rested the hat against her stomach and gently, gently touched his neck. He quivered but didn't pull away from the oats.

Glory laughed softly. "See, it's not so scary after all." She touched him again, thrilling at this victory.

He snuffled up the last of the oats and trotted away to watch her from a safe distance.

Glory couldn't stop grinning. "You and I are going to be great friends once you learn you can trust me."

Trust. She knew it took a long time to prove to an abused animal trusting was okay. Her thoughts filled with questions from her past and promises from God's Word, entwined together like a ball of knotted yarn. She sat in her favorite spot to consider the tangle.

Levi had said he cared and then changed his mind.

She wasn't sure he was a preacher or a crook. Plain and simple, she didn't trust him. And yet he said to search the Bible and find God's promises. He assured them all they could trust those promises.

She thought of some of the ones that had found their way into her heart. A promise to love her—*"I have loved thee with an everlasting love"*—a promise to hear when she called on Him, to draw near to her, to answer her requests. Dare she trust Him?

The words that Levi had brought that first Sunday came to mind. *"God is not a man, that he should lie; neither the son of man, that he should repent: hath he said, and shall he not do it? or hath he spoken, and shall he not make it good?"* The next Sunday he had given even more promises from God's Word, but she wasn't sure she was ready to thrust herself wholly into someone else's care. Not even God's. Life had disappointed too often for trust to come readily.

A horse approached, and she scrambled to her feet.

The man drawing near was a stranger. In a fine suit. With a round-topped black hat that looked like it had just been plucked out of a store display. He rode well, though in a stiff manner. Not like a cowboy who spent hours in a saddle. He drew to a halt before her. "You are on my land."

Not now. Her heart reached bottom and lay there limp. She'd hoped this day would never come. "Who are you?"

He pulled off his hat to reveal blond hair slicked back with plenty of pommade. "Master Marcus Milton." He returned his hat to his head and looked almighty pleased with himself, as if she should rejoice at meeting such a fine, pompous man.

She bit the inside of her lip in order to keep her opinion to herself.

When he realized she didn't plan to comment on the privilege of meeting Master whatever, he gave a decisive nod. "Do you have plans to purchase this land?"

"How much?"

He named a sum likely fair enough but far more than she had in her tin can. Even selling her current half-dozen horses wouldn't bring in enough money. "I could pay part now and part later."

He sniffed. "I am a businessman. Borrow the money from a bank. In the meantime, either buy the land or move your horses off it."

"They're not hurting anything."

"You're trespassing."

"I need time to find another suitable location. After all, I can't keep them tied up in town, now can I?"

"Very well. I am a reasonable man." He looked like it pained him to say so. "I will give you two weeks." He beamed at her.

She stared, suddenly realized he expected her to thank him. "You'll have your money in less time than that."

"Or you will remove your animals." He jerked his mount around.

It was all Glory could do not to order him to keep in mind the horse's tender mouth. She watched him until he disappeared from sight then sank back to the ground and moaned. "How am I supposed to get that kind of money in less than two weeks?" Dare she pray about it? Would God listen to a foolish, selfish request? What did she have to lose?

God, help me out here if You care about me at all. You say in Your Word You care. But everyone who says they care about me takes it back one way or the other. But You aren't a man to change Your mind. So if it's true, if I can trust You, make a way for me to buy this piece of land.

She didn't say amen. Just finished and sat there, a little seed of hope sprouting.

Later, she returned to town, curious as to whether or not Levi was back. Or was he out taking advantage of innocent people? Perhaps even planning to rob a bank or something equally as dreadful. Her mistrust of

Levi was at such odds with the step of trust she'd taken up the hill. But trust did not come easily, and she'd learned it shouldn't be given freely.

She half expected to see Levi striding into the saloon, despite Bull's continued threats and warnings. Once she'd seen Bull pushing him out the door, growling and saying all kinds of horrible things, but Levi seemed to be hard of hearing. Why would he even bother going there when he knew it meant nothing but trouble from Bull? Was it part of a ruse? Or for real? She wished she knew. But it didn't make any difference to her. Not really. He couldn't or wouldn't care about her. And she didn't care about him.

There was no sign of him at the saloon. She stopped and dismounted, checked to see if Toby was inside. He wasn't. Maybe the two of them were together someplace, though she'd seen no sign of Levi's big horse outside Mr. Phelps's house. Not that she had looked. She was only being observant.

She swung back into the saddle and headed for her shop. Sometimes he sat on the step talking to Toby as they waited for her. No one sat on the step. No one waited for her.

And why had she expected anyone would? It was only because she was angry at him for saying something he didn't mean. Just proved he was like every other man she knew.

She unsaddled Pal and turned him into the pen. Time to head to the stopping house and take care of the chores.

Toby was already there, already had the wood box full and the ashes cleaned out and was about to tackle the bucket of potatoes as she approached.

She sat on the bench and started peeling a wrinkled potato. "What have you been doing today?" It was normal conversation. No reason to feel all jittery about asking such a question. She stifled a desire to groan. It wasn't the question that bothered her. It was the curiosity behind it. *Where is Levi?*

"Been hanging about waiting for Levi to get back."

"Where did he go?"

"Only thing he said was he had something to attend to up the trail."

"That doesn't make a lick of sense. Is he trying to make us think he has legitimate business?"

"Maybe."

"He's got you convinced he's really a preacher, hasn't he?" She pointed out he was the first one to suggest the Rawhide Kid. After hearing him preach again each Sunday, she was almost ready to believe it. Almost.

"Glory, you should talk to him. Then you'd be convinced, too."

"I've talked to him, and it surely didn't convince me."

He stopped peeling potatoes to study her. "What did he say to upset you so much?"

"Enough for me not to trust him."

He returned to his task. "You'll see sooner or later."

"I expect I shall." As usual, she sat so she could see the comings and goings on the ferry. And not—she informed herself—because she hoped to glimpse Levi returning without a posse on his tail.

The vegetables were prepared, the table set when she saw him on the ferry. Or at least she saw an animal like his horse. But this man had two children with him. Where did he get two children? He hadn't killed their parents in a robbery or kidnapped the children hoping for a ransom, had he?

He rode slowly toward the stopping house. At the hitching post, he reached behind him and swung a small boy to the ground. Then he lifted the child from in front of him and leaned over to deposit the second one beside the first.

Glory stepped from the dining room to watch.

A small boy with a defiant look on his face clutched the hand of a smaller girl who looked as if she'd been crying recently.

Levi swung to the ground and pushed his hat back on his head in a gesture speaking worry and confusion better than any words could have.

She crossed the porch and faced him squarely. "Where did you get these children?"

He grinned as if reading her suspicious thoughts. "I didn't steal them, and I know that's what you're thinking. I found them. Rescued them." He told of finding the pair at the side of the road, waiting for their father to return. Waiting for four days without losing hope.

Their fear and pain drew deep lines in both little faces. It was too much like her own experience, and Glory had to turn away, pretending an interest in something inside the dining room while she gathered up her self-control. "You couldn't just bring home a lost dog like everyone else. Oh no, you have to find two lost children."

"We weren't lost," the boy protested. "Was waitin' for our pa. He won't be happy we didn't stay where he told us to. But"—his sigh was half shudder and perilously close to a sob—"we was getting hungry and tired and my sister was afraid. We could hear the coyotes howling so close at night."

Glory pressed her lips together and stilled her emotions. These children were even younger than she had been and without a protective older sister. She looked at Levi in silent protest, hoping he saw nothing but shock and dismay that these children had been abandoned.

Levi's expression revealed an equal amount of both plus a healthy dose of anger. "It took me all afternoon to persuade them to come with me."

The little girl stuck out her chin in an act of such defiance Glory had to press her lips together to keep from smiling. "He said he'd take care of us and find our pa."

Glory shook her head as she turned back to Levi. "Sounds like a mighty big task."

He shrugged. "How hard can it be? Besides, I couldn't leave them there another day. I doubt you could have either."

She forced all emotion from her eyes and answered cooly. "I suppose not. After all, they are just children."

The boy widened his stance. "I'm Jack Templeton. This is my sister, Emmy. I can take care of her."

Glory recognized his determination and admired it. "How old are you?"

"Ten." A boy with a tangle of straw-colored hair and brown eyes. "Emmy's—"

"I'm eight." Similar in looks to her brother, only her hair was longer and her eyes wider and filled with forced bravery. And as afraid as any child.

Glory straightened and met Levi's eyes. "What are you going to do with them?"

"Exactly what I said. Take care of them and try to locate their father."

She nodded and without another word went back inside. She went directly to the kitchen where Joanna and Mandy waited.

"What's going on?" Joanna asked.

"He found two kids." She repeated his story.

Joanna sighed. "Familiar story, wouldn't you say?"

Mandy moved to the doorway so she could watch them. "He's washing them up. The little girl is so tiny. She looks up at him with big trusting eyes." Mandy's words choked. "I can't imagine leaving such a sweet pair behind."

Glory snorted. "What? Were we ugly? And even if we were, did that make it all right for Pa to leave us time and again?"

"I'm sure he didn't mean to. He just got busy."

"Mandy, when will you learn we just didn't matter to him? Still don't, if one goes by the evidence." She waved her hands to indicate the room. "You see him here? Did he tell us where he was going? No. I say forget about him and get on with our lives."

"Hush, girls." Joanna as always played the peacemaker. "We are doing the best we can. All of us. Only time and God's love will heal some wounds."

Glory and Mandy exchanged surprised looks then faced Joanna, who laughed awkwardly.

"Ma taught us to obey God and trust Him. I guess it's about time we all did."

"I'm trying," Glory mumbled.

"I feel close to God when I'm out in the woods." Mandy sounded confused.

Joanna patted them both on the back. "We need to look to the future, not the past." She sniffled and wiped her eyes on a corner of her apron. "Now let's serve our guests."

Glory helped carry in the full platters and mounded bowls. Not until the food was on the table did Joanna signal at the door for the guests to come in. As they filed by, they dropped their coins into her hand.

Glory watched as Levi dropped in coins for three.

He looked tired and worried as he found room for himself with a child on each side. But Emmy trembled when a strange man sat beside her.

Glory caught Levi's eyes and signaled to him to check the child at his elbow.

He did so, saw how frightened she was, and changed places with her so she sat between himself and Jack. He glanced to Glory, said a silent thank-you.

She turned away, pretending she didn't notice. It was almost more than she could do to watch his tenderness with the children. She forced steel into her thoughts. Would he tell them the same thing he'd told her? That he couldn't care about them and that he took back his promise?

She was quite prepared to ignore the three of them. But against her will, her gaze returned to them over and over, watching as Levi cut Emmy's meat, as he refilled their water glasses. Like a father with his children.

Determinedly, she closed her eyes. She would not be like Mandy, always hoping Pa would return and somehow be changed into an ideal father. Nor would she look for the tenderness and caring she'd missed from her father in some other man. She understood how even a whisper of that kind of thinking made her vulnerable to more hurt and disappointment. The best thing she could do would be to stay as far away as possible from Levi and these two little ones until such time as he reunited them with their father.

A thought ached through her. What if they didn't find the missing father? Seems if a man didn't want to be found, he had a hundred different ways of disappearing.

As soon as the meal ended, she hurried to the kitchen to start washing dishes, determined she would not watch what Levi did with the children. Not that she had to. Mandy gave a running account.

"He's making sure they wash up again." "He's sitting on the bench outside with them. Looks like he's telling them a story. Both children are staring at him with such big eyes they practically eat him up."

Glory could take no more. "I don't want to hear about him."

Mandy laughed. "You're jealous because he's spending time with those kids. You want him to spend time with you. I saw him follow you into the trees the other evening. And why is he always hanging around the farrier's shop? Not because he has dozens of horses to take care of."

Glory threw the wet dishrag into the water with a splash and spun around to face her sister. "That's stupid talk. You be quiet."

Mandy wrinkled her nose. "I will say what I want."

"No, you won't." Glory jumped for her, intending to forceably shut her mouth, but Mandy guessed her intent and raced out of the house.

"You can't stop me." She laughed as Glory tore after her.

"When I catch you, you'll be sorry. I'll hurt you real bad."

Mandy had always been faster than Glory, but Glory was more desperate, more angry, and she did not give up the chase for half a mile. Finally, winded and knowing she didn't have a chance of catching her sister, Glory ground to a halt. "You have to come back sometime," she shouted.

Mandy stopped to face her, a good distance separating them. "You have to stop being mad sometime."

Glory laughed. Her anger had already fled.

She marched back to the house, humming to herself, and stared at Emmy, watching her with wide-eyed fear. She shifted. Saw how Jack looked ready to flee. She recalled her threatening words, the anger that no doubt had been evident on her face, and wished she could recall the past few moments and do them over.

Although she vowed she would not look at Levi, her eyes somehow shifted his direction and their gazes collided. His look burned. Accused.

"Nice example," he murmured.

Two seconds ago she'd been wishing she'd acted differently. Not frightened the children. Now she wished she'd caught Mandy and wrestled her to the ground just to prove to Levi she didn't care a thing about his opinion.

"You were mad," Emmy whispered.

Glory's stubborness warred with her concern for two innocent children. The latter won out. "Only for a moment. My sister knows that. It's a game we like to play."

"You shouldn't say bad things."

Glory grinned at the little girl. "So I'm told." She flounced around and headed for the kitchen to finish her chores.

Joanna watched her return. "Will you ever learn to be a lady?"

Glory gave her an unrepentant smirk. "When you do."

Joanna glanced down at her split skirt and laughed. "I'm as ladylike as I can be. No wonder they call us the buffalo gals."

"It could be a lot worse." They grinned at each other. "I'm happy enough to be a buffalo gal."

"Me, too."

Mandy returned a little later, and the three girls worked in happy contentment.

At bedtime, Levi found a corner and bedded the two children down at his side.

Glory tried to ignore them, but it was impossible not to hear him reading aloud from the Bible then see him kneeling with them to say their prayers. He tucked the covers around them firmly.

Glory could almost feel the comfort of those blankets holding her close. He wasn't even their father. Why was he acting like he was? Did some men simply react to children in a tender way?

She fled to the bedroom she shared with her sisters. Mandy was wrong. She wasn't jealous. She didn't want him to give her the same kind of attention. Yet there was no denying the long, echoing ache inside her yearning for something.

Chapter 7

L evi lay back on his bedding and let out a long sigh of relief. It had been a difficult afternoon. The children didn't want to disobey their father and leave the spot where he'd told them to wait. They flat out refused until Levi said he would scratch a message in the rock at the side of the road. It had taken him a long time to do so. But that gave him an opportunity to explain how he would send a message up the line and see if they could locate their pa. He talked about the good meals at the stopping house and the nice ladies who ran it.

Eventually, they agreed to come but only after checking and approving the message on the rock. He'd gathered up their sack of belongings—a few items of clothing and one set of bedding he knew they shared, likely clinging to each other for security and warmth.

He hadn't taken into account the variety of men who clustered around the table morning and night. Some fine gentlemen. But also some rough characters. After supper, Emmy confessed they scared her. Levi didn't know what else to do. He had no home. And knew of none suitable to keep them in. The hotel certainly wasn't. The men he'd seen leaving that place convinced him it was not fit for decent people.

Staying with the buffalo gals seemed the best idea except it brought him back to the initial problem—Emmy was uncomfortable among so many strange men. And he didn't want to be forced by such circumstances to spend more time with Glory. His wayward thoughts far too often drifted toward her, recalling his pleasure when he kissed her, remembering how she challenged a man about how he treated his horses, how she—

No, he must keep his hands and mind to the task before him. He had made a bargain with God and intended to keep it.

The men around him settled down. There was a constant sound of shuffling and snoring, but he was too tired to be bothered by it. He silently prayed for God to help him find the children's father then rolled over and fell asleep.

A scream jolted him awake. He reached for his rifle, found only bare wood. Felt about him, remembering he slept in the stopping house and his rifle was with his saddle and other things. He sat up as did several others. Someone lit a lamp and held it high.

A bewiskered man who had spat out a steady stream of black tobacco juice all evening bolted to his feet, revealing a very dirty undershirt. He grabbed the lamp and shone it into every corner of the room. "Who screamed?"

The flickering yellow light stopped at Emmy, who sat up, tears streaming down her face, and as everyone stared at her, her sobs grew loud.

Jack pushed from his slumber and reached out for his sister. "You had a nightmare. Go back to sleep."

She didn't move.

Levi urged her to lie down. Covered her tightly. Patted her back gently, murmuring soft sounds. "It's all over, folks. Go back to sleep."

But he spoke too soon. He had no sooner fallen asleep again when another scream rent the air.

"Make her stop," someone called in the dark.

"I'm trying to get some rest," another growled.

Murmurs and snarls came from various corners.

Levi again soothed the child. When he heard her soft, steady breathing, he allowed himself to fall back asleep.

But again his peace was shattered by Emmy's screams.

The protests from the other guests grew louder, more abusive.

Levi knew it would be impossible for him to sleep if he meant to keep the child quiet. He pulled on his trousers, scooped Emmy into his arms, and escaped outside. He got as comfortable as possible on one of the narrow benches, resting his back against the rough wooden wall, wrapped one of his blankets about Emmy, and settled down for a restless night.

Twice more she cried out, loud enough to bring a muttering of protests from inside.

Finally dawn eased across the hills and turned the air pink. Geese came awake on the river, honking in joyful song. Birdsong filled the air. So peaceful. Why couldn't man enjoy nature and stop hurting themselves and each other?

Inside came the sound of one of the women—likely Joanna—in the kitchen, rattling pots on the stove. And men started to surface from their sleep.

Two men passed him, muttering about how their night had been so disturbed.

Jack came out and sat by Levi. "She was scared being with so many strangers."

"I know."

He felt Emmy stir, knew she wakened. But she seemed content to remain curled in his arms. And he was too weary to move.

One by one, or in pairs, the men left the room to allow breakfast to be set out. Not a one had a kind word about Emmy's upset. All they seemed to care about was their disturbed sleep.

"I'm hungry," Jack said.

"Did you roll up your bedding?"

"Uh-huh."

"Bring your things and mine out to the porch then wash up."

Emmy sighed, sat up, and rubbed her eyes.

Levi took her to wash.

"Breakfast is ready," Glory called and stepped aside to allow the men to reenter. Joanna waited to take their coins.

The crude man from the night before stepped forward. "I don't intend to pay for a night when I wasn't allowed to sleep. I want my money back."

Others crowded about him, and their discontent rumbled.

Glory pressed to Joanna's side. She gave Levi a look full of accusation.

He didn't need her to silently inform him this was his fault. He already knew it and intended to make it right. He pushed his way to the front. "I'll pay for everyone's breakfast to make up for last night." He counted heads then dropped the appropriate amount into Joanna's palm. It made a dent in his funds, but it couldn't be helped.

Joanna turned to the waiting men. "Is that acceptable?"

Seems they were agreeable, and they trooped inside.

Levi took the children in, well aware Emmy squirmed in discomfort. This arrangement wasn't going to work. He'd have to figure out something else.

The others left before Emmy finished. In fact, she didn't start eating until they departed.

Joanna stood in the kitchen doorway. "Levi, can we talk to you?"

He knew what she wanted. "I'm sorry about last night."

The three women faced him. Even Glory looked regretful. For one second only, he allowed himself to look into her pale brown eyes and believe he saw understanding.

Of course he did. For the children. And what more did he want or expect? Nothing more. Nothing at all.

"I'm sorry," Joanna said, as the spokeswoman for the trio. "But if we let you stay here, we'll ruin our business."

"I know. I'll find something else."

"Where?" Mandy demanded. "I don't know of any empty place in town."

"Except—" Joanna turned to stare at Glory.

"Of course." Mandy gave Glory her attention as well.

"Your room behind the shop," they said in unison. "It's furnished and everything."

"No. It just wouldn't work."

"Why not?" Again the pair spoke at once.

"She's right," Levi said, but they didn't hear him. He did not intend to move into her shop. See her at work every day. Be aware of her comings and goings. Be tempted to watch her. Speak to her. Wonder if she would perhaps drop in for a cup of coffee and a visit. How could he keep his mind on his task under such circumstances? "She's right," he said again, louder, more insistent.

All three stared at him.

"She is not." Mandy seemed shocked he would agree.

"Yes, I am." Glory's expression was rife with anger. He'd agreed with her, hadn't he? No reason she should be upset about it.

Joanna looked from Glory to Levi and back again. "You two fighting about something?"

"No, ma'am." Levi was firm in his denial.

Joanna turned to Glory and waited for her answer. When it wasn't forthcoming, she planted her hands on her hips. "Don't tell me. You've done something so outrageous you offended him."

"I did not." She glowered at Levi.

He couldn't help but grin. No, she hadn't. But he had. He'd kissed her. Told her he was sorry. But was he? Not completely.

Joanna saw his grin. "Something is going on between you two. I can tell."

Levi shrugged, and Glory glowered, but neither offered an explanation.

Joanna sighed. "If that's the way you're going to be. . . Then what are you going to do with the children?"

"I'm not sure. Nothing seems ideal. But then anything is better than sitting alone at the side of the road." The thought cheered him. "We'll manage."

Only one option presented itself. He'd throw himself and his charges on Mr. Phelps's mercy. His house was tiny, but they could squeeze in.

He gathered up the children and their belongings and headed out. He'd check on Widow Kish first.

As he approached the house, he saw the door open. But as he drew closer, he saw the door was not just open. It was missing. Something was wrong. "Stay here," he told the children and dropped to the ground to ease forward.

A big sign had been nailed to the side of the shack. No TRESPASSING. Who would want to trespass, and who would care? But someone obviously did.

He stepped inside. "Mrs. Kish? Are you here?" The place felt as empty as a licked-out tin can, but he investigated every corner and searched the clearing around the shack. Nothing. Nobody. What happened to the widow? All sorts of scenes raced to his mind. Someone had hurt her. She'd fallen somewhere and hurt herself. But none explained the absence of her belongings. Had she suddenly decided to move? But she said she had no family.

He mounted his horse again and turned back to town.

"Where's the lady we was supposed to see?" Emmy demanded.

"She's gone."

"Where?"

"I don't know."

"You gonna find her?"

Jack spoke from behind Levi. "Emmy, you ask too many questions."

"Well, if he's gonna find our pa, maybe he can find the lady, too."

They turned off at Mr. Phelps's house.

"Who lives here?" Emmy asked.

"A friend of mine."

"Will I like him?" She twisted around to look at Levi, forcing him to grab the back of her dress to keep her from falling.

"She talks too much," Jack muttered.

"Do not."

"Yes, you do. Even Pa said so."

Emmy's face grew instantly sad, and tears filled her big eyes. "Is that why he left?"

Jack relented of his scolding. "Course not, silly. He had something to do. Remember?"

Levi wanted to find their father and demand an explanation. Why would he leave his children even for a moment? But right now he had to do something to restore Emmy's cheerfulness. "Probably right now he's wishing he could hear your voice." And if he wasn't, the man didn't deserve to be a father. Forbidden, his thoughts went to Glory. Seems her father didn't deserve the privilege either.

He took the children with him to the door, knocked, and went inside at Mr. Phelps's call to enter. He went into the kitchen and blinked. Widow Kish sat across the table from Mr. Phelps, and they were both drinking tea.

"Join us," Mr. Phelps called. "Though the children will have to share a chair."

Levi pulled out a chair for the children and sat on the fourth, all the while trying to make sense of this situation. He turned to the widow. "I was at your place. It looks deserted."

"It is. The man who owns the land came by yesterday and said I had one hour to vacate his property. And let me tell you, he wasn't prepared to listen to reason. So I gathered up my things under his eagle eye and marched out without so much as a backward look." She gave a laugh, half-bitter, half-grateful. "I stopped to say good-bye to Mr. Phelps."

"I said I could use a housekeeper if she was interested."

"So here I am."

"It's good to know you're safe and sound. I had all sorts of thoughts about what happened to you."

"I'm sure I shall enjoy it here. Like the good Lord says, 'The lines are fallen unto me in pleasant places.'"

"I'm most grateful to have someone care for my home," Mr. Phelps said. He cleared his throat and looked embarrassed. "We're hoping you'll agree to marry us."

Levi grinned. "It would be an honor." His first wedding in Bonners Ferry. "Why don't we meet at the lawyer's office in a couple of hours?" It was indeed good news. . .for the widow and lonely Mr. Phelps. But it left Levi with no place to shelter the children. There would not be room for them here now.

But—he cheered up—if the Lord could provide for a widow woman,

He could certainly provide for two abandoned children.

They visited awhile then Levi headed back to town.

He slowed his horse as he neared Glory's shop. The door was open, a man and four horses in the pen. Glory glanced up from her work, saw him, and straightened to study him. Her gaze darted to the children then back to him. Then she turned to her work.

But had he seen regret in her gaze? Was she thinking of the sparsely furnished room at the back of her shop? It sounded mighty appealing just now. But he knew what would happen to his vow of service if he moved into it. He would not be able to keep his thoughts focused on working for the Lord. He'd think far too much about how he could show he cared for Glory.

Because, despite taking the words back, he cared.

And it could not be. He thought of Matt the last time he'd seen him, in leg irons and chains, a mask of toughness almost hiding the hurt and fear beneath. Perhaps only Levi saw it, but it was enough to convince him to help his brother. And he knew how. Serve God wholly and exclusively. Trust God to soften Matt's heart.

He hadn't changed his mind.

He rode on. Unless something else turned up in the next few hours, he would be making camp for the three of them among the trees. In fact, there was no point in delaying the inevitable. First, he needed to meet Mr. Phelps and Widow Kish at the lawyer's office.

A little later, having duly married them, he headed for the store and some much-needed food supplies. Then he followed a little trail leading up the hillside.

"Where we going?" Emmy demanded.

"Would you like a picnic?"

"Yes."

He found a grassy clearing large enough to allow the sun to warm the air early in the morning. Trees surrounded them at a distance, and the blue mountains filled the horizon. "This will do." He set the children on the ground.

Free from the presence of strangers, Emmy let out a deep sigh and with a shriek of delight started to run around the clearing.

Jack started after her then grew serious. "She's just little." He turned, somewhat reluctantly Levi thought, and reached out to take the gunnysack as Levi removed it from the back of the horse.

"I'm going to need some help building a shelter."

"This isn't just a picnic, is it?"

"It's where we'll sleep until I find something else."

"Or find our pa."

"I'll get at that right away." He would give the ferry man a message to hand off to someone he considered trustworthy enough to deliver to the North-West Mounted Police across the border.

He cut branches, and Jack helped him fashion a shelter. They found more branches to create a bed for them. The nights would cool off, but with a fire in front of the open side, they should be fine. And if it rained? Well. . .he hung a roll of canvas on the open side just in case.

He wasn't much of a cook, but they enjoyed pieces of cheese and biscuits, both of which he'd been able to purchase at the store. They remained there all afternoon, the children playing so happily he couldn't bear to take them away to return to town and check on. . .things. Mostly he thought of Glory and warned himself to remember his vow. Later, he fried up some salt pork for supper. If he felt comfortable leaving the children, he'd hunt some fresh meat. But he was reluctant to leave them.

The next morning, they had more biscuits and some canned peaches. The children ate heartily without complaint.

"I need to do some things today," he informed them after they'd eaten and cleaned up. "You'll have to come with me."

Emmy stuck out her chin, prepared to argue.

Jack grabbed her hand. "Come on."

"I don't want to. I'm having fun."

Jack faced her and grew very serious. "Emmy, you must not make him regret taking care of us."

"We was doing fine by ourselves, weren't we?"

"You were scared."

"Only at night."

"And when you saw people coming."

Her bottom lip quivered. "I was only hoping it was Pa."

Levi decided it was time to intervene and clear up any fears triggered by the suggestion Jack had made. "I'll never regret helping you two, but I need to send a message about your pa. You want to come with me?"

That brought an eager response from them both.

Their first stop was the ferry where Levi wrote the message on a piece of paper. The ferry man promised to see it into safe hands.

Chapter 8

For two days Glory watched Levi ride through town with the children. If she thought it would make him change his mind, she would track him down and insist he move into the little room adjoining her shop. It galled her to think of the children camping out, though they no doubt considered it an adventure.

Joanna had learned they had a rough camp up the hill. "That's no place to have children. Glory, you should persuade Levi to move into your room."

"You heard him. He doesn't want to." She managed to keep the bitterness from her voice. He made it clear he regretted stealing a kiss, saying he cared. Even living in a room she owned was too much. As if he couldn't abide a hint of her presence.

"Did you two argue about something? Did he say something when he stopped your horses?"

Joanna could be so dense sometimes.

"Of course he said something. Told me I was foolish."

Joanna chuckled. "You're certainly foolhardy. Even you can't deny that."

"I don't care what anyone thinks."

"Exactly. And Levi is a preacher. I expect he does care what people think. He must be circumspect."

"Or real good at fooling people."

Joanna jerked about to face her. "Glory, you don't believe that." Her eyes narrowed. "I suppose you accused Levi of being false. No wonder he avoids you."

"Does he? I hadn't noticed." She stomped away to take care of her chores. Not for anything would she let Joanna guess how much it stung to realize even her sister was aware of Levi's attempt to stay as far away from her as possible. "I don't care." She said the words time and again but couldn't force herself to believe them.

Truth was, the dining room table seemed empty without him. The breakfast table lacked something.

She sat beside Toby now to peel potatoes and turnips.

"Levi said he's trying to find the children's father," Toby said. "Sent a message up north. Hopes he'll hear something soon."

Glory grunted acknowledgment of his statement.

"He says the children keep asking after their pa. They're afraid he won't know where to find them."

"Any father who cares wouldn't have left them in the first place."

"Levi says they had been traveling with some others and parted ways. Then their father realized his friend had left behind a sack of things. He had to ride hard to catch up and told the kids to wait for him. Said he'd only be half an hour or so."

"Long half hour."

"Levi says something must have happened."

Levi said. She didn't want to hear it again. Why did everyone else champion him while she felt dismissed, invisible? She hated the feeling. Hated that she couldn't control it.

"I've got something to do." She hurried to her shop, saddled Pal, and headed for the pen where her other horses looked up, anxious for their oats.

She had noticed the No Trespassing sign on Widow Kish's shack. No doubt put there by the same man who threatened to kick her and the horses off his land. Sure he had the right. But she didn't want to move. This was convenient. Had good grass and a beautiful view. But she didn't have enough money to purchase it.

And little faith God would help her.

She had barely arrived at the pen when it started to rain. She hadn't given the weather any thought and glanced around. The sky was heavy, threatening a downpour. Meant soggy wet clothes and muddy shoes around the table tonight. The air would be heavy with the smell of wet leather and damp wool.

But it wasn't the stopping house that was utmost in her mind. . .Levi and the children were camped out. According to both Toby and Joanna he had only a rough shelter. It would not be waterproof. The three of them would be cold and wet.

They'd be okay. She said the words over and over as if by repetition she could convince herself. But her efforts proved futile.

She pulled her slicker from where she kept it tied to the saddle, slipped it on, and headed back to town. Rain came down in sheets. It dripped from her hat brim, slashed against her face, drizzled down her neck. Spring rains could be awfully cold. Her hands were like winter ice, her legs as cold as yesterday's coffee.

Her thoughts had gone to a defenseless little girl. A boy who, no matter how miserable he felt, would not complain. And Levi's concern at knowing both children were suffering from the cold and wet. He wouldn't take them to the stopping house because of Emmy's fear of strangers, but there was one place where they could find protection from the elements and privacy from strangers. The room at the back of her shop. It was a perfectly good room. Seemed a shame for it to be empty. No need for them to get in each other's way.

She stopped at the house and stood in the doorway. "Jo," she yelled, not wanting to take off her wet things to go inside.

Joanna stuck her head from the kitchen. "What?"

"It's raining."

Joanna shook her head. "I know. Is that all you want?"

Glory hesitated. She wanted to let Joanna know where she was going. But she wanted more. Perhaps assurance she wasn't being a fool. "I expect the children will be wet and miserable."

"What children?" She leaned against the door and grinned. "Oh. You mean *Levi* and the children."

Glory wrinkled her nose at the way Joanna emphasized the word *Levi*. As if it had special importance. But she decided not to defend herself at the moment. "I'm going to persuade them to use the room at the shop. At least it's dry."

"About time you came to your senses."

"What's that supposed to mean?"

"If you can't figure it out yourself, I'm not going to waste my breath explaining. Go on. Get out of here."

As Glory turned to leave, Joanna called, "I'll send Mandy to fill the wood box and take up some things you'll be needing."

It wasn't until Glory rode from the yard that she realized Joanna had said "you," as if taking for granted Glory would help Levi care for the children.

"About time," she'd said. "Figure it out yourself."

Glory grinned. She had it figured out already. She intended to make Levi take back his words about not being able to care. She pretended it was only out of spite, because it had hurt to have him take it back, but it was more than that. She wanted him to care about her.

She needed him to, even though she wanted it to be otherwise. She was more than half certain she would regret cracking open a long-shut door in her heart.

The trail to the ferry had turned into mud. She slogged through it and turned off at a narrow path. It, too, was slippery with mud. She spoke reassuringly to Pal. At least there was still light to pick her way cautiously.

A few minutes later she broke into a clearing. Immediately she saw a shelter made out of branches with a piece of canvas over the open side. The wind battered it, allowing rain to blow in at the ends. A campfire sputtered, sending out nothing but dank smoke. They would be cold and wet.

The damp grass muffled her approach. She reined in before the flapping canvas. "Hello. Anyone home?"

A faint sound came from behind the canvas.

She called out again, louder this time. "It's raining, in case anyone cares to notice."

"We noticed." Levi lifted the corner of the canvas. "You rode out here to tell us that?"

She studied him. His hat was off, his hair darkened by dampness. A poncho draped over his shoulders. "Where are the children?"

"In here." Jack's voice seemed to come from under Levi's arm.

"We're trying to keep dry." Emmy's voice came from under his chin.

"And are you? Keeping dry."

"No," Emmy said. "I'm cold, too."

"It seems a shame to sit out here and suffer when there's a dry, warm room back in Bonners Ferry."

Jack's face appeared beside Levi's. "There is?"

"Yup. Back room of my shop is empty. And I'm pretty sure there's a stove belching out heat right now."

Jack turned to Levi, his eyes wide with longing. "Emmy's awfully cold."

Glory guessed she wasn't the only one. The three of them looked like they'd been plucked from the river and left to drip in a brisk wind. She didn't feel much better herself, and the idea of a warm, dry room made her want to ride back to town without pause. But she couldn't leave the children to suffer any more than she could look at the discouragement in Levi's expression and not do something about it. "If you hand Emmy up to me, I'll tuck her under my poncho and take her to that room. You and Jack can follow."

Levi hesitated about one second then whipped his poncho off and wrapped it around Emmy, handing the child up to Glory.

"You have no protection." She saw the argument in his eyes. He'd suffer for the sake of the little girl. "Jack should be protected." She edged Emmy under her slicker and handed Levi's back. "Now let's get into some decent shelter." She didn't wait for Levi to call Billy Bob. Didn't linger to see if he and Jack would follow. She knew Levi could manage. Glory's greater concern was getting Emmy into a warm, dry place. The child was like a block of ice in her arms.

Pal fought for footing on the slippery trail.

"Be careful," Levi called from behind her.

"Always am." But it took a great deal of effort to hold Emmy close and guide Pal. She knew it would have been harder if she'd been on a horse with less common sense.

They reached the main trail, now a sea of mud, and sloshed through it to the shop. She'd left the gate open and rode straight in, Levi right behind. She didn't stop to take care of Pal or even close the gate but slid from the saddle with Emmy in her arms and raced into the room. The heat from the stove welcomed her.

Levi carried Jack inside and stood him on the floor.

A stack of towels and bedding waited on the bed. Joanna must have sent them with Mandy.

"Take Jack through to the shop." She handed him a towel and indicated the door. "Strip his wet things off and rub him dry."

"What will I wear?" Jack clutched at his wet shirt, not wanting to be seen naked.

"We'll have to dry your clothes. In the meantime, wrap up in this." She tossed Levi a blanket. "Now get so I can take care of Emmy." Already she had begun to peel off the child's wet garments.

Emmy's eyes were big and as full of misery as an old hound dog's. She shivered and her teeth chattered enough to keep her from talking.

"You'll soon be warm." Glory tossed her wet things to one side to hang later and scrubbed Emmy dry, rubbing her hard to get her blood flowing. They stood inches from the stove. . .close enough that Glory's own damp clothes steamed.

She expected Emmy to stop shivering, but the child continued to quake. "Let's wrap you up in this blanket." She bundled up the child and drew a chair close, holding Emmy as close to the stove as she could stand. Still she shook. Glory held her tight and hummed softly, thinking she only needed to calm down. She should have insisted they use her room before this, but she'd let her pride get in the way.

Jack and Levi returned. Jack's color was good. He sat cross-legged on the floor, two feet from the stove. He let the blanket drape from his shoulders. Obviously he was warmed.

Levi knelt at Glory's side. "You still cold, little one?"

Emmy nodded, her eyes wide.

Levi turned his gaze toward Glory. "I shouldn't have been so stubborn."

"Me either."

Emmy continued to shiver.

They silently shared their concern. "Maybe a hot drink would help?"

Glory nodded. "I see Mandy left water and some supplies. Knowing Joanna, there's likely tea and sugar there."

Levi hustled about filling the kettle and finding tea and sugar, but his gaze darted to Emmy every few seconds and then connected with Glory's eyes.

She tried not to watch his every move or admire the efficient way he did everything. Told herself his worry about Emmy was natural and normal. Nothing to make her insides feel empty. And when he looked into her eyes, silently letting her see his concern, there was no reason it felt like a warm, sweet drink. Except it did, and even though she told her brain not to read so much into it, her heart stubbornly followed its own way.

He poured hot water over the tea leaves and stood waiting for the tea to steep.

"Doesn't have to be too strong for her," Glory said after a moment.

He jolted like his thoughts were elsewhere. "Of course." He poured tea into a cup and ladled in a heaping spoonful of sugar. Tested the temperature of the liquid and grimaced. "Too hot." He added a bit of cold water, tested it again, and then, satisfied, he brought it over. He again squatted at Glory's side and held the cup to Emmy's mouth. "Drink some, sweetie. It will make you feel better."

He bent close to Emmy, giving Glory plenty of opportunity to study his profile. Strong jawed as she already knew. Little contrasting lines fanning from the corners of his eyes from squinting into the harsh sunlight. An outdoor man. A tiny doubt niggled. Wasn't a preacher an inside sort of man? The thought barely had time to surface before she continued her study. Long, dark eyelashes. His hair was almost dry, thick and untamed. Like Levi himself. He didn't let Bull stop him from going into the saloon. He stood up to Glory even in her most angry defiance. Even said he cared. Though he'd taken it back.

Levi glanced up, caught her studying him, and sat back on his heels to match her look for look. Neither of them spoke. The only sounds were the crackle of wood in the stove, Jack's low murmur as he played with a bit of leather he'd found in the shop, and the chatter of Emmy's teeth.

It was the latter sound that made Glory blink and turn her attention to the child. "Aren't you getting warm yet?"

"My stomach is cold."

Levi looked startled. "That doesn't sound very good."

Glory wished she could say it was okay, but she didn't know. "All I know is to give her warm drinks and keep her wrapped warmly. Sooner or later she'll start to get warm." *Don't you think?* she silently asked Levi. Too bad there wasn't a doctor nearby.

He lifted one shoulder to indicate he didn't know. "Seems you're doing all that can be done." He urged Emmy to swallow the rest of the tea. He straigthened, walked to the door, and stared at it then strode back to her side. "I should have found better shelter for them before this happened."

"How were you supposed to know it would rain?"

"Children deserve to be in the care of adults who know how to provide for them."

She held his gaze, seeing his frustration, understanding his feelings of inadequacy. Her own thought echoed his words. "Children need people to care for them." She'd let her feelings toward Levi make her neglectful of these children.

His eyes narrowed as if he thought she accused him of not caring. "I care about them. And even though I might have given you cause to think otherwise, I care about you."

Despite the shivering child in her arms, Levi's words warmed her. She ducked her head lest he see how pleased she was and delivered a firm warning to her heart. Likely by tomorrow he would be taking the words back again.

She continued to hold the child. Levi hovered at her side, touching Emmy's head every few minutes as if to check to see if she still shivered though one only had to look to see it.

His hand brushed Glory's shoulder as he reached for Emmy yet again. The nerves in her skin lit like a streak of lightning. She half expected Emmy to jump from her lap, complaining she was too hot. But Emmy continued to shiver, and Glory knew the heat came from her own reaction. Levi was so close, his presence so overwhelming.

He crossed the room again, spun around, and hurried back. As if afraid to take his gaze from Emmy, as if unable to stand by and helplessly do nothing as she continued to shiver.

Glory wanted to ease his mind. "I'm sure she'll warm up soon. Won't you, Emmy?"

Emmy nodded without speaking, her eyes even wider than before if such a thing was possible.

"In fact, I think she's shivering less now."

Levi rushed to her side and dropped to a squat. He cupped the child's head in his hands and looked at her face, taking in each feature.

Glory wanted to close her eyes at the tenderness in Levi's gaze, but she couldn't deny herself one bit of it. Maybe Mandy was right. Maybe Glory was a tiny bit jealous of the attention he gave these children. Attention she'd never had from her father.

But it wasn't fatherly attention she longed for from Levi. She wanted him to see her as a woman with—

She daren't think of what she wanted. She had other things to occupy her time and thoughts. Like getting Emmy warmed. Like earning enough money to buy that piece of land. Like—

Levi pulled the covers tighter around Emmy, his knuckles grazing Glory's arm.

She suddenly couldn't remember anything more important than this moment and sharing it with Levi.

"She's still shivering."

She ducked her head and cradled the child close.

Levi paced the room, pausing at each passing to touch Emmy's head.

His restlessness scraped along her mind. She glanced at Jack. He had fallen asleep on the floor. "Best put him on the bed."

Levi scooped up the boy and laid him on the bed, covering him with the blanket, tucking it around him tightly as she'd noticed him do before.

Again, she ached deep inside for such comfort.

Levi pulled a chair up beside Glory. "Do you want me to take her?"

"She's fine here." Glory needed to hold the little girl. Needed something in her arms. Needed the weight of her body against her chest. She felt so empy inside, Levi's voice reverberating back and forth from one side of her rib cage to the other. She had to find a way to put this agony to an end. "How did your parents die?"

"Influenza."

"And you and your brother didn't get sick?"

"No. Thank the good Lord."

"Where's your brother now?"

For a moment he didn't answer, and Glory shifted so she could watch his expression. Pain flickered through his eyes, and she wondered at the cause. Then his eyes hardened. "He's away. He'll be gone for some time."

A traveler then. "I suppose you miss him."

"A lot."

She shifted to a more comfortable position. "I always wished I had a brother. What's it like?"

He laughed softly. "Sort of like having you for a sister, I expect."

"What's that supposed to mean?" She gave him a hard look, prepared to defend herself.

"Don't get all prickly on me. But I've seen you and your sisters teasing each other and laughing at shared jokes. And"—his eyes darkened with their own teasing—"I've seen you angry enough at Mandy to try and chase her down. I expect you wanted to tie a lickin' on her."

She drew her chin up and gave him a dismissive look. "I would never beat her up."

His laughter deepened, sending ripples through her insides. "If that's true, I would venture to guess it's only for two reasons."

She wouldn't give him the satisfaction of asking what they were. She wouldn't. Un-uh. But the words burst from her mouth. "What two reasons?"

His satisfied grin notified her he had been aware of her futile mental struggle. "First, you couldn't catch her, and second, if you did try, Joanna would separate the two of you."

She sniffed. No way would she admit he was correct. Never.

He chuckled softly, a sound as full and rich as thick, sweet chocolate. "I see I'm right."

"You see nothing."

"You're wrong there. I see a lot of things."

Dare she challenge him? No. She wouldn't. She wouldn't invite him to make observations. But she couldn't let it be. "What things do you see about me?"

He shifted to face her, his gaze exploring her chin, skimming her cheeks, coming to rest on her eyes. Indeed, he seemed to see way deeper than what most people saw. His look probed the secret places of her heart.

She held her breath as he contined to study her.

"I see a beautiful woman who is as prickly as a pincushion. And as cautious and fearful as a trapped fawn."

She swallowed hard, unfamiliar emotions clogging her throat.

He touched her cheek, brushed aside a strand of hair she hadn't been aware of. "I see a woman who is afraid to let herself feel. She's afraid to be real, let her feelings have expression because she's so often been disappointed and hurt."

She wanted to narrow her eyes, deny his words, laugh them off as false, but she couldn't. No more than she could pull back from his probing, owning look.

He sighed and sat back, freeing her from his scrutiny. "Unfortunately, I fear I will only add to your hurt."

"Excuse me?" What on earth did he mean?

"Yes. You see, I care about you. Far more than I have a right. I think you might end up hurt and disappointed."

"Really." She put as much sarcasm into the word as she could muster, but it still sounded far too begging for her liking.

"Yes. You see, I have a purpose that leaves me no room for anything else."

He as much as admitted he wasn't a preacher like he said. She tried to put that thought on top of her confusion, but it sank, leaving her staring at the things he'd said about her. He understood her as no one else did, not even her sisters. Why couldn't he simply be her friend and maybe more? She licked her lips and forced her wooden tongue to work. "A man can always change who he is and what he does."

For a moment he didn't answer. She held her breath hoping he would agree. Instead, he shook his head. "Not always, I'm afraid." He planted his palms on his knees and slowly pushed to his feet. "How's she doing?"

"She's quit shivering. In fact, she must be getting hot." She folded back the blanket. "She's flushed." She lowered the woolen cover. "She's burning up." The child was naked. Glory grabbed a towel to cover her.

She saw an old nightie Joanna must have stuck in and pulled it over Emmy's head. "Do you suppose she's taken a chill?"

"I don't know. What do we do?"

She'd never nursed a child. Only animals. She tried to calm her thoughts and think how to handle this situation.

The door crashed open, and Mandy strode in with more wood. "Joanna sent me to see if you were okay. You've been gone a long time. I took care of the horses."

Glory and Levi exchanged guilty looks. They'd forgotten the horses. For the first time she could remember, Glory had neglected an animal.

Mandy took in the pair of them huddled over Emmy.

Glory groaned. No doubt Mandy would read a lot more into the scene than it deserved. "I think Emmy's sick."

Mandy dropped the wood in the box and crossed to Levi's side. "How do you know?"

"She's so hot."

"Well, it is like a furnace in here." Mandy cracked open a window.

Levi scooped Emmy from Glory's arms and took her to the bed. She opened her eyes at the disturbance.

Jack groaned and rolled toward the wall.

"Don't her eyes look glassy?" Glory asked.

The three adults stood gazing at her.

"You ever been sick?" Glory asked Levi, hoping he might have some personal experience with this sort of thing.

"Wouldn't dare."

"What's that supposed to mean?"

"My grandparents thought it a sign of weakness. Before that I only remember my ma giving me sweet licorice tea if I didn't feel well. You?"

"Never had time for it." And hadn't paid much attention when she'd seen little ones ill. Glory turned to Mandy. "You once had the measles. Ma made you stay in bed in a dark room and insisted you drink lots of water." She bent close to Emmy. "Would you like some water?"

Emmy groaned and turned her head away.

"I don't suppose that's a good sign," Levi said.

"What do we do?" Glory looked from Mandy to Levi, wanting an answer.

They both shook their heads.

She faced Levi. "You say you're a preacher. Shouldn't you know how to help people?"

He lifted his hands in a helpless gesture. "I've never been responsible for someone so young."

"What are we going to do?" Glory didn't know if she was more scared or more angry that none of them knew. "I don't know if we should wrap her up and keep her warm or uncover her and cool her off, but there's one person who will know. Joanna. Mandy, run and ask her what we should do."

Mandy was gone before Glory finished speaking.

Suddenly she noticed how Emmy's breath whistled in and out. She turned to Levi. "Is she going to be all right?"

Levi reached for Glory's hands. "We're going to do all we can."

She sought and found comfort in his eyes, in his promise, and in the strength of his grip.

Chapter 9

L evi held Glory's hands and looked deep into her eyes—almost golden in the last of the watery daylight. Apart from worry about Emmy, he had enjoyed the afternoon with her. He'd likely not get another and would forever cherish the few hours they'd been able to spend together in harmony.

When she rode into the wet campsite, he'd never heard a more welcome voice. For the sake of the children he went with her, though it wasn't hard to make the choice. Yes, he knew he couldn't offer her anything more than an afternoon or maybe two. Maybe three or four.

He stopped right there. No more counting. No more giving himself excuses. Or reasons. He'd been as honest with her as he could be, but still, he had no intention of hurting her.

Her eyes filled with worry and—dare he think it?—trust. Just a hint of such. He gripped her hands harder, vowing he would do all he could to deserve that trust. Which meant not caring for her, not allowing her to care for him.

For two heartbeats he considered changing his mind about devoting his life to serving God. But recalling the misery in Matt's expression and knowing nothing would change unless Matt's heart changed, Levi knew he must keep his bargain with God. At whatever cost.

"Is she going to be okay?" Glory demanded again.

"I am at a loss to know what we can do except for one thing and perhaps the best thing. Pray."

She sucked in a sharp breath. "Of course. I keep telling God I am going to trust Him more. Believe His promises and all that sort of stuff. Then I forget." Her grin was crooked, her expression regretful.

"He understands our humanness and doesn't judge us for it. All He asks is that we turn back to Him after every lapse."

"Sounds awfully forgiving."

"Always. After all, God loved us enough, was forgiving enough to pour the punishment we deserved on His sinless Son."

She swallowed hard. "Makes me think how much I owe Him. A debt I can never repay."

"But that's the wonder of it. God doesn't expect us to try and pay it back. It would be impossible. God's love and forgiveness are gifts." Something about what she said tugged at his thoughts. As if he missed some detail, overlooked an important connection. But he couldn't find the elusive thing, and let it go. This was not the time to explore his own problems.

He shifted his hands and held both of Glory's in one and rested the other on her shoulder, feeling her quiver beneath his touch and then calm as she drew in a deep breath. "Shall we pray?" It took every ounce of self-control to remember his responsibility here—to act like a preacher—when his heart called out for him to pull her into his arms, press her to his chest, comfort and hold her. He stiffened his arm and bowed his head. "Lord God, the One who loves us, touch little Emmy's hot body and cool it. Help no harm come to her. Amen."

He kept his eyes closed and silently prayed for strength and self-control to keep his eyes on the task set before him, the road he had chosen. He needed it as never before as Glory leaned into his touch.

Time to shift things before he couldn't control his emotions. He withdrew his hand from her shoulder but continued to clasp her hands. "Tell me how you came to be a farrier."

She blinked, obviously startled by his sudden shift of focus.

He grinned. "I'm only trying to get us thinking of something else. Maybe ease our worry."

"Isn't prayer supposed to do that?"

"I simply thought it would help the process."

She studied him a full ten seconds until he wanted to squirm.

"Stop looking at me like that. It reminds me of my grandmother."

Glory blinked then patted her face. "I've got wrinkles?"

His chuckle came from deep inside, a place where he stored secret pleasures. "Not wrinkles. Just a way of looking at me that makes me think you can read my mind."

"Maybe I can." She looked mysterious as if trying to convince him she saw many secrets.

He met her look without flinching, not caring if she saw secrets. He longed to open his heart to her and share the hidden contents with her. But he had made a vow, and God did not look kindly upon people breaking vows made to Him.

"How did you become a preacher?" she asked, her quiet voice pulling him from his mental wandering.

"I'll tell you if you answer my question first."

"What question would that be?" Her look of confusion didn't convince him she'd forgotten, and he only grinned for answer.

"Very well. When I was about thirteen, our pa left us with a couple who ran a livery barn. We were expected to work to earn our keep. So I learned to look after the horses and bothered the man to teach me how to trim hooves and shoe the horses. He might never have done so except one day he cut his hand badly and needed my help."

"I'm sure he never regretted it."

She lifted one shoulder in a gesture of uncertainty and indifference. "Couldn't say. Pa showed up shortly after that and dragged us off to another place. Where he promptly left us high and dry again. This time we refused to live with the family he'd stuck us with. One thing about having to work for our keep, we'd learned lots of things, so we started working for ourselves."

"You did farrier work?"

"Or whatever would bring in a few coins. Like train horses who had been ruined by mistreatment."

"That blue roan wouldn't be one of them, I suppose?"

"Yup. Pal, too. Horses can develop some very bad habits."

"Just like people." They searched each other's eyes. He found himself going deep, into her hurt. "You rescue hurt horses because they remind you of yourself."

Shutters blocked her feelings. Her eyes darkened. "It's your turn."

"Actually, becoming a preacher was almost natural. My grandfather was one. Several times as he grew older and was too weak to stand behind the pulpit, he asked me to do it. I guess you could say I inherited the job."

"I expect you had a choice in the matter."

"Don't we always?" Matt had the same choices as Levi and had chosen the opposite.

Again, he and Glory looked at each other. Studied each other. Her brown eyes revealed wonder at his question as if the idea of a choice was new to her. "Most times our choices are driven by what others choose to do."

He struggled to pull himself back from the pain and anger in her voice and in her eyes. If he didn't step away mentally, he would pull her into his arms and hold her tight, promise he would never do anything to hurt her, always protect her. "Others do things that impact our lives. . .sometimes in a cruel way." *Lord, keep me from hurting Glory.* "Seems to me we still have a choice about whether to let it make us bitter or whether to rise above it."

She sucked in air hard. Blinked. Again shuttered her emotions. "Maybe so."

The door banged open, sending a rush of cold, damp air across the room.

Glory sprang away from him, clutching her hands to her waist.

Joanna strode in, Mandy at her heels. "I hear the little one is sick."

Glory nodded. "Burning up. I didn't know what to do." She tossed a glance over her shoulder at Levi. "None of us did."

Did he detect regret in her gaze? Was it regret at their discussion being interrupted? Or regret at the choices flung into her life by others? He hoped it was a tiny bit of the former, even though he knew he must guard his feelings very carefully.

Joanna leaned over the child, pressed her hand to Emmy's forehead.

Emmy stirred and moaned.

"Get me a basin of lukewarm water."

Mandy hurried to do so.

"And a washcloth."

Glory plucked one from the pile.

"You have to get the fever to break. Sponging her to cool her body is the only way I know." She pushed the baggy nightgown out of the way and set to washing Emmy's chest and legs, letting her skin dry in the warm air.

The adults hovered at the side of the bed as Joanna sponged Emmy over and over.

Thankfully, Jack crowded to the far edge of the bed and turned his back toward them, able to sleep through the disturbance.

Time ceased to exist for those watching Joanna work and waiting for her to declare Emmy was going to be okay.

Twice, Glory looked at Levi, her eyes wide with appeal. He nodded. And at her silent urging, prayed aloud for the fever to leave.

Suddenly Mandy straightened. "It's stopped raining."

They glanced at the window. Saw it was dark outside.

Joanna paused from her task. "Mandy, you'll have to go back to the stopping house so people can bed down."

Mandy hesitated.

"I'll let you know as soon as Emmy is okay."

"You won't forget?"

Joanna spared her a quick look. "I won't forget."

Mandy slipped away.

"I can take over," Glory said and edged Joanna aside. "You sit down for a while."

Joanna looked about ready to argue.

"I'll make tea," Levi offered.

"Has anyone eaten?" Joanna, always concerned about caring for everyone.

Glory's attention was on the child, which left Levi to answer Joanna. "We haven't had time."

Levi made tea and poured Joanna a cupful where she sat at the table. He offered to take Glory's place so she could sit with her sister.

"I need to do this."

Levi sat across from Joanna. Need? Why did she say it that way? As if it was her responsibility.

Joanna sipped her tea. "She can't stand to see any living thing suffer without doing something."

"She told me about the horses."

"I tell her she's taking care of her own hurts by helping them."

Levi chuckled. "I said something similar."

He and Joanna smiled silent understanding at each other.

"I'm right here," Glory groused. "I can hear every word you say."

Joanna and Levi grinned at each other. He couldn't speak for Joanna, but he'd wanted Glory to hear every word.

Glory sat back on her heels and released a gust over her teeth. "I don't think she's so hot anymore."

Joanna sprang to her side, ran her hands over Emmy's body. "Her fever has broken. Thank You, God."

"Amen," Glory and Levi chorused and grinned at each other in shared joy.

Joanna pulled a sheet over Emmy. "She'll have to be watched carefully to make sure the fever doesn't return."

"I'll watch her," Glory said.

Joanna studied Glory. Levi wondered if she would tell Glory it was inappropriate to stay here with him after dark.

Glory must have expected the same thing. "I can't leave until I'm sure she's okay."

Joanna nodded. "I know. I understand. But I must get back to the stopping house." She hesitated. "I'll send Mandy back with supper. She can stay with you." She hesitated and looked as if she wanted to say more then shook her head and ducked out the door.

Glory straigthened and met Levi's look. The air between them grew still as if neither breathed.

He couldn't say what she was thinking, but for himself he felt as if they shared a special moment, a special awareness of each other, of having shared a common concern and conquered it. He shifted his gaze to Emmy—their common concern. She lay peaceful, her color normal.

He brought his eyes back to Glory. She watched him, waiting.

He closed the distance between them until they were only inches apart. Everything in him wanted to pull her into his arms and hold her close. Let his heart thud against his chest in acceptance of his feelings. He reached out and caught a strand of hair from off her cheek. Silky. He curled it around his finger and tugged at it. Strong. Just like Glory. Tough and resilient. Yet fragile. She'd been hurt in the past, and if he wasn't careful, he could very well hurt her yet again.

Sucking in every bit of self-control he could muster, he freed his finger from her hair and dropped his arm to his side. "Are you hungry?" A stupid question when his mind burgeoned with so many more demanding things, like what did she feel toward him?

"Now that you mention it, I suppose I am." She spun away and went to the table, gathering up the cups used when they had tea. "Mandy will be back soon with food."

Although he was hungry, he didn't care about food. So many things crowded his heart and mind. Things he couldn't voice. He forced forward the reminder of Matt in chains. Now in a tiny prison cell. Slowly, determinedly, he brought his vow into focus. For Matt, for his salvation, for his redemption, Levi would give up everything but service to God.

⚭

When Mandy returned, her arms full of food and other things Joanna thought they might need, Glory let herself draw in the first full breath she'd taken since Joanna left.

Why did Levi touch her and then pull back? Not that it mattered to her. It was strange, that was all. Reminded her of Big Gray, the gelding who shivered when she touched him.

Had Levi been hurt by something? That piqued her curiosity.

Mandy put a pot of stew on the stove and a plate of biscuits on the table. She lifted the lid off the pot and sniffed. "I'm hungry."

The aroma of the stew filled the room, and Glory realized she was, too.

Jack sat up. "Is that food?"

Glory stared at the boy. Startled, she turned toward Levi and saw a matching expression.

Levi blinked. "Nothing will disturb that boy's sleep but the smell of food." He held Glory's gaze as he laughed.

She laughed, too, her tension disappearing. She'd let her imagination and her innate wariness make her see things not there. Maybe she was the one like Big Gray.

The four of them sat at the tiny table, enjoying the food and laughing as Mandy told them of the near riot at the stopping house because the men had to wait while she prepared the room for sleeping.

Later, Jack crawled back into bed and fell asleep. Levi watched him in wonder. "You'd think he hadn't slept in days."

"When was the last time he slept in a bed?" Glory asked. "And apart from the unsettling night in the stopping house, when did he last sleep in a room with four walls? I'm guessing he feels safe for the first time in many a day."

Levi continued to study the sleeping Jack. "Trusting us to take care of him." He slowly faced Glory, a look of determination hardening his eyes.

She couldn't pull away from that look. Could not think what it meant.

Mandy yawned loudly. "I know how Jack feels. I just want to curl up somewhere and sleep."

Glory checked Emmy. "She's still okay. Sleeping like a baby. Perhaps we should waken her and give her some broth."

Levi sank to the edge of the bed and shook Emmy gently. "Wake up, little one."

Emmy cracked open her eyes and allowed Levi to hold her upright while Glory spooned in the warm liquid. Soon her head lolled to one side, and Levi laid her down again.

Mandy grabbed a blanket and a pillow and settled in a corner. She was soon breathing deeply, though Glory knew she was a light sleeper.

She would waken instantly and be completely alert if any sudden noise disturbed her.

She and Levi sat at the table. Glory tried to keep herself amused and her thoughts distracted by tracing the cracks on the tabletop.

"I had hoped to hear something about their father by now." Levi's voice was soft.

"It's hard to find a man who doesn't want to be found."

"I can't believe he would abandon the children at the side of the road. Not intentionally. Something must have happened."

A thousand arguments sprang to her mind. But obviously he didn't understand how leaving was easy for some people. That not everyone had someone to fall back on apart from brothers or sisters. And when they were as young as Jack and Emmy, that wasn't much more than comfort. "You must have been grateful your grandparents took you in when your parents died."

For a moment he didn't answer, and she studied him. What she saw was not gratitude but regret.

"I appreciated having a home, but they were very strict. Our parents had allowed us a lot more freedom than our grandparents were prepared to give us." He paused. "It was hard to adjust."

"But you did."

"I tried. It was harder for Matt. He was seventeen and thought he was an adult, had to answer to no one. The only reason he hung about was to make sure I would be okay. And then he left."

"Did you see him again?"

"Off and on."

The man must travel a lot. Not unlike Pa. And maybe for the same reasons, adventure but also escape from responsibility. "You miss him."

"Yes. I'll do anything to get him back."

"What can you do? Like you said, he's a man now. He makes his own choices."

"I'm trusting God to change him."

She studied that for a few minutes. "Does trusting come easy for you?"

A chuckle rumbled from his chest. "Not always. You work with mishandled horses, right?"

She nodded.

"How hard is it for them to learn to trust? And then how often and how quickly do they retreat if something frightens or threatens them?" He gave another deep-throated chuckle. "Guess I feel like one of those horses. I trust God, but every time something challenges it, I have to learn to trust all over."

"It's hard for a mistreated horse to learn to trust at all."

The way he looked at her, she knew he understood she wasn't talking solely about animals. "So what do you do?"

"I just keep proving they can trust me. I just keep being kind. Giving them oats. That sort of thing."

"Not unlike how God treats us."

She checked Emmy as she contemplated his words. Liked how they made her feel about God. "I'm trying to learn to trust." The child's skin felt a normal temperature, and she returned to her chair.

"Me, too."

As they sat in the yellow light, the quiet around them as cozy as a blanket, it was easy to think of him as honest, a real preacher. She let herself be lulled by the atmosphere as they talked about things they did as children, about horses they had known, and various other topics. They took turns checking on Emmy and sighed with relief when her fever didn't return.

The sky lightened.

"It's morning." Levi sounded as surprised as she felt. It was impossible they had spent the whole night talking.

Glory stared out the window. Something had changed in her feelings toward him. She felt as if she had tasted the oats he'd offered. Wanted more. But she wasn't sure she even trusted him. Was he who and what he said he was? She tried to reconcile her doubts with the things she'd seen—his prayers, the way he took care of those in need, his own struggles with trust. . . .

She didn't know what to believe.

Mandy tossed aside the blanket and scrambled to her feet. "Is little Emmy okay?"

"Slept all night. No fever."

"Good. Then if you and I know what's good for us, we better get back and help Joanna."

Glory needed no more excuse to head for the door. She barely glanced at Levi, not trusting herself to hide her confusion and uncertainty.

Outside, she and Mandy strolled toward the stopping house.

"I heard you and Levi talking all night." Mandy nudged Glory and giggled. "Seems you've changed your mind about the man."

"We were talking about horses. He knows a lot about horses for a preacher." She forced suspicion into her voice.

"Well, he rides. I would hope he knows something about the animal under his saddle." She moved far enough away to be out of reach. "I heard you talking about trust. I guess you're learning how to trust a man instead of shoving him into a naughty corner along with Pa. Where, I might point out, he doesn't belong, just as lots of the men don't. I like Levi. He's a good man."

"You're so willing to trust every man that you scare me."

Mandy stopped and stared. "I am not."

"Always ready to give Pa an excuse for leaving."

Mandy snorted and stomped onward. "At least I don't run from every man like he was poison."

"I just find it hard to trust all the words that come from a man's mouth."

Mandy, several steps ahead, turned to face her. "Now there's a sudden revelation." She wrinkled her nose in mocking.

Glory laughed. "Guess I'm pretty obvious, aren't I?"

Chapter 10

L evi got the children up, helped them put on their clothes that had dried overnight, and made a simple breakfast from the supplies Joanna sent over. He'd make a point of going by later in the day and paying her for them. After watching Emmy carefully for an hour or more, he came to the conclusion she had recovered from her illness the night before.

What a night it had been. He'd cracked open his heart to Glory, tentatively sharing things with her, knowing he must maintain strict boundaries and yet finding such sweet solace in telling her of his childhood.

She told story after story of the horses she'd worked with—abused, mishandled, neglected. Levi wondered if she realized how much she revealed of herself when she told about earning an animal's trust, the way the animals tested her. He guessed she would have stopped talking if she had.

He watched Jack and Emmy play at the table. Seems they could amuse themselves quietly if they had to. Could he persuade someone else to watch them while he crossed the river to go look for their father? He knew one person he would trust to have consideration for their feelings—Glory. While he waited for her to open the shop, he tended to dishes and generally made the place livable. He heard her at the shop door. "Come on, kids. We're going out."

Jack dashed to the door as eager as a young kitten to be outside. Levi carried Emmy.

Already the sun had dried the tiny pasture next to the shop where Billy Bob and Pal grazed. He edged around to the front of the shop.

Glory had stepped inside and didn't noticed his approach until his boots thumped on the step. She spun around, and when she saw it was him, her expression went from welcome to caution.

He had business to attend to. For a moment he diverted himself as he put Emmy on her feet. He focused on that in order not to think of the gentle hours of last night. He removed his hat and turned it round and round in his hands. "How much is the rent on this place?"

She hesitated. He could practically see her thoughts churning. "I'd let you stay for free, but I need money to buy more oats for my horses."

"I can afford it," Levi assured her. He had funds left from the amount he had set aside for living on. He didn't intend to dip into the money he'd earmarked for starting a permanent work here—money he'd use as he felt the Lord direct.

"Two dollars for the month."

"Two dollars?" he sputtered. "You sure?" It was far less than he knew she could reasonably ask.

"You ever known me to lie?"

He correctly read the challenge in her voice. "No, ma'am. Not once. Didn't mean to imply otherwise. Promise you won't challenge me to a shootout at high noon."

Glory rolled her eyes to let him know just what she thought of his foolishness, noticed the worried look on the children's faces, and leaned close to whisper, "He's just being silly."

Emmy shrugged one shoulder. "I knew that. Sort of."

Levi whispered to the children as well. "I was just being cautious. She's not the sort you want to fool around with."

Emmy giggled.

Jack took a minute to decide if they were joshing or serious, but when he saw the pleased look on Levi's face at making Emmy laugh, he chuckled.

Glory tossed her hands skyward and let out a groan. "I can see I'll get nothing but silliness from the three of you." But she grinned, ruffled Jack's hair, and squeezed Emmy's shoulder.

Levi met her look and held it. He didn't free her from his intensity as he leaned back on his heels and studied her.

She shifted her eyes past his shoulder, but her gaze returned as if she couldn't look away.

"This room will be just the place for us until I find their pa."

"Yup," she said. "Might teach you a few important lessons."

"Like what?" She sounded almighty pleased about something, and he suspected it wasn't about last night.

She half turned away. "Things like nightmares, silly fears, foods that gag certain people, and. . .things like saying something then taking it back. You don't get to do that with kids."

So they were back to the start. He caught her shoulder and spun her about to face him. "Glory, I didn't mean to hurt you. I don't plan to hurt you again." Why then did he allow an evening of quiet talk, sharing memories and experiences, and why above all was he so stupidly happy to rent a room from her? A room sharing a wall with her business where she would show up every morning?

"I wasn't talking about me."

"Yes, I think you were." But he had already gone over the line and he must stop right there and retreat. He pulled two dollars from his pocket and handed it to her.

She hesitated as if reconsidering.

"Take it."

She grabbed the money and stuffed it in her pocket.

He grinned, knowing she fought a desire to tell him to pack his bags and leave. She might have except for the children. He didn't doubt she cared about them. She understood how it felt to be waiting for their pa, afraid, uncertain, and with no place to belong.

Just thinking of it made his insides twist like he'd swallowed a bitter drink. Though it was as much on Glory's behalf as the children's. "I need some help," he murmured.

Glory chuckled softly. "I'm sure you'll manage just fine, Mr. Preacher Man." She turned her back. "I need to attend to my chores."

She'd misunderstood him. Thought he meant with looking after the children. It was sort of what he meant, and he decided to push the idea and grabbed her arm. "Have mercy on three poor souls."

She froze in place, one hand extended toward her worktable, her head half-turned toward the window.

A snap of silent power blazed up his arm and pooled in his heart like he'd barely missed being struck by a bolt of lightning. He'd touched her before, several times last night, but this time was different. This time it was daylight. There was no crisis with the children to excuse his touch. He pulled back and forced his tone to remain teasing. "You wouldn't leave us to manage on our own, would you?"

The children watched in confusion.

Glory blinked, seemed to shake herself. Her gaze went only as far as the children, and she seemed to struggle to remember their presence. Then she grinned down at them. "Do you think he's being silly again?"

They nodded, still not quite sure what to make of it. Emmy looked up from under her thick eyelashes. "Maybe he could use some help. He can't cook."

Levi couldn't believe his ears. "I haven't let you starve."

Emmy sighed. "'Preciate your kindness and all, but I'm getting a mite tired of hard biscuits and jerky."

"Shush, Emmy," Jack warned.

Glory tipped her head back and laughed.

Levi shoved his hat back on his head to hide his confusion. He thought he was doing just fine at looking after the children even though he was admittedly inexperienced.

"Where's my pa? Why didn't he come back for us?" Emmy choked out the words.

He reached out to pull them close. "Something must have happened to detain him. I'm sure we'll hear from him soon. Likely he's on his way back for you right now."

Glory nudged him aside. "Don't make promises you can't keep or have to take back."

Her words stung. "I didn't."

"Yes, you did. You can't know if he'll come back or not."

Emmy wailed louder. "I want my pa."

Glory knelt before the pair. "I can't say what happened to your pa. Seems you'll have to wait and find out. But right now you have a safe, warm place to stay."

He was surprised she didn't tell them to buck up. Not that he had anything to offer them but words of assurance he based on nothing more than hope and goodwill.

Emmy scrubbed at her eyes with her fists. "How long has your pa been gone?" she asked Glory.

Glory's expression hardened. "He's been in and out of my life since I was Jack's age."

"Don't it bother you?"

Levi watched, wondering how she would answer. Would she admit it did, made her wary, defensive?

She leaned forward, bringing herself to eye level with the children. "I can't say it doesn't bother me, but that's just how it is. I can't change anything."

Emmy nodded. "I guess not." She sucked in air. "I'll be okay."

Glory lifted her face toward Levi, a look of admiration on her face at the child's sudden acceptance of the facts.

Levi wanted to protest. Do something to prove to them all they could trust a man. A father. He addressed Glory. "Tell you what. If you would watch the children for me, I'll go and find their pa."

Glory took two steps away and looked at Levi with eyes darkened with suspicion.

"I'll be back. I promise."

"How can I look after them? I've got my work." She waved an arm around the little shop. "My horses." A vague wave to indicate some place beyond town. "My chores at the stopping house."

"They're right here. You can keep an eye on them as you work. Take them with you the rest of the time. Just spend the night here so they aren't alone."

Two pairs of big brown eyes begged her to do it, far more effectively than any words he could utter.

She sighed. Gave him a look of warning.

He read her loud and clear. *You better not run out on this.*

"I'll be back unless I'm dead. You can count on it. In fact"—he opened the notebook she kept on her worktable, tore out a page, and wrote on it—"I will carry this in my pocket just in case." He handed the note to her.

She read aloud, her voice growing incredulous by the end. " 'In case of my demise, please return my body to Miss Glory Hamilton at Bonners Ferry. Inform her of the circumstances of my death and tell her I tried to get back.' It doesn't matter to me. I just don't want to see the children building false hope." With a flick of her wrist, she tossed the note at him.

He caught it and stuck it in his pocket.

She gave him a look fit to crispy-fry bacon. "I'll watch them. You go find a missing father."

"Which one. Theirs or yours?" He didn't know what possessed him to say such a thing, but now that he had, he waited to see her reaction.

She pulled the two children to her side. "I don't need a father. They do." Her eyes challenged him to think otherwise.

Wisely, he held his tongue, but as he crossed on the ferry, he prayed not only to find Mr. Templeton but also Mr. Hamilton. He'd demand both men return and face their children.

∽

"If anyone can find Pa, Mr. Powers can," Emmy insisted as Glory prepared her for bed.

"I'm just saying don't get your hopes too high."

"Mr. Powers told us to pray. He said God listens to even little girls."

Glory closed her eyes for a moment. She used to believe it without question, but her prayers for her pa to come back and take care of them had never been truly answered. Now she was trying to learn to trust God all over. Right now her fervent prayer was for God to provide a way for her to buy the land where she was keeping her horses.

Jack sat on the edge of the bed, waiting for Glory to read them a story and tuck them in. "I remember Pa saying sometimes it's hard to trust when it seems things are going wrong, but that's when we need to trust the hardest."

Glory glanced at the boy. Where did such a young person get such wisdom? Did he suspect Levi would not return with the hoped-for, prayed-for result? Was he preparing himself for the worst? "Trust is indeed hardest when we need it worst." And when she needed it most she'd let it go. No more. Levi was right. God's promises weren't subject to change.

She tucked the children in and listened to their breathing grow deep as she sat at the table and read from the Bible. But her thoughts kept drifting. Would Levi be able to find their father? Would he happen to run into her pa, too? And if he did. . . ?

She would not allow herself any dreams or hopes. Instead, she prayed for Levi to find the children's father and bring him back to claim his children.

Two days later and she waited impatiently for the answer to two prayers—a way to buy the land and a man returning on a black horse with a second man at his side.

She sat helping Toby peel potatoes while Emmy and Jack perched a few yards away, watching the ferry.

All her old doubts and fears returned. Rawhide Kid disguising himself as a preacher. "Looking for someone has given him a handy excuse to disappear for a few days. Maybe I'll ask the ferry man to get someone to pick up a newspaper from up in the territories. Might provide interesting reading."

Toby grunted. "I think the man could live a pure life for ten years and you'd still be looking for signs of something unlawful. Maybe even that wouldn't be enough." He suddenly faced her, his expression half-mournful, half-accusing. "Glory, what would it take to make you trust a man?"

His question caught her off guard. She had to think about it. Finally, she realized she didn't have an answer. "Don't ever plan to need to trust a man." A tiny voice deep inside reminded her of how nice it had been to share those hours with Levi not so long ago. For a little while, she'd let herself forget her doubts and suspicions.

Only because Emmy's illness and the darkness had lulled her. It wouldn't happen again.

Emmy and Jack crossed the yard and stood before her. "Why hasn't Levi come back?" Emmy demanded, the momentary spokesman for the pair.

The question echoed inside Glory's head, reminding her of all the times she had asked the question about her pa. But she didn't want to be the one to shatter this pair's world. Life would surely do it soon enough. "He promised he'd come back, didn't he?" Dead or alive.

Toby snorted at how her words contradicted what she'd said only a moment before.

"You just have to be patient."

After supper, the children returned to their station, wanting to watch until the last ferry crossed.

Glory let them. After all, she had chores to do and wasn't anxious to be shut up in the tiny room, wondering and waiting.

Later, she returned to the room and put the children to bed. She was tired, but sleep did not come easily as her thoughts chased down blind trails. *What if he doesn't come back? What will happen to the children?* She'd make sure they were safe. Joanna and Mandy would surely welcome them to stay at the stopping house. Emmy would get used to all the people coming and going.

It should have calmed her. It didn't. She kept seeing the words of that stupid note. *"In case of my demise"*—who ever used such a word?— *"tell her I tried to get back."* Dead or alive, he promised he'd get back.

Who wanted him back dead?

She flung over to her side, trying to get comfortable, and mentally counted her savings. Calculated how much she would need to earn in just over a week. It was hopeless, but nevertheless, she considered every possibility. It was not something that particularly soothed her thoughts, but it beat thinking about Levi.

Next morning the children could barely wait to get their clothes on before they begged to be able to hurry down to watch the ferry. "He'll come today," Emmy insisted.

"We can't be sure. We'll have to wait and see." Glory wanted to prepare the child for disappointment.

Emmy simply tossed her head and ignored Glory's warning. "I'm tired of waiting."

If only life were so easy. Even trusting God appeared to come with challenges and disappointments. Last night she'd read a verse in Job, chapter thirteen, verse fifteen, *"Though he slay me, yet will I trust in him."* And seems God almost slew Job. Took his children, his cattle, everything. Still Job trusted God. Glory didn't know if she could do the same given the same circumstances.

The kids scampered ahead of her to a spot where they could watch people crossing on the ferry, mostly heading north. She sat with them to watch. And wait. So Emmy was tired of waiting, was she? Glory could tell her she might be in for a lifetime of waiting unless she put the past behind her.

And yet, Glory prayed inwardly that Levi would return—alive. With Mr. Templeton at his side.

Midmorning she watched him ride to the landing site of the ferry on the far side of the river. He looked like he'd been battered mercilessly. It showed in the way his shoulders slumped, his hat tipped forward over his forehead hiding his eyes from onlookers. He rode alone and Glory knew it meant bad news of one sort or another.

The children had grown bored and played with rocks in the grass, pretending to herd them like a bunch of horses.

Glory didn't point out Levi to them. They'd have to face the bad news soon enough.

At the sound of the ferry beaching on this side of the river, they sat up and immediately saw Levi on Billy Bob. As quickly they saw that he was alone.

Jack sprang to his feet.

Emmy shrank into the grass, her hand pressed to her mouth.

Glory waited, not sure if she should urge them toward the ferry or wait for Levi to ride to them. But already Levi was headed their direction. She rose to wait by the children.

Levi swung from his horse and made the last few steps on foot. He stood before them, pushed his hat back to reveal a face wreathed in anguish and disappointment.

"You didn't find him, did you?" Jack's voice rang with resignation.

Levi squatted to Jack's level. "I'm sorry. I did find him. But he won't be coming back."

"He's dead, ain't he?" Jack bunched his fists at his side. He tried for anger, but his voice quivered.

"Yes." Levi pulled the boy into his arms and let Jack weep against his shoulder.

Glory sat beside Emmy and opened her arms.

Tears streaming down her face, Emmy climbed to Glory's lap and wrapped her arms about her neck. Hot tears soaked Glory's shoulder.

She didn't mind in the least and held Emmy close, her own eyes clouding with tears. It was even worse than knowing her pa was out there and didn't care to come back. Their pa would never come back. No false hopes. No eternal waiting.

She closed her eyes and rocked the child.

Now what?

Chapter 11

L evi scrubbed his chin, noted the rasping. He needed a shave. But it was the least of things he needed. He'd hoped for a different outcome, but there was no way to change things.

It had been a tough day. The children were understandably upset and required attention from both him and Glory.

"I couldn't have made it through this day without you." His weariness made his voice hoarse.

They stood at the side of the bed watching the children, who had finally fallen asleep. His shoulder almost touched Glory's. He wanted to find comfort in holding her, wanted to tell her the whole sorry story. "Let's go sit outside. We'll be able to hear them if they call out but won't disturb them as we talk."

She nodded, grabbed a chair, and carried it to the side of the shop.

He followed, also carrying a chair, and parked it close to hers, grateful when she made no protest or shifted farther away.

For a moment they sat in silence. The lowering sun sent pink coloring into the clouds. The tree-covered hills turned a deep green, almost black. He leaned back and tried to think of nothing but the beauty of the sky, the sureness of God's love. It was hard to concentrate on either after his trip.

"Was it awful?"

Glory's quiet question shuddered through him. "It wasn't fun. I don't know what I expected. Maybe he was injured and couldn't get back."

"I guess dead is about as injured as you can get."

He understood that she hoped to make him smile and he appreciated her efforts, but he wasn't ready to enjoy any humor.

She studied him, and he let her without meeting her look. "What happened?"

"The children told me he'd hurried away to return a package a fellow traveler had forgotten. That much I knew. What I didn't know, and neither did he, was the package had been stolen from a rough pair of men. When they saw Mr. Templeton with it, they took him as well as the package. According to what others had observed, they had crossed into the British territories. I followed, always asking about the three men I sought. I heard clues but never saw them." He closed his eyes and tipped his head back. "I kept thinking how desperate Mr. Templeton must be, knowing his kids were waiting for him back near Bonners Ferry. Knowing how small and vulnerable they were."

She touched his arm. "Too bad he couldn't have known they were safe with you."

He lowered his head to see her hand on his arm. It steadied him, made it possible for him to fill his lungs without the air catching halfway down. "I went to the Mounted Police to ask if they had any word on the man I sought. Unfortunately, they did. They'd buried the man."

She pressed her hand more firmly to his arm, causing his blood to flow more smoothly through his veins. He knew he was imagining it, but that was how it felt.

"They had written a report. They gave me a copy." He touched the inner pocket of his vest where the pages waited to be passed on to someone who would someday tell the children the whole truth. "There was a fight. It seems Mr. Templeton saw his chance to escape his captors and stood up before a crowd of witnesses and said he was being held against his will. He had two children needing a father and waiting for him to return. They'd been waiting ten days and it was too long for youngsters to be alone. He had to get back to them and called upon those present to witness his escape and help him return. Of course the crowd surged forward, intent on punishing the two culprits, but they escaped, leaving Mr. Templeton behind. People provided him with a horse, supplies, and everything else he needed to get back here." It should have been the happy ending to the whole affair. "He was found two days later. Shot in the back. He was on his way here."

"Did they catch the men?"

"No, but the Mounted Police vow they will be captured and brought to justice."

"Good." She leaned back and pulled her hand away.

His arm felt cold and heavy. His heart empty just because he no longer had the comfort of her touch. He thought of the time he had taken a kiss. Wished he could take another.

"I'm sorry," she murmured. "Sorry for you. Sorry the man died. Sorry for the kids." Her voice choked off.

He turned to her and opened his arms, more than half expecting she would laugh and jerk away, but she came readily, wrapping her arms around his waist and holding him. He pressed his cheek to her hair and breathed in the warm, earthy scent of her. He couldn't say if she held him or he held her, only it eased the pain that had become a knot in his chest.

He didn't want to let her go, didn't want to tell her what else he'd learned, but she shifted and tipped her head to look into his face. Did he see longing in her eyes? Or was he only dreaming it, wishing for it?

"Glory," he whispered and slowly lowered his head, giving her a moment to pull away if she didn't want him to kiss her. She didn't move, and he almost smiled before he caught her lips in a gentle kiss. This one was mutual, not stolen. Prickly Miss Glory was kissing him.

She broke away. Sat up. Patted her hair and faced forward.

He cupped her shoulder. "Thank you."

The look she gave him encompassed so many things. Surprise, denial, and a healthy dose of interest causing her to glance at his mouth and jerk away as soon as she did, as if denying she might have liked it just a little.

"Glory, I appreciate your kindness in offering me sympathy." It was best for them both if they believed it had been nothing more.

But she snorted. "Is that what it was?"

It's what it had to be though Levi wished otherwise. He hoped Matt would appreciate the sacrifices Levi was making on his behalf. He had chosen a hard road but would not forget the verse that said, *"No man, having put his hand to the plough, and looking back, is fit for the kingdom of God."* He would not look back or regret his vow. "I asked about your pa while I was up north."

She stiffened and her expression informed him she didn't care. Almost he believed her, but she could not hide the flash of pain in her eyes.

"The Mounted Police had heard of him. Said he was headed for the gold fields farther west. I asked them to forward a message if they heard anything more."

Glory pressed her palms together and clamped her hands between her knees. She sat forward not moving, not saying anything, not revealing a single emotion.

"Glory, at least you know he's still alive."

She flung him a gaze rife with anger and pain and so much more. "It would be easier if he was dead. No more waiting. No more wondering if we might get a message like the one you brought the children. It would be over." She bent over her knees and sat as still as a statue.

He could see only the back of her neck and the heavy brown braid hanging over her shoulder. He lifted the braid and moved it to the other side, hoping he could see her face but got only a glimpse of her profile as she shifted away. "Glory, it's always better to know."

She didn't reply or even move.

"Glory?"

Slowly she sat upright, and when she looked at him, her face was set in a hard line, silently informing him she didn't want to discuss it. She didn't thank him for asking after her pa and definitely did not agree it was better to know. "What are you going to do about the children now?"

He sucked in air, found the knot in his chest had returned. What had he expected? That she would throw herself in his arms in gratitude? Yes, he would like her to be a little grateful. God forgive him. He couldn't seem to remember his vow when he was with Glory. Nor was it possible to avoid thinking of her more deeply than he should.

He was still certain she was part of his mission in Bonners Ferry. But he no longer knew how. To reform her seemed unnecessary. She had simply adjusted to her life in the only way that made sense to her. And it now made sense to him as well. She rescued horses because she knew what it was like to be hurt and afraid. And despite the way his heart ached to rescue her, it wasn't possible. He would never regret his vow or change his mind about it.

He forced his thoughts to her question. "I asked Jack about family. He said they have grandparents back in San Francisco. I'm going to write them and inform them of the children's situation. If they are the caring sort, they will make arrangements."

"Let's hope they are."

"More than that, let's pray they are."

She studied him a moment. "There are times I forget about prayer." She continued to look into his eyes as if searching for a hidden truth. "I have trouble believing in prayer when things don't go the way I think they should."

"There's a verse in Psalm one hundred and thirty-nine that comforts me when I feel like I'm alone in the dark, that God has forsaken me. It says, 'The darkness and the light are both alike to thee.' He is still there even when we can't see it. Sometimes He is perhaps testing us to see if we love Him only for what He can give us or because of what He's already done for us."

"I read something in Job." She told him of the verse. "I don't like to think God would send trouble to my life just to see if I will continue to love Him."

"I don't have the answers. I wish I did. But I struggle with the same things. Are troubles meant to test us? Or are they simply a part of living on this earth and God gives us what we need to get through them?"

"Maybe it's both."

"Maybe." He recognized something still troubled her.

"What if. . ." Her voice fell to a whisper. "What if God is like Pa and can't be counted on?"

He reached for her hands and held them between his. "God is not a man that He changes His mind or has regrets. He says He loves us with an everlasting love. He is the same yesterday, today, and forever. His love is the one constant that never changes."

A slow smile drove away the tension in her face. "Everlasting. Always the same. I can trust Him whatever happens."

"You can indeed." He released her hands and let the words sift through his own thoughts. Whatever God had in store for him, however hard it was, he did not face it alone. God would guide him through this long ache of wishing he could love Glory. Knowing he could not and still keep his vow. And he intended to keep his vow.

My service for Matt's salvation. That's what he'd said and renounced all else, including love and marriage.

∞

Glory had sold two of the horses and put the money in her coffee can, but the two weeks was up and she did not have enough to purchase the land. *Master* Milton had left town days ago. *God, help the man to stay away until I can earn enough money.*

She had neglected the horses while caring for the children, and much of the work she'd accomplished with Big Gray had come undone. But she had plenty of patience to continue winning the animal's trust. She'd considered other pieces of land and dismissed them for various reasons—not enough pasture, too far from town for her to go back and forth each day, down in the flats where it was damp underfoot. She wouldn't put her horses there and risk damaging their hooves.

As she worked, she mentally recounted the events of the previous days. The children alternately played happily and then retreated into sadness. Levi was good with them. Holding them as they cried. Not telling them it would be all right. Losing both parents would never be all right, and if the grandparents didn't come, life could get much harder.

These kids were innocent and didn't deserve this misfortune. Sometimes it was hard to trust God. But she could hardly blame God that wicked men chose to do evil. Or even that ordinary men did ordinary things that hurt others. Like Pa chasing after fortune and leaving three little girls to fend for themselves. Despite the neglect, the three little girls had grown into three self-sufficient women. So she had that to be grateful for.

She finished working with the horses and went to her favorite spot to sit and look over the valley. The sound of an approaching horse drew her attention to the trail. It was a big black horse carrying a man wearing a buckskin vest. What was Levi doing here? He'd never visited this place before. She watched him unobserved for a few minutes. She no longer doubted he was a real preacher, even if he did wear a fringed vest. It was just something he liked wearing even as she liked wearing britches. Britches were convenient, too, when working with the horses.

She allowed herself to admire the way he sat Billy Bob. The way his eyes roamed his surroundings, how the blue of the sky reflected in his eyes as he turned toward the light. He had a good face. One that would grow old in a good way. For the first time in her life, Glory thought about growing old with such a man at her side.

She jerked her thoughts back to being sensible. He'd made it as clear as the air around her he had no such interest in her. Even apologized for saying he cared. A man couldn't get much more direct than that. It didn't matter to her. She would not be trusting a man to love her always.

But if she did, it would be a man like Levi.

Her throat closed off, and her eyes grew damp. Even though she vigorously denied it, she could imagine sharing her life with Levi. Actually ached to do so. It took half a dozen deep breaths to cleanse herself of such nonsense.

And just in time.

Levi saw her in the shade of the tree and slid off his horse without using the stirrups in a way that seemed impossibly smooth. "Didn't expect to see you here."

"I could say the same about you."

"Thought I'd ride up and have a look around. May I join you?" He indicated the ground beside her.

"Ground is free," she said, "just like the sky and air. Help yourself."

He chuckled. "It would kill you to say, 'Please, sit down, and welcome,' wouldn't it?"

"Not quite." She grinned at him. They seemed to have arrived at a new place in their friendship—acknowledging it existed, setting boundaries to protect them both. Boundaries of humor and common interests.

He sank down beside her, his shoulder pressed to hers as they shared the support of the tree. She allowed herself to enjoy the strength of him at her side.

Neither of them spoke, and Glory enjoyed a sense of contentment. He was a good man. Caring. Willing to go the extra mile for others. The sort of man a person could learn to lean on. And she let her body settle toward him. "What did you do with Emmy and Jack?"

"Left them with Toby. He was building a fort in the trees behind the stopping house when I left."

"Sounds like fun."

"All three were excited about the prospect."

It was pleasant and warm. She was glad there seemed nothing to disagree about at the moment. "No word from the grandparents?"

"Not yet."

"What if—"

He squeezed her hand. "Let's not build bridges across rivers before we need them."

Her heart curled around his fingers and settled down for a long stay. Her head told her it was only a friendly gesture, but inside her heart something more was going on. She had to know why he couldn't care about her because, frankly, she didn't believe it. He cared even as he denied it. "Why did you decide to become a preacher?"

"I told you. My grandfather was a preacher. I sort of inherited the job, I suppose."

She shifted so she could see his face, study his eyes. "I don't see you deciding to do something simply because your grandfather did. There's something more, isn't there?" The way his eyes flicked toward her and then jerked away, she knew she had guessed correctly. "I'm right. I know I am. So what's the big secret?"

He slowly brought his blue gaze toward her and searched long and hard. She allowed him to explore deeper into who she was than anyone had ever before. He held her in his steady look and slowly nodded. "I made a vow."

A vow? "What sort of vow?"

"I want my brother to come back."

"I don't understand."

"I can't explain." He jumped to his feet. "Come on. Let's look around." He pulled her to his side.

So he didn't want to tell her. No reason it should matter. But it did. She didn't care for secrets. They made a person uneasy. Distrustful even. Not that she was prepared to trust him.

Except she was. At some point, and she couldn't say when or where it had happened, she'd decided the man was too kind to be the Rawhide Kid. She'd let herself trust.

A shiver of fear trickled up her spine. Trusting opened the door to disappointment. "You plan to be around here long?"

"Thinking of staying a long time. I'd like to start a mission. You know, a home for unfortunates like Widow Kish, children like Emmy and Jack, and even sick people needing care like Mr. Phelps. Right now there is no place for them. If I had a little piece of land, I'd build such a house and a church."

Would he want a wife to share the work? She glanced down at her britches. Like Joanna said, Glory wasn't the sort of woman a preacher man would choose. Perhaps it explained why he couldn't let himself care. Maybe if she wore a dress...

"I heard there was a piece of land up here for sale."

She ground to a halt and tore her hand from his. "Who said?"

"There's a notice in the store. Owner is a Mr. Milton. It's this land right here. It's a perfect place for a mission. Close enough to town to go back and forth, high enough to be dry, and a beautiful view. Look, there's a FOR SALE sign on it."

She pushed by him and stared at the sign nailed to the tree of her pasture. When had it been plastered there, and why hadn't she noticed it?

Because the man had been careful to nail it just out of sight of a person going to the pasture where she kept her horses. She ripped the sign from the tree and threw it on the ground. "This is my land. Look." She pointed. "Those are my horses." The animals grazed contentedly a few yards from the trail.

"I don't understand. Why would someone try and sell land you own?"

"Because," she spat out the words, "I haven't come up with enough money to pay for it."

"So it is for sale?"

She faced him, letting every disappointment, every failure of every man she'd ever experienced burn across his cheeks. "If you buy my land, I will never forgive you. Never."

He reached for her, but she sidestepped, avoiding his touch. "Glory, I'll find another piece of land."

"You won't find one as nice as this."

"Probably not, but I have no desire to hurt you. Only thing is. . ."

She waited for his excuses.

"What's to stop someone else from buying it?"

"I'm praying for God to help me. Surely He'll answer." She hated how desperate she sounded.

"Glory, I—" He lifted his hands in defeat. "God doesn't promise to always give us what we want. He promises to give us what we need. And to always love us."

Her heart faltered as she thought of Job's words. "This is what I need. I'm sure God knows it."

"I guess the question is, will you still trust Him even if you don't get the land?"

Her eyes grew brittle. "Will you still trust Him if your brother doesn't come back?"

She wanted to feel victory at the uncertainty in his face, but all she felt was a long ache. "Trusting isn't so easy, is it?"

"I never said it was. But the option of trusting no one and nothing isn't appealing. Far better to trust a God of love."

All her fight evaporated. "I will continue to pray."

"I will pray for the same thing."

"What about your mission?"

He smiled. "There must be something almost as nice as this. Will you help me look?"

"Of course." Her world felt brighter. Her land was safe for now, and Levi wasn't angry with her.

"Then let's go."

"Right now?"

"You got something better to do with your time?"

She could think of nothing at all she'd sooner do, so she whistled for Pal, and sid by side she and Levi rode higher looking at other sites. They crossed back and forth. She'd looked at all this and knew her way around. But it had not been nearly as much fun when she'd ridden around these places on her own. Now discussing the land, the view, the possibilities with Levi made it much more interesting.

By the time the afternoon headed toward supper, they had examined much land.

"There's a few places that could work. But you're right, nothing is as nice as your pasture."

"I told you so," she crowed.

"I'm sure we'll find something. Will you help me again tomorrow?"

They had reached the shop and headed the horses into the little bit of pasture. He dropped to the ground in the same fluid motion she'd admired so many times and reached up to lift her down. She wanted to protest. Hadn't needed anyone lifting her down for many years. But he didn't give her a chance.

He lowered her to the ground and stood facing her. "Thank you for your help, and I hope you get your dreams. I really do." He bent closer.

She knew he was going to kiss her and she welcomed it. But he only brushed his lips to her forehead. Annoyed, she demanded, "What was that?"

"Just a thank-you."

"Huh." She gave him a good view of her back as she turned to remove Pal's saddle. Just a thank-you? She deserved a whole lot more than that. And wanted it.

She hustled her gear into the shop, resisting the urge to kick herself at each step. What she wanted was contrary to all the promises she'd made to herself. And he'd made it clear he wasn't interested in the likes of her. She was not suitable as a preacher's wife. She understood it. Too bad he didn't think to ask if she could change, because she just might be willing to give it a try.

If he needed her to be a lady, she could do it.

Chapter 12

They spent three days riding about the country looking at land. Glory realized at some point finding a suitable location for his mission had taken second place to spending time together, although Levi didn't say anything or give her reason to think he was reconsidering his earlier declaration that he couldn't care about her. He didn't try and kiss her again. . . .and she told herself she wasn't disappointed because the way he looked at her made her feel ten feet tall. She often brought along a light lunch and they shared it, usually with their backs pressed to a tree, their shoulders brushing.

Today he suggested they go to the pasture where she kept her horses. "I like the view from there."

So they rode up the hill and returned to her favorite spot. They sat and enjoyed the scenery for about thirty seconds then Levi pulled a letter from his inside vest pocket. "I heard from the grandparents."

Did he sound pleased or disappointed? She couldn't tell, but then it could be that her own fears for the future of the children made her blind and deaf. "I'm afraid to ask what they said." So many times she'd seen a letter arrive and Joanna tear it open. Each time she'd crossed her fingers behind her back and hoped it was from Pa, saying he would be there within the week. Seldom did they receive such welcome news. Almost always he was simply informing them he was going somewhere else, leaving them to either stay where they were or find a way to follow him. They usually did the latter, never quite catching up to him but being on his heels.

"It's good news. They're coming to personally get the children. That way we'll be able to meet them and judge for ourselves if they'll make a good home for the children."

"And if you think otherwise?"

"It's not like we could do anything about it, but I hope and pray they are kind. It would make it easier to let them go if we could think they were."

She thought of his statement. *"It's not like we could do anything about it. . . ."* She knew it revealed a lot about Levi. From the little he'd said, she knew life with his strict grandparents had been difficult. But it was a home, and he'd made the best of it. It made her feel a strange twist of both admiration and sympathy. "When are they arriving?"

"They'll be here tomorrow."

"Do they say how long they'll stay?"

"No. It's going to be hard to say good-bye to the kids." He faced her. "But at least they have family. What about those who don't? I have such a burden for orphaned children. And for people like Widow Kish with no home. Not every widow ends up remarried and taken care of. I want to help people who need it, but I need a place for them to live."

Seeing the way his concern drove worry lines across his forehead, she squeezed his forearm, liking the warmth of his skin through the fabric of his shirt.

He glanced about. "I need to find suitable land and build a house."

"We'll find something suitable. I know it." She pressed harder against the tree as she thought of how the land she hoped to buy was so ideal.

He chuckled and reached for her hand. "I'm not going to steal your land. I promise."

She let him take her hand. Pushed aside her fears and doubts. After all, hadn't she decided to trust God? And somehow that enabled her to trust Levi.

"I haven't told the children yet. I suppose I should." He pushed to his feet. "Do you want to come with me?"

"Yes. . .but I can't. I have to feed the horses and see they have water." And spend some time working with them. She'd neglected them the last few days.

"Of course. Come and see me when you get back to town, and I'll tell you how it went." He stuffed the letter back inside his vest and strode away.

She remained where she was, soaking up the view and remembering all the other views she and Levi had enjoyed. A sense of peace and rightness filled her. But she couldn't sit there all day dreaming. The animals did need attention. She pushed to her feet, dusted her backside, and headed for the pasture.

Something on the ground next to where Levi had tied Billy Bob caught her attention. A piece of paper. He must have dropped the letter when he tried to put it in his pocket.

She scooped up the paper. It was the wrong shape and size to be the letter. Curious, she unfolded it. It took her several seconds to believe she held a wanted poster. Even then she couldn't believe the identity of the man on the poster.

Her heart stopped beating. Her lungs stopped working. Seems her ears must have stopped working, too, because a vast silence surrounded her, and then everything started up with a bang. She gasped as her heart kicked against her ribs and her ears roared.

"It can't be," she whispered. But there was no mistaking the likeness, even though it was only a drawing. It was Levi. The Rawhide Kid. Reward of $500. Toby had been right in his first observation.

She stared at the poster a long time, her thoughts scrambling in a thousand different directions.

He was living a lie.

But he was a good man.

The reward money would buy her land.

Who would do the good things he did if she turned him in for the money? Who would be her friend?

What was she going to do?

Finally, she folded the poster and carefully slid it into her pocket. Levi had obviously changed his mind and left his life of crime. Didn't everyone deserve a chance to start over? If he could do it, so could she.

After taking care of the horses, she returned to town, went immediately to the store, and placed a mail order for a dress. The storekeeper promised he wouldn't tell anyone.

Only then did she go to find Levi.

∽

Levi waited for the grandparents in front of the store. They would arrive by private buggy, hired out of Sandpoint. Being reunited with the grandparents was best for the kids. Yet he hoped the grandparents weren't like the ones he'd had to live with.

He often wondered how his fun-loving, happy ma could have been the product of that home. It had been all about rules governing every minute of the day. As if making any sort of decision was a sin.

Small wonder Matt had rebelled. Trouble was, Matt's rebellion had gone too far. He could have left home and sought his own path without crossing into lawlessness. Levi sighed. Anger had driven Matt to make foolish choices.

A buggy approached, and Levi snatched his hat from his head. He squinted, trying to see the couple, gauge what sort they were. But dust billowed up as the buggy slowed, obscuring any sight of the occupants. He stepped back and waited for the dust to settle and glanced back to the figure watching out the window.

He'd asked Glory to join him, but she'd laughed and refused. She'd said, "I might ruin your good impression on them," then glanced down at her britches. "After all, they'll be measuring you up as surely as you're measuring them." So instead of being by his side, she watched from the protection of the store. He'd wanted to say she would pass inspection just as she was, but she hadn't given him the chance.

He smiled at her now, hoping she would read in his look his acceptance. He didn't know when he'd decided he didn't have any intention of trying to reform her. She was fine just the way she was. . .britches and all.

By the time he turned back to the buggy, a stately looking gentleman assisted a black-clad woman from the back. He strode forward and introduced himself.

It was much later, after supper taken at the stopping house, before he got a chance to speak to Glory alone.

"They seem nice enough, don't you agree?" They had left the grandparents to put the children to bed and spend the night with them. Levi would sleep under the stars. Not something he minded at all.

They had walked to a place overlooking the river and found a spot to sit and watch the sun set.

Glory didn't answer for a moment, as if considering her words. "I guess we have to trust what they are when they're here is what they are when they aren't here."

He chuckled. "And you don't know if you can trust them or not."

"Trust is a pretty fragile thing. I don't give it easily."

"But when you do?" Did he hope to hear her say she trusted him? Yes, he wanted it, but for all the wrong reasons. Maybe not wrong, but not available for him. He would not forget Matt in prison, not even for the joy of knowing a woman like Glory—spunky, free-thinking, and independent. A rescuer of abused animals. . .and so much more he couldn't let himself enumerate because of the way it made him struggle to remember his vow.

"All I can say is there are no second chances."

She must mean her father. "That's pretty harsh. What if your pa comes back a reformed man? Wouldn't you give him another chance?"

"I no longer even think about Pa that way. He's just a person we're related to. Nothing more. As such, if he came back half-dead, I'd care for him. Just as I would any sick or injured person or animal."

"But without forgiving him?"

She didn't answer, and he supposed that was her answer. Then she spoke, quietly, softly. "I will never say never."

It was a huge concession on her part. One that made him realize just how much she'd grown in her faith. He reached for her hand. "Perhaps you will get the chance to take never out of your life one of these days."

She gave him a long, considering look. "Maybe I already have."

"Really? How? When?"

She shrugged. "Can't say. Just have."

He wanted to hug her, dance her across the prairie, but he didn't have the right, so he squeezed her shoulders with one arm. "You've changed, Glory Hamilton."

"You have no idea how much."

He ached clear through that he didn't have the right to ask if her change included trusting him. Instead, he shifted the conversation back to the children. "The children are a little tense around the grandparents, but that would seem normal considering they haven't seen them in several years and it signals the reality of their father's death."

"How long are the grandparents staying?" she asked.

"Mrs. Templeton said she needed a few days to recuperate before she makes the return trip. They said they'd like me to show them around, explain the work I want to do."

"They'll be here Sunday then?"

"At least that long."

"So they'll hear you preach?"

He wondered why the caution in her voice. "Don't you think that's a good thing?" Did she consider him a poor preacher? It wasn't something they'd ever discussed, and suddenly he longed to know. "You think they'll be disappointed when they hear me?"

"No, I didn't mean that. I think you're a very good preacher. I remember the first Sunday." She gave a low laugh. "I thought you'd preach fire and brimstone and warn people like me we needed to toe the line."

His laugh was mocking. "I wanted to. But I couldn't. Now I know you only want to shock people to keep them at a distance and protect yourself."

She grew very still. "Is that what I do?"

Had he gone too far? Crossed her solid fence lines?

A deep sigh shuddered from her. "I suppose I do. I just never thought of it. Maybe I can change."

"How?"

"You know. Be more ladylike. That sort of thing." She sounded as if the words burned her tongue.

"Glory, who you are is who you are and is just fine. All you can do is learn to trust others. Or at least God."

"You think that's all I need?"

"I know it."

She sighed, a sound as full of uncertainty as any he'd heard.

By the time Sunday rolled around, Levi had taken the Templetons around the country. They'd discussed the mission he wanted to start. They'd enjoyed several picnics with the children. Levi was convinced they would be good with the children, who were anxious to get to their new home.

Mr. Templeton had promised they'd leave the next day if all went well. "I have some business to attend to before we leave."

Levi couldn't help wonder what business he could possibly have, but it wasn't his place to ask and he didn't.

Attendance had grown steadily at the Sunday service. From his place before the gathering audience, he looked about, saw the usual townspeople, as well as a number of people passing through, many who had spent the night at the stopping house. Glory and her sisters had not yet appeared.

He picked up his Bible and quickly reviewed his notes.

A sudden rumble of murmurs made him glance up. He saw people looked to the right and followed the direction.

Three women approached. He recognized Mandy and Joanna, but the third was unfamiliar. No. Wait. It was Glory. In a dress. A very pretty dress. She had fashioned her braid around her head in a coronet.

Levi stared.

Glory sent him a defensive, vulnerable look then stared straight ahead.

Glory in a dress. He tried to think if he liked it. He didn't. Glory belonged in britches. Was there something wrong with him to think so? Shouldn't he be glad to see her in something more conventional? But he wasn't. This was not the Glory he knew and loved. Why would she change?

The question badgered the back of his thoughts as she and her sisters found a place to sit, as he led the singing, and even as he delivered his sermon.

He wanted to ask her, but several people spoke to him after the service, and he had to watch Glory and her sisters slip away. As soon as he could get away, he hurried to the stopping house and burst into the kitchen. "Where's Glory?"

Joanna looked up from doing some mending. "She left. Try her shop."

He raced to the shop. Pal was gone, but he checked inside anyway just to make sure Glory wasn't there. She wasn't. He wanted to ride out and find her, but he'd promised the children to spend the afternoon with them.

And then Mrs. Templeton prepared a nice supper. "If all goes well, this will be our last day here. I hope we can start our return journey tomorrow."

Levi could not excuse himself without seeming rude. But as soon as he could get away, he ran back to the stopping house, again demanding to see Glory.

Joanna shrugged. "She's not here."

"Is she avoiding me?"

"I'm not sure. Maybe she's avoiding everyone."

"Why?"

"Why is she avoiding people, or why did she wear a dress?"

"Yes."

Joanna chuckled. "The first is because of the last. But why she felt the need to don a dress? Well, I expect it has something to do with you."

"Me?" He backed up two steps as if she'd punched him in the chest.

"You being a preacher and all, I'm guessing she thought she had to be a proper lady before you'd look at her in that. . .you know. . .special way. And if you hurt my sister, you'll be answering to me."

Levi stumbled from the house. He'd told her he wasn't free to care. How had his vow turned into such a sacrifice? Was this God testing him?

He'd find her tomorrow and explain his vow. Tell her the whole truth. She'd understand.

Only the next day turned into a blur of activities he couldn't escape.

Mr. Templeton disappeared right after breakfast, and when Levi tried to slip away, Mrs. Templeton begged him to wait. "He'll be back soon, then we must be on our way. He'll want to see you before he leaves."

Levi expected the man wanted to say a last good-bye, but it was all Levi could do to endure the wait.

Mr. Templeton strode in a short while later, a glow of victory on his face. "I did it, Mother. Just as we planned."

The pair grinned at each other then faced Levi. Mr. Templeton spoke, but it was obviously for the both of them. "We appreciate how you rescued our grandchildren, and we think you are doing a good work here. So to show our gratitude and help your cause, we bought land you can use to start your mission."

Levi knew his mouth hung open. He cranked it closed. Forced himself to speak. "You bought land?"

"We studied the options as you showed us around, and did some asking around. There's one piece of land that seemed superior to all the others. It's close to town, high enough to not suffer floods, and it's beautiful. We purchased it and have put your name on the deed."

Levi's heart thudded to the soles of his boots and lay there quivering. "What land did you buy?"

"A piece owned by a Mr. Milton." They handed him a piece of paper he knew was the deed.

The deed to land he had promised Glory he would not buy.

She would never understand.

He must find her and explain before she heard the news from another source. But he could not rush away until he'd helped the Templetons pack up everything, until he'd seen them safely into the hired buggy, until he'd said his final good-bye. His heart felt pulled in two as he kissed the children good-bye. "I'm going to miss you both."

Emmy hugged him tight. "I wish you could go with us."

He nodded and hugged Jack, who tried to be brave about this parting, but tears glistened in his eyes as he broke away from Levi's arms. Levi's own eyes weren't without unshed tears. "Keep in touch," he said to the grandparents, and they promised they would.

He waved to them through blurry vision until the dust obscured them from sight. Then he drew in a deep, steadying breath and turned his heart toward the other half of his pain. He must find Glory.

He'd bought the land. Everyone in town knew it. And everyone seemed to think it was a good idea. Not one person, apart from her sisters, expressed concern about what she'd do with her livestock. They all agreed the work Levi intended to do was so noble it deserved every bit of sacrifice necessary.

She was the only one making any sacrifice. And not willingly. What would they all think if she posted the wanted poster by the door of the general store? They wouldn't likely be so oh-isn't-Levi-wonderful then.

The paper practically burned a hole in her britches. She'd kept his secret because she thought he deserved a second chance. Now she knew he was more false than any of them knew.

There was something better than tacking the poster to the wall. She dug out an envelope and paper from the drawer where Joanna kept such things. She wrote a short note, addressed the envelope to the territorial marshal, and put in the wanted poster. Her footsteps driven by anger and a sense of betrayal, she delivered the letter to the ferry man.

She then rode out to her horses and led them from the pasture. For two cents she'd ride five days and disappear into the mountains far to the north.

Just like her pa.

She swallowed a bitter taste. If she left, it would be to run from deceit and lies. Why did Pa run when he had three daughters who had once longed for him to be part of their lives?

No more. No more trusting anything a man said or promised. She should have learned that lesson well enough from her father. Only it appeared she hadn't, and now she had to learn it over again. . .thanks to Levi.

Levi. She tried to think his name with the same coolness she thought of Pa, but instead it caught like a burr in her brain and scratched along her thoughts, leaving a trail of scraped flesh. She narrowed her eyes, ground down on her teeth, and tried to ignore it, but she suspected it would take a long time for the bruises to heal.

She left the gate of her pasture open and headed away from town without a backward look, her horses trailing after her. Properties she'd dismissed as being too far from town now seemed not nearly far enough, and she rode for two hours before she turned off the narrowing trail and ducked through crowded trees with barely enough room for a horse.

Fifteen yards later she broke into a grassy clearing. It didn't receive as much sunshine as her former pasture and would likely be dampish, but it was the best she could do. She strung rope from tree to tree, creating a temporary enclosure for the horses, then pulled her camping supplies from Pal's back. She hadn't come right out and told Joanna she wouldn't be back but had given enough hints that when she didn't return Joanna would understand.

Not until she sorted out her feelings, her sense of having been dealt a dirty deal, would she return to town. Treacherous Levi intended to stay in town, but soon the marshal would ride in and take him away. Only then would Glory go back.

She sat staring at the horses munching down grass with little concern for their future. Her heart felt like a giant fist grinding against everything she valued, trusted, or even dreamed of.

Was she as much a traitor as Levi to turn him in?

But he was a criminal with a price on his head. And she needed the money to buy land. Perhaps she could even buy back *her* land.

If he had known she found the wanted poster, would he have trusted her to keep his secret?

Just like she'd trusted him. And look how that turned out.

She would never trust again.

What about God? Did her decision include God?

The words she'd read so many times in Job, and wondered at how the man could still trust God, crowded her mind. *"Though he slay me, yet will I trust in him."* Job was a better person than she. She couldn't find it in her heart to say, "Okay, it's fine," when everything was wrong.

⚭

She spent her days working with the horses and sitting next to her campfire, which for the most part remained dead, and staring into space. She was healing, she told herself. Rebuilding the protective barriers around her heart she'd foolishly let crumble under Levi's influence.

Three days later she still had not returned to town. She'd worked with the horses all morning and at high noon sat by the cold fire chewing on dried biscuits when the sound of a footfall only inches away brought her to her feet, her hands out ready to defend herself.

Mandy broke into the clearing, laughing at Glory's alarm. "I almost snuck up on you."

Glory blew out air as her lungs started to work again. "One of these

125

days you're going to get yourself shot."

"You think I'd sneak up on someone I didn't know?"

"What are you doing here? How did you find me?"

Mandy snorted. "I could have tracked you across rocks. If you really wanted to disappear, you wouldn't have dragged a herd of horses after you."

"I wasn't trying to disappear." At least not permanently.

Mandy looked around the clearing. "Not a bad place you got here. Maybe I'll join you." Then as almost an afterthought, "There's someone looking for you in town."

"Levi? I don't care to see him."

"It's a marshal. He says he needs to see you."

Glory jerked back. "Did he—?" Arrest Levi. But she couldn't say the words aloud. "Did he say what he wanted?"

Mandy widened her stance, crossed her arms over her chest, and studied Glory with narrowed eyes. "What have you done? Shot someone for whipping their horse? You haven't stolen a horse, have you?" She studied the placidly grazing horses as if trying to recall where Glory had gotten each. "Joanna sent me to find you and said if you did something that's going to get you arrested to shoot you on the spot. Do I need to get my gun?"

Glory laughed. She knew Joanna didn't mean it. It was her way of saying how angry she would be if Glory did something so stupid. "I didn't break any laws." She glanced around. "I guess the horses will be okay for a few hours." But there was only a rope keeping them from wandering away. "I'll have to come back as soon as I speak to the marshal."

In no hurry to return, welcoming any excuse for delay until it was almost three hours later, they rode into town.

A tall man, gun strapped to his hip, a star on his chest, rose from a chair tipped back in front of her shop as they approached. He strode to the street and waited for them. "You must be Miss Glory Hamilton."

"Yup."

"You and I need to talk." He glanced about, suggesting they needed to talk in private.

"I'll let Joanna know I found you." Mandy rode toward the stopping house.

Glory slid from Pal's back and led the way to her shop. "We can talk here."

The marshal pulled the poster from his pocket, unfolded it, and spread it on her worktable. "This is the Rawhide Kid."

"I can read. I can also see the picture."

"The man in this picture is Matthew Powers."

It took a moment for the news to sink in. He lied about his name, too?

"Levi Powers's brother."

"Matt?"

"That's right. Though I can see why you might mistake the two. Heard they look a lot alike. Had to come and see for myself if it was true." The marshal folded the poster and handed it to Glory. "The Rawhide Kid is in prison as we speak."

She took the slip of paper with fingers almost lost at the end of arms that were long and heavy.

"I'll be leaving now." He paused. "Sure beats me how you couldn't see Levi Powers is a man you can trust." His departing footsteps echoed inside her hollowed-out thoughts.

Why couldn't she trust Levi?

She hadn't even given him a chance to explain about the wanted poster. Even as she hadn't given him a chance to explain about the land.

Sounds from the other side of the door to the room he rented indicated he was there.

Swallowing her wrongful pride and hurt feelings, she acknowledged her lack of trust stemmed from years of learning she couldn't count on her father. Levi was not her father. And she was no longer a child.

She went outside and around to the outer door of the room. She knocked, and he called for her to enter.

She stepped inside and saw his saddlebags packed. A quick glance revealed he'd removed everything belonging to him. The room already had a deserted air. "Are you going somewhere?"

His face could have been a wooden mask for all he revealed. "I can't believe you thought I was the Rawhide Kid and sent for the marshal."

"It looks like you."

"Is that what you think of me? Is this because of the land?"

"You promised you wouldn't buy it."

"And I kept my promise."

"Funny then that there is a deed somewhere with your name on it."

"Mr. Templeton bought it as their way of saying thanks. I had no idea they planned to do so, and of course they had no way of knowing of my promise to you. Glory, I'm sorry it turned out this way." He took a step toward her, his expression regretful and so much more.

For a moment she let herself believe she saw caring and love in his face. Then he drew back and grabbed up the saddlebags and tossed them over his shoulder.

"Where are you going?" Was this how it would end? And it was all her fault. "I'm sorry. I realize I have to separate my experience with trusting Pa and being disappointed from other people." She swallowed hard knowing she had to say more. "From you."

"Glory, I have to go. There is something I need to do."

She couldn't beg. It made her too vulnerable.

He paused at her side. Again she let herself believe she saw tenderness and longing. Then he put that wooden mask in place again. "I'm going to see my brother. Feel free to take your horses back to the pasture. I won't be using it anytime soon."

Her feet might as well have been riveted to the floor. She couldn't make them move even when she heard him saddle his horse. Not even when she heard him mount, the leather creaking beneath his weight.

"Good-bye, Glory."

The words scraped her insides hollow.

The thud of Billy Bob's feet thundered through her, and she cried a protest. "Wait." She dashed for the door and around to the pen just in time to see him ride down the street, away from town.

He had not said if he would return.

She lurched against the splintery wall of the shop and leaned over as pain grabbed her insides. He was gone, and it was her fault for not trusting him.

Chapter 13

The realization she'd allowed her feelings about Pa to cloud her reason had come too late. She should have trusted Levi. It was time to grow up. Even if it was too late with Levi, she had to stop looking at everything through the disappointment of Pa's continual disappearances. She had to trust God. Just like Job. Even when things weren't going the way she wanted.

Day after day Glory hurried through her chores. She did her work as always but far faster than before. All she wanted was to spend time with her horses and her thoughts. Joanna allowed her to take the Bible with her, and she spent hours reading it, finding solace in the words, the promises, God's love.

One side of her heart was empty and barren, filled with wind-driven regrets. The other side grew strong and sure of God's faithfulness.

The pasture was a temporary fix, but so far she had not come up with a permanent one. But she prayed about it and tried to trust God. Trusting still did not come easy. Perhaps it never would. She would always have to choose trust over doubt.

One question continued to weigh on her mind. Did she have the right to ask God to bring Levi back? Perhaps *right* was not the word she meant. Seems she didn't deserve anything from God, but He gave out of love. Maybe the question was, did she have the faith to ask God? More importantly, did she have the faith to trust God even if Levi didn't come? If her prayer wasn't answered the way she wanted?

It was a choice. And she chose to trust God no matter what the answer.

God, I messed up with Levi. I didn't trust him, and I should have. I'd like a chance to try again so I'm asking You to give me that chance. Send Levi back. Remind him of the work he has to do here. But whatever happens, I will trust You.

She sat as blessed peace filled the half of her heart that didn't miss Levi. Trust might be hard, but it sure felt better than anger. Feeling more settled than she had in a very long time, she returned to town to help Joanna.

As the days passed, she promised herself she wouldn't check down the road hoping to see Levi riding toward town, wouldn't check the horses hitched at the side of the street for Billy Bob, but she couldn't help herself. Each time she did and didn't see what she wanted to see, she reminded herself she would trust God no matter what.

Her inner peace grew, spilling into the empty half of her heart. But she knew it would never be completely satisfied without Levi to share her life.

∞

Levi had returned from his trip. He'd been gone only ten days, but it seemed a lifetime, and he could hardly wait to see Glory. He hoped to find her up the hill with her horses and went there first. She sat on the edge of the property where they had shared so many good times, and he stood hidden in the shadows of some trees so he could watch her unobserved, gauge how she was. Whether or not she would give him a chance to explain himself or chase him off with a big stick.

She turned her face toward the sky. Her expression made his pulse feel as if he had been riding a smooth trail and suddenly his mount stepped into a dip, leaving his heart to follow in a desperate dive.

He had never seen her more beautiful, as if she captured the sunshine inside her but couldn't keep it there. It breathed through her pores. He couldn't stop staring, couldn't move toward her. In fact, he couldn't think.

She grew watchful, seemed to listen to some silent voice within her.

He knew the moment she grew aware of his presence. She splayed her fingers to her chest as if she wondered if it was her imagination and she wanted to capture it and make it real. At least that was what he hoped the gesture meant. Then she jerked to the right and stared into the shadows.

He edged forward, hesitantly, not wanting to shatter the moment. It felt sacred, as if he'd entered a place of worship. *God, help me speak clearly and plainly. Help her understand.*

"Levi?" His name was a gentle whisper fluttering through the air and landing in his heart with force enough to make him think it should have been shouted. "I've been waiting for you," she murmured.

He didn't know what to make of that and couldn't ask. "Can we talk?"

She grinned. "Far as I know we're both very capable of it." She shifted and indicated the grass beside her.

"I want to explain."

"Sit down before I get a crick in my neck."

He sat though he wasn't sure she'd be so welcoming once he told his whole story.

"Go ahead and explain." She sounded half-teasing, half-exasperated.

"You had a right to wonder about me. I didn't tell you everything."

She sat quietly, giving him plenty of time to sort his thoughts.

Not that he needed time. He'd practiced his speech over and over since he left Matt at the territorial prison. Suddenly words seemed so inadequate. But words were all he had at this point.

"I should have told you the whole truth about Matt. How he didn't just rebel against our grandparents' rules. He rebelled against everything and became the Rawhide Kid, a wanted man. I suppose I didn't want to admit who he was. I didn't want people to think I was like my brother."

She drew in a breath as if she meant to speak.

"Let me finish before you say anything."

She nodded and let him go on.

"I should have told you the rest of it, too. You see, when I watched them drag Matt away in chains to serve his sentence, I made a vow to God. I said I would devote my life solely to serving God if He would work on Matt in prison. It was a foolish vow, one I probably shouldn't have made, but I did and I couldn't back out without perhaps angering God."

He held up a hand to silence her as she again started to speak. "It was foolish because I started to care about you and knew I didn't have the right. I had no idea how to change my vow. You don't vow something to God and then say, 'Oops, I changed my mind.'" He sorted out his thoughts, wondered how he could think this would be simple.

"When you thought I was the Rawhide Kid, I was shocked. I don't blame you. Matt and I do look alike. I understand your anger and how hard it is to trust. But how was I to tell you to trust me when I had no right to offer you anything? I had to find an answer or leave for good." He had struggled so hard, knowing he had made a vow with no reservations but aching to be free to love Glory. "I went to see Matt. I told him of my vow, told him that I had fallen in love and didn't know how to get out of the vow."

Her quick intake of breath brought a fleeting smile to his lips. Then he gave a sharp laugh. "Seems odd to seek counsel from someone in prison, but that's what I did."

"And?" She sounded as if she couldn't wait to hear if he found a solution.

"Matt had a good laugh at my expense. He wanted to know why I thought God owed me anything, and when I tried to deny it, he said that's what my vow was. He said I thought if I served God in the way I chose, sacrificing my chance to love and have a family, then God owed it to me to make Matt become a Christian. Boy, did Matt laugh at that. 'Ain't nobody going to make me become a Christian,' he said."

"I'm sorry." She squeezed his arm.

"He was right. I wasn't trusting God to work in His way and His time. Any more than I was serving Him out of love. God didn't ask me to do things so He had to repay me. He only asks me to serve Him out of love." It had taken him days to come to the conclusion, but when he did, he knew such sweet peace he wondered why he'd fought it so long.

He took Glory's hands in his and faced her full-on. "Glory, I am now free to tell you I love you and want to spend the rest of my life with you at my side."

She studied his features, her gaze searching his eyes, examining his cheeks, his chin, his mouth.

He couldn't read her mind. He feared she was angry at him and couldn't trust him after all the secrets he'd kept.

She lifted her eyes to him. He detected a twinkle in them. "You would marry a woman wearing britches?"

"If you'll have me. I love you, Glory."

Wonderment filled her eyes. "I love you, too. And yes, I'll marry you."

He kissed her smiling mouth. A little later, he told her the rest of it. "I want you to be my partner in every way. My land is your land."

Her eyes widened. "You mean—?"

"Your horses have a home here, too."

"It is more than I asked for or hoped for. God is good."

"He has given us both what our hearts need." Levi kissed her again.

Mandy and the Missouri Man

Chapter 1

M andy Hamilton squatted down on her haunches in the shadows and stared at the intruder invading her bit of land. No, she didn't have a deed saying it was hers, but it was the site she'd chosen. She had a secret ritual she did no matter where she lived. She found the best spot to build a home and in her imagination created a house for her family to live in. . .her sisters and their pa. A place where they would finally be together, safe and secure.

This man had no right to pitch his tent in the sunny little clearing nor build a campfire where she pictured the front step. Somehow she must convince him to leave. "It's mine," she whispered, as she slipped away as silent as the shadows hiding her, knowing he hadn't noticed her presence.

Soundlessly she circled the area until she reached a slight hill where she could operate without fear of discovery. Again she settled on her haunches—a position she had grown to prefer. It allowed her to gain her feet quickly yet provided relative comfort as she studied whatever she desired to watch. Wearing trousers made the position easy to maintain. There were those who frowned on her wearing them, but she'd long ago learned they made life in the woods a lot easier. She pushed up the sleeves of her white shirt to cool her arms and settled back to watch. The man tramped about the clearing as if measuring it. Like he thought he owned it. Nothing had been said around town about someone filing claim on any land in the area, so she guessed he was only a squatter.

On *her* land.

If her gaze could cross the distance, she would fry him in his tracks, but all she could do was narrow her eyes and stare.

If she had anything to say about it, he'd soon change his mind about thinking he owned the land.

She pressed deeper into the shadows, lifted her head to bark and howl like a wolf—many wolves. All the while she kept her attention on the man below. He jerked toward the sound, and she grinned with satisfaction. All those hours prowling the woods had taught her many valuable skills, but she'd never imagined imitating a wolf would come in so handy.

Moving quickly to the left, she climbed higher and repeated wolf sounds as if animals circled the clearing.

The man strode toward the tent and snagged up a rifle then headed straight toward her. His wide-brimmed hat sat low on his forehead so she couldn't see much of his face, but the set of his jaw informed her he meant to put an end to any threat from a marauding pack of wolves.

She didn't intend to wait to see what he'd do if he realized he'd been duped by a woman. Fact is, she didn't intend he should find out. If she could convince him wild animals objected to his presence, making it an unsafe place, then she would have accomplished what she set out to do.

Soundlessly she slid away before he neared her location.

A few minutes later, she sank down in another place and waited, watching his shape slip through the trees. For a time he disappeared and she tensed, hoping he wouldn't shoot willy-nilly into the bushes. But in a bit she detected him returning to the camp. He was almost as quick and silent as she was. She allowed herself a fleeting moment of admiration then dismissed it. Neither stealth nor skill mattered. He didn't belong here.

He reached the open and studied his surroundings. She didn't move, knowing she was invisible among the trees. He removed his hat and brushed back a mop of dark blond hair. She took the opportunity to assess him further. From what she could determine at this distance, she guessed he was close to her age. She'd seen every sort of man go through the Bonners Ferry Stopping House. Every shape and size, so she eyed this one up with a practiced look. He wore a yoked western shirt, such as she'd seen on bow-legged cowboys passing through. He looked solid. Muscular. Like a man who worked for a living rather than push a pen across paper. Probably a man seeking gold. But then why was he in her clearing? Shouldn't he be headed for the ferry and the gold fields to the north?

He jammed his hat back on his head, cradled the rifle in his arms, and returned to pacing out the clearing.

She again climbed the hill and made wolf calls, grinning at the way the man jerked toward the sound. She moved away. Should the man decide to fire blindly toward the source, she didn't intend to be within range. A few minutes later she leaned against a tree to observe the clearing.

A movement at the tent caught her attention, and her mouth fell open. Someone was inside. And it wasn't the man she'd tried to scare off. She sought his figure just to make sure, but he'd disappeared. She rubbed her eyes and stared. Had he moved into the tent so quickly she'd missed it? Impossible.

The person in the tent inched out far enough for Mandy to see it was a woman. Or a girl, who clutched a poke bonnet to her cheek and hunched her shoulders forward. Someone ought to warn her about bad posture. The girl—or woman, if she be that old—seemed afraid. At least, that was how Mandy read her furtive movements as she jerked little peeks about her then retreated into her rolled forward shoulders.

Mandy hadn't had something so interesting to watch for a long time. She sat back again to observe.

∞

"You stay out of sight while I take care of this," twenty-year-old Trace Owens told his sister. It was no wolf harassing him. At least not the four-legged kind. He knew plenty of the two-legged variety. Could his treacherous associates have followed him here? He'd seen no sign of them in weeks. But whoever it was would soon discover Trace had no patience left for people bothering them. He'd run so far he felt like a foreigner in his own country. Seemed this distant corner of America was not involved with the civil war. He hoped it was true.

He cast a glance over his shoulder to the clearing. This little spot—a pleasant distance from the nearest town of Bonners Ferry—suited him just fine, and he wouldn't be harassed away by some mischief-making person.

It would take more than a fake wolf to drive him onward. But he prayed to God they'd outrun the dogging threat of troublemakers. Not that he prayed much anymore. Didn't seem to be any use in it. Except for Cora's sake.

He'd listened to the wolf call as the person circled the camp. Knew whoever did it would move away, figuring Trace would go toward the sound. He went the opposite direction, moving silently among the trees, pausing often to listen for any rustle to indicate movement.

137

His opponent was good—he'd give him that. But after a bit he was rewarded with the sound of a little gasp. He wondered what caused it but didn't let curiosity distract him. He focused on the sound and edged closer.

There he was. Squatted down, looking toward the clearing. Trace wondered what held his attention so completely but didn't shift his concentration as he narrowed the distance between them.

He was close enough now to spring, and he did, bowling the spy over and pressing his slight frame to the ground. Their hats fell off, and he looked into the face of—

A woman! In man's trousers!

A woman with a thick, untidy braid of dark brown hair and dark brown eyes that widened in surprise then narrowed, filling with anger and purpose.

He realized his peril just in time and clamped her hands to the ground beside her head. He kept her body weighed down so she couldn't kick or hit or. . .

He jerked back as she reared her head, intending to do damage to Trace's face. Did she realize it would hurt her as much as him?

She bared her teeth and flung about, trying to get a mouthful of flesh.

He leaned back as far as possible while still restraining her. "Why are you spying on me? Pretending to be a wild animal?" He snorted. "Guess it isn't much of a pretense. You *are* a little wild animal."

That certainly did nothing toward calming her. She kicked and reared and flung her head some more.

He tightened his hold. "Answer the question. Who are you, and what do you want?"

Lifting her head, she gave him a look that practically peeled the skin from his face. "Get off me."

He considered his options. If he let her go, she'd either run away or attack him. He intended to find out why she was spying on him before he let her escape. But he had no desire to be the target of her feet and fists and teeth and goodness knows what else if he released her. Likely a knife and certainly a gun, though he saw her rifle had been kicked aside in the scuffle.

She followed the direction of his gaze, but the distant rifle did nothing to mellow her. "Let me go." After a few minutes fighting to escape him, she grew still. "I have never been treated this way by a man. And I will exact justice."

"I didn't know you were a woman." Still he didn't move, knowing once freed she posed a risk to his safety.

"Well, I am. And now you know."

Yes, now he knew. That didn't make her any less dangerous. But he couldn't stay where he was. It was indecent. He clamped both her wrists in one hand and leaped to his feet. Just as he guessed, she kicked and twisted and fought. But he held on. Not until she told him why she spied on them would he let her go. He repeated his questions.

"I could ask the same of you." She spat the words out in between jerks and twists.

"Fine. I'm—" Did he want his name known? Not that it wasn't a good name. Why, his father had been a hero in the Mexican-American War, which was the cause of all their trouble. But he'd lost enough. He wasn't going to lose his name, too. "I'm Trace Owens."

"What are you doing here?"

"You mean besides trying to calm you down?" He panted from the effort of restraining her.

"Sure picked a strange way of doing it." She swung her foot and connected with his knee.

He grunted. At least she wore moccasins, not hard boots. He might survive a kick or two.

"I aim to build me a house and live here." Fighting with her had deepened his consideration into determination.

"Yeah." She twisted full circle, forcing his hands to burn a ring around her wrists. "You own the land? Got a deed to it?"

"Nope. Figure building a house makes it mine." He'd see about filing on the land after he got settled. Didn't seem to be any rush to go into town for the task. The longer he kept his presence a secret, the better he'd feel.

The kick she aimed at him was meant to do serious damage. He managed to jump aside and still hold her wrists.

"You can't have the land. It's mine."

He hadn't considered someone might own the property. "You got a deed?"

"No. Don't need one."

"Neither do I." He jerked her wrists upward, forcing her to stand on tiptoes, effectively making it impossible for her to kick or bite. He realized she was almost too tall for him to be able to do so. Tall and tough. Bold and beautiful. "What's your name?"

139

"I ain't telling."

"Expect I could go to town and ask. Maybe tell everyone about this little incident."

She looked about ready to spit. "It's Mandy Hamilton. Not that it's any of your business."

"Suppose not. But seems we both figure we got a claim to the same piece of land." He lowered her slightly, as much to ease his arms as hers, and leaned in closer, hoping she wouldn't break his nose with a head bunt. "Seems the one who builds a house first is the rightful owner, and that will be me."

He was ready for her explosion, but even so it was all he could do to hold her at arm's length. He'd long ago started to sweat from the effort. Beads of moisture dripped from his forehead. He bent to wipe his face on his sleeve.

She took advantage of the movement to jerk back hard enough to make him stagger forward, close enough for her to bring her knee into his middle. He groaned but held on. Would she buy his declaration that building a house established a claim? Or would she only pretend to and head off to town to file on the land?

"Mister, that's my land. I saw it first, and I aim to keep it. You won't find it easy to build a house there. I'll see to it."

He straightened, forced her to face him. "Lady, I'm claiming that land. See, I already live there." He twisted to glance at his tent and the horses tethered a distance away. "It's mine." Cora peered from the tent flap, watching the tussle. He couldn't see her face but knew she'd be frightened. They'd both hoped they could find seclusion here. This feisty woman could make that dream an impossibility. Maybe he could bargain with her. "What would it take to persuade you to leave us alone?"

Another look that made him fear for his safety. "What would it take to persuade *you* to get off *my* land?"

So that's the way she meant to be? So be it. She wasn't the first challenge he'd faced nor likely would she be the last.

He tossed her arms free.

She rubbed her wrists and favored him with a dark scowl.

"Have it your way." He jammed his fists to his hips. "Turn this into a fight, but I won't be driven off. Seems to me whoever is living here and building a house would be declared the official owner." He didn't know if the law would support him in that claim, but it seemed reasonable.

"Fine. You want a fight, mister, you've got a fight. But I intend to fight fair." The look on her face made him wonder what she meant. "First one to build a house and live in it gets the land. Agreed?" She stuck out her hand.

He drew back, expecting her to engage in another tussle.

She shoved her hand closer. "You willing to shake on it?"

"Agreed." He was ready for the way she squeezed his hand and squeezed back equally hard.

She jerked free and strode away, chin in the air.

He stared for a moment then chuckled. With her baggy trousers and overly big shirt it was no wonder he'd thought her a man at first glance. But she was most certainly a woman. And he didn't have to wrestle her to the ground to know it. She had a face of unusual beauty.

She moved with stealth and disappeared into the woods like a shy deer.

He snorted. Mandy Hamilton was no shy deer. More like the wolves she imitated.

How much risk did she pose? Could he trust her to keep their presence quiet? Not likely. He did not intend to trust anyone for anything from now on.

First one to build a house owned the land, she said. Who could say if she meant it or only meant to trick him? But if he had a house built, he would have a reason to dispute anyone filing on the land.

He jogged down the hill to his campsite.

Cora stepped into the sunshine. "Who was that?"

"Nobody. You'll be okay. But I got to hurry and start a house."

"So we're staying here?" She glanced about as if taking real stock of her surroundings.

"It's a fine place. We'll be safe here."

She sighed. "Already one person has found us. How soon until more come to stare?" She pulled her bonnet closer to her cheek.

He hesitated, caught between the urgency of getting trees chopped down and trimmed for a house and the sad note in his sixteen-year-old sister's voice. Cora's need won out. He went to her side. "Cora, baby sister, you are still a beautiful girl." With a great deal of self-control, he stilled the anger souring his insides. The treachery of people he'd once trusted brought them to this place and made his sister endure her disfigurement.

She pushed her bonnet to her shoulders and faced him full on. "So long as you don't look too closely."

141

He'd learned not to flinch at the sight of the scars on the side of her face, but it never failed to sear his insides. He touched her shoulder. "You're lucky to be alive." He'd do all in his power to protect her from prying eyes. But how was he to keep Miss Hamilton away?

Emotions worked across Cora's expression—anger, sorrow, denial, and finally, resignation. "I suppose some would think so." The flatness of her tone denied the truth of her words.

No need to agree or disagree on the subject. He knew she didn't count herself lucky. Often enough she'd said she wished she'd died in the fire along with their parents. No amount of reassurance on his part changed her mind. He seemed the only one happy that she'd lived.

"I just wish people would leave us alone."

He hated the harsh tone of her voice and hoped changing the subject would lighten her mood. "The house I'm going to build will be small to begin with, but it will be warm and dry and better than sleeping on the ground under dank canvas."

She sighed. "I suppose so."

"Do you want to come with me into the woods? I'm going to start cutting down trees."

She looked wistful, and for a moment he thought she might agree. Then she shook her head. "I'll stay here."

"You'll be okay by yourself?"

"You won't go far, will you?"

He thought of what he'd seen in his earlier scouting trips. Seemed there might be enough suitable trees within shouting distance to start with. "You'll be able to hear me working."

"Then I'll sit here and read."

He hated to leave her. Anytime she said she'd read he figured she mostly stared into space, but he had to get a house started if he meant to beat Miss Hamilton. "I'll be back before dark. If you need me, just come or call out." He grabbed his ax and headed for the woods.

∞

Mandy fumed all the way back to Bonners Ferry then pulled up hard. If she steamed into the stopping house, Joanna would start asking all sorts of questions. Joanna could get very nosy. Four years her senior, Joanna had been the mother figure for both Glory and herself since their ma died eight years ago. Joanna had only been fourteen at the time, and she'd done a good job of taking care of them. But she took her responsibilities very seriously. And heaven forbid she would encounter her other sister. Ever since Glory had fallen in love with the preacher man, Levi, why, Glory had been too high-and-mighty for her own good. As if she had figured out the answer to all life's problems just because she'd succumbed to love.

A couple of times, Mandy had challenged her to an Indian wrestle, but Glory only laughed and said, "Poor Mandy."

Mandy ground about and headed up the hill away from *her* place. She needed to think and plan. That miserable cur of a man thought he could claim her land, did he? Well, she'd show him he didn't stand a chance against her.

A part of her brain mocked. *Yup, you showed him good who was boss, didn't you? He had you sprawled helplessly on the ground. Then practically hung you from his hands.*

She admitted with some reluctance that it took a mighty big man to lift her to her tiptoes. Mandy Hamilton was tall and had more muscle per inch of body than half the men she'd met, and she'd met plenty. Her insides burned with humiliation at the way the man had roughhoused her. She forced that insult aside to contemplate the urgency of building a house. She plunked to the ground to consider the quandary the man had forced upon her.

No time for a real house, even though her dreams included a tidy little dwelling with at least two bedrooms, a kitchen and a front room, and a stoop big enough to hold buckets, shovels, and a supply of wood.

She smiled. A stoop would serve as a cabin for now. No one said it had to be fancy. Just a place to live. That's all she needed to gain ownership of the land. Of course, she could walk down to the lawyer's office and fill out a claim, but it didn't sound like half as much fun as beating the man at a challenge.

A frown drew her mouth down. She needed to beat him to salve her pride.

A little later she sashayed into the stopping house with several dressed grouse for tomorrow's meal.

Joanna glanced up. "I was beginning to think you got yourself lost."

Mandy chuckled. "When was the last time I got lost?"

Joanna grinned. "So long ago I can't remember. Glory seems to have disappeared though."

The sisters looked at each other and sighed.

"No doubt helping Levi put up his mission house," Mandy said unnecessarily. Both knew where she was and why.

"Says they won't marry until the place is finished." Joanna giggled. "Seems she's in a big hurry to get hitched."

They both had a good laugh and then sobered.

"It won't be the same without her," Mandy said.

Joanna hugged Mandy then broke away. "We still have each other."

Mandy developed a sudden interest in the array of pies on the table. What would Joanna do if Mandy built a house and moved into it? But it wasn't as if she planned to stay there day and night. She'd still provide food for the stopping house and come every day to help. "You need anything done?"

"You could haul out the ashes, fill the wood box, and sweep the lean-to floor before people start arriving."

As she did the chores, Mandy planned her house.

Chapter 2

M andy hurried through her morning chores at the stopping house then called, "I'll be back later."

Joanna waved her away. Nothing unusual about Mandy's announcement. Almost every day she went hunting, keeping the place supplied with fresh meat. But today she swung her rifle over her shoulder and detoured by the woodshed to pick up the ax. On second thought. . . She took a few steps away and then backtracked. . . . She would take along a hammer and nails, too.

Glory had chosen the moment to get an armload of wood. She stared. "You're going hunting with an ax?"

"Aren't you supposed to be helping Levi?"

"He's ordering supplies. I'm going up there later." The way she eyed the ax, Mandy knew even mention of Levi hadn't distracted her.

"You're letting him order supplies on his own?" She hoped the doubt in her voice would trigger concern in Glory and send her after Levi.

"I think he can manage. What kind of animal do you hunt with an ax?" Her eyes narrowed. "You aren't going to go into hand-to-hand combat with a bear, are you?"

Mandy laughed. "I might."

Glory snorted. "Even you aren't that stupid."

"You calling me stupid?"

Glory shrugged. "I'm not going to fight with you."

"Cluck, cluck." Mandy made flapping motions with one arm, the other otherwise occupied with holding the ax.

Glory simply shrugged again. "You can't provoke me today. I'm in too good a mood."

"Well, ain't that sweet?"

"Unlike you, who seems determined to be miserable."

"Am not." Didn't take any effort at all to be grumpy with an intruder

145

on her land. She strode away.

"So where are you going with the ax?" Glory fell in at her side.

"You sure are hard to figure out, Glory. When Joanna needs you to help, you can't be found anywhere—"

"I can always be found helping Levi."

"Then when I have something to do that I don't need help with, you stick to me like a bad smell."

Glory punched her shoulder. "I don't smell. At least, not bad."

When Mandy ignored Glory's attempt to start a tussle, Glory deliberately bumped into her, making her sidestep off the path.

"Stop it."

"Tell me where you're going with the ax."

Mandy drew to a halt and faced her sister. Glory was a year older and a daredevil who liked to ride wild horses and challenge any man who abused his animals. Did Levi have any idea what he was getting himself into by marrying Glory? She sighed. Her persistent sister would not give her any peace until she found out what Mandy intended with the ax. "If you must know, I'm going to build a house."

Glory roared with laughter then seeing Mandy's frown, sobered. "You're serious, aren't you?"

"I've always wanted a house."

"Yeah. And no doubt you think Pa will come and live with you, and you'll be a happy family at last."

"So what if I do? I don't hate Pa like you do. I wish he would come back."

Glory lifted her hands in a sign of defeat. "I don't hate Pa. I just don't have any expectations of him. I no longer hope and pray he'll come back and make a home for us. Besides, in case you've forgotten, I'm going to make a home with Levi. He'll never walk out on me the way Pa always does."

Mandy kept her mouth clamped shut. They'd had this argument before.

"You don't need Pa anymore either. We're all independent, full-grown women now."

Mandy hurried away.

Glory followed.

"I guess it's too much to hope you might leave me alone."

Glory ignored Mandy's dig. "Where are you going to build this house?"

"I got a place picked out."

"Oh yes. I remember. Every time we move, you pick out the place where we will suddenly become a happy family with Pa living contentedly with us."

Mandy didn't slow down. Not that it discouraged Glory.

"So where is this place you got picked out?"

"If I tell you, will you drop the subject?"

"Maybe."

Mandy stopped, pointed up the valley. "On that hill over there. A nice flat clearing with hills rising on one side."

While Glory studied the place Mandy pointed out, Mandy resumed her journey.

Glory hurried after her.

Mandy sighed loudly.

"You've always had this dream but never before built a house. Why now? Is it because I'm getting married? Does that make you feel like our family is falling apart even more than Pa leaving all the time? Because I'm not leaving. I'll be real close. You'll probably get downright tired of me being so close."

Mandy ground to a halt and stared at Glory. "Are you out of your mind? This has nothing to do with you." A blast of exasperation exploded from her lungs, and she lifted a hand in defeat and amazement. "If you must know, it's because someone else thinks they can own my land. If I build a house first, it will be mine."

"Why don't you just file on it?"

"Because. . ." It made perfect sense but completely eliminated any possibility of besting the man. "I intend to claim it fair and square by getting my house up first."

"What do you know about building anything? Seems to me any time that kind of work came up you disappeared."

"Someone had to find food."

"Yeah, but using a rifle isn't a skill that will help you build a house."

"How hard can it be?" She steamed onward, Glory sticking to her side like a burr.

"Who is this person who wants your land? A man, I assume."

"A man by the name of Trace Owens."

"So you've met him?"

Mandy's insides flared hot at the memory.

"Is he alone, or does he have a family?"

Mandy jerked to a halt so fast that Glory had to retrace her steps. "There was someone. A woman or girl, I couldn't be certain."

Glory tapped her chin and considered this newest bit of information. "Did you ever think he might need the land more than you do?"

It was enough to make Mandy want to wrestle Glory to the ground until she hollered stop. "Look around you." She waved her arm in a wide circle. "There's plenty of other places." She pushed past her sister and hurried down the trail. "Let him find something else."

After a bit she realized Glory hadn't followed. About time. She went directly toward the clearing where she would build her house.

Trace swung his ax again and again, the shudder racing up his arm a constant reminder of his despair. No point in crying over spilled milk, as Ma would say.

He lowered the ax to the ground and bent over, moaning as pain with no physical cause clenched his innards.

Bad enough Ma and Pa had died. But the reason, the treachery behind it. Behind Cora's scars...

He lifted the ax and attacked the tree, welcoming the ache in his limbs from the hours he'd devoted to this kind of work.

But pain in his body did not neutralize the pain in his heart.

He knew nothing would. Not time. Not drink. Nothing but death, and he was too stubborn, too proud to let his enemies drive him to that. Besides, what would happen to Cora if he weren't around to care for her?

The tree fell, and he set to peeling it, sweat pouring from his brow and soaking his shirt.

No one would drive him from this place. Certainly not a woman who could pass for a man. A grin skated across his lips. No way could he be fooled into thinking she was a man. Not with those full lips, wide eyes, and feminine body.

The ax slipped, but he caught it before he did himself damage. He needed to focus.

No man or woman was driving him away. He was through running. And hoped they were far enough from his past that no one would bother them.

He secured a chain to the logs, attached it to the horse, and dragged them to the camp.

There she was. Mandy Hamilton. Complete with ax and rifle and, if he wasn't mistaken, a hammer in the pocket of her baggy pants. She circled the logs he'd already placed.

She turned a jaundiced gaze toward him as he drove the horse close to the house. "See you've been hard at work."

"You'll never catch up."

"Sounds surprisingly like a dare."

He grunted. Seems they'd already established it was a competition, at the very least. "What's to stop either of us from going to the land title office and putting our name on the deed legal-like?"

Her look shot daggers at him. "On my part, honor. I said first one to build a house—and live in it—gets the land. When I say something, I do it. I keep my word."

The words came out like hot bullets. He wondered if she meant them as strongly as she spoke them. "I ain't got much use for words. Easily spoken. Easily forgotten or excused."

She lowered the ax to the ground, carefully eased her rifle to rest against the logs. "Mister, them are fighting words. That's not the first time you've offended me. How do you propose to give me the satisfaction of justice?"

He rolled his eyes at her drama. "What? You want a duel? Swords at sunrise? Pistols at noon?" He snorted.

A muffled giggle came from the tent where Cora listened to everything.

Mandy's gaze shifted that direction, filled with curiosity, then returned to him, as harsh as before. "I demand satisfaction."

Trace shook his head back and forth. "No way I'm fighting a girl."

She sputtered. "I'm as good as any man."

"At what?"

"Everything."

He simply stared at her. "I can't believe we're having this discussion."

Another muffled giggle from the tent. No doubt Cora was enjoying her brother's discomfort at being challenged by a woman.

Mandy stared toward Cora's hiding place. "Your wife?"

"My sister, and I'll thank you to stay away from her."

"'I'll thank you to stay away from her.'" She mocked him. "I saw her from up the hill yesterday. She looked perfectly ordinary to me. What are you trying to hide?"

"Mind your own business."

Her eyes hardened. "Mister, you have offended me yet again. It's about time we dealt with this."

"Okay, fine. What do you have in mind? Another wrestling match like yesterday?" He grinned, letting her see just how much fun it had been to subdue her.

She blushed clear to her hairline. "A shooting match."

He chortled. "You're on."

They reached for their rifles in one fluid movement.

She cradled hers in the crook of her arm. "First, let's be clear about what's at stake."

"I'm sure you're going to tell me."

"Yup. You win, I forgive your insults. But when I win, which I will, you let me meet your sister."

They both heard the gasp from the tent.

"'Fraid that's not my call."

"Ask her if she's willing."

He could almost hear her asking if he was afraid. He was certainly not afraid of her. She was a woman. If he couldn't outshoot a woman, he better put on a dress and grow out his hair. "Cora, what do you think? You don't have to agree."

He waited, picturing the struggle his sister would be enduring.

"If I refuse it sounds like I don't think you'll win. But I know you will, so I agree."

"Done." Mandy held out her hand.

"Done." This ought to be fun. Like taking candy from a baby. Her firm hand in his reminded him he was not dealing with a helpless child.

They agreed on targets and took their places.

"Ladies first," he said generously. After all, he didn't want to intimidate her with his skill.

Her face hardened, and he sighed. He didn't need her to step back and refuse to lift her rifle to know he'd be the one shooting first.

"Don't say you didn't ask for it." He lined up a bead.

Mandy stood back to watch. The man had loads of confidence. It showed in the way he widened his stance and pressed his cheek to the stock. It revealed itself in his assurance he could outshoot her. In fact, if they weren't in competition, she might admire his self-assurance. He was going to need it. 'Cause she intended to beat him soundly.

He curled his finger around the trigger, and a shot rang out. The piece of wood serving as target exploded. Five more times without a miss. He lowered his rifle and stood back, grinning as if he'd already won the contest. "Ready to concede defeat?"

She flicked him the barest of glances. Defeat? He'd soon be crowing out the other side of his mouth. She knelt on one knee and rested her elbow on the other, eased her sights on the target, and squeezed off a shot. The chosen wooden target exploded. She reloaded five times, and five more targets followed suit. She rose and faced him. "Ready to concede defeat?"

"Not a chance." He glanced about, pointed out a dead tree branch a fair piece away. "I'll get that in the first shot."

"If you don't, I will." She indicated he should go ahead. He took his time lining it up then fired. At first she thought he missed, but then the branch cracked and fell to the ground. He was good. She'd give him that.

Just not good enough.

"See that branch?" She indicated one several yards past where he'd shot. "I'll take it down first shot."

He hooted disbelief. "Lady, if you do, I will concede defeat."

"Prepare to concede." She knelt again, studied her target, shifted when the sunlight glinted off the barrel. She pushed her hat back and steadied her arm, drew in her breath, held it, and squeezed very slowly. At this distance, she couldn't afford the least mistake. The rifle cracked. She pushed to her feet, her eyes never leaving the branch she'd aimed for. It exploded from the tree.

Ears ringing from so many shots, she bent enough to rest her rifle against the logs then turned to face Trace, a grin threatening to split her face in two.

His mouth hung open, and he stared toward the now-missing branch.

She whooped. "I win."

His attention jerked toward her. Admiration replaced surprise, albeit reluctant admiration. "That was a fantastic shot." His gaze held hers, exploring, she supposed, what kind of woman could shoot like that. Better than any man. But he continued looking at her, causing her insides to shift as though he offered something she hungered for.

How stupid. She didn't need anything. Especially from a man. Hadn't she proven over and over that she could manage without her pa, without any man? Hadn't all the Hamilton sisters?

She shifted her gaze and did a little victory dance up to him. "I won.

I won. I won." She danced back to where she started. Only then did she face him again, wondering what she would see. No doubt anger, displeasure at being beaten by a woman.

But he grinned widely, his eyes flashing appreciation.

Her words died on her lips, and her feet ceased dancing. The only part of her body that still moved was her heart, and it rattled against her ribs like a trapped animal trying to escape.

"No one likes a sore winner," he groused, still grinning. His gaze trapped her. Then he glanced toward the tent, freeing her to suck in air and shake herself inside for being so easily affected by a smile. Like she was some sort of foolish female. She followed his gaze and waited.

"Cora." He sounded so regretful she almost backed down from their agreement. But curiosity overrode any weakness. What kind of woman hid in a tent?

"I know." The disembodied voice sounded uncertain, maybe even a little unsteady. "I can't believe you let a woman outshoot you."

"I can't believe it either," Trace said. "But she's awfully good."

Mandy faced him. "I tried to warn you." Whatever silly thing she'd felt must have been only fleeting foolishness. But then his gaze collided with hers, and her heart dipped like it had broken free from its hitching post. She jerked away. What was wrong with her? "I won fair and square."

"No argument with that. And we'll live up to our agreement. Won't we, Cora?"

"We're honorable people no matter what others might say."

That was a mighty peculiar observation, but before she had time to consider it, the tent opening flapped. His sister edged out, though she clung to the bit of canvas as if it served as an anchor. "Hello, I'm Mandy Hamilton. I'm pleased to meet you." If you could call this a meeting.

Cora hunched forward as she had the first time Mandy saw her. She pulled the poke bonnet close to her face. She didn't even bother to look at Mandy. Wouldn't allow Mandy to see her. A sting of sympathy caught Mandy's heart. "I know what it's like to be shy. I'm not much good around people myself. Kind of prefer being out in the woods watching the animals. Do you like animals?"

A brief nod acknowledged the question.

"I can move through the woods so quiet I can get right up to a deer. Maybe I could show you how."

The girl jerked toward her, allowing her a brief glimpse of her profile, then turned away before Mandy could garner any details. From what she could see, the woman was barely out of childhood. "How old are you?"

"She's sixteen," Trace said.

"Can't she talk for herself?"

"Course I can. I'm sixteen just like he says."

"I'm eighteen. Perhaps we could be friends. Apart from my sisters, I've not had a friend for a long time."

"Why not?" Cora asked.

"Mostly because we move around too much."

"Why do you move?"

"It's a long story. Sure you want to hear it?"

One shoulder lifted in a shrug. "I wouldn't mind."

"Very well." She sank cross-legged to the ground. "Our pa is always chasing off after one adventure or another. Ma and us girls would follow after him. Ma died eight years ago, but we still tried to keep up with him. Gotta tell you it wasn't always easy to track that man. He moved so frequently we were often two stops behind him. Guess if a man isn't interested in keeping his family together, he doesn't really have anything to keep his feet in one place. Pa's been everywhere, tried everything."

"Like what?"

Mandy shot a glance at Trace to see what he thought of this mostly one-sided conversation.

He smiled encouragement, and her heart again lurched inside her chest.

Hoping to save her heart further wear and tear, she shifted her attention back to Cora.

The girl didn't hunch quite as markedly. Guess she was enjoying the storytelling, so Mandy continued. "He worked on building railroads, hunted wolves, hunted buffalo. . . ." She laughed a little. "Right now he's off hunting gold in the Kootenais."

"Why didn't you follow him there?"

"I wanted to, but Joanna—that's my eldest sister—she saw the chance to run the Bonners Ferry Stopping House. Said we could support ourselves nicely. Glory agreed, so I was outvoted."

"Who is Glory?"

Trace settled on the ground close by. She studied him, wondering if he'd had enough. He nodded. "Go on. This is the most she's talked to anyone but me in a long time."

"Glory is my sister. She's a year older." She paused.

The girl remained on her feet, her back to Mandy, her shoulders hunched. She must be getting uncomfortable.

"Cora, why don't you come over here and sit with us? I'll tell you more about Glory."

For answer, Cora ducked back inside the tent and pulled the flaps tight.

Mandy sought Trace's eyes, wanting to apologize. "I only wanted to make her welcome. Be a friend." Such sadness and regret filled his expression that her exuberant heart spasmed hard.

"Leave her alone. We don't need friends."

His harsh tone scraped raw wounds to her heart. But what did she expect? Pa had taught her well not to ache for anything from anyone.

He pushed to his feet. "Time to get back to work."

"Right." She hurried to the spot she'd chosen for her house. Too bad he'd already claimed the best site. But never mind. Once she had title to the land she'd use her cabin as an outbuilding and build a real house where she wanted it.

Chapter 3

Trace turned his back to Mandy, ignoring her as she paced out the perimeter of her house and used the butt of her ax to drive in posts.

He harbored a deep desire to kick himself in the behind all around the outside of his house. For a few moments he'd allowed himself to think he was an ordinary man like he'd once been, enjoying friendship with a beautiful woman, listening to her talk, enjoying the sound of her voice. Had he so soon forgotten the lessons he'd learned? As if such were possible with Cora hiding only a few feet away. It knotted his insides to see her go from a buoyant young girl on the cusp of womanhood to this fearful person.

If he had any gumption he'd forget about a race to build a house, march into town, file a claim on the land, then post No Trespassing signs around the whole area.

Except his honor insisted he live up to the agreement they'd given their hands on.

Not for all the gold in the Kootenais would he admit he rather enjoyed the idea of Mandy's company despite her somewhat prickly attitude.

Determined to bring his wayward thoughts into submission, he bent over the log he wanted to place next and set to trimming and notching it. He and Austin had often talked about building their houses. They had promised to help each other. His stomach filled with bile. He never thought his best friend would turn into a lawless Bushwhacker. Thinking about it made his muscles twitch, and he forced his thoughts away from the memory. He could build this house without help.

He might have succeeded in ignoring troublesome Mandy, except she stepped into his peripheral view.

He glanced up to see her studying his place and then hers—which was nothing at this point—with a speculative expression on her face. Only his upbringing stopped him from suggesting she move along and mind her own business. And—a grin tipped one reluctant corner of his mouth—the memory of how quickly she'd taken offense to him saying so a short time ago.

His words and the resulting contest had cost Cora, though Mandy had been nothing but kind and generous—willingly telling Cora all sorts of details about her life.

Letting his ax rest motionless, he considered the woman before him as something she'd said tugged at his mind. He tried to recall what it was. Something about her pa. Then he remembered. "Didn't you say you wanted to go after your pa?"

Her attention jerked toward him, her expression rife with challenge.

He sighed. "Do you walk around looking to be offended, maybe hoping to draw someone into a gunfight?"

Her mouth fell open. She struggled momentarily to close it, and then the burning in her eyes brought him to his feet, ready to defend himself.

"I do not." Her fists clenched and unclenched. "You take that back."

"Nothing to take back. You just proved it." He closed the distance between them until he was just out of reach of her arms. "It might be interesting to know why Mandy Hamilton is so defensive."

She glowered, fit to start his hair on fire. Then she settled back on her heels and gave a mocking smile. "Might be interesting to know why Trace Owens says he doesn't want friends." She correctly read his unspoken denial and grinned in triumph.

"You sure like to get people riled with you."

She lifted one shoulder. "Not normally."

"So it's just me."

"Yup."

He held her gaze as he considered her confession, trying to decide if she wanted to annoy him or. . . Caution forced him to guard his reaction. "Nice to know you've picked me as your number one enemy."

"'Twas you who said you didn't want a friend. What else is left?"

He recognized her challenge and decided to ignore it. "There's something about you building a house I don't understand. If you're keen to follow your pa, why would you want something as permanent as a house? Doesn't seem to fit. You sure you're not a wanderer like your pa?"

Denial darkened her eyes, followed swiftly by a flash of confusion as if she'd never considered this conflict between what she said and what she did. Then her lips softened, her eyes glistened.

Mandy looked about to cry.

He couldn't imagine her allowing such weakness.

She blinked away all signs of tears and turned her mouth into a stubborn line. Obviously she would not allow any weeping. "Maybe. . ." She breathed hard. "Pa might settle down if he had a nice house to live in. You ever think of that?"

He fought between laughing at her question and wanting to somehow assure her that dreams didn't always come true, but a person must go on, making the best of what life handed out.

"Mandy, I. . ." He had no idea what he meant to say. Only that she brought forth a reaction similar to what he felt when he considered Cora. He chuckled at the idea. Cora, hiding from view in the tent, and Mandy, challenging everything he said, had nothing at all in common. And yet his heart felt the same sort of tightening.

He resisted an urge to pound his closed fist on his forehead.

What was wrong with him today? He returned to shaping the end of the log, pointedly ignoring Mandy while she watched him work. Finally he couldn't stand it another second and glanced up. "Can I help you with something?" He meant the words to be dismissive—a kinder version of *mind your own business.*

"Nope." She didn't move away.

He turned back to his task. Whatever she wanted, she would have to come right out and voice it. He wasn't prepared to play at guessing games.

At last she spun around, grabbed her ax, and stomped into the woods.

Finally. He sat back and drew in a long, refreshing breath.

"Is she gone?" Cora asked after a moment of silence.

"She's taken her ax, so I expect she's off to get logs."

Cora edged back the flap and poked her head out. "You really let her beat you at shooting?"

"I didn't let her. She's a good marksman."

"Don't you mean *markswoman?*"

He turned and caught the flash of mischief in Cora's face. They laughed. "She seemed to want to be friends with you."

Cora shook her head. "I saw her. She's beautiful. She'd be repulsed to see my face. Beautiful people always are."

"I know I'm not beautiful." He pretended a sad note into his voice.

She giggled. "I think you see me the way you want me to be. Maybe the way you remember me."

"I see my little sister. All I have left of my family."

She lowered her head, but not before he caught the glint of tears. Again he vowed to protect her from ignorant people.

"Trace, I'm scared she might lead people here," Cora whispered.

"I've wondered about that, too. Not much I can do about it so long as I don't have title to the land. Except keep a sharp eye out and discourage any visitors."

Cora snickered. "Like you have with Mandy. She's outshot you and outsmarted you. Wouldn't surprise me none to see her outbuild you, too."

He dropped his ax and pressed his hands to his chest. "Oh such little faith you have in me. I am mortally wounded by your doubt."

She laughed then jerked back inside the tent, pulling the flaps almost closed. She would be able to see out through the tiny opening and watch without anyone being able to see in.

His arms hurt, but it wasn't from work or the heaviness of his ax. It came from regret pulsing from his heart, knowing his little sister would watch life from a protected place, hiding from others. Sweet, funny Cora.

The pain raced both inward and outward until his heart seemed to beat fire and his hands and feet stung as if burned. He should have protected Cora and their parents.

Mandy returned to the clearing, dragging half a dozen spindly trees after her.

"You going to build a log house or a twig shack?" His laughter earned him a look of disdain.

She marched past without answering.

"Hey, Cora, you ought to see this. It reminds me of that fairy tale Mother read. Remember? *The Three Little Pigs.* The middle pig built a house of sticks."

"A house is a house," Mandy muttered. "Don't think we mentioned what we could use to make one." She released her collection of trees and stared at him, hands on hips. "It sounds suspiciously like you've called me a pig."

"Oh brother." He took off his hat and scrubbed his hair. "Here we go again. What's it going to be this time? Swords? Knife throwing?"

She tossed her head, and her thick braid swung over her shoulder.

She caught it and returned it to her back.

He followed the movement, suddenly imagining the heavy waterfall of brown waves that would cascade to her waist should she free her hair. He frowned and forced his thoughts back to reality.

"I haven't got time for silly games or silly fairy tales." She gave him a good view of her back and her swinging braid as she bent to lift one of her trees.

He took a step forward, intent on lending aid, then stopped and returned to his own building.

"You know," Cora's low voice reached him. "If she's one of the three pigs, that makes you the big bad wolf."

Dare he hope Cora's voice went no further than his ears?

Mandy's roar of laughter dashed his hopes. "Big bad wolf?" She chortled the words. Sucked in air to stop her amusement, made a few wolf-sounding yaps, then dissolved into another fit of laughter.

Cora's muffled giggles wafted from the tent.

Trace tried to be annoyed at her derision, but her full-throated laughter was contagious. He quit resisting and chuckled.

Mandy stopped laughing and dried her eyes. She grinned widely at him.

He couldn't tear himself from her gaze, full of challenge, laughter, and something that dropped into his heart with a warm splash and filled it with sweetness. He hoped she wouldn't see all the things he failed to suppress—hope and despair twisted together like some odd twine. Surely she would look away, free him from this expectation he couldn't stifle. But she only continued to grin at him.

She quirked one eyebrow. "A wolf? Seems we're pretty familiar with them."

"You never once fooled me with your imitation."

She looked not at all dismayed. "Drew you from the camp though, didn't I?"

"You did a better job at convincing me you were a man."

Faint pink stole up her cheeks. "Didn't take you long to see your mistake, did it?"

His face grew hot, and he wondered if he'd turned as pink as she did.

She jerked away the same instant he turned from her, and gave every bit of his concentration to preparing each log. In the silence that followed, she grunted and scuffled as she moved her twigs about.

Mandy smiled as she tugged her trees into place. A piggy and a wolf. It was ludicrous. She wondered about this piggy story. Maybe Joanna would know of it.

She should have thought to bring a horse to pull out larger logs, but like Glory said, what did Mandy know about building? She'd studied how Trace constructed the walls on his house. Of course, he had newly peeled logs that were much larger than the ones she'd chosen for hers, but the method was surely the same. So she notched her unpeeled logs and laid them out in the square she'd measured out. Big enough for a bed, a table, and a small stove but not much more. Live in it. That's all they'd stipulated. But she could see Trace planned a larger, more substantial house. As if he meant to put down roots like an old oak tree and stay forever.

Mandy paused as she tried to imagine a man who stayed because he wanted to. Planned to. So a person could count on him from one day to the next. She understood there were men like that, but her pa had taught her well to question her assumptions.

She placed all her logs and headed back to the woods for more. She hadn't gone far when she realized Trace was also setting out for more logs.

He overtook her as she applied her ax to another tree and stopped to watch, making her too nervous to continue. She straightened and faced him. "You want something?"

"If you notch the tree like this"—he swung his ax to show her what he meant—"the tree will fall that direction. Always check to see what the tree will hit. For instance, you'll want to miss that tree."

"What makes you think so?"

He shrugged. "The branches will get hung up, and you'll have an impossible time getting it down. Besides, look in that crotch. A nest. If I'm not mistaken, it has baby birds in it."

She stared at the spot and tried to reconcile her varying views of this man. A big bad wolf concerned about baby birds and a younger sister. She didn't know what to make of him.

Trace had moved higher up the hill and paused as if something caught his interest. "Mandy, have a look at this view."

It was likely something she'd seen before. In fact, there wasn't a view around here she wasn't familiar with, but she wondered what drew his admiration and climbed to his side.

"You can see up and down the valley for miles. It looks like a good country."

"As good as any, I suppose. There's plenty of game, not too many people, and if I believed all the tales, rubies and gold and other treasures ready for the picking."

"Sounds like you don't believe it."

"Just 'cause someone says it, don't make it true."

He pulled his gaze from the view to study her.

She met his look, letting him know she would defend her statement if need be.

"You're one suspicious woman, you know that? Don't you trust anyone?"

"Only God and my sisters." Though sometimes she found it easier to trust her sisters. At least she could demand an explanation from Glory or Joanna. Seems with God you just had to accept what He sent your way, even if you didn't understand the whys or wherefores. Levi said that's what faith was.

Trace continued to study her. "Guess we're in much the same situation. I only trust my sister, and I try to trust God." He looked regretful. "Sometimes it's not easy to do."

Their gazes went on and on, silently sharing secret doubts and fears, and so much more she couldn't begin to understand. "So what's your reason?" she asked.

"For what?"

"Being so narrow in your trust." She almost shivered at how quickly his expression changed before he turned back to eyeing the view.

"I guess everyone has their grounds."

"True." But not everyone's reasons made a sister hide inside a tent during the heat of the day nor turn a man's expression to granite in the blink of an eye.

"I see someone riding up the other side." He pointed. "Riding like a madman."

She moved closer. Saw the rider. "It's Glory. She always rides crazy. She's going to see her preacher man."

Trace chuckled. "You say that with a great deal of expression, but I can't tell if it's pride or regret or something else."

She tipped her head to consider it. "I suppose it's both. Glory is too wild to marry a preacher, but Levi doesn't seem to mind."

"So what's the regret?"

She thought she'd spoken both, but his question forced the truth to the surface. "Our family is getting divided into pieces. I'm not sure I like it."

"It's part of life. I thought all girls looked forward to growing up and getting married. I know Cora did."

The way his voice dropped and he clamped his mouth shut, Mandy knew he meant she had at one time, but that time was over. She wondered why. Tried to think of a way to frame a question. But he spoke again before she could.

"Now we have a new home to look forward to and a new life. At least if I don't spend my days staring out at the view." He clucked at the horse and moved on.

Mandy stayed where she was, watching Glory until she raced out of sight. Good thing Joanna couldn't see her reckless haste, or she'd worry. With a deep sigh, she turned away.

Trace had chosen a tree not far away and tackled it with the ax. A wide stance allowed him a generous swing at the trunk. She watched the muscles across his back work with each swing. A strong man. A gentle man who considered the safety of tiny birds. But a man with a secret that made him deny friendship and keep his sister in hiding.

The sort of man she would do well to steer clear of.

And yet. . .

She pushed her hat more firmly on her head. What did it matter? She'd build her house, sleep in it, and win the land. He'd have to move somewhere else. He and his secretive sister.

Mindful of the lesson on falling trees, she cut down more spindly things and dragged them back. By the time Trace returned, she had several more in place. He might bring in bigger ones, but she could set six for every one of his, so it equaled out.

She stared at the position of the sun. Time to return to the stopping house and help Joanna. Which left Trace plenty of time to continue building without competition. "I have to go help my sister."

He nodded. "Fine by me."

"Well, it's not fine by me. It's not fair. You can work several hours more a day than I can."

He spared her the briefest of glances. "Don't remember anything in our agreement about having to work the same hours."

"A gentleman would offer."

He didn't even bother to lift his head but continued trimming the log. "A lady would honor her word."

"Surely you don't expect me to neglect my duties at home? That wouldn't be fair to Joanna." She loaded every word with as much guilt as she could dredge up, hoping to persuade him to agree he wouldn't work when she wasn't able to.

"Mandy Hamilton, I can't believe you're trying to change the rules after we've agreed. You could have specified any conditions before the fact. But not after."

"Oh." She clenched her hands into fists. "I perceive you are a most unreasonable man."

That brought him to his feet to stride toward her. He didn't stop until they were toe-to-toe. She met his glare with one equally as narrow eyed.

"I do not consider it unreasonable to expect a person—man or woman—to honor an agreement. To live up to what they've promised. Or to be loyal to another."

She stared, surprised at his words, then backed up a pace. "I will indeed honor our agreement if you are unwilling to concede to changes. As to promises and loyalty, I think you are not talking about me."

He pulled himself taller and crossed his arms over his chest. "I expect nothing less than complete trustworthiness."

Again she wondered if he meant her. But how could he? He had no more reason to trust her than she had to count on him.

She didn't trust easily. Certainly wouldn't be opening her heart to a man full of dark secrets. A man who said promises had no value, loyalty was to be questioned, stated he didn't need friendship. . .and was hiding his sister.

He turned back to his task. Clearly he could not be trusted.

She would not let little hints of kindness and brotherly loyalty cause her to think otherwise.

Chapter 4

The evening chores done and the guests settled down for the night, the three sisters withdrew to their bedroom.

Joanna opened up their mother's Bible. Shortly after Levi had shown up in Bonners Ferry, they'd begun the habit of reading from the scriptures. Joanna sat on her bed facing Glory and Mandy, who shared a bed—at least, until the wedding in a few more weeks.

Mandy tried not to think of one of her sisters moving on. The bed would seem wide and lonely without Glory. Glory was a year old when Mandy was born. She couldn't remember a time she wasn't able to reach out and touch the comforting presence of her sister. Or turn to their eldest sister for comfort and guidance.

Joanna studied each of them as she spoke. "Levi read from the Psalms on Sunday. I enjoyed it so much I thought I'd read there tonight." She turned a few pages. "Psalm one hundred forty-six." And she read.

Mandy listened, hoping for an answer for the turmoil in her heart. She didn't want Trace on her land. She didn't want to be his friend, even though she offered to befriend Cora. And why did Cora hide? Most of all, why did Mandy's thoughts head one direction then switch to something else whenever she was around him? In fact, he was nowhere near, and it was happening again.

"'Put not your trust in princes, nor in the son of man, in whom there is no help.'"

Mandy pressed her fingers to her mouth to stifle a giggle.

Joanna stopped reading. "What's funny?"

"God telling us not to trust men." Her chuckle was half snort.

Glory pushed her, causing her to fall over on the pillow. "Not all men are untrustworthy. . . ."

Joanna and Mandy knew what was coming next. They chorused the words with her. "Levi's not."

The three of them grinned at each other.

Mandy righted herself. "Glory, I wish you weren't leaving."

"We can't stay like this forever."

Ignoring them, Joanna finished reading the psalm and closed the Bible. "Mandy, what's this about a man up in the hills?"

Glory nudged Mandy, signaling she'd told Joanna.

Mandy jabbed her elbow in Glory's ribs, thanking her for interfering. "All kinds of men in the hills."

"And building a house? What's that all about?"

Mandy gave Joanna her best innocent, wide-eyed expression. Not that she expected Joanna to be fooled. For half a penny, Mandy would love to tell her to mind her own business. Remind her she wasn't Mandy's mother. But she knew it would hurt her sister's feelings, so she held back the words.

Glory decided she had the right to answer for Mandy. "You know how Mandy always picks out a spot for a house. She can't stop thinking Pa will come back and we'll be a family." She turned to Mandy. "I keep telling you to give up on Pa. He ain't got time for us, and besides, it's too late. We're grown up. Ready to start our own homes."

Mandy tightened her jaw. Knew she looked stubborn and petulant but didn't care. "I'd welcome Pa back if he came."

Glory grabbed Mandy's shoulder and shook her a little. "Think. When has Pa ever come looking for us? Never. We follow him. Or we used to. But no more. Stop pinning your hopes on him."

Joanna's soft voice interrupted. "About this man. . ."

"He's on my land." She ignored the way Joanna's eyebrows went up. Glory snorted.

"I tried to chase him off, but he wouldn't go. So we agreed that whoever builds a house first can file for the deed."

Joanna leaned forward. "Exactly how did you try and get rid of him?"

At the same time Glory groaned. "You don't know how to build a house."

Mandy chose to hear only Glory's words and waved her hand dismissively. "We didn't stipulate what sort of a house it had to be. Only that we had to live in it."

"Let me guess." Glory sounded resigned. "You're not building a regular house."

"Well. I'll be able to live in it. That's all that matters." She described the rough structure she intended to put up. "Trace is putting up a real log house." She told of his work.

"Trace is the man?" Joanna prompted.

"Trace Owens. And he has a sister who hides." That brought a burst of interest from both sisters. "I've had only two glimpses of her. One from the hillside. And one when I won a shooting match with him." Another flurry of interest and more explanation.

When she finished telling how she'd outshot the man, Joanna and Glory laughed.

Mandy waited for their amusement to abate. "Joanna, did you ever hear a story of the three pigs and a big bad wolf?"

"Yes, I read it when I worked for the Johnsons. Mrs. Johnson bought a new storybook for Sally. That was one of the stories."

"Tell me what it was about."

Joanna told of three pigs who built houses—one of straw, one of sticks, and one of bricks. A big bad wolf blew down the first two houses, hoping to eat the pigs, but they found shelter in the brick house and captured the big bad wolf in a pot of boiling water.

Mandy grinned. She liked what happened to the wolf. It meant she won.

Her sisters demanded an explanation.

But she would never admit he'd likened her to the middle pig. "He's so confident he'll beat me. But I can out do him without even trying." She snorted. "The arrogant man." Joanna and Glory chuckled and exchanged knowing looks.

"What?"

"Nothing—except he sounds like the perfect man for you." Glory had the nerve to speak the words, but Joanna nodded.

"He is not." Mandy bounded off the bed and faced her sisters with clenched fists.

Glory nodded, too. "Yup. He is. He shoots almost as well as you. Enough to earn a bit of admiration. And he's building a solid house. What you've always wanted."

"You. Are. So. Wrong. This man has all kinds of secrets. Why his sister refuses to leave the tent. I don't trust him. The last thing I need is a man I have to guess about."

Joanna gave her serious study. "I wonder if you'll ever let yourself trust a man no matter how noble and true he is."

"Course I will." But he'd have to prove himself able to live up to her expectations. "I'm going to bed." She stripped off her trousers and shirt and pulled on an oversize man's nightshirt.

Glory shook her head sadly. "Better start wearing something a little more feminine than that if you ever expect a man to look at you."

Mandy's face burned like fury. She grabbed a pillow and whacked Glory on the head. "No man better see me like this unless he's married to me."

Glory fell down on the bed, giggling madly. "You'll want to look all pretty and nice for the man you marry. You wait and see."

Mandy whacked her again for good measure. "You still wear trousers. Besides, how many fancy nightgowns have you made?"

Glory grabbed the pillow and tucked it under her head. "I might make a couple. You never know."

Joanna turned off the lamp. "Girls, go to sleep."

Mandy and Glory giggled just like they always did when Joanna grew motherly.

But Mandy couldn't fall asleep as a thousand questions raced through her mind. What did Cora hide? Why was Trace so touchy about friends and loyalty? Was he really intent on staying or just unable to re-sist a challenge? Where did he come from and why?

And what made her heart float high up her throat just thinking of him?

The next morning, she hurried about her chores, chomping with im-patience, knowing Trace would spend these hours raising the walls of his house higher and higher.

But finally she could leave. As usual, she called, "Be back later."

Joanna came to the door. "Hunting for meat or for men?" She laughed.

Mandy flicked her the barest protesting glare then hurried up the trail. She wasn't hunting any man.

In fact, she was doing her best to drive him away.

Trace had been up since before dawn. After Mandy left yesterday he'd raised the walls by four logs, but he had a long way to go and planned to use every hour to his advantage.

"Breakfast is ready." Cora sat by the campfire, her bonnet hiding her face.

"I don't have time to eat."

"You must eat. You can't keep working so hard while starving your-self." She paused. "I wish you'd let me help."

She'd offered several times, but Trace's imagination pictured her being crushed by a runaway log. He would never let anything harm his little sister again.

"It would go faster with two of us working. We'd be sure to win the contest and get the land. Otherwise. . ." She left the rest unsaid.

"I have no intention of losing this place and my house to Mandy." He turned to study Mandy's structure.

Cora joined him. "It isn't much of a house."

"Like she said, we didn't specify the sort of house it should be."

"Maybe you should do something similar. Just to win the land."

He contemplated the idea for several moments, shifting his gaze between the two houses. "No. I think I can win and still build a solid structure. Something we can live in for a long time."

"Do you suppose we will be happy here?"

"As happy as we dare."

"Life will never be the same." She hunched forward, clutching her bonnet closer. "Do you think the Bushwhackers will follow us?"

"They got what they wanted. They got rid of the Owenses. I don't expect we'll hear from them again."

"Then why do you always keep the rifle so close and jerk up from bed at the slightest sound?"

He would not admit his fear that one of the marauding bunch would take it upon himself to track down Trace and Cora and finish what they'd started. "There could be wild animals around."

"Like Mandy pretending to be a wolf?" She giggled.

"Glad you find it amusing."

"Admit it. She's funny. I can never guess what she might say or do next."

"About as funny as a case of cholera."

Cora laughed.

Trace tried to recall the last time she'd shown so much pure, sweet enjoyment. He allowed himself a brief moment of appreciation for Mandy if her presence allowed Cora to laugh.

"She doesn't put up with any nonsense from you."

Trace faced his sister. "Are you saying I'm overbearing? Difficult to get along with?"

Cora backed up a space and held her hands up in mock defensiveness. "Heaven forbid. But. . ." She slowed her words. "Since the fire, you have grown. . .well, hard."

"Guess I've been forced to get that way."

"I know. And I'm not condemning you. But when Mandy is here, you seem to forget about the past. For just a bit."

"Maybe because she forces me to be on my toes. She continually surprises me." He shook his head. "Who'd ever think she might put up a twig house?"

"Like the second little piggy. Don't think she fancied being called a piggy."

"Don't imagine she would. But at least she didn't challenge me to a gunfight at high noon."

They both laughed. It felt good and cleansing.

"Let's eat breakfast." Cora took his arm and guided him to the fire to dish out thick oatmeal mush and fresh biscuits cooked in the outdoor oven. "I put stew to simmer. It will do us for lunch. You'll have to bring me some if Mandy is here."

"Cora, I don't like you being holed up in the heat of the day."

"I'm fine. I stay close to the flap. I get air there."

Meaning she didn't intend to venture forth and allow anyone to see her.

"I'd sooner take the heat than have people make faces or call me names."

They'd ridden through one town during daylight hours, and a woman had screamed and called Cora a witch. They would have been run out of town except they left as fast as they could.

He pulled her close. "People like that don't matter." Except they both knew they did. "Just as soon as I finish this house you'll have a nice place to stay. I'll put in windows to let in air."

"I'll put up curtains to prevent prying eyes."

He hurried through breakfast and returned to the house. Not only did he need to beat Mandy, the sooner he completed it, the sooner Cora could get out of the inadequate tent and have decent shelter.

Somewhere to his right, a wolf yapped. "Mandy's coming," he warned. Cora ducked into the tent.

She didn't show up right away, but the sound of an ax and the crack of trees falling echoed through the woods. She was working on her stick house, but he intended to beat her. He bent his back to preparing and placing the logs he'd dragged in late last evening.

Mandy grunted as she dragged in her twigs.

"Why don't you use a horse?"

She dropped her load and shrugged. "Prefer to prove I can win by my own efforts." She dusted her hands and strode toward him. With a measuring glance she studied how much he'd done since she left. "Thought you'd have it up to here by now." She indicated her shoulder. "Been slacking off, have you?"

"Didn't want to get too far ahead of you. Didn't seem gentlemanly, and it seems I have to prove I'm that."

She grinned as if she knew something vastly amusing at his expense then bent to examine the notching of his logs. "You did a fine job. A fine job. Can't say as I mind seeing the house built soundly." She faced him, her eyes flashing challenge.

Good thing he had stopped using the ax. He might have cut his hand, because his heart stuttered at the way her eyes blazed, filling him with a strange sensation. Like he'd been riding along mindlessly and his horse had dropped over a sharp edge, taking him along for the descent and leaving his heart to follow.

She didn't blink. "You realize the house will be mine when I win this little challenge?"

"Not when. Not if. When I win, your little pile of twigs will be nothing more than a corn crib or"—he tried to think of some use of significant unimportance—"pigpen."

"Speaking of pigs. . ."

Why did she continue to grin so triumphantly? And why did he feel as if he'd been invited along for an adventure?

No way. He would guard against any invitation from any source from now on.

She continued. "You do know what happened to the big bad wolf in your story of the three pigs, don't you?"

"He had pork dinner. Yum. Yum." Only he knew it hadn't ended well for the wolf, and he wondered if he should heed the warning.

"Nope. The pigs outsmarted him. Sometimes it isn't the biggest or the baddest who win."

"I'll take that under consideration." Too bad he couldn't believe it. Seems the biggest and the worst did win. And the small and decent lost. . . . Paid with everything they had. He straightened.

"I've only got a few hours to work, so no time for idle conversation."

But did she walk away and tend to her own affairs? No, she stood staring at the walls of his house.

"Seems to me it's going to be a lot of work for one man to get the logs up to roof level. Hmm. Let's see how the big bad wolf handles that."

And she marched away.

He knew she wasn't wishing him well. "Takes longer for one man, but by applying some basic mechanical know-how, it can be done." More time, more physical effort, but he could and would do it.

"If you say so." She chanted a tuneless ditty as she worked.

After a moment, he made out the words.

"I'm not afraid of the big bad wolf."

"Psst." Cora called for his attention.

He left his work to see what she needed.

"Why is she so confident?"

He wondered the same thing. "It's all bluff."

"I don't know. I don't trust her."

"I'll keep an eye on her." Neither of them said they weren't ready to trust anyone.

He returned to his work, doing his best to ignore the endless cycle of words coming from Mandy as she worked. "I'm not afraid of the big bad wolf." He could almost believe she repeated the singsong dirge without thought. . .but not quite. It was part of her strategy. And he didn't like it one bit.

He pried the next log into place, struggling to raise it to the next level. Sweat poured from him as he worked.

The endless tune from Mandy came to an end but only because she watched him lifting the heavy log. It would have made a world of difference to have someone hold one end steady while he hoisted the other, but he wouldn't ask her for help if his life depended on it and was equally certain she'd refuse if he did.

The log slid into place, and Mandy clapped.

Not about to let anything she did annoy him—or rather let her know it did—he bowed deeply then headed for the water bucket. He downed two dipperfuls, took off his hat, and poured another dipperful over his head.

Mandy stared as he shook the water from his hair, then spun away as if he'd splashed her. He knew he hadn't.

But she didn't return to her own house. Instead, she sidled up to Trace. "It must be awfully hot in that tent. Why don't you let Cora come out?"

"Let her?" He sputtered. "You think I'm forcing her to stay there?"

"Nothing else makes sense. It must be hot as an oven. If you let her sit in the shade, she'd be so much cooler." There was no gentle pleading in her voice, only hard, accusing tones that stung Trace clear to the tips of his ears.

"I am not making her stay. She doesn't want to come out." He shot out each word with fury. How dare she accuse him of such unkindness?

"Prove it. Tell her she can come out."

"Mandy Hamilton, there are some things you should stay out of, and this is one."

She jammed her fists on her hips. "So you can't prove it."

"I don't need to prove anything to you. Best you just leave this alone."

"So you've said, but I take orders from no one."

"Kind of figured that was your problem."

"Don't consider it a problem."

"Think what you want, but Cora won't come out even if I beg."

"Prove it."

He took a step toward her. "If you were a man—"

"Don't let that stop you." She widened her stance and held her hands in front as if she truly expected him to engage in another wrestling match with her.

He turned his back to her, thought better of it considering some of her little habits like kicking and biting and goodness knows what else, and faced her again. "You are the most infuriating woman I have ever met."

"And you are the most devious man I've ever met, and that's going some. I've met a lot of male creatures, especially in the stopping house, and I gotta say some are pretty nasty people."

He'd only once before seen a red haze in his vision. And it had taken a whole lot more than one woman to cause that. "Cora, come out and prove to this. . .this. . ." He refused to say *woman*. ". . .person that you are not some sort of prisoner."

Cora gasped. Next followed a silence so deep he could hear the beat of his own heart and the flap of wings on a bird passing overhead.

"She's accusing me of forcing you to stay in the tent."

"I don't want to come out. I won't." Cora's voice trembled. "Mandy, Miss Hamilton, believe me, it's not because of Trace. It's my own choice. Please, just leave me alone."

"There." Trace had never glared at a woman before like he glared at Mandy. "Are you satisfied?"

She didn't look one bit convinced. "There's something mighty fishy around here, and it ain't fish." But she strode over, picked up her ax, and headed for the woods.

He waited until she crashed out of sight. Allowed himself a small smile. Not like her to be so noisy. She must really be annoyed. But she had no reason. Any more than she had any need of the truth.

He brought his attention back to his sister. Cora would be in fear and trembling until she knew she was safe. "She's gone."

"Why is she so set on seeing me?"

"I can't say. Maybe she's truly concerned about you staying in the tent in this heat." Or maybe she thought she had a right to know everyone's business. Or maybe she suspected them of some deep, dark secret, though he couldn't imagine what two travelers—a brother and sister with nothing more than what they could carry with them in way of belongings—could be suspected of concealing.

Except Cora was hiding, and that piqued Mandy's curiosity.

He didn't trust her to let it go, but he didn't know what to expect next.

What an unsettling woman.

Chapter 5

M andy worked like a fiend putting up log after log. Never mind that Trace called them twigs. They were making walls, and that's all she cared about.

She tried to ignore him as he worked, steadily building the walls higher on his house. It was a fine-looking building. She'd be right proud to be its owner in a short while. She tried hard not to think about his sister, Cora, while the sun beat down. Even out in the open with a breeze against Mandy's hot skin, the heat was close to unbearable.

"Aren't you afraid she'll perish from the heat?" she demanded as she paused to down some tepid water from her canteen. She thought longingly of the cold water in the river not far away. But she wouldn't waste time to fetch it.

"She's fine."

"How do you know? Did you check to see? How can you ignore her?"

He flung around. "Seems you worry about her enough for the two of us." But he stomped over to the tent and ducked inside.

She listened shamelessly.

"Mandy is sure you're going to die in here. Are you?" As he spoke the anger in his voice fled and his words gentled. "It is dreadfully hot. Cora, let me take you to the shade."

"No. I'm fine."

"Cora, you'll be just as fine outside."

"No I won't."

Mandy held her breath and leaned close to catch Cora's whisper. "She'll see me."

"I'll hide you by those bushes up the hill a ways. No one will see you."

"No. Just leave me. I'm fine."

"Fine." The word sounded angry.

Mandy stepped away and bent over one of her logs.

174

"She's fine." Trace's tone did not indicate any relief, but he, too, returned to shaping logs.

Even at lunchtime, Cora refused to leave the tent.

Mandy grew more and more curious. She'd seen glimpses of Cora and could think of no reason the girl would be afraid for others to see her.

Something was not right here.

And Mandy intended to find out what it was.

The afternoon sun, unrelenting in its heat, headed for the west. Time for Mandy to return to her chores back in Bonners Ferry. She stood back to study the progress on her house.

"One good wind and it will blow away." Trace sounded downright happy about the idea.

"Wouldn't gloat just yet. Unless. . ." She spun about to eye him with suspicion. "Seems in the story the wolf had something to do with the fall of the first two houses. Don't you be planning to do something to my house."

He let out a *tsk*. "You are one mistrustful woman. Fact is, it never crossed my mind." He tipped his head one way and then the other as he studied her house. "Looks a little askew to me."

"It's a good enough house for me. I guarantee it won't disintegrate in the wind or the snow. What it lacks in beauty it makes up for in strength."

He had the gall to laugh openly.

"A gentleman would show more respect."

"Ah, but you forget, I'm really the big bad wolf." He puffed out his cheeks and blew at her house then faced her, his gaze filled with teasing.

She gasped. Not because he pretended to blow her house down but because like sunlight on water, his eyes flashed with blue brightness, allowing her to see something she'd not noticed before.

The man was as handsome as any man she'd ever seen. And when he smiled like that, he seemed to make the world a happy place.

She forced her unwilling attention to something beyond his left shoulder. Tried to think what she was supposed to be doing. Her gaze settled on the ax. Then the walls of her house. Drifted onward to the hill beyond, where the trees glistened with heat and birds twittered softly. A chickadee flitted between branches seeking food for her nestlings.

Food. Mandy's thoughts slowly righted themselves. "Time for me to go. The stopping house is in need of fresh meat." She brought her gaze back to Trace, relieved to see he had returned to his usual guarded look. "See you tomorrow. Bye, Cora," she called.

"Bye." Surprise filled the single word coming from the tent.

Mandy strode off, grinning, though for the life of her she couldn't explain why.

A little later she took game to Joanna then slipped noiselessly back up the narrow trail toward Trace and Cora's camp. She circled to a hill overlooking the site where she knew Trace wouldn't bother her. The trees there were too small for him to want to chop down. The brush allowed her to edge close to the clearing for a good view.

She found a spot allowing her to see the front of the tent and settled back to watch.

Trace worked on a log. Did the man ever leave off building the house?

Mandy measured his progress, checked it against what she'd accomplished earlier, and nodded. She still held her own.

There was no sign of Cora. Surely she didn't remain in the tent after Mandy left. But Trace seemed to be talking to someone.

Mandy edged to her left until she could see around the log wall. Cora was there all right, sitting with her back to the wall, plucking blades of grass and examining them. Her mouth moved as she talked to Trace, but Mandy was too far away to hear her, and she'd never learned to read lips. Too bad. It would have come in handy at the moment.

Trace dragged the log to the wall, rolled it into place. He dusted his hands as he stood back and admired his work, obviously well pleased with his efforts.

Huh. It was way too soon for him to think he could gloat.

He took his horse and headed back up the hill for another log. Good. Now she could watch Cora without the distraction of Trace.

She edged closer until she couldn't go any farther without fear of discovery. Cora still sat against the log wall, her bonnet practically covering her face.

In the distance, the ringing of an ax informed her of Trace's whereabouts. The thump of a falling tree soon followed. He would be busy trimming and barking it for some time.

Mandy simply had to wait and watch Cora.

Cora stretched her arms skyward as if embracing the world or imploring God to change it. Mandy couldn't say which. A breeze fluttered the leaves. Cora shoved her bonnet to her shoulders and shook her head as if inviting a breath of coolness. She bent to get a pot off the ground and take it to the fire where she hung it to cook the contents.

That's when Mandy saw her face. One cheek beautiful as china. The other red and puckered.

"*Oh no.*" She mouthed the words. *So this is what she doesn't want people to see.*

"I guessed you wouldn't let it go."

She jumped to her feet like a frightened deer and jerked around to stare at Trace. "Where did you come from?"

"You're not the only one who can tiptoe through the trees." His narrowed eyes warned he wasn't pleased to see her.

She saw his anger and something more. Something that made her want to reach out and touch him, assure him things weren't as bad as he and Cora seemed to think. But tension vibrated through him, and she knew any sudden movement on her part would bring forth some sort of eruption. Instead, she leaned back, hoping her attempt to appear relaxed would neutralize his tautness.

"Now you know why she doesn't want anyone to see her."

She nodded. "What happened?"

"She was burned."

"How dreadful for her."

"She will never forget it. And if she tried, neither her mirror nor other people's stares would let her."

"I didn't mean her scar. I meant being burned. It must have been painful."

"More than you can imagine." His eyes lost their anger and flooded with despair. "She deserves to be left alone."

"Deserves? Or do you mean desires? But she's a beautiful young woman. I can't imagine she wants to spend the rest of her life hiding."

"What she wants and what she has to deal with are entirely different things."

Mandy sat on the ground, cushioned with old leaves and pine needles, and turned to watch Cora.

"Can't you show a little decency and leave us in peace?"

"I'm not bothering anyone. Just sitting here enjoying the afternoon shade." She wanted to say something more, but she didn't even know what it was. She needed time to clarify her thoughts and put them into words. "You're welcome to join me." She patted the ground beside her.

He grunted. Or was it a groan? "What have I done that deserves this kind of torture?"

"Are you referring to the heat? Or the flies? Maybe the work of building a house?" She knew he meant none of those things, but she would not give him the satisfaction of acknowledging what he meant.

"I mean you. From the first day you have tormented me."

She grinned up at him. "You're just sore because I upset your plans."

"I couldn't have said it better." But the anger and despair fled. He glanced at the spot she'd indicated beside her and shrugged as if to say he didn't have much choice because he expected she wouldn't leave him any peace until he sat. With a great show of reluctance he joined her. "I don't suppose it would do any good to suggest you forget you've seen her."

"Why would I want to forget it?"

"She doesn't want people to know."

She understood he meant know about her disfiguring scars, but she wouldn't accept it. "I am not repulsed by her face, if that's what you expect."

He didn't say anything, which she found oddly touching. But when she turned to study him, his face was a mask of disbelief.

"Her face is scarred horribly."

"Only part of one cheek, not her whole face. And it's only a tiny fraction of her physical body and nothing to do with who she is."

"Huh."

"I've seen people who are whole and even beautiful, but their spirits are scarred terribly by greed or bitterness or cruelty. I've seen people who are ugly and deformed but have such an inner beauty you never think about how they look." The words she'd been trying to sort out tumbled forth in a tangled rush. "Where we once lived there was a bent little man who had a hump in his back and one side of his face twisted all out of sorts, but Old Terry was the sweetest person I've ever known." Her voice tightened, revealing how fond she had been of the old man. "He understood how three girls forced to live with an unwelcome family could feel abandoned and unloved. So every day as we walked to school, Old Terry would meet us. He'd walk a little ways with us. We had to slow down for him to keep up, and he only went a short distance before he was out of breath. But every day he gave us something. Maybe only a pretty rock to put in our pockets."

She sniffed, hoping he wouldn't notice as unshed tears clogged her nose. It had been a long time since she'd thought of Old Terry, and she wondered how she could have forgotten him and the lessons he'd taught them—like finding happiness and joy in little things, accepting the bad without letting it destroy them. If only she could make Trace and Cora see life like Old Terry had. "Sometimes he found a wildflower or a bit of pretty glass. Many times it was only a kind word, a reminder of better things."

She'd been lounging over her knees but suddenly sat up straight and blinked back her threatening tears. "I just remembered. One thing Old Terry would bring us was Bible verses written on a scrap of paper. I used to keep them in a little cigar box." She turned to look at Trace. "I can't believe I forgot that." A sudden rush of memories washed over her. "He said we should always trust God no matter what happened, believe God had nothing but good planned for us."

Trace watched her closely, a flicker of amusement in his eyes. But she saw something more and recognized it as the same mixture of despair and hope Old Terry had noticed in her and her sisters.

"I remember the verse he gave us one day and made us promise to memorize. For days afterward he would make us repeat it until we could say it easily."

"What verse was that?" Trace's voice sounded as thick as hers had felt a few seconds ago. "Do you still remember it?"

"As if I could forget. Jeremiah twenty-nine, verse eleven. 'For I know the thoughts that I think toward you, saith the Lord, thoughts of peace, and not of evil, to give you an expected end.' He said it meant God had nothing but good for us in His thoughts."

Trace's gaze held her firm. Searching, hoping, delving into her heart as if seeking some balm there.

She let him look his full, prayed God would comfort and encourage him with the verse as it had her when Old Terry gave it to her.

He blinked and shook his head. "Hard to believe God has anything good in mind in what happened to Cora."

"Let me meet her. Really meet her."

"I can't do that. I promised to protect her."

"By hiding her?"

He closed his eyes as if to shut out her demands.

"She shouldn't hide from people. What a lonely life. I would think it might be a worse fate than being burned."

"Mandy." He groaned. "You don't know what you're talking about."

"Yes, I do. For instance, if Old Terry had hidden just because some people were unkind. . . Some threw rocks at him and called him a devil. But if he'd let them turn him into a recluse, who would have helped and encouraged three lonely girls?" She touched Trace's arm in an appeal to give her words consideration. "Let me meet her."

He covered her hand with his, a warm sense of connection flowing through her arm to her heart. She wanted to help him, ease his pain, help Cora.

"You almost persuade me, but it's not my decision."

"You know, I can steal in silently and meet her if you don't warn her of my approach."

"And be a traitor to my own sister?" He shook her hand off and scrambled to his feet. "If she can't trust her own brother, who can she trust?"

"She can trust me. You can, too."

He bent close. "Can I trust you to respect Cora's desire to be left alone?"

She rose to her feet to face him squarely. "I will not agree to something I am so opposed to."

"Then don't ask me to trust you." He stomped into the woods and disappeared.

She stood still for a moment then nodded, having come to a firm decision.

She would not take no for an answer.

∞

He heard her following him. Obviously she meant him to, or she wouldn't have made so much noise. He returned to where he'd left the horse, but he wouldn't go back to the camp with Mandy trailing after him like a lost dog. He faced her. "Why are you following me?" The stubborn set of her jaw made him want to grind his teeth. With two steps he closed the distance between them and grabbed her shoulders to shake her. "Mandy, leave us alone."

Awareness hit him on several levels. Her shoulders were firm. Muscles twitched beneath his palms. She was a strong woman, and he meant both physically and morally. He stopped shaking her but did not pull his hands away.

She pressed her hands to his shoulders in a manner imitating the way he'd captured her, and he wondered if she felt aggravation as well or something else. Her expression hinted at patience and understanding.

"Trace, if I came across an injured animal in the woods, I would not walk away until I'd done all I could to help it." Her smile flashed with unspoken promises. "Why would I do any less for a hurting person?"

He forced words from his thick brain. "Because people have the ability to say whether or not they want help."

She nodded, holding his gaze in an unrelenting grasp.

He couldn't break away even if he tried. But he discovered he didn't want to. Something in her look offered him hope, healing, or. . . He couldn't say what. He didn't try to make sense of his mixed-up thoughts.

She patted one shoulder. "You know I won't let this go, so you might as well accept it."

He shifted his gaze, freeing himself from her power. "It isn't just about you and me. It's Cora and her wishes."

"You know it's wrong to keep her like this." She tilted her head toward the camp.

He'd thought it himself a time or two. But. . . "You haven't seen the way people react to her."

She shrugged her shoulders, sending a thousand sparks into his palms.

He dropped his hands and spun away. What was he to do? Not that she was giving him any choice. She would follow him, dog him, harass him, spout forth insults until she got her way. Might as well get it over with.

Ignoring her, neither giving her permission to follow him or ordering her not to, he led the horse back to camp.

Of course, she followed as he knew she would.

They broke into the clearing. Cora glanced up. Her gaze went past Trace, and she bolted to her feet.

"I couldn't get rid of her," Trace said, regret and sadness making a twisted rope of his insides.

Cora clutched at her neck, looking for her bonnet, but it had fallen to the ground. Gasping, pressing her hand to her cheek, she started toward the tent and ground to a halt when she saw Mandy blocking her path.

"Don't be afraid," Mandy soothed.

Cora whimpered. "Go away." She ducked, giving Mandy a view of the top of her head.

"I don't aim to hurt you."

Trace watched. Part of him wanted to bodily remove Mandy from the face of the earth—or at least return her to Bonners Ferry and nail her to the floor of the stopping house. Another part wanted to see how this played out. Could she persuade Cora not to hide?

Mandy caught Cora's chin and tipped her face up. She stroked one cheek and then the other. "You are much too young and beautiful to hide."

Cora's blue eyes widened. She looked hopeful, as if she wanted to believe Mandy.

Trace could not get in a satisfying breath. His little sister had been born with a halo of golden-white hair. It had darkened slightly as she grew. In the fire she'd lost much of her hair on one side, but no one would know it to look at her now. It had grown back enough for Cora to braid it into tidy submission.

But despite her beautiful eyes and hair, Cora would never be the same. He recalled something Mandy had said. Cora was scarred both inside and out.

Trace admitted he was equally scarred inside. Nothing could change that.

With a muffled sound—half groan, half cry—Cora broke free of Mandy and scrambled to find her bonnet and tie it tight. She glanced at the tent, stole a fleeting look at Mandy, then turned her back to them and walked to the half-built log house. She slipped around the corner and sank to the ground, holding the edge of her bonnet to her cheek.

Mandy shifted her attention to Trace, her eyes brimming with sorrow and sympathy. She smiled. Did he detect a quiver in her lips?

"It's a start," she murmured.

Why did her words fill him with hope such as he'd forgotten existed? It pushed at the bottom of his heart, sought to escape into his thoughts, his feelings, his life. He tried to shake himself free of her gaze and failed.

He dare not allow himself such a measure of hope.

He could not, would not let himself trust her. "Time to get to work," he muttered. He dragged the log to the house, unhitched the horse, and set it free to graze. All the while Mandy remained, watching. And no doubt scheming something.

He could hardly wait to see what it was. Mocking, silent laughter caught halfway up his throat. So far her schemes had brought him nothing but trouble.

So why then did he grin?

Chapter 6

M andy tried to make sense of what happened up the hill. Why had he touched her? Why had she grabbed his shoulders in a similar gesture? The way her insides bucked at his touch should have warned her. But did she listen to the signals? No. She was far too intent on convincing him it was wrong to let Cora hide. But when she'd felt his warm flesh under her palms, recognized the strength there, acknowledged the twitch of his muscles, and experienced a helpless tangle of thoughts and emotions, she realized she had stepped into something she was at a loss to control.

Even now, after focusing her attention on Cora, her insides contained a whirlwind of confusion. Cora. She pushed her thoughts, her attention back to the girl who again wore her bonnet like a helmet of steel. At least she hadn't retreated to the heat of the tent.

Mandy nodded decisively. She knew what to do next. Hang about for a time to prove to Cora she posed no harm.

Trace sat astride the log, about two feet from where Cora hunkered against the wall. Neither spoke, though the air was heavy with silent words.

Mandy grabbed her ax and plunked down on the other end of the log, imitating Trace's movements as he stripped bark from the tree.

He stopped work.

She felt his demanding look. "What? You've never seen a woman debark a tree?"

"I never thought to see Mandy Hamilton assisting Trace Owens."

She shrugged and returned to her task. "Consider yourself fortunate indeed, because you won't see it very long."

"Why am I seeing it at all?"

"You looked like you needed help." She slid him a teasing glance. "No need to let a little competition stop us from being neighborly."

Trace choked like the idea strangled him.

She pretended great concern. "Do you need me to pat your back?"

He waved her away and shook his head, starting another bout of coughing.

"Aw. I just want to help."

"I don't think I need the kind of help you're apt to dish out," he managed to say.

She chuckled and was rewarded by an echoing giggle from Cora. Mandy turned her attention to the girl. "He sure gets all cautious at times. You think he's afraid I might hurt him?"

Cora met Mandy's eyes full-on for a moment, long enough for Mandy to see the brimming humor and take hope the girl still knew how to enjoy life. Then Cora ducked away, hiding behind the flaps of her bonnet.

"Not afraid," Trace protested. "Only realistic. After all, you have an ax in your hand. My motto is 'Never take chances with a woman wielding an ax.'"

That brought another giggle from Cora, and Mandy grinned widely at Trace. *See*, she said silently. *Isn't life better when you stop hiding?* Only she meant when Cora stopped hiding.

Trace quirked an eyebrow. Not necessarily in agreement though.

They both bent to their work until they met in the middle. Their foreheads touched. Mandy dared not continue to use her ax. Not for the reasons Trace insinuated but because her hands weren't steady. She edged back, pushed to her feet, and glanced at the sky. "Oh my. I didn't realize it's so late. I gotta go before Joanna sends someone looking for me." She jogged to the path, paused to look back and wave. "See you both tomorrow." And then she sped toward town and her worried sisters.

A few minutes later, Mandy raced by the men congregating outside the stopping house. Several of them looked startled. She didn't care if they were surprised at her haste or the fact she wore trousers. The Hamilton girls did things their way.

"Where have you been?" Joanna demanded as Mandy skidded into the dining room. "I was so worried I haven't served the meal yet."

Glory came from the kitchen to watch. "I was about to ride up the hill and drag you home."

"I'm sorry. But you'll understand when I tell you what happened." She pushed past and grinned at Glory. "Don't say a word," she whispered then grabbed up a big bowl of potatoes and headed back to the dining room. "Let's get this bunch fed."

"I can hardly wait to hear what kind of a story you concoct," Glory whispered as they passed again. "But it better be good."

Mandy shook her head.

She didn't get a chance to say anything further until the meal was over and the men departed outside to wait for the dining room to be cleaned up and the table pushed against the wall, creating an area in which they could spread their bedrolls. The girls used the intervening time to wash the stack of dishes.

"I'm waiting for your excuse," Joanna said as she scraped the leftovers into a bucket. Someone usually begged for scraps to feed their dog.

"I saw Cora today." She told the whole story. "I don't think her burn is that disfiguring, but she is very conscious of it."

"The poor girl," Joanna said.

Glory hooted. "I was thinking that poor man. Mandy has not given him a moment's peace since she discovered him."

Joanna and Glory looked at each other and grinned like they shared a secret.

"What?" Mandy demanded.

"We never said anything."

"I saw the way you looked." She planted her hands on her hips and gave them each her most insistent look. "You were thinking something."

Glory nodded. "But you don't want to know what it was." She bounced away, holding up her hands, ready to defend herself. She tipped her head with a come-on-I'm-ready gesture.

Mandy ignored the taunt. "I do, too."

"You're sure?"

Joanna watched the pair sparring with a look of patient endurance.

"Of course I am."

"Very well. But remember you asked for it."

Mandy grunted. What could they possibly think she'd get upset about?

"It sounds very much like you can't stay away from this Trace Owens." Glory began edging toward the door. "I think you've found a man you're interested in. Love is in the air." She ducked out the door, calling over her shoulder. "Mandy and Trace. Mandy and Trace." She raced across the yard and headed for the road, thinking she could escape.

Mandy threw the towel on the table and took off in hot pursuit. "You take that back."

She didn't catch up until they reached the little shop where Glory shoed horses. By then both were out of breath and collapsed to the step.

Finally Glory was able to speak. "Don't you think it's about time we met Trace and his sister?"

"That's a good idea. I'll see if I can persuade them to come. But I wonder if Cora will be ready to let others see her."

"Are you really beginning to care for this man?"

Mandy considered Glory's question. "He is annoying and bull-headed, but I do admire how gentle he is with his sister." She gave Glory a little shove. "People who treat younger sisters kindly can't be all bad." She shoved her harder. "Too bad you didn't realize that."

Laughing, Glory pushed back. Soon they were both giggling.

Glory glanced up. "Here comes Levi." She sprang to her feet and waited for him to reach her side.

Levi stepped close and stole a kiss in the shadow of the doorway.

Mandy groaned. "Such inappropriate behavior especially for a preacher and his fiancée. You're fortunate no one saw you."

They both looked unrepentant.

Glory chuckled. "I'll never be appropriate. Look at what I wear." She indicated her tight dungarees. "Levi loves me anyway."

"You're exactly what this preacher man needs." He took Glory's arm and the pair wandered away.

Mandy watched for a moment. Somewhere deep in the inmost parts of her heart, she felt a longing for something similar.

Like Glory said often enough, Mandy was always looking for what her pa failed to give her. Only she wasn't picturing Pa at this particular moment.

"Shoot. I must be losing my mind." She stalked back to the stopping house to help Joanna.

⬯

For some inexplicable reason, the next morning she took her time about returning to the building site. She cut down a number of trees and bundled them together to drag to her house. But still she didn't take them there.

All night she'd thought of Trace, even in her sleep. She dreamed of his gentleness and loyalty to Cora. She relived the way his hands felt on her shoulders, the way his eyes flashed bright blue or darkened according to his mood. The sudden awareness of something inside her she didn't know existed until now. . .a jolt of an emotion she couldn't name. But it seemed to have a Trace-shaped hollowness to it. Or so she'd decided in the middle of the night.

In the light of day, she decided she'd been more than slightly crazy.

But the remnants of the feeling lingered, making her uncertain how to face him.

She chewed on her lips. Mandy Hamilton never let anything upset her equilibrium. It was not about to happen now either.

Grabbing the rope, she pulled her load toward her house. Yeah, even she had a hard time calling it a *house,* but she'd never admit it. "Morning," she called, as she entered the clearing.

Only after she dropped her burden did she bother to look around.

Trace, who'd been notching a log, straightened to greet her. Did she detect the same guardedness she felt?

For some reason, the thought gave her courage. She grinned. "Hard at it still? Not ready to concede defeat yet?"

"Not a chance." He tipped his head toward the tent.

She was afraid to look. Had Cora holed up in there, prepared to sweat out the hot sunshine? When she saw Cora bent over the cooking fire, stirring a pot of something, she almost cheered. Yes, she still wore that silly poke bonnet as if it were armor, but she was outside.

Mandy sent Trace a wide smile.

He nodded, happiness wreathing his face. *"Thank you,"* he mouthed.

She tipped her head in acknowledgment. Though he might not be thanking her by the end of the day. Leaving the tent was only the first step for Cora. "Morning, Cora."

Cora glanced at her. "Hi, Mandy. You've come back to torture Trace?"

"It's the driving force of my life."

They both chuckled.

Trace groaned. "Sounds like you two plan to make my life miserable."

"Not me, dear brother." Cora pressed a hand to her heart. "Why would you think such a thing?"

He shifted his gaze to Mandy, and she simply smiled. "I've made no secret of it from the beginning, have I?"

He gave a long-suffering sigh, but he favored her with a look that was rich with amusement.

If she wasn't mistaken, he enjoyed her form of torture. "You better get to work, big bad wolf, before this little piggy finishes her twig house."

He laughed and bent to continue notching the log.

She stared as pleasure warred with a hundred cautions she'd developed over the years, and for a fleeting moment she wondered if this was how Glory felt around Levi.

Then she realized her thoughts again bordered on foolish or worse. They weren't enemies per se, but neither were they exactly friends. In fact, she couldn't say what they were, apart from competitors in trying to establish a claim to this piece of land.

The thought straightened out her confusion immediately, and she turned her attention to building her house.

The heat grew as the day lengthened. But Trace did not slacken his pace. Neither did she.

Midday, Cora announced, "I've plenty of stew for all of us. You might as well take lunch with us, Mandy."

Mandy gratefully accepted. She was famished, hot, and thirsty.

The three of them dished up the stew and moved away from the cooking fire to eat. They chose a shady spot where a cooling breeze blessed them.

Cora carefully kept her face turned from Mandy, but at least she sat with them.

The meal finished, the three of them leaned back against the trees, Trace between Mandy and Cora.

"Where have you come from?" she asked.

The air stiffened. She didn't need to look at either to know the question made them nervous.

Then Trace eased back into an indolent position. "Missouri. We're from Missouri."

She tried to think what she knew about Missouri, but it was embarrassingly little, never having paid much attention to such things. The political discussion she'd overheard at the stopping house centered mostly on the Civil War. She couldn't imagine friend fighting against friend, or worse, brother against brother. "We sometimes see families moving West to get away from the war." She assumed they were doing the same.

Neither of them answered.

"Is it possible in Missouri to avoid being affected by the war?" Mandy asked.

Cora gave a strangled sound. Trace bolted to his feet and strode away.

"I've got a house to build."

Mandy rose more slowly, fully aware she'd said something to upset the brief spell of contentment among them. "I was only trying to make conversation."

"We know," Cora murmured. "But it's a touchy subject for us." She took the dirty dishes and hurried to clean up.

Mandy supposed she should drop the subject and promise to forget about it, but their reluctance only served to make her more curious.

The Owenses certainly had their share of secrets. And she didn't like secrets. Reminded her too much of Pa. He would have his little secrets and wouldn't tell the girls even though they knew something was up. Then one day he'd be gone. Most times with no warning. No forwarding address. No invitation to join him. They'd be left in the care of anyone he could interest in the idea.

No, she didn't like secrets one little bit.

"I was only showing a little interest in you," she muttered as she returned to her house. "It's not like I'll condemn you for what side you support." *Whack, whack.* She adjusted the supporting posts.

No answer from either Owen except for a muffled sound from Trace and a vicious swing of the ax.

He better be careful, or he'd injure himself.

"I guess it has something to do with why you're here."

Trace lowered his ax to the ground, wiped his brow, and glowered at her. "Now why would you say that?"

She studied her house as if it required all her attention, but she couldn't have said what she saw. "I don't know. Intuition maybe. Or because"—she glared at him till her eyes stung—"when I mentioned the war, both of you bolted like I'd thrown scalding water on you."

He stalked over to plant himself directly before her. "Mandy Hamilton, you are the most persistent woman I've had the misfortune of meeting. Once you get an idea in that. . .that"—he sputtered—"that head of yours, you worry it to death like an old hound dog with a rank bone."

"My, but you do know how to sweet-talk a woman." She ground about on her heel, putting distance between them for his safety. "First a pig, and now an old hound with a smelly bone." She gave the wretched building before her careful consideration. "I wouldn't be surprised if you offended some pretty little gal back in Missouri with your sweet talk, and she ran you out of town."

Cora, scouring dishes, giggled.

"Yes, I'm persistent," Mandy continued, her anger fueling heated words. "Let that be a warning to you, Trace Owens. Right now I've got my mind set on owning this land, and like you said, I don't give up."

She grabbed her ax and headed for the woods to find more trees. But amid her anger, Mandy felt scraped to hollow rawness. She was only trying to be friendly. Something she thought he would welcome after he'd almost hugged her yesterday.

Just went to show how far you could trust a man to have regard for your feelings. About as far as she could throw him with one hand tied behind her back. Which wasn't very far.

∞

Trace couldn't believe only this morning he thought she was sweet and pretty. Believed he'd felt attracted to her as they stood arm to shoulder.

They worked throughout the afternoon in silence as his heart continued to vibrate with anger. Anger at the deceit of those who'd forced him into this position and made it impossible for him to trust anyone, but especially anger at Mandy with her persistent prodding. Unknowingly, she'd picked a newly formed scab off a fresh wound.

As if she had any right to stick her nose into their business. He'd never met a more annoying woman in all his born days.

It was a relief when she tossed aside her ax, called an abrupt, unfriendly good-bye, and disappeared into the woods. Finally he could take in a decent lungful of air and edge aside his anger.

Thankfully, Cora kept her opinion about the whole episode to herself, though he felt her measuring look more than once.

∞

Next morning, the events of the previous day lingered like a persistent headache. He downed two cups of coffee without relief.

Cora sat back watching him, well aware of his unsettled mood. "Why don't you tell her what happened and get it over with?"

"Because I don't trust her. Don't trust anyone."

"What's she going to do? Announce it to the whole town?"

"Maybe."

"I wonder if people here will care. Didn't Mandy say she's seen people heading West to avoid the war? Maybe they'll understand our desire to be neutral."

"I simply can't see any benefit in telling our story."

Cora shifted closer. "I am not the only one scarred by what happened."

He jerked up to stare at her, letting his gaze drift to her burn.

She brushed it with her fingertips. "I know you don't have an outward scar, but both of us have damage here." She pressed a palm to her chest. "No one can see it. But it hurts as much as anything on the outside. And makes us want to hide from people every bit as much as my face does. I understand. You don't want to open up to her because you're afraid of getting hurt again. But I don't think Mandy is like Annabelle." She settled back to cradle her cup of coffee. Then she chuckled. "She isn't anything like Annabelle."

"Good morning," Mandy sang out.

Trace stilled the surprise jolting along his nerves. How had she managed to step into their camp without him hearing her?

Because he was so busy trying not to think of her.

"Looks like it might be a little cooler today. That's good news."

Neither Trace nor Cora had answered her yet. He guessed Cora was as surprised as he at having the object of their discussion show up unexpectedly.

He glanced around. Either he'd spent a lot of time drinking coffee or Mandy was earlier than usual.

"Trace? Cora? Is something wrong?"

He shook away his mental fog. "Good morning, Mandy."

Cora greeted her, too.

"Aren't you early today?"

She leaned back, her arms across her middle. "Got to get my house built." But she stood there grinning, not even looking toward her twig house.

What was she up to?

Her shirt billowed and wiggled.

He bolted to his feet. "Mandy, what's in your shirt?"

"Oh, that." She dug inside. "A little something for you. Not you exactly. It's for Cora." She brought forth a black-and-white ball of fur.

"A cat?"

"A kitten." She cupped it in her palms and held it out to Cora.

Cora took the kitten and cradled it to her cheek. "He's so soft." She laughed. "He's purring." Eyes shining, she looked at Mandy. "Where did you get him?"

"A man left five kittens at the stopping house. He said they were weaned now, and he didn't want to take them farther. He took the mama cat with him. Joanna picked out one to keep. Said she wouldn't mind a cat to keep the mice down. The others found new homes almost immediately. I claimed this one for you." She beamed at Trace, saw his watchfulness, shifted her attention back to Cora, and was rewarded with nothing but pleasure in Cora's expression.

"You're sure it's okay if we have him?"

Mandy nodded. "He's yours."

The cat played with the strings of Cora's bonnet.

"What did the others look like?"

Mandy hunkered down at Cora's side, teasing the kitten with a blade of grass. "Joanna kept one that is more black than white. Then there was one almost all white. This one, though, had a nice balance of both. The fourth was all mottled looking and the fifth striped."

"This is the best one of the lot, then."

"I thought so. Glad you approve."

Cora favored Mandy with a smile.

Trace held his breath and waited for Cora to realize her bonnet had fallen to her shoulders and jerk it back up. Instead, she dragged one ribbon toward the kitten, laughing when he caught it between his paws and growled.

"Look at that. He's a born hunter." Cora lifted her face to Trace. "Isn't he sweet?"

It wasn't the kitten he thought of. It was Cora, seemingly forgetting her burned cheek for the first time since the fire. And Mandy, who'd worked this little miracle with her gift. He squatted beside Cora and scratched the cat's head. The impossibly tiny creature grabbed his finger and licked it.

"He likes you," Cora said.

Trace didn't know if it was true, but for sure he liked what the cat had wrought in his sister's behavior. "What are you going to call him?"

Cora grew thoughtful. "I don't know. But not a silly pet name. This cat deserves a noble name."

Mandy chuckled. "He's so tiny. Why not call him Goliath?"

The three of them laughed at the idea. But Trace knew before Cora announced it. The cat was stuck with the name.

"Goliath it is," Cora said. She grew serious. "Mandy, thank you for bringing him."

Mandy draped an arm across Cora's shoulders and gave her a little hug.

Trace's throat tightened.

"You're welcome. I thought he might provide you with some company."

The teasing look she gave Trace sent a thrill through his veins. He knew she expected him to object, as if he weren't enough company for his sister. But he was too pleased with the situation to rise to her bait. In fact, he feared his eyes might reveal far too much of what he thought and felt toward Mandy at the moment. He pushed to his feet and went to work on constructing a fine log house, determined he would think of nothing else until he finished.

At that time, Mandy would leave them alone.

When had the word *alone* ever sounded so barren?

Chapter 7

Trace looked up as Mandy grabbed her ax and strode into the woods in search of more twigs. He needed to cut more trees, too, and headed the same direction. His path took him past Mandy, and his steps slowed. He dropped the reins of his horse. But still he didn't move toward her. Something inside him had shifted hard to the right at her kindness to Cora. The same feeling that shifted the opposite direction yesterday when she'd been so annoyingly persistent. In fact, he felt bruised on either side of his chest from the way his emotions bounced back and forth.

But he couldn't pass without acknowledging what she'd done for Cora. He went to her side, being careful to stay away from the swing of her ax. "Mandy?"

She rested the ax head on the ground and faced him, her expression guarded as if she expected another insult or angry retort.

To his shame, he knew she had reason for her caution. He had not been a gentleman. And why she brought out the worst in him, he couldn't explain. But at this moment he felt nothing but goodwill toward her. "It was kind of you to bring Cora a kitten."

"You're welcome," she said, even though he hadn't exactly said the words *thank you*. "You needn't be surprised that I can be kind."

"Mandy, I'm not at all surprised."

"Really? Aren't I the most persistent, annoying person you've met? A hound and a pig?"

He hadn't said those *exact* words, but it didn't matter. He'd hurt her feelings and regretted it. He moved in cautiously, afraid of her reaction if she objected. But she only watched with guarded eyes. He grasped her shoulders simply to make sure she wouldn't attack him. Inwardly, he grinned. He knew self-defense wasn't his only motive. He wanted to touch her, feel her warmth beneath his palms. Most of all, he needed to erase the flash of pain he'd glimpsed. "Oh, Mandy. I don't mean to call you names. But you must accept there are things I cannot tell you."

She stiffened. "Secrets make me nervous."

"No need for this one to."

Her gaze searched his, reaching deep for answers, not finding all she wanted because he couldn't let her. There was a time he'd trusted a woman to hold his dreams and desires gently. He'd gone to visit her when he knew the Bushwhackers were looting in the area. He should have realized his family was in danger, but he blindly expected his friendship with Austin to protect them.

She must have seen his guardedness. "I thought you would see by now I am not your enemy, but I fear you are more cautious than Cora. She hid in a tent. You hide out in the open."

Her words were true. "I'm sorry." He dropped his hands but did not step back, struggling between a desire to hold her close and derive some comfort and yet somehow maintain mental, emotional distance.

For several more seconds their gazes connected, searching, as the air between them shimmered with promises, hopes, and—invisible walls. He understood she could not trust him while he kept secrets. But he couldn't allow himself to break his code of silence on certain matters.

"Mandy?" The word shifted the air, breathed open a clarity between them. If things were different. If they'd met at a different time, a different place. Before life had turned sour for him.

She stepped back. "It's never mind to me what you're hiding." The way she hoisted her ax warned him she intended to get back to work. And if he was smart, he would step out of ax range.

"Thanks for your kindness to Cora."

She snorted.

He picked up the reins and moved away. Life was what it was, and he couldn't change the fact.

By the time he got back to the campsite Mandy had already returned and added another layer of branches to her—whatever it was. He couldn't dignify it by calling it a house. He dragged a log to where he needed it and stood back to admire his work. Now *this* was a house.

Mandy and Cora were both out of sight on the other side of Mandy's building. He heard shrieks of laughter; then Cora and Mandy raced around the corner, chasing Goliath. The cat ran between Trace's feet and crouched behind the log, watching for the girls.

Mandy touched Cora's arm. "Shh. You go that way, I'll go this. We'll corner him."

They tiptoed forward. The kitten picked up his ears, well aware of their every movement.

Cora crept up beside Trace. Mandy edged to the other end of the log. She nodded her head, and both sprang toward the cat. Goliath jumped over the log and darted back toward Mandy's house, Cora and Mandy in hot pursuit.

Trace leaned back and laughed heartily. Cora ignored him and continued the chase, but Mandy drew up short and faced him. She glanced toward Cora, who disappeared around the corner. Then her gaze rested on the twigs she'd dragged in.

He waited, wanting her to look at him, wanting to assure himself she held no ill will toward him. Finally, almost reluctantly, she rewarded his patience and studied him as if seeing him for the first time.

What did he want? Forgiveness? For what? For not being open with her? Yes, he realized. Because she was hurt by his secretiveness.

"Maybe someday," he murmured, not certain she would understand his meaning.

She flashed a smile and nodded.

His lungs expanded fully as if a weight had been yanked off his chest.

"I'm not only persistent," she said. "I'm patient."

"Nice to know." Their gaze held until he felt hope building in his heart and jerked away. "Got to finish my house." His words sounded thick.

"Yup. You get right at it. I want it as near completion as possible when I sign the deed." She laughed.

For some reason her remarks amused him. He couldn't say why, except it felt a whole lot more like they were partners than rivals.

The morning passed pleasantly enough as they worked side by side. Again Cora invited Mandy to share their lunch, and she agreed.

"Tomorrow I'll bring something," she promised.

"Can you cook?" He tried to picture her over a stove with an apron about her waist.

"Depends what you mean by cooking." Her smile teased.

"Normally, I would mean put a pot on the stove, fill it with meat or potatoes, and cook them. Maybe put a pie in the oven."

"Well, Joanna is the pie baker. None of us can do near as well as her."

He waited. Nothing. As if that answered his question. "So you make the best"—he left plenty of time for her to insert something, anything—"uh, pudding?"

She shook her head.

"Mashed potatoes?"

A little one-shoulder shrug as if anyone could do mashed potatoes.

He looked at Cora for suggestions, but she had nothing to offer.

"Biscuits? Bread?"

"Nope."

"Then what?"

"I can turn a venison roast into the tastiest bit of meat you've ever imagined."

"Really? And how do you do that?"

She leaned forward, spoke close to his ear. "'Fraid I can't tell you. It's a secret." She leaned back, a satisfied look gleaming from her eyes. "You know how it is with secrets."

Yes, he did. And he understood she'd gained a little victory by refusing to share one with him, even though it involved nothing more important than meat.

Silently, they challenged each other. Then she grinned. "Tell you what I'll do though. I'll cook a nice big roast for you so you can see for yourself." She sprang to her feet, humming as she returned to her work.

Despite the cooler morning, the afternoon grew still and hot, forcing them to retreat to the shade several times for a break.

Cora offered to help Trace but he refused, telling her to stay away from the logs. He hated seeing the flash of hurt in her face as she backed off. Thankfully, she turned her attention to the kitten and enticed it into the shade. A few minutes later Mandy and Trace flung themselves down on the grass beside Cora to cool off.

Mandy shifted to look across the valley. "I wonder if Levi and Glory are able to work."

"What are they doing?" Trace lounged back, knowing this guileless woman would share the information freely.

"I told you Levi's the preacher man Glory is going to marry. She was certainly suspicious of him to start with." She told about a sister who rode like a wild man, who shod horses and worked with the abused ones. She told of a preacher who came to town. "Glory said he dressed more like a cowboy than a preacher. But now they're crazy in love." She rolled her eyes. "I do mean crazy. They don't even mind kissing in front of others."

Trace laughed at the way she wrinkled her nose.

"They're building a mission house to care for orphans, the sick, and the elderly. As soon as they're done, they're going to get hitched, though Joanna thinks they should wait until the town builds a church."

"No church?"

"Nope. Sunday services are held outdoors. If it rains, we cram into the stopping house. Say. . ." She craned her neck to look at him. "You and Cora ought to come to the Sunday service and meet my family."

Cora gasped.

Trace shook his head. "'Fraid we aren't planning to go out in public now or at any time in the foreseeable future." He could see arguments building in Mandy's head. "Cora's not comfortable around others." He wasn't about to try and change her mind either. He didn't want to go to church. Didn't want to be reminded that his anger toward those who hurt him was wrong. Didn't want to be told God was in control and he should forgive.

Mandy shifted her attention to Cora. "Cora, you should reconsider."

Cora lifted her bonnet from where it rested on her shoulders, tied it to her head, and pulled the sides close around her face.

Mandy sighed. "Forget church, then. Come to the stopping house and meet my sisters. They've asked after you. I'll do my roast for Sunday dinner. How's that?"

Cora shook her head. "Trace, you go. I'll be fine here. I have Goliath to keep me company."

"I don't think that's wise." But at Mandy's expression—gentle pleading, hopeful anticipation—he added, "I'll think about it." Victory and pleasure gleamed in her eyes, and he almost regretted giving her any encouragement. She would likely take it as an open invitation to badger him into agreeing.

And yet he realized he didn't mind the idea of her trying to persuade him. Not at all.

∽

I'll think about it. She'd make sure he did. Today was Friday. If she couldn't convince him to come and at least visit her sisters by Saturday evening, she might as well stop being Mandy.

Satisfied she'd find a way, she returned to work, finished for the day, and headed back to Bonners Ferry and her chores.

Before daylight the next day she was out in the woods with her rifle. Deer stole through the pink dawn to water at the river. She waited until most of them finished and moved away. Then, feeling the same reluctance she always did at killing such an innocent, beautiful creature, she downed a young buck. The shot echoed through the trees, sending protesting birds from the top branches. She dressed the animal, quartered it, hung the pieces from the back of her horse, and carried it back to the stopping house.

"Good." Joanna took the bounty. "We were starting to get low on meat. Have to feed the men well if we expect to keep in business."

Mandy refrained from pointing out they could serve hard beans and people would eat there because they had no other option, but she knew what Joanna meant. They had a reputation of good food to maintain. "Save a nice big roast for Sunday."

"Oh?"

"Yup. I'm expecting company." She grinned at Joanna's surprise.

"Trace and Cora?" Joanna asked.

"Yup."

Glory's arrival was announced by the pounding of horse hooves then she rushed in, her hair in disarray, smelling of horseflesh. She caught Joanna's question. "Ohh. Trace is coming to visit."

Mandy ignored her teasing grin. "I told him I cook the best venison roast in the world. So now I have to prove it."

"I'll be happy to meet them," Joanna said, turning her attention to the meat. "I'll have to can most of this to keep it from spoiling in the heat." She looked toward the river. "We need to build an icehouse."

"I'll be happy to meet them, too," Glory said, grinning from ear to ear. "I can't imagine a man who can divert Mandy from pining for Pa." Her boots thudded on the floor as she crossed to scoop a dipper of water from the bucket on the cupboard and drink deeply.

"Who says he has?" But it had been days since she'd thought of Pa. It had nothing to do with Trace. She'd simply been busy.

She gave Glory a wide view of her back. "Joanna, maybe you could make a pie or two?"

Joanna jerked about from tending the meat, stared at Mandy, then a slow smile started at her eyes and edged toward her mouth. "Sure. I'll make pies. Any particular kind?"

Mandy squinted at her eldest sister. Why did she grin about nothing more than pies? Nothing special about wanting a pie for Sunday dinner.

"I've always thought your dried apple pie was especially good. Probably the best you make." She turned her full attention to the task of washing breakfast dishes, though she couldn't help but overhear whispers between her sisters. Knew they talked about her, but she wouldn't give them the satisfaction of giving it any heed.

She washed the stack of dishes then grabbed a loaf of bread. "I'm going to take a lunch with me today." She sliced the entire loaf, grabbed the leftover bit of grouse from last night, and made thick sandwiches, liberally salted and peppered.

Joanna kept busy slicing venison and setting the pieces to soak in a brine solution in readiness for a hot, steamy afternoon of canning. But she spared many a glance at Mandy.

Glory made no pretense of doing anything but watching. She leaned against the table and studied every movement. "You sure must plan on being hungry."

"Cora and Trace have shared their lunch these past two days. I figure it's time for me to contribute." She reached for a syrup pail, removed the lid, and took out a handful of cookies and then another. "Don't worry, Joanna. I'll help you bake more."

"Uh-huh." Joanna sounded doubtful. "I've heard that before."

"I have helped."

"Never mind. You bring in meat and do other chores. I'm not complaining if my job is to do the cooking."

Mandy wrapped the sandwiches in brown paper, did the same for the cookies, dug a sack out of a cupboard, and settled the whole lot carefully so she wouldn't arrive with nothing but crumbs. "I'm going to work on my house."

Glory straightened. "I think I'll come along and have a look at your house. And your Trace."

"No, Glory. Please don't. Not yet." Both sisters looked at her like she'd said something foreign.

Joanna washed and dried her hands and stood before Mandy. "What's going on? We don't keep secrets among ourselves."

"No secret. I've told you everything." Except for the foolish way her heart jumped around when Trace looked at her, but Joanna didn't mean that. "You have to understand, Cora is only beginning to feel comfortable around me. I fear if I brought someone there she would retreat." Trace had no reason to hide, and yet she wondered if he wouldn't view a visitor as a betrayal on her part. "Wait until Sunday, and you'll meet them."

Joanna studied her a moment longer then finally nodded. "Until Sunday."

Mandy recognized it as a warning. She silently appealed to Glory, who would not think twice about choosing a different direction than Joanna.

Glory considered her a full moment then nodded, albeit reluctantly.

Neither of her sisters liked secrets any better than she did. What would it take to persuade Trace to open up?

She bid them farewell and headed up the trail to her house. Only it wasn't her twig shack she pictured; it was the fine log house Trace built.

Trace was missing when she arrived. Cora played with the kitten and glanced up. "Trace has gone for another log. He's been working since dawn."

The walls were higher than when Mandy left yesterday. He was determined to win. She left the lunch in a shady spot to keep cool and grabbed her ax. She would never let him beat her.

They passed each other coming and going, pausing only long enough to say hello, even though she wanted so much more. But at a loss to say what she thought she wanted, she merely nodded and continued on her way.

All morning she worked. Steadily the walls grew higher. At noon, she retrieved the lunch sack. "Time to eat. Come and get it."

Trace washed, filled the dipper from the bucket, drank deeply, and dumped water over his head. Then he shook like a dog after a dip.

She watched shining droplets cling to the ends of his hair. One ran down his cheek. He dashed it away.

Their gazes caught and held. She swallowed back a thousand unnamed emotions clogging her throat, thickening her thoughts until they were immobile. In the back of her brain she ordered herself to stop staring openmouthed. Stop embarrassing herself. But she lacked the power to do so.

Cora dashed between them, chasing little Goliath and freeing Mandy from her foolishness. Mandy's fingers felt thick as sausages as she handed out sandwiches, barely able to refrain from jerking back like an idiot when Trace's fingers brushed hers.

What was wrong with her? Was she sick with something? But apart from these occasional lapses of good sense, she felt fine.

Trace settled back against a tree, and she relaxed inch by inch. After a bit, the quiet heat calmed her brain, and she recalled her plan. "You know that venison roast I mentioned?"

"You mean the one you're famous for cooking?"

"Yup. Well, it's definitely on the menu for Sunday dinner. This is your chance to see if it's as good as I say. Join us for the afternoon."

Cora, who had been distracted by feeding the cat bits of her sandwich, jerked her attention to Trace. "Go."

"I might."

Mandy dared not look at him. Didn't want to know if he appeared reluctant or pleased about the prospect. It was enough that he considered it. But despite her resolve, she slid a glance at him.

He watched her, his gaze steady, searching. She let him see a welcome and maybe more, though she couldn't imagine what more he'd want from her. Or what more she could offer.

With an effort she pulled her gaze away and settled it on Cora. "You ought to come, too."

"No. I couldn't." She touched her scarred cheek.

"Cora, only my sisters and Levi will be there, and they won't care about your cheek."

Cora ducked her head. "I couldn't."

"Maybe next time." She returned her attention to Trace, wondering if he felt the same promise in the words as she did.

Not giving him a chance to change his mind about coming, she handed out cookies.

"You make these?" Trace asked.

"Joanna did, but I promised her I'd do some baking." Right then and there she decided she would bake cookies at the first opportunity so she could hand some to Trace and say she'd made them.

∞

Trace studied his face in the tiny mirror. Shaved, his hair combed back, he looked his very best. But what did Mandy see? A man with a secret, certainly. But did she see the man he'd once been? A man with normal hopes and aspirations? He touched the edges of his damp hair. Maybe he should get Cora to trim the ends. He jerked his hands from his head. Why had he agreed to go to the stopping house for dinner? "I should have told her I changed my mind."

Cora peered over his shoulder, checking his every move, pointing out a missed whisker, an untidy bit of hair. "Can't see any reason why you would."

He faced her. "I don't like leaving you alone."

"You aren't. I have Goliath with me."

"Some protection that is."

"If I hear anyone approaching, I'll slip away and hide." She patted his arm as if he needed reassuring. "Don't worry. I'll be fine. Besides, don't you think it's time you met Mandy's family?"

"Why?"

"Seems the next logical step."

"To what?"

She chuckled softly. "Your growing fondness for her."

"Fondness?" He sputtered. "How can you say that? All we do is fight. Or at least spar. So far we haven't resorted to fisticuffs. Or gun-fights." Though their first meeting had involved him wrestling her to the ground. But then he didn't know she was a woman, so he could be excused.

"You're both dancing around what you feel. Not quite certain if it's real. Or if you want it to be. I think she is as cautious as you about letting herself care about someone. But she is sweet, don't you think?"

"No. She's anything but. Try sharp, annoying—"

"Once the two of you decide to trust each other, that will all be nothing."

"Cora, you're sixteen years old. I hardly think that qualifies you as an expert on romance."

"Almost seventeen, dear brother. And I don't have to be an expert to see what's right in front of me." She patted his arm in a motherly gesture that made him want to gnash his teeth. "Now you go meet her family and make a good impression."

He slammed his hat on his head, but his anger had already burned itself out. "I won't stay long so—"

"I am not worried. I am not afraid. Bye."

He paused to kiss her cheek and pat Goliath on the head. "Take care of her," he murmured to the cat. But as he strode down the path toward town, he fought his doubts. Having Cora turn this into—what? Romance? Well, what did he think it would be? A business meeting?

No. He knew it was more. But he couldn't say what. Or if he welcomed more. All he knew was he longed to know about Mandy Hamilton.

He approached the town as the ferry crossed the river with men and horses on board. More prospectors seeking gold in the Kootenais. He had no such aspirations. All he wanted was peace and solitude.

He chuckled. Mandy had made both impossible, but he found he didn't object.

This being the first trip to Bonners Ferry since he'd passed through on his arrival, he glanced about. The typical frontier town, thrown up in haste with little preplanning. The houses and businesses clustered close to the river were built on stilts, indicating the problem of spring flooding. Other buildings higher up the hill seemed safe from the threat. The stopping house sat solidly above the marsh area. He paused to consider what he was about to do.

Meet Mandy's family. Risk people knowing of his presence. Unintentionally inviting them to visit as western people were wont to do by way of hospitality. Cora did not want company. Nor did he. Company meant friendships. Friendships were not to be trusted.

He reminded himself he would see only Mandy's family.

Perhaps it was worth the risk.

He adjusted his hat and crossed the last few hundred yards to the stopping house. He'd soon find out if this was a mistake or not.

Chapter 8

"Thought you might put on a dress," Glory said. "In honor of this occasion."

Mandy pretended she needed to put a spoon in the washbasin. At the same time she glanced out the window to see if Trace headed down the path. She'd never admit she'd wondered if he'd look at her differently if she'd found a dress and worn it. "You're going to marry a preacher. Shouldn't you start wearing dresses?" She carried a jug of water to the table.

Glory snorted. "Can't work with my horses in skirts and petticoats."

Mandy hesitated, trying to come up with an excuse to return to the window. She failed to find one so simply walked over and looked out. Still no sign of Trace.

Glory laughed. "You can hardly wait to see him again." She danced around on the floor. "Mandy and Trace. Mandy and Trace."

Rather than give her sister reason to tease, Mandy forced herself to stay away from the window. So she didn't see Trace approach.

"Here he comes," Glory called, all triumphant because she'd seen him first.

Mandy took her time about going to the window. Took too long. He'd almost reached the house, so she missed her chance to assess his attitude as he approached. Was he eager or reluctant? Or somewhere in between? It didn't matter. The important thing was he'd come.

She moseyed toward the entrance, determined no one would guess she longed to run and pull him inside before he changed his mind.

"Maybe I'll get the door," Glory said, taking two hurried strides that direction.

"Glory, stop teasing her," Joanna murmured.

"Can't. It's too much fun."

Levi chuckled. "Not to mention it would feel too much like defeat if you stopped."

Glory laughed. "She wouldn't know what to do if I didn't tease her, would you, Mandy?"

"I might be willing to find out. Just don't get carried away with Trace here."

"Oh, I'll be very good. I promise."

"Is that even possible?" By the time she opened the door, Trace had his hand raised to knock. "Hello. Come in." Her voice sounded high and thin. Thankfully, Glory didn't point it out to everyone present.

Trace stepped over the threshold, jerked off his hat, and stood there.

Mandy pointed to the row of hooks, and he hung his hat. She waved him toward the kitchen where the others waited. "My sisters, Joanna and Glory, and Levi, the preacher."

He shook hands all around.

"Welcome. It's nice to have another man present," Levi said.

Joanna and Glory measured him discreetly but thoroughly.

What had she expected? Of course they would. Just like she'd made her own personal assessment of Levi before she was prepared to let him befriend Glory. Ironically, both she and Joanna saw how things were between the pair before Glory did.

Her thoughts stuttered. Did they see something she didn't? It wasn't possible. Her cheeks burned to know her sisters might think so.

Joanna invited them all to sit at the smaller kitchen table, and in the ensuing shuffle she forgot the question.

Joanna indicated she and Trace should sit on one side of the table, Glory and Levi across from them. Joanna sat at the end. The food was ready and waiting. Mandy's sisters must have placed it on the table while she invited Trace in.

Joanna nodded in Levi's direction. "Would you say the blessing, please?"

Levi stood as he prayed.

They passed the food—mashed potatoes, gravy, cooked carrots, and succulent roast venison.

Trace tasted the meat and sighed. "You're right. It's delicious."

"Best you've ever tasted?"

"Think so. How do you do it?"

"It's a secret." She felt him stiffen and knew he'd caught the little emphasis on the final word. Yes, it was silly and probably childish to keep harping on the subject of secrets, but she couldn't stop herself.

"I see. An old family secret, I suppose."

Glory laughed. "She doesn't even want us to know, though all we have to do is watch her. It's something she learned from an old man who showed her how to cut up a deer."

"Took a little practice to get it perfected." In truth, it wasn't that difficult. She soaked the meat in a brine solution, seared it, and rubbed a mixture of herbs and spices into it. The old trapper had told her his mixture, but she had experimented and created her own special blend.

Glory leaned toward Trace.

Mandy didn't like the look in her sister's eyes and knew she was up to no good. She reached out her foot under the table and nudged Glory's leg, but her sister ignored the warning.

"Mandy tells me the two of you are in a race to see who will get that piece of land. Tell me why you don't leave her have it and find another piece. Seems it would be a lot less trouble."

Trace's laugh rang with wry amusement. "At first, I only saw it as a challenge. Not a very tough one either, I figured in my innocence. I realize now it would have been a lot easier to walk away, but now I have a house started. A very nice log house. In fact. . ."

Mandy's heart sank. She should have warned him not to call hers a twig house and mention the three pigs. It was too late. All she could hope for was to change the subject. "He should have known I wouldn't be bested when I outshot him in a little contest we had."

Levi chuckled. "They're called the Buffalo Gals for a good reason."

Mandy groaned. Even Joanna looked like she wanted to stuff something into Levi's mouth to shut him up. But Glory grinned.

Trace rose to the bait as nicely as a river trout. "Buffalo Gals?"

"Yes, indeed. A well-earned title." Levi's gaze adored Glory. "It started when they trailed after their father. When they asked if people had seen him, one man asked if they meant the buffalo hunter. That's when people started calling them the Buffalo Gals. But they rightly earned the name. They wear pants, they look tough, and they are. There's nothing these three won't try and succeed in doing."

Mandy shifted a little so she could see Trace's reaction without looking directly at him.

His eyes found hers and wouldn't let her go. "I have seen it first-hand with Mandy." His grin didn't mock her. In fact—her breath caught midway up her chest and refused to budge—she could almost think his gaze was as admiring as Levi's.

No reason it should be.

But at least he didn't mention her twig house.

Levi finished his meal and pushed away his plate. He'd seen the pies and no doubt decided to save some room for a slice. "How is your house coming?"

Determined to prevent Trace from repeating some of the things he said about her construction work, she answered first. "The walls on my house are five feet high or so."

"Yes, indeed, the walls of her house are coming along quickly. Keeps me hopping to stay ahead." Trace, bless his heart, laughed—a sound so full of mocking Mandy expected everyone at the table would wonder what was so funny.

Glory leaned forward. "She can cut logs and place them as fast as you?" She shot Mandy a look of pure disbelief.

"Why should that surprise you?" Mandy demanded.

Glory shrugged. "For one thing, you aren't all that great with an ax. Joanna asks me to chop the wood for a very good reason. So either you have improved a great deal or"—she shifted her gaze to Trace—"you aren't a skilled axman." She ran her gaze up and down his arms and across his shoulders. "Something I would find hard to believe." She leaned back and crossed her arms across her chest. "I think you aren't telling the whole truth."

"Sure sounds like you're calling me a liar." Mandy jerked forward, reaching across the table toward Glory, who simply backed away with a wicked grin.

"Girls," Joanna chided. "Please remember this is Sunday, and we have guests."

Levi chuckled. "Don't let our presence interfere with a little family discussion." He turned to Trace. "I've learned to stay out of their arguments and as far away as possible."

Both Glory and Mandy settled back in their chairs. Glory continued to grin while Mandy scowled.

When Glory turned her attention to Trace, Mandy guessed her sister didn't intend to heed her silent warning.

"So what is the whole truth and nothing but the truth about these houses?"

Trace spared Mandy a quick glance, but she didn't look his way to see if he intended to throw caution to the wind or guard his tongue.

"Well," he began slowly. "There is something unique about Mandy's house. You see..." He had the full attention of everyone around the table.

"Mine is a fine log house that will stand for years. I intend to add on to it once I've completed the terms of our agreement and have the deed to the land."

"But what will you do with two houses?" Joanna asked.

Under the table, Mandy kicked Trace's ankle, which only brought a chuckle from his traitorous lips.

"Mandy's house will be a perfect storage shed." His demanding gaze informed her he'd been as kind as possible.

But Glory wasn't about to let it go. Talk about a hound dog with a smelly bone. Her sister qualified far more than Mandy. "You said there was something unique about her house. What?"

Trace hesitated.

Mandy tried to kick his ankle again, but he'd shifted his legs out of her reach.

"Maybe you'd like to tell them yourself?"

If looks could do damage, his cheek would be as scarred as Cora's. "Don't think so." She knew Glory would not be satisfied with that. Nor Joanna, though *she* would wait until they were alone to turn the thumbscrews.

Glory shrugged as if it didn't matter.

Her pretended indifference made Mandy's nerves twitch. What was she up to?

She didn't have to wait long to find out.

"I don't need anyone to tell me. All I have to do is walk up the trail and see for myself. In fact, I don't know why I haven't done so already."

Trace jerked halfway to his feet then subsided. "I'd like to ask you to respect our privacy."

"Mandy told us about Cora. I won't bother her. Won't even let her know I was there."

Mandy lifted her palms toward the roof in surrender. "If you must know, Miss Nosy, my house is built of—" She struggled for the right word. One that sounded better than—

"Twigs," Trace supplied.

"Twigs?" Glory hooted. "How are you keeping them stacked? With fence posts?"

"It's not twigs. It's small trees, and I'm putting them up in the same fashion Trace is using to build with thick logs." She sounded every bit as aggrieved as she felt and wanted Glory to know it. No reason to inform them she'd had to drive some poles in upright to hold her logs in place.

"It will be a perfect storage shed," Trace soothed.

The way he patted her arm and spoke so kindly did nothing to ease her anger.

Joanna, seeing Mandy's expression, tried to change the subject. "Levi, that was an excellent sermon." She shifted her gaze to Trace. "Too bad you missed it. It was about Jesus calming the winds and the waves on the sea." She returned her attention to Levi. "I like how you reminded us that God is in control of nature."

Glory tore her gaze from Mandy to Levi, and her expression changed from teasing to pure adoration so fast Mandy blinked to assure herself she wasn't seeing a mirage.

"What was that you said about the water in the ocean?" Glory asked.

"All the water in the ocean cannot sink a ship unless it gets inside." His look included everyone at the table. "All the trouble in the world cannot harm us unless it gets into our spirit."

Trace had been enjoying the teasing between Mandy and her sister. He'd been silently pleased when Mandy nudged his ankle. Okay, it was more than a nudge. More like a sharp kick. He'd have a bruise, but Levi's words brought Trace back to reality with a thud that hurt his head. Certainly he'd been taught to believe God was in control. He'd even believed it at one time. But then he realized how truly awful life could be. If God was in control of those things, then God couldn't be loving and kind, as he'd once believed.

Levi continued to speak. "Bad things happen. There is evil in the world because of sin. But faith enables each of us to rest in God's care."

Pat answers. Easy for a preacher. For a person who likely knew nothing of the sort of evil Trace had witnessed firsthand. Lies. Theft. Arson. Murder.

Joanna glanced around the table. "Anyone for a second piece of pie?"

Trace would gladly have taken another but didn't want to seem greedy. However, when Levi handed his plate forward, he did the same, thanking Joanna.

Suddenly Glory leaned forward so far she almost upset her chair. "That's why you wanted to know about the three little pigs."

Uh-oh. He couldn't imagine Mandy letting this go unchallenged. "This is really good pie, Joanna. I haven't had pie in so long I almost forgot what a treat it is."

"He said you built a house of twigs—like one of the three pigs—didn't he?"

Mandy didn't answer, but her glower was enough to tear strips from Glory's flesh, though Glory seemed unaware of her danger. She turned her burning interest to Trace.

He ducked and wished he had more pie to concentrate on, but he'd eaten the last bit and had to settle for scraping together a few flakes of pastry.

"You said that, didn't you?" Glory persisted.

He shrugged. Allowed himself one quick glance at Mandy. She studiously avoided looking at him.

"I know you did." Glory leaned toward him. "And she let you live? Amazing." She tapped her finger on her chin. "Or maybe not." She grinned at Mandy. "Maybe not so strange at all."

Levi draped an arm across Glory's shoulders. "Give your sister some peace."

Trace wondered if Glory knew the meaning of the word. He began to feel sympathy for Mandy. No wonder she was always so ready to defend herself. Seems she'd have little choice around Glory.

But before either girl could take the conflict to another level, someone threw open the door. "Fire. Up at the Murray house. Hurry. We need all the help we can get."

Fire! Trace couldn't breathe.

Mandy and the others bolted for the door. She paused, saw him frozen in place. "Trace, aren't you going to help?"

"I'll be there." He was hot on her heels in a matter of seconds. Time was of the essence in rescuing the inhabitants and saving their belongings.

The group raced toward the center of town. Smoke billowed behind the lawyer's office. Flames shot from the window of a small house—hungry, angry flames. Consuming.

A bucket brigade formed under the shouted orders of a large man. Mandy fell in line, Glory at her elbow, then Levi and Joanna. Trace raced past and stopped before the man in charge. "Is everyone out?"

"Don't know."

Trace stared into the flames, holding up a hand to protect his face from the heat, and cocked his head. Did he hear a call for help? He moved closer to the house.

Mandy appeared at his side. "What are you doing?"

"I have to make certain there's no one inside." He inched forward, but the heat was intense.

Mandy grabbed his arm. "No, you can't go in there. You'll die."

"I can't stand by and not do something. Listen. Do you hear that?"

"How can you hear anything but people yelling and the flames crackling? It's not possible. Trace, you aren't thinking right."

He tore away from her grasp and raced around to the other side of the house. There had to be another door. A window. Mandy followed him. "I'm going in." He grabbed a rock and broke the glass. Hot air whooshed out.

"Trace, no. It's too dangerous." But she turned, hearing the same thing he did. A call for help.

"I must." He used the rock to remove the sharp fragments of glass in the frame then swung his leg through the hole. "Wait here."

"If you're going in there, so am I."

He reached through the window and grabbed her shoulders. Shook her hard. "Do as I say. Stay there."

He recognized the stubborn set of her chin. "Please, Mandy. I couldn't bear it if you got burned." A thousand pictures filled his mind. The fire that had destroyed his home. Killed his parents, Cora screaming as he pulled her from the flames. "Please wait." He dropped his hand. He must get to that voice. He crouched low and pushed into the smoke and heat.

He made his way through the room, following the call for help, reached a doorway, and paused. The fire raged to his left, sizzling angrily as bucket after bucket of water reached it. For a moment, the flames died back as if beaten then roared to life again. He turned to his right, down a hall. Through the smoke he made out another doorway and crept through it.

"Help me." A woman saw him, grabbed an arm, and dragged him forward. "My husband. He isn't moving."

A man lay on the floor.

"What happened?"

"He fell. Banged his head on the dresser."

Trace grabbed the unconscious man's shoulders and, keeping low, dragged him toward the door.

The woman whimpered, rooted to the floor.

"Follow me. I'll get you out."

She moaned, but her feet didn't leave the spot.

"Lady, we have to get out."

"I'll get her." Mandy crawled past him, pulled the woman to her knees, and pushed her toward the doorway.

"I told you to stay."

"I never agreed, did I?"

He pulled the man; she pushed the woman until they were back near the window. He wanted to be angry at Mandy, but he couldn't. All that mattered was getting the four of them out safely. Someone jumped through the window and grabbed the injured man. Many hands reached forward to take him.

Mandy pushed the woman forward, and hands pulled her to safety.

The heat grew intense, the smoke so thick Trace's eyes streamed with tears. Between the tears and the smoke he couldn't see Mandy. Couldn't see the window. "Mandy," he rasped. "Where are you?"

She coughed. Couldn't stop.

He reached out. Connected with her arm. Dragged her to where he knew the window had to be. Flames licked overhead, crackling like the laughter of the devil. "Get out." He didn't let go of her arm until he felt another hand, heard a voice saying, "We got you." The hands ripped her from his grasp.

The noise overhead roared. Flames surrounded him. He coughed, choking. His eyes streamed.

Then everything went black.

Chapter 9

M andy stared up into the sky, her lungs searing from the smoke she'd inhaled. Joanna bent over her on one side, Glory on the other.

Joanna's hands examined her, stroked her hair. "You'll survive."

"I know you're crazy," Glory said, her voice heavy with concern despite the anger she tried to convey. "But I never thought I'd see you dive into a burning building."

Mandy gasped, tried to speak but discovered her voice had disappeared in the pain of a burned throat. She reached for Joanna's shirt front and pulled her close, barely able to focus through the sting of her eyes. "Trace?" She mouthed the word. "Is Trace okay?"

"He's fine." Joanna was the world's worst liar.

Trace wasn't fine. Panic stole her strength, and she lay like an old rag. But she must find him. She tried to sit up. Got as far as one elbow. Ignored her dizziness, her seared throat, her ineffectual lungs.

Where is he? She begged Joanna silently.

Joanna nodded to a group of men beyond them.

Help me. She appealed to both sisters.

Joanna and Glory exchanged a look.

"I know how I'd feel if it were Levi," Glory said and pulled her to her feet. She'd have never made it without their help. With a sister on either side, Mandy stumbled through the men.

The men parted. Trace lay on the ground.

"Trace." The groaned word ripped her frightened heart every bit as cruelly as it scraped up her damaged throat.

She jerked from her sisters' arms and fell to her knees beside Trace's inert body. With arms so weak and trembling she didn't recognize them as her own, she pressed palms to his chest. A cry of relief escaped when she felt it rise. He was alive.

She leaned over, pressed her face to his smoke-streaked shirt front, and cried. She hoped everyone would think her eyes were streaming from the smoke.

Hands pulled her back, and she collapsed to the ground, one hand clinging to Trace's as he lay motionless at her side. Motionless except for the rise and fall of his chest.

She coughed again and again. Joanna eased her to her side.

"Cough it all out."

Like she could stop. She coughed until she wondered her lungs didn't come out. She drank cupful after cupful of water.

In the meantime, several people hovered around Trace, discussing what they should do.

"He got clunked on the head when the beam came down. He needs to lie still until he comes to."

"No," another "expert" said, "he needs to hang his head over a bench or something to clear his lungs."

"My old granny said there wasn't nothing that couldn't be fixed with a good dose of salts."

Mandy met Joanna's gaze and rolled her eyes.

Joanna chuckled. "Sounds like Mrs. Ester."

Mandy nodded. They'd once been left in the care of a woman who treated everything from cough to tummy ache to tardiness with a dose of salts. The girls had quickly learned nothing hurt as much as the result of that particular medication and never complained about any ache or discomfort.

Bull, from the saloon, joined the circle, a bottle in his hand. "A snort of whiskey will set him right."

One of the men jeered. "He can't swallow when he's out cold."

Feeling a little stronger, Mandy edged to Trace's side. She managed to whisper his name. She stroked his cheek, streaking the smoke smudges. She breathed a silent plea. *Trace. Don't die on me. Not just when I discover how much you mean to me. Please, God. Don't let him die.*

Levi pushed aside the men and knelt at Trace's side. He gave him careful consideration then reached for Mandy's hand. Glory joined him and took her other hand. Joanna stood behind her and rested her palms on Mandy's shoulders. Then Levi prayed. "Father in heaven, we ask for the life of this good man. He's saved others. Please save him."

"Are Mr. and Mrs. Murray okay?" Mandy whispered.

Levi answered her. "Mr. Murray has a lump on his head, but they'll be just fine. Thanks to you and Trace."

"It's thanks to Trace. He was certain he heard someone. I only followed him in to make sure he got out safely." It hurt to talk even at a whisper, but everyone needed to know Trace was a hero.

She couldn't take her eyes off his still face. Even streaked and dirty, his was the most handsome face she'd ever seen. Why had she wasted their time together fighting with him? What if she didn't get a second chance?

His eyes fluttered.

"Trace." She wanted to hug him and kiss him.

He coughed, gasping for air. Levi sat him up as he coughed out the smoke in his lungs.

Trace pushed Levi's steadying hands away. Jerked about as if seeking something. His gaze rested on Mandy. He stopped searching and reached for her hand.

"You're safe." The words croaked from him.

"I'm safe. The Murrays are safe. And you're a hero."

"No hero," he managed. "Is the fire out?"

"Dowsed, and nothing else affected."

He nodded and, with a strangled moan, reached for his head.

"The roof came down on you," Levi said.

A crowd gathered round to see for themselves the man who'd risked his life to save Mr. and Mrs. Murray.

"Who is he?"

"Where did he come from?"

"What's your name, mister?"

Mandy turned to Levi and spoke quietly. "He doesn't want people to know he lives here. He thinks he has to protect Cora." For now they wouldn't argue about whether or not he was right.

Levi nodded and got to his feet. "Folks, give the man a chance to rest. His name is Trace, and he was visiting at the stopping house."

Trace relaxed visibly.

Mandy realized she clung to Trace's hand and jerked away.

Levi signaled to a couple of men. "Let's get these people to the stopping house to rest."

Joanna and Glory helped Mandy to her feet. She shook off their assistance. "I can walk on my own." And she hurried to Trace's side, hovering close to make sure he didn't fall as Levi and another man half carried him to the stopping house.

Joanna dashed ahead to set up a cot for Trace.

Trace shook off helping hands and refused to accept the comfort of the narrow bed. "I must get back."

But it was obvious he was too weak.

Mandy knew that fact wouldn't deter him. "I'll go to Cora and explain what happened. You better not leave while there are so many people milling about. Unless you want someone following you." She stared into his eyes, hoping he might reconsider his need to hide. Cora's desire to hide.

But he only nodded.

She wondered how long he could continue to conceal his whereabouts. People weren't stupid, and if they wanted to find him for any reason, good or otherwise, they would. But now was not the time to discuss differences of opinion. "I'm not leaving until I see you on that cot."

They dueled with their gazes, his rapier sharp despite the smoke and streaks on his skin.

"And wash your face."

He chuckled. "Maybe you should look in a mirror."

She dashed to the mirror in the bedroom and groaned. She looked down. Her clothes were as soiled as her skin. She went to the kitchen and washed her face and hands then ducked into the bedroom and slipped into a clean shirt and trousers.

When she stepped into the big dining room, Trace lay stretched out on the cot, an arm thrown across his eyes. He shifted his arm so he could watch her. Grinned at her clean clothes. "That's better."

"Can't say the same for you."

"I'll have to wait until I return to camp." His voice was hoarse. He had to pause to catch his breath. "Tell Cora I'm safe. Tell her—"

"I'll tell her the truth."

"Don't frighten her."

Feeling sorry for his predicament, she crossed the room and squatted at his side. "Trace, trust me to take care of this little thing."

He reached for her hand. "I know you don't agree, but promise me you'll keep Cora's whereabouts a secret."

She examined their joined hands. Allowed herself to likewise examine her feelings. She cared about him enough to accept his way of thinking on this subject even though she thought he was mistaken. She would do as he asked even though it was in her power to choose whatever direction she wanted. However, when she tackled the situation, she would do so openly. No sneaking around doing things behind his back. "No one will know where I've gone. You can count on that."

"Thank you." He squeezed her hand. "For everything."

"Everything? I'm only making one promise." She didn't want him to get the idea she vowed eternal silence on anything.

"For being you."

His words fell into her heart with a sweetness that stung her eyes and threatened to make her start coughing again. "I best be going." She slipped her hand free from his grasp and headed for the door without a backward look. If she looked at him—saw the tenderness she hoped and feared she'd see—she would embarrass herself by weeping.

Sneaking away from the stopping house was no problem. Any more than taking a roundabout trail through the woods that left no clue of her passing.

She approached the camp in silence and looked around for Cora. At first she didn't see her; then she heard a whisper and detected a movement up the hill in some underbrush. She caught a flash of black and white as Goliath chased something. Cora was hiding there, but the kitten gave away her position.

Mandy straightened and walked into the camp as if everything was normal. "Cora? Where are you? It's me."

Cora scampered from the bushes, scooping up Goliath as she descended the hill. She was five feet from Mandy before she glanced up and looked past Mandy. "Where's Trace?"

"He'll be along later."

Cora's face wrinkled into a map of worry. "Why isn't he here now?"

"He's resting."

Cora cried out. "What happened?"

"Come, sit down, and I'll explain everything." She led the girl over to the log house and pulled her down to sit side by side with their backs against the wall. "Trace is a hero."

Cora nodded. "I know."

Mandy smiled. Of course he was a hero to his sister. "Because of him two people are alive today."

"Two? But. . ." She turned to study Mandy. "I meant when he rescued me. But we aren't talking about the same thing, are we?"

It would be interesting to know the details behind Cora's words. "There was a fire in town today."

"A fire?" Cora pressed the cat to her chest with both hands. Little Goliath seemed to sense his job was to provide comfort and didn't protest.

"He insisted on going into the burning house and helping the two occupants escape. He took in a lot of smoke and got a bang on the head, but he's okay."

Cora moaned.

Mandy rushed out the last words. "He's resting for now." She didn't say Trace would find it impossible to leave without one of the curious or grateful following him.

Cora rocked back and forth. "Poor Trace. Poor Trace."

Mandy reached for Cora's arm, trying to still the frantic movement. "He's okay."

Cora turned wide-eyed shock toward her. "But it will remind him of everything." She touched her cheek. Her face crumpled, and a sob shook her.

Mandy pulled the girl to her and patted her back. "He was very brave."

"He always is. Our parents were killed in a house fire. He tried to save them, but they were already gone. He pulled me from the flames." Every word was punctuated with a sob. "I don't know if he'll ever stop blaming himself."

"Why should he blame himself?"

"He just does." Cora wailed and clutched Mandy's arms, squeezing Goliath between them. The cat meowed a protest and wriggled free to sit at Cora's knees and groom himself.

Cora quieted then sat up. "You're sure he's okay?"

"I wouldn't have left if I wasn't."

Cora nodded. "He protects me by keeping us hidden. I appreciate it. I don't want people to stare at me and call me horrible names."

Mandy squeezed Cora's arm. "You need to give people a chance to see past your burn to your sweetness."

Cora watched the cat. "Trace is hiding as much as I am, you know."

"What's he hiding from?"

"People."

"But why?"

Cora grew still. Stared into the distance, past the trees, past the present. "People are not always who you think they are. Sometimes friends turn out to be enemies. How do you know who to trust?"

"Someone turned against him?"

"Friends, supposedly. A good lesson not to trust anyone."

The blanket decision stung like hot smoke. It seared right to the pit of her stomach. "You don't trust me?"

Cora gave her a crooked smile. "You're the exception."

Mandy knew her smile was equally uncertain. She didn't want to be the only exception. There were plenty of good, decent people out there if only Trace would give them a chance. Surely he'd seen that today. First, at the stopping house where only good honest people sat around the table then later, when many hands had dealt with the fire and many people had expressed concern and gratitude for Trace.

Cora gathered up the kitten and moved to the edge of the clearing. She picked up a basket of mending and examined a tear in one of Trace's shirts.

Mandy knew the chance to press for more information or to suggest a flaw in her thinking had passed. . .for now.

"When will he be back?" Cora asked.

"I don't think it would hurt him any to spend the night. I'll stay until he returns."

She leaned back to watch Cora, who kept her attention on threading a needle. For the first time since Mandy had been pulled from the burning building, she had a chance to examine her feelings. To admit without pressure or fear that she had grown fond of Trace. Extremely fond. Now what did she intend to do about it? She shifted to study her twig house. If she really wanted to, she could finish the house in a matter of days— hours, even.

The question was—did she want to beat Trace? Did she want to take the land from him? Would he leave if she did?

She sprang to her feet and circled her house and then the one Trace built. Her thoughts raced ahead as she worked out a plan.

∽

Trace slept in restless fits, waking often to cough. His lungs burned. His head felt like a beam had landed on it. Which was exactly what happened, according to Levi.

Glory and Joanna bustled about the kitchen. Men mingled outside, waiting for the meal to be served.

Trace pushed himself to the side of the cot, sat until the dizziness passed, then made it to his feet.

Joanna noticed and hurried from the kitchen. "You need to rest."

"I'm not going to lie here in the middle of the room and be an object of interest while those men come in to eat. Thank you for the meal and for your kindness in providing me a place to rest, but I'll be heading on home now."

Joanna gave him serious study. "You're sure you can make it on your own? Glory could help you."

He held up a protesting hand. The movement caused his head to pound, and he choked back a groan. "No need."

"Very well."

Glory joined her sister in the doorway. "Sure wouldn't want to be in your shoes if you collapse on the trail and Mandy finds you."

"I can handle anything Mandy hands out."

Joanna and Glory laughed.

He smiled weakly. "Maybe not at the moment though." He stepped out to the porch and went to a washbasin to clean up.

Two men moved in to shake Trace's hand and thank him for helping fight the fire. But the majority of them were simply passing through. Many weren't even aware there'd been a fire. He made his way to the edge of the yard and leaned against a shed as if waiting with the others for supper to be announced.

Finally, Joanna came to the door and rang a cowbell suspended on a hook, signaling mealtime. They paused at her side to drop coins into the can she held. Trace hung back, and when the last man stood before her, he ducked out of sight and headed up the trail. He paused several times to let his heartbeat slow to normal and to listen for anyone following him. Satisfied he had no company, he did his best to hurry onward.

A few feet from the clearing he stopped and listened. The girls laughed. Perhaps playing with Goliath.

Then Cora screamed.

He charged into the clearing. "What's wrong?"

Cora and Mandy stared at him with wide eyes.

"Goliath scratched me," Cora said. "Trace, you look awful."

Mandy rushed to his side. "You better sit down."

"I'm fine." But he let her lead him to their usual spot and gladly sank to the ground.

Cora hung over him. "For a hero you look pretty grubby."

"You should have seen me before I cleaned up."

"I can't believe you went into a burning building." She sat facing him, her knees drawn up, her brow knotted. "You could have been burned." She pressed her palm to her cheek.

He hadn't stopped to consider the risks. He'd simply acted. Determined not to let a fire claim another life. Or two. But now he realized how close he'd come to dying. How close Mandy had come. His gaze sought and found Mandy's. "You were supposed to wait outside. Where it was safe."

Cora gasped. "You went in, too. Why would you?"

Mandy's gaze held Trace's like a vise. "I had to make sure Trace was okay."

The sound coming from Cora's mouth rang with disbelief and likely a lot of fear. "I can't believe either of you. If something happened. . ."

She grabbed the ever-present kitten and stalked up the hill to the thicket, where she disappeared.

Trace continued to drown in Mandy's look. He remembered the moment when he'd regained his senses. "I thought you were gone." His voice grated as he recalled that initial fear. He touched her cheek, assuring himself that she was, indeed, okay.

She pressed her hand to his, keeping his fingers against her warm skin. "I thought the same thing about you. You gave me quite a scare." She shook her head back and forth. "After Cora told me your parents died in a fire, I found it impossible to believe you would dash in to rescue strangers."

"She told you about our parents?" He withdrew his hand and shifted his gaze. How much had Cora revealed?

Mandy nodded. "She said friends had turned against you. Seems it had something to do with the fire."

He recognized her pause as invitation to tell her what happened. But his emotions were too raw, his head hurt too much. Opening those wounds would take more effort than he could handle at the moment.

"According to Cora, your experience has taught you both not to trust anyone."

Again, she waited for him to add something. What could he say? He'd learned the cost of trust. He leaned his head against the log wall. "I'm tired."

After a moment, she slipped away. He wondered if she would go home. Instead, she joined Cora, and the girls chased the kitten through the trees.

Half his heart ached to let Mandy in. Allow himself to love her.

The other half remembered the price he'd paid because he'd so blindly trusted those he loved. Or supposed he'd loved.

How could he ever take that chance again? Even with a woman like Mandy who risked her life to make sure he was safe.

He shifted so he could watch her play with Cora, making her laugh like a young girl. His eyes ached with longing.

His heart quivered with caution.

Chapter 10

The next morning, he forced his reluctant body to get up and return to work on the house, though at the moment he didn't care whether or not he finished it.

Cora followed him around, keeping a close eye on him.

He stopped to face her. "You can quit worrying. I'm not hurt."

"Trace. . ." Her pause lasted several beats. "Oh, never mind. There's no use in saying anything." She turned to walk away.

He caught her arm and stopped her. "About what?"

She considered his question and met his gaze. "About everything. About Annabelle and Austin. Mama and Papa. About the fire. And most of all, about you and Mandy."

"Wow, little sister, that's quite a mouthful. Seems you've covered about everything in our lives."

"It is everything in our lives. And it's all gone, destroyed by a stupid fire."

"And the treachery of so-called friends."

Cora pressed Goliath to her cheek. "Will we never again have a normal life?"

Brother and sister studied each other. "Are you saying you want to go to town? Let people see you? That's normal."

Her eyes flooded with tears. "So is letting yourself care about someone."

"I care about you."

"I mean someone outside the family. Like Mandy."

He opened his mouth then closed it. There was nothing to say. He cared for Mandy, but his feelings scared him. Made him feel as if he were the traitor. Turning on his own resolve. He had vowed to never trust another person—man or woman. Apart from Cora, he would live with his heart closed to anything but the most surface of acquaintances. But Mandy with her persistence had forced her way past those barriers.

He resented her doing so.

At the same time—stupid as it was—he ached to open his heart and invite her in.

"I've got work to do." Cora, already mixing up corn bread for lunch, would be okay. He headed for the woods, supposedly to find and cut another tree. In truth, he hoped he could flee his thoughts.

But escape was impossible. He had gone but ten yards when he realized he'd forgotten his ax. He retraced his steps and arrived in the clearing at the same time as Mandy. She saw him and stopped dead still.

His boots refused to take another step. He told his eyes to look for the ax, but they wouldn't leave Mandy's face.

Her expression revealed nothing. Which told him a lot. That she was guarded after his refusal to talk to her last night. Perhaps wondering if he considered her a friend.

His heart said she was so much more.

But he couldn't admit it. Not because he didn't trust her. She was as guileless as a baby.

He didn't trust his feelings.

Last time he'd trusted in the word *friend* it had cost him everything but his life and Cora's. Last time he trusted a woman, she'd been part of the plan to destroy him.

Confusion knotted his throat, made it impossible to talk, almost impossible to breathe.

Mandy broke the silence. "Morning, Trace. How are you feeling today?"

"Good," he managed to choke out.

"No ill effects from yesterday?"

"Sore throat." It was true, and he hoped she put his hoarseness down to that.

"Mine, too. Joanna made a little honey tonic that calms it. I brought you some." She handed him a flask. "Have sips of it every so often." She pulled a second flask from her pocket and proceeded to take a sip.

He could not force his eyes to leave off watching as she tipped her head back and swallowed.

She capped the flask, returned it to her pocket, and picked up her ax. She noticed he didn't have his and looked around. She spotted it and handed it to him. "Ready to get to work?"

He tried to think what she meant. Finally decided it didn't make any sense. He hoisted his ax to his shoulder. "I was just on my way." He turned and retraced his steps into the woods.

She followed hard on his heels.

He stopped.

She stopped.

He waited for her to pass or head off a different direction, but she didn't. It seemed unusual, but what could he say? She had as much right to walk the ground as he did.

He reached the place where he'd chosen a tree, and set to work.

Mandy hovered close by, watching.

He paused. "You taking lessons?" Maybe she wanted to start a proper building. But she didn't stand a chance at catching up.

"Guess you could say I am. I've decided to help you finish your house."

"That knock on my head yesterday must have affected my hearing. Seems like I heard you say you were going to help me."

"You heard right."

It must have affected his reasoning, too. "Why?"

"Because you need it."

"Where do you get that idea?"

"You and Cora need a home. I have one. You want to stay. Seems like a good idea. Besides, seems to me you need to learn that it's possible to have friends and trust them." She measured a tree with her eye. "This looks like a good one. What do you think?"

He'd already picked it out as suitable. "It looks fine."

She set to work.

All he could do was stare. None of what she said made sense. Oh, it made a degree of sense. He needed a house. He had decided to stay here, more out of a need to beat Mandy at her own game than any real conviction that the land was the best in the world. But the rest of it? Total nonsense. "I know how to have friends. Just don't think I need them." He swung his ax at the tree.

"Everyone needs them." She didn't stop swinging her ax. "Everyone needs people they can trust." Several more swings by each of them. Then she added, "Person just needs to learn which ones are safe."

"Maybe the safest thing is to trust no one."

"Nope." She continued working. "Not safe." *Chop.* "Lonely." *Chop.* "Unnecessary." *Chop.* "Judgmental." *Chop.*

He echoed each of her words with a swing of his own ax. His tree went down first with a ground-shaking thud.

Hers followed two blows later, and she stood back in triumph.

"First real tree you ever felled?"

"Yup." She grinned at him. "Did okay, didn't I?"

"You sure did."

He set about trimming off the limbs. She followed his example. He slowed his pace, afraid she would try and keep up. He didn't want to risk her slipping and cutting herself.

He closed his eyes and sucked in air, stilling the tickle in his raw throat. He didn't know if he could live through another scare with her.

It didn't escape him that a man determined to keep a wide distance between himself and others had a strong reaction to the thought of Mandy being hurt.

"Well, shoot," he muttered. Of course he cared. That wasn't the point. It was all right to care. Just not all right to. . .well, to rest his heart in the hands of another.

"Something wrong?"

"Nothing. Nothing at all." He bent his attention to his work, aware she watched with avid curiosity. Try as hard as he could, he could not ignore her. He stepped away from the tree to go to her.

She rose, her ax hanging from her hand.

He grabbed her shoulders. "But if I were to trust anyone, it would be you."

There. He'd said it.

The ax slipped from her fingers. She lifted a hand to his cheek. "Why Trace Owens, that's the nicest thing you've ever said to me."

"Don't get too excited."

"Oh no. Heaven forbid." Her eyes shone.

He couldn't think. All he saw was the gentle kindness of her expression, a look reflecting the soul of the woman. He curled his finger and ran it along her jawline. Paused at her chin. Slowly, as if he moved only in his imagination, he tipped her chin upward and caught her mouth with his, lingering a heartbeat, feeling so content nothing else mattered.

She jerked back. "Why did you do that?"

He stepped away, considering her. Unable to read her expression. "Seemed like a good idea at the time." Now he wondered if it was a mistake. He didn't allow his grin to surface. He still wasn't certain about Mandy's reaction. But kissing her was no mistake. He'd learned something. Like how much he cared about this woman.

She planted her fists on her hips. "You shouldn't have done it."

"Why not?"

"A kiss is supposed to mean something."

It did. But he wasn't about to say exactly what. "What's it supposed to mean?"

"I don't know." She grabbed her ax and whacked off a branch. "That there's something special between a man and a woman. Not just a grudging confession that you might trust me." She attacked several more branches. "Might. *Humph*."

He laughed, earning a scalding look.

"And now you mock me?"

"Heaven forbid," he murmured, inordinately pleased by her ire. "But I can't help wondering what the kiss meant to you."

She straightened and glowered at him.

"Well?" he prompted.

She bent her head so he couldn't see her expression. "I don't know."

"Be sure and tell me when you figure it out."

She didn't answer, but a few mutters drifted his way.

He grinned but contained the laughter filling his lungs. She might not take kindly to what she perceived as his enjoyment at her expense. But it felt mighty good to see her at a loss for words.

∽

Mandy's arms ached from the effort she put into swinging the ax—effort driven by frustration. First, Trace reluctantly admitted he might allow himself to trust her. Then he kissed her. On top of that, he had the nerve to laugh. What kind of game was he playing? *I don't think I can trust you as a friend, but I can kiss you?* That was simply wrong to her way of thinking. The trusting and friendship came first. Then the kissing.

At least he hadn't apologized or said he regretted it, or she might have done something *she'd* regret.

Like plant her hands on either side of his face and show him what a kiss really meant.

She chuckled. In fact...

She stalked over to where he worked at wrapping a chain around the log to haul it to the house. "I have something to say to you."

He took his time about straightening, and if she wasn't mistaken, he pushed his shoulders back as if preparing for a showdown. He took even longer turning to face her. She almost laughed at the way he glanced at her hands to see if she held a weapon of any sort then searched her eyes, trying to guess what she wanted.

She closed the three feet separating them until they stood toe-to-toe. She reached up and planted her palms on his cheeks, felt the roughness of his whiskers, noticed for the first time the way his skin gathered days of sunshine and pocketed them in each pore. She saw the tightening of his mouth as he waited.

No anger remained in her. Not even a smidgen, though she tried to summon the feeling. Her heart beat with a force that made her wonder if it had ever worked at capacity before. A thrill of anticipation skittered up her throat. She didn't know how to contain it. Feared it would take off the top of her head or scorch the soles of her feet. She sucked in air to clear her thoughts. Didn't succeed.

She pulled his face to hers and lifted her lips to his mouth. Felt him start with surprise and then kiss her back.

Oh my. This was supposed to prove something to him. She couldn't remember what. All she knew was this kiss meant something to her besides guarded trust or reluctant friendship.

To Mandy, it meant he'd stolen a place in her heart.

She couldn't say who broke away first, nor if he was as breathless as she, but neither stepped back. Somehow his arms had closed across her back, and hers were pressed to his shoulders.

"You kissed me." He sounded like he'd run a hundred miles through ice and snow, his voice thick and breathy.

"I'll let you try and figure out what it means." Suddenly aware her eyes and expression would likely give away her feelings, she ducked away. "Don't you think it's about time we got these logs to the house and finished the walls? Never know when it might rain. Rainy weather is miserable when you're living in a tent. Far better to be safe and dry in a real house." She knew she rattled out words like some lonesome old woman, but she didn't want to give him a chance to talk about the way she'd kissed him.

"Right. It's time we got a house built."

She wondered at the way he said it, as if they had suddenly become partners. Nor did she want to point out that partners normally trusted each other. She'd decided to help him complete his house, and that's all that mattered.

Yes, she hoped if he stayed around, lived in the house, he might learn to trust people. Trust her. Enough to kiss her for all the right reasons—because he loved her wholly, completely.

They dragged the logs back to the house and notched them.

Together they lifted each into place. She tried to think of nothing but the task at hand, but again and again she stole glances at him. What was going through his head? Several times she caught him watching her, and she jerked away. Then she wondered if he was still watching her.

She was glad when it was almost time to return to the stopping house. But when the sun reached the spot midway down the western sky, signaling her need to return, she said, "We can get one more log before I have to go."

"You're sure?"

"I wouldn't say it if I wasn't."

He gave a tight grin, but his eyes smiled more fully. As if he read more into her offer than she wanted him to.

She held his gaze unblinkingly, daring him to say anything. She told herself she only wanted to help complete the house as quickly as possible. In case it rained.

She wondered if she failed to convince him as completely as she failed to convince herself.

The task took longer than she'd anticipated. When they returned to the clearing, she had no choice but to hurry away before Joanna came looking for her. "I've got to get back."

"See you tomorrow," Trace said.

In her imagination his voice rang with a hundred promises of many tomorrows after tomorrow. She was building possibilities in her mind that were more fragile than the twig house.

Trace watched until Mandy was out of sight then sat on the log and contemplated the day. He'd kissed her. He cared about her. . .a fact he wasn't ready to welcome.

She had kissed him again after spouting off about a kiss meaning something special.

He leaned back, a smile on his lips. She obviously cared about him, or she wouldn't have kissed him.

With a mutter of disgust, he sprang to his feet.

Cora stood close by, leaning over the tree stump that served as a table, scrubbing a baking pan. "Trace, what's wrong?" Her words were shrill with worry.

"Nothing. At least nothing I can do anything about." He wasn't making a lick of sense.

Cora came to his side. "You're upset about something."

He couldn't explain to her when he didn't know himself what bothered him. Was he upset because Mandy cared about him? Or that he cared about her, and the idea scared him?

"Are you thinking about Mama and Papa?"

He wasn't. He'd buried them and moved on. Driven not by sorrow, but by anger.

If he let go of his anger, would his parents' deaths be in vain?

"Cora, I don't even know what I'm thinking. I don't want our mother and father to be forgotten as if their lives and deaths meant nothing. But—"

"What do you think they would want us to do? How would they want us to live?"

"I don't know. I simply don't know."

"I miss them." Cora sniffed back a sob.

Trace pulled her into his arms and patted her back. "I do, too."

"I'm glad Mama didn't see my scarred face though."

Cora's muffled words against his chest sent a shock through his insides. "Mama wouldn't care. She'd love you just the same."

"I don't know. She used to say I was far prettier than she'd ever been. I think she would be disappointed I no longer am."

Trace pushed her back to look into her eyes then at her burned cheek. He remembered it as fierce red and distorted. When had it started to fade? "Cora, come here." He drew her away from the bench toward the tent, opened the trunk that held his belongings, and pulled out his shaving mirror. "Look at yourself."

She shied away from the mirror and covered her cheek with her hand. "No. I've seen enough of it."

"It's been weeks since you last looked at it." He held the mirror directly before her face.

She closed her eyes.

He shook her gently. "Cora, look at yourself."

She squinted one eye and peeked at the mirror. Drawn perhaps by curiosity, she slowly opened both eyes and peered at her likeness, dropping her hand away from her face. She stared for a long time then looked at Trace. "It's fading."

"Yes, it is." He squatted to face her. "Cora, Mama and Papa would not want you to think you are no longer beautiful. Because you are. I think they would want you to live a full life."

She rocked her head back and forth. "I'm not sure if I can face people."

They studied each other, a great ache consuming Trace's insides. They had lost so much. More than parents. More than a home. More than Cora's unmarred beauty.

They'd lost faith. In people. In life.

Perhaps even in God.

He tried to put his thoughts into words.

Cora nodded as she listened, her expression wavering between miserable agreement and fragile hope. "Do you think the scars inside us will fade in time like my burn?"

"I can't say."

"This Levi, the preacher man, do you suppose he could tell us?"

"Maybe."

"Then you must talk to him."

He chuckled. "Cora, when did you get so decisive? So bossy?"

She nodded her head like their mother did when she'd made a decision and would accept no argument. "Mandy makes me see how strong a woman can be. I want to be like her."

He bolted to his feet. "Heaven forbid."

But as he strode over to the house, intent on escape, Cora's laughter followed.

His little sister was growing up. Perhaps the lessons she absorbed from watching Mandy would serve her well, make her grow strong.

He grinned. Mandy was strong, independent.

His smile flattened. She was also an idealist—especially when it came to matters of the heart. From what she and her sisters said, she hankered for a father who often left them on their own. He turned to stare at her twig house. Why would she be willing to give up her goal of persuading her pa to settle down here?

Or had she?

Hadn't he learned what happens when people must choose between two loyalties? Friendship held a flickering candle to the strong light of family and obligations.

Where did that leave Trace?

He straightened his shoulders. He'd given his heart to a woman, trusted her, and she'd used his weakness to draw him away from his home. His absence made it possible for the Bushwhackers' attack. How could he ever trust again?

Chapter 11

Trace's self-constructed inner path grew more and more narrow by the day as Mandy worked at his side, ever cheerful, usually teasing, often amusing, and sometimes downright confrontational.

The house was about ready for a roof.

Would she stop visiting once it was finished?

The idea brought on a feeling of emptiness.

Mandy stood back, admiring the structure they had worked so hard to build. "It will be a fine house."

"Good enough for Cora and me." Why did his mind picture someone other than Cora sharing the rooms? Someone like Mandy?

"Tomorrow is Sunday," she said.

"So it is. A day of rest."

"And worship." She turned to give him a serious look that unsettled every effort he'd made to push her away. "Trace, why don't you come to church with me? You and Cora?"

Cora, listening nearby, said, "I told him he should go and talk to the preacher man."

Mandy grinned. "There you go. Cora has a reason for you to talk to Levi."

He didn't bother to correct her. "I don't have to go to church to talk to Levi, do I?"

"Wouldn't hurt you none."

He laughed. "You calling me a sinner?" He didn't need her accusation to know he was—and the worst sort. Hadn't Jesus said if he didn't forgive, he couldn't be forgiven? Or something like that? He couldn't recall the exact words.

She grinned without apology. "We're all sinners. That's why Jesus came. That's why we need to gather together and be reminded how to deal with the problem."

Cora joined them and nudged Trace. "Go. Mama and Papa would want you to."

He frowned at her. "Cora, you are spending too much time with Mandy and learning some of her underhanded tricks."

"Me?" Mandy sputtered. "Underhanded tricks? You take that back."

He didn't know what she intended to do to him for his remark, but he didn't plan to hang around to find out. He raced for the woods. She'd have to catch him to exact payment, and he didn't intend to let her.

"Cora, help me catch him," Mandy called, already hot on his heels. Then silence. Did he hear whispering? He edged around a tree to see what they were up to.

Mandy had her back to him, but the way their heads bent together, it was obvious the two of them planned something. Something that involved catching him.

Not if he could help it.

He slipped away, silent as a shadow, circling higher and then cutting down the hill to backtrack. He passed beneath them. Cora's passage was unmistakable, the way she crunched over the pine needles. She was no hunter. He had to concentrate to hear Mandy, but after a moment he did. Both of them still followed his path.

He wondered if Mandy would be good enough to pick up his back trail.

A few minutes later he returned to the clearing and moved to the far edge, where he hunkered out of sight behind some bushes. He made himself comfortable. After all, he might be there some time.

He leaned his head back against the trunk of a tree, his thoughts racing. Go to church? His anger and the resulting guilt would surely make him uncomfortable, but all this talk with Cora about what their parents would want had him reconsidering some of his decisions. They would expect their offspring to attend church. Even more, to live Christian lives. He might force himself to go. But he wouldn't force Cora.

He sensed someone watching him. Not moving, careful not to give away any indication of his notice, he scoured the surrounding area thoroughly. Had to stifle a laugh of amusement as he made out Mandy pressed to a tree trunk, invisible to a more casual observer.

He wasn't surprised she'd found him without giving away her approach. In fact, he expected it. But he intended to let her make the first move.

He tipped his head back, lowered his hat to shade his eyes, and pretended to sleep. All the while he watched her, saw how she studied him as if she wanted something from him. Or to give him something.

Her posture relaxed. She knew he'd seen her.

"Okay, I'll go to church with you," he said.

"Great. Cora," she yelled, "he's over here."

Cora tripped through the woods, not at all concerned about how much racket she made.

"He said he'd go to church. You're coming, aren't you?"

Cora stopped still. She shot a look toward Trace so full of longing and aching it brought him to his feet. "Cora, come with me."

Then she closed up like a locked door. "I couldn't."

How he hurt for the pain and isolation his younger sister endured.

Mandy slipped to his side. "One day she will realize people will care about her if she gives them a chance. In the meantime, I mean to be her friend."

Trace reached for Mandy's hand and squeezed it, welcoming her steadfastness.

Cora looked at their joined hands and grinned.

Trace couldn't say who pulled away first, but he and Mandy sprang apart with a sudden need to return to the clearing.

∞

Sunday dawned clear and sunny—perfect for an outdoor service. Mandy had wondered more than once if Trace would truly come. But now she sat on the grassy slope with Trace at her side, waiting for the service to begin. He wore an especially fine white shirt and black trousers she'd never seen before. With a start, she wondered if he'd worn them to his parents' funeral. She shifted her hand, intending to squeeze his and offer silent comfort. But they sat in plain view of a whole bunch of people, and even though they were outdoors, this was church.

Besides, what was she thinking? It seemed ever since she'd kissed him, her heart did strange things. Like give her this sudden urge to comfort him. Or the inner demand he attend church with her. So many other things, too, like dreaming about him at night. Often in her dreams they were sitting side by side under the stars, his arm around her, holding her close. She would tip her face to him, and he would kiss her. A couple of times, Glory had kicked her awake. Demanded to know why she laughed in her sleep.

It would take four Glorys and half a dozen strong men to pull the truth from her. Likely even then she wouldn't confess.

Any more than she'd admit how longingly she looked at the almost-finished house and imagined cooking over a stove, sitting before the fire with Trace and reading to each other.

At last Levi stood, drawing her away from thoughts of sharing her life with Trace.

Levi welcomed everyone, opened in prayer, then announced a hymn. There were no hymnbooks, so they sang from memory. And no musical instruments. But Mandy enjoyed hearing the voices next to her. Mr. Phelps had a deep voice like a bullfrog. Joanna sang clear as a bell. Levi carried them all along with his strong voice. And Trace...

Mandy decided he must have the voice of an angel—a man angel, if there were such things. A solid, pleasantly mellow voice. She had to force her attention to remain on Levi while her errant, willful heart longed to look at Trace, meet his eyes, and join her voice to his as if there were no others present.

The hymn ended, and her heart knocked at her ribs. Such a demanding part of her body. She hadn't noticed it till lately.

They sang three more hymns, Mandy's enjoyment growing with each verse. Then Levi opened his Bible.

"Today I am reading from Matthew chapter five, verses one to twelve, what we commonly call the Beatitudes."

Mandy leaned forward as he spoke on the blessings of doing things God's way.

Could she possibly expect to be blessed when she constantly insisted on doing things her way? When she chafed at God for allowing Pa to abandon them?

The service ended. Many recognized Trace from last Sunday and crossed to his side to speak to him and thank him for rescuing the Murrays.

"How are they?" he asked one man.

"Fine. Temporarily living in the back of the office while they rebuild. Mrs. Murray says now she can have a house with a little more style."

Mandy stayed close to him, proud to be his friend. Even if he wanted to hide Cora, there was no need for Trace to secret himself away from others.

He joined them again for dinner.

"Mandy made the dessert," Glory announced as if she'd done it specially for Trace.

"It's only a chocolate cake pudding." She tried to find Glory's ankle under the table, but Glory stayed out of the way and grinned with a great deal of triumph.

Trace tasted it. "Fantastic."

Levi echoed his comment. "Maybe you could teach Glory to make it." Which earned him an elbow to his ribs.

Unrepentant, he laughed.

Trace let out a deep-throated chuckle, and Mandy angled her body toward him. She quirked an eyebrow.

His eyes shone like summer sunshine. "I find you Buffalo Gals amusing"—he must have read her warning not to mock them—"in a purely delightful way." He shifted his gaze to encompass the other sisters. "You're all as strong as any woman I've ever met, and many a man. You're adventuresome, hardworking, and not afraid of risks. Quite unlike the young women I knew back in Missouri. I admire you." His eyes made their way back to Mandy and probed deep into her thoughts.

It felt as if the words were meant for her alone.

"Thank you," Joanna and Glory said. "We try our best," Glory added.

"I couldn't agree more," Levi added. "Though you forgot one important characteristic."

Trace turned toward Levi, and Mandy turned her attention to him, too, with some reluctance.

"Yup," Levi said. "You forgot wild and rebellious." Which earned him another jab of Glory's sharp elbow and a chuckle from Trace.

Mandy and Glory studied each other, plotting revenge.

"Oh, oh," Levi said. "I'm going to pay for that."

"Unless you can outrun them." Trace's voice rang with amusement.

"I'm not even going to try." He leaned toward Glory and kissed her on the nose. "I don't want to miss the fun."

It didn't take a genius to see Glory had forgotten any thoughts of payback.

Mandy couldn't drum up much interest either.

They finished the meal and worked together to clean up the kitchen. Both Trace and Levi offered to help with supper preparations; then they all escaped to the sun-filled yard.

"We're going to check on the folks at the mission." Although the building wasn't finished, Levi had taken in an injured man and his very pregnant wife. "Anyone want to come along?" Levi asked.

Joanna shook her head. "I have a few things I want to do on my own." She emphasized the last two words as if indicating she would be relieved to be free of them all.

Mandy studied her eldest sister as tendrils of worry and fear threaded through her heart. "Are you getting tired of us hanging about?"

"Mandy, I didn't mean anything except I don't mind being here on my own. Now off you go, and enjoy the afternoon." She waved them away.

Trace said he wouldn't mind seeing the mission. Mandy remembered Cora wanted him to talk to Levi about something. But she wanted to show Trace some of the special spots around Bonners Ferry. "We'll be along in a bit."

Glory planted herself in front of Mandy, ready to tease her.

But before she could spit the words out, Levi grabbed her hand. "Come on, Glory." Glory jerked back, unwilling to give up her plan so quickly.

"Let it go," Levi said.

Glory squinted at Mandy then allowed Levi to lead her away.

Finally Trace and Mandy were alone except for those going about their business, unmindful of the pair. And Mandy couldn't decide where to look. Certainly not at him. What if he saw the burst of joy blaze across her face?

"Come on," she murmured, hurrying in the general direction of the ferry.

"Aren't we going with Levi and Glory?"

"In a roundabout way. I want to show you something first. Is that okay?" She finally turned, finally met his gaze. Almost wished she hadn't. But not quite. She could swim in the blue of his eyes, drown in the fondness she saw. . .or let herself think she saw.

They walked side by side past the scattered buildings at this end of town. She led him up a rocky path until they met up with the narrow stream and stopped at its bank. The water chattered noisily across rocks. She wanted to say something about how she found the noise of the water both cheering and calming. But she couldn't find the words. So she let him look and listen without comment.

"The sound of running water is hypnotizing." His voice was all soft and mellow.

"I like it."

"Me, too." He reached for her hand. "Me, too."

She wasn't certain if he still referred to the running water. And didn't care. Being here, sharing her love of nature, feeling at peace with herself and this man—it was all that mattered at the moment.

"Let's keep climbing." She indicated the path by the stream, and they moved upward, their feet padding softly on the leafy ground, the sun warming them despite the canopy of trees crowding toward the stream. In many places the passage was too narrow to walk side by side, and he led the way. As soon as the path widened, he waited for her and again took her hand.

Mandy discovered something satisfying, and at the same time frightening, about the clasp of her hand in his. It made her want things she thought only Pa could give—home, belonging, and so much more.

In a short time they reached a wider spot where the water had spread into a pool. "This is my favorite place." She led him to a fallen tree where she often sat to watch the animals tiptoe in for water. "I've seen so many animals. I never shoot anything here. Seems the animals deserve to know this place is theirs."

They sat side by side, the quiet sifting into her thoughts, her soul. She wondered if he felt the same blessed peace. Her hand lay in his.

He shifted. "Mandy, what did you think of the sermon?"

She gathered her impressions into some sort of order. "I know I should trust God more. Like when I get upset and sad because I miss Pa. I wonder why God doesn't stop him and make him come back and live with us."

Trace threaded his fingers between hers and curled his over the top, protectively—or so she let herself think. "I suppose it's because God doesn't force us to do anything."

"But He could stop Pa, couldn't He?"

"He has the power to do so, of course. But not the will."

She understood, but. . . "Sometimes it's hard to trust God."

He examined each of her fingers then stared at the shadowed water. "Blessed are the merciful, for they shall be shown mercy."

"That's one of the Beatitudes Levi read, isn't it?"

She felt Trace's tension. Knew something about the words bothered him.

"I don't know if I can show mercy."

"To whom?"

"I told you my parents died in a fire." His voice seemed heavy with sorrow.

"Yes." She had nothing to offer by way of comfort but her quiet presence.

"What I didn't tell you was the fire was deliberately set."

She gasped. "They were murdered?" A shudder raced through her. "That's terrible."

He gripped her hand so hard her fingers hurt, but she didn't pull away. "My best friend was one of those who did it."

She could feel his pain like sharp needles all over her body. "That's why you don't trust people."

He nodded. His shoulders slumped forward the way Cora's often did.

"Trace, I'm so sorry." She rubbed his back, trying to soothe him like Joanna did for her. "Why would your friend do that?"

"Because he wasn't really a friend." Bitterness edged each word.

"I'm sorry." The words were inadequate, but she had no others to offer.

"Just because my father was a hero in the Mexican-American War."

Mandy didn't see how that constituted a reason, but it seemed to make sense for Trace.

"Everyone assumed he was Unionist because of that. He did his best to stay out of the Civil War. Said he'd seen enough fighting to last ten lifetimes. Said problems should be dealt with by negotiations, not by killing each other."

The pain pouring out with each word scraped at the inside of Mandy's heart until she wondered it wasn't in shreds.

"My friend"—he made the term sound positively hateful—"joined the Bushwhackers for the Confederates. As if it made running with a bunch of lawless renegades somehow more legitimate. They loot, burn, and take advantage of defenseless women. They honor no law, nor any person's rights apart from their own." He spit out each word like the pit from a sour fruit.

She continued to rub his back, though she ached to do so much more. Pull him into her arms and hold him tight. But no amount of comfort she offered would erase the pain from his soul.

Only time and God's love could do that. Not something she'd given a lot of thought to until this moment. But seeing Trace's misery, knowing how it felt to be mortally disappointed by others whether a close friend or a pa, she knew healing lay outside human resources.

"I knew a girl back then. Annabelle Jones. I thought she had some regard for me. But it was all pretend. Austin—the man I thought was

239

my friend—got Annabelle to lure me away from our house. While I was gone, they set it afire. My mother and father were resting and died on their bed."

His body shuddered.

Mandy pressed her cheek to his shoulder. "Cora?" she whispered.

"I heard people rushing to fight the fire. Didn't even consider it might be my own home. Annabelle tried to hold me back. 'It's too late,' she said. But I wouldn't be stopped. Even when men tried to prevent me from going in, I pushed them aside. I found Cora trying to get to the door and pulled her to safety. She was burned. But you know that. Oh, Mandy. It was awful. How will I ever forget?" He faced her, his eyes brimming with sorrow.

Although her heart gathered up his pain until every pulse hurt, she did not shrink from meeting his gaze. She hoped he could read her unspoken thoughts of comfort and caring.

He wrapped an arm around her shoulder and with a muffled groan pulled her to his chest. "Mandy." That was all he said, her name a sound of despair.

She edged her arms around him and held him close. Sharing his sorrow as best she could.

He shuddered again then his breathing evened out. "Mandy." This time her name carried something more.

She couldn't let herself think what.

His arms tightened. "I cannot forgive them. I cannot show mercy."

What she heard was not unforgiveness but lostness. She had no words for him on either subject, but she recognized them as her own. She often felt that sense of lostness about her pa. Only she'd never truly recognized it. Needing guidance, she offered up a tentative prayer. *God, I don't often come to You for anything, but Trace needs Your help today.* She should try and get him to walk with her toward the mission. Levi could help him.

But he showed no sign of releasing her, and she didn't intend to free herself.

"I wish I could forget the whole thing. My so-called friends, the way the community turned a blind eye to the fact two murders had been committed. . .everything. But I can't."

She offered up another silent prayer. Trace must find a way to forgive those dreadful people, or his own soul would suffer. "The trouble with bitterness is it hurts the man who carries it. Not the person to whom it is directed. It's like drinking poison."

"I'm learning that. But I don't see any way out of it."

She edged back to look into his face. "What if this Austin fellow repented of what he'd done? Could you forgive him then?"

He searched her gaze. "I simply don't know."

"What if"—she could barely bring the name to her lips—"Annabelle came to you and said she was sorry?"

She felt his careful consideration of her question. Would he decide to return and explore this possibility? If he did, she could have the house. Not even a flicker of joy accompanied the thought, because she didn't want it. She wanted Trace. Wanted him to stay here. Live here.

"I think I can forget Annabelle's part in this treachery. She is a silly girl who doesn't know what she wants. Likely she'll marry someone who appreciates her charm and simplicity."

Mandy's heart lifted with relief.

"But Austin and I grew up together. I always thought we would stand shoulder to shoulder in any challenge and fight side by side to the end."

Mandy tried to imagine how she'd feel if Glory or Joanna had betrayed her. Couldn't picture it. But even the thought made her insides feel like they'd been melted and poured out.

"How do I forgive and forget?"

"I don't have the answers. Maybe Levi does."

But neither of them made a move toward resuming their journey. Instead, they shifted to contemplate the pond and their thoughts. Trace's arm remained across her shoulders, and she clutched his other hand.

"It's peaceful here," Trace said after a bit. "The troubles of the world seem far away."

"That's why it's my favorite spot."

He caught her chin and tipped her face toward him. "What troubles do you have, Mandy?"

She hesitated, deciding to trust him just as he had trusted her. "I struggle with forgiveness, too. It's nothing like what you have to deal with, but I'm often angry with Pa for leaving us." She wondered if he heard the quiver in her voice. "It's something I only recently realized. I always believed what Glory said. . . . I was trying to make him into an ideal parent. But it's far more than that." She sat up and faced him, finding courage in the steady way he regarded her. "I'm angry at him."

Trace nodded. "Sometimes it's hard to forgive."

"But not impossible."

"How is it possible? Tell me. I want to know."

How could she explain when she didn't understand it herself? "I think it has something to do with allowing a different feeling to control me."

"Like what?"

Like my growing feelings for you. Trace, I think I love you. But she couldn't say the words. Feared that doing so would put a vast gulf between them. "Maybe being in competition with you over building our houses made it possible to forget my anger. It lost its hold on me." She concentrated on the trees beyond his ear, unwilling to meet his gaze directly, lest he guess the truth.

He chuckled. "I, too, forgot to be angry while you were around building your twig house."

She laughed along with him, wondering what he felt about her.

A duck quacked across the pond, her gaggle of ducklings paddling after her.

With a sigh of regret, Mandy realized how long they'd lingered. "Glory will come looking for us any minute."

"Let's be on our way." He reached for her hand and pulled her to her feet.

Hand in hand, they walked back to the roadway and within minutes reached the mission.

Mandy hadn't been to visit in some time, and the amount of work accomplished stunned her. The main building was almost finished. "You two have been busy."

"We've had lots of help," Levi said. "It will soon be ready. I can hardly wait."

But the way his eyes rested on Glory, bringing a pink blush to her cheeks, Mandy knew his impatience was more about wanting to marry than wanting to open the mission.

She didn't envy her sister's happiness, but would she ever know the same? She didn't dare look at Trace nor any of the others for fear they could read her longing.

Chapter 12

T race accompanied Levi on a tour of the frame construction. Large enough to house a number of people in need of care, with living quarters for Levi and Glory as well. Trace heard the explanation with half his attention.

Something had happened between himself and Mandy as he confessed his feelings about the incident that took his parents' lives. Something warm and wonderful and full of promises for the future. But had she felt it, too?

He almost hoped she hadn't, because until he could get rid of his bitterness toward Austin and the others—a bitterness that boiled over toward God—he could not offer her unfettered love.

They left the building and walked across the yard until they came to a corral of horses.

"These are the animals Glory works with, healing abused and neglected horses."

"Does a horse always recover from such things?"

"With enough kindness. Glory is willing to give what it takes."

"Can people recover from similar misfortunes or treachery or. . ." He didn't know what he wanted to ask.

Levi faced him. "Are we talking about something specific, or just general conversation?"

"Do you have time to listen to my tale of woe?"

"Always." They leaned against the top board of the fence as Trace retold his story.

"Can a man forgive such things?" Trace gripped the railing, hoping for an answer but unable to see a way. "Can I trust a God who allowed it? Can I ever love again after experiencing such betrayal at the hands of people I considered friends?"

"The short answer is yes. But I think you know that. What you really want to know is how."

"Exactly."

Levi took a deep breath, watching a gray mare canter around the fence. "Again, the short answer is by trusting God. But that's too simplistic. Perhaps I should tell you my own experience. My brother and I were orphaned as youngsters and went to live with my grandparents, who were very strict. My brother refused to adjust. He threw their rules over his shoulder and left. But he wasn't content with walking away from their rules. He also ignored man-made rules and God's rules and ended up in prison, where he is even now."

"I'm sorry to hear that. It must be hard."

"It is." Levi turned to Trace, studying him. "But my reaction was to bargain with God. Tell Him if I served Him as a preacher, then He was obligated to turn Matt around. I made a vow that almost cost me a chance for life with Glory. In hindsight, I can't imagine how I could have even thought God wanted me to do such a thing."

Trace wondered what this story had to do with him.

"My whole point is this—God is not responsible for the choices people make, but He is faithful to what He has promised."

Trace tried to think of a promise to cover the betrayal of friends, the murder of his parents, and the anger in his heart. He shook his head.

"I don't have any cure-all answer for you." Levi stared into the distance. "But remember Jesus was betrayed, murdered, and yet allowed it so He could provide salvation for us all. 'With God all things are possible.' Even impossible things like forgiveness."

Trace's jaw clenched. "My friends are responsible for murder."

"I agree. But justice will prevail. If not in this life then in the next."

"That hardly seems like justice."

"God is never early and never late."

Glory called out an invitation for refreshments, and the conversation ended. They joined the sisters and visited over tea and cake.

Mandy glanced at the position of the sun. "We need to get back and help Joanna."

"And I need to get back to Cora," Trace said. He and Mandy headed down the trail, leaving Glory to say her good-byes.

Mandy barely waited until they were out of earshot to speak. "Did Levi say anything helpful?"

He wished he could assure her that, thanks to Levi, all his problems were gone, but he couldn't. "He said, 'With God all things are possible.' I haven't figured out how that helps me. I guess it doesn't."

"But maybe it will. Seems it's impossible for us to forgive some things. Maybe only God can forgive."

"But who is He to forgive—Austin, for his treachery, or me for not forgiving Austin?"

Mandy stopped in front of him, preventing him from continuing. She faced him. "Why not both?"

"Austin doesn't deserve forgiveness."

"True. But if he repented?"

"Mandy, it makes me angry to think he can just say sorry and be done with it. That's not fair."

"I suppose not." She studied the sky for a moment as if seeking answers from above. "But when you think about it, all of us are undeserving of God's forgiveness." Her gaze returned to his, warm and gentle. "We don't deserve His love, but He gives it anyway."

He couldn't resist the look of peace on her face and cupped his hand to the back of her head. "Mandy, if I were free to love. . ." Why go on when he wasn't?

"Why aren't you? You still in love with Annabelle?"

"No." He scowled. "I never loved her."

"Then what's keeping you from loving?"

Did she have any idea how appealing she looked as she probed his heart? Was she suggesting she loved him?

"Mandy, how can I love freely when my heart is consumed by bitterness? Hate? Hate has the power to poison love. I don't think there is room for both. Until I can deal with it, I cannot offer my love." He should break away, put distance between them, but she clamped her hands to his shoulders and smiled so sweetly and gently his heart threatened to melt. "When I sort this out. . ." His throat had grown so tight his words came out husky. He could speak no promises, but he could let her get a glimpse of the love in his heart.

He bent and kissed her, breathing in her wildflower scent until he could barely think. But he must think. He must be rational. Until there was nothing in his heart competing with his love for her. He slowly lifted his head.

Her eyes were dark pools of emotion. She opened her mouth, and he feared she would demand he speak the words his kiss hinted at. He could not. Before she could say anything, he took her hand and continued down the trail.

Mandy knew Trace's kiss was a silent promise of love. But he feared what lay in his heart. Who could blame him for his bitterness? Why did such awful things happen?

As Levi often said, it was easy to blame God for what man was responsible for. She could do nothing more than pray for Trace to find healing. And continue to show her love for him.

But he sure knew how to make it difficult.

The next morning she raced through her chores at the stopping house and hurried up the trail.

Perhaps by now he'd sorted out his feelings and was ready to move on.

She stepped into the clearing and halted. Cora huddled by the fire, sobbing. Trace knelt beside her.

Mandy rushed to them. "What's wrong?" She squatted beside Cora and rubbed her back. "Cora, what happened?"

Cora sobbed harder, unable to speak.

Mandy hadn't allowed herself to look directly at Trace yet and steeled herself to meet his gaze. She'd hoped for signs of love but saw only raw anger. She asked her question again, directing it this time at Trace.

He sprang to his feet, shoved his hand through his hair, strode three feet away, then turned. "Some young fella saw the smoke from our campfire and thought he'd pay a neighborly visit. No one invited him, but I suppose it's a free country." He reeled about and walked the same three feet, spun around, and stomped back to his original spot. "He saunters in here all friendly. Asks if he can join us for breakfast. I tried to shoo him off, but he saw Cora at the fire and wouldn't pay any heed to me."

Cora sobbed harder.

"Cora had left her bonnet off. She couldn't get it before the young buck sauntered up to her, bold as brass, and said he'd like to make her acquaintance. I grabbed a branch, prepared to persuade him to leave us alone. But then he saw her face and changed his mind so fast he almost tripped over his feet getting out of here."

Trace kicked dirt into the fire until it was buried.

Mandy pulled Cora into her arms and patted her back. But a suspicion grew in her mind. "Is this where you were sitting?"

Cora nodded.

"Trace, is that the branch you picked up?" She pointed to one a few feet past Cora.

"I should have applied it to his backside."

"Did the young man come from up the trail or down the trail?"

"I suppose down. He stepped into the clearing over there and made his way to the fire." Trace pointed.

"Oh, honestly, Trace." A bubble of amusement rose to the back of her throat, but she feared her laughter would offend Cora. "Did you ever consider it wasn't Cora's scars he saw but a big, angry man with a fat stick in his hands?"

Trace scowled.

But Cora sat up, wiped her eyes, and sniffled into a hankie. She looked from the branch to the place where the man had stood. She glared at Trace, his face twisted in anger. "You scared him off, you big oaf." She started to laugh.

Mandy could no longer contain her amusement.

Trace frowned at the pair of them, laughing hard enough to bring on tears. He stalked into the woods without a backward look.

Mandy scrambled to her feet and followed.

She found him deep in the woods, slamming his fist into a tree. She choked back a scream. Why was he throwing a temper tantrum? She stepped forward and grabbed his arm before he could hit the tree again. His knuckles were bloodied. Her own anger flared. "What is this accomplishing?"

He jerked his arm free and turned his back to her. His neck muscles corded. His shoulders pulled forward.

"Trace, it was a mistake. Anyone would have fled when they saw you approaching. I doubt it had anything to do with Cora's cheek."

"You can't say that with any certainty."

She glared at him. "Just as you can't say with any certainty it was Cora's scars that scared him away." She crossed her arms, waiting for his anger to abate, but he remained as rigid as any of the logs he'd cut for the house.

"This is what I mean about hate poisoning everything. Including me. I am so angry I am on fire inside." The words ground out so hard she wouldn't have been surprised to see bits of tooth enamel accompany them. "I know it can consume me." He strode away, resting one hand on a nearby tree, blood oozing from his knuckles. He let his head fall forward. "Until I find a way to erase it. . ."

She heard what he didn't say. Until that time, he would not allow himself to love. And yet. . . She forced some patience into her voice and repeated an idea she'd expressed yesterday. "Perhaps the way to get rid of hate is to replace it with something." She waited, but he gave no indication if he heard or understood her meaning. Pain or no pain, she had absolutely no sympathy for letting events control him. Enough was enough. "Look, if you want to spend your life wallowing in your hurts, fine. But did it ever occur to you that maybe letting love into your heart can rid it of hate and anger?" She moved to his side and touched his arm, felt him twist beneath her palm. "Trace?" Was he ready to quit being an idiot?

He faced her, his eyes dark as still, deep water, his mouth drawn back into a thin line of despair. "Don't you see," he whispered. "I love you, but love hasn't erased my hate."

"You love me?" Did she sound as surprised and happy as she felt? Annoyed, too. This was not the moment he should have confessed his love.

"Forget I said it. I can't love you, can't offer you what you deserve until I do something about this." He slammed his bloodied fist into his chest. "I don't recognize myself when I'm like this. I don't trust myself."

Unbelievable. Part of her ached to tend his wounds—hold him close and assure him he was fine just the way he was. But she sensed he was as angry at himself and his inability to handle his emotions as he was about his past. She wondered if anything she said at this point would make a difference. Likely not. Besides, another part of her wanted to shake him hard and tell him to look at what the future held for those ready and willing to forget the past. But what was the use? She shook her head. "Let's go work on the house." She headed toward the clearing.

With a heavy sigh, he followed.

They soon settled into a soothing rhythm of work.

Cora, Goliath in her arms, sauntered over to watch. "What are you going to do with Mandy's house?"

"You mean the twig house?" Trace teased.

Relieved to see his normal good humor restored, Mandy pretended to get all defensive. "No wolf is going to blow it down. It will suit just fine for an outbuilding."

"I don't know." Trace circled her little shack, touched each corner, and each time jumped back as if afraid it would come crashing down.

"Let's see how hard you can blow," she challenged.

His eyes crinkled at the corners in a hidden smile; then he blew and blew until he had to bend over his knees to get his breath.

"See, I told you."

"I doubt if my little puffs will be the worst thing this shack has to endure. What about the winds, the rain, the snow?"

She went to his side and contemplated the building. Wasn't much to look at, but she wasn't going to confess it to him. "It'll stand the winter."

"Maybe. Then crumble into the soil."

"Dying a natural death as all things do." She cocked her head at Trace and added, "All things pass. . .even emotions. If we give them half a chance."

He lifted his eyebrows skyward as he understood her message. "But this has the elements to wear it down."

"And you have God's love and forgiveness to wear down your hate."

"Hasn't helped much so far." He wheeled around and bent over a log, notching it.

☙

Day after day they worked on the house. The roof would soon be finished. It was satisfying to see progress.

But despite Mandy's reassurance that his emotions would change, Trace saw no progress in conquering his hate and lack of forgiveness. Every time he looked at Cora, he remembered Austin and the others. Even building this log cabin was a reminder. They'd once had a fine, big house.

Cora wandered around the interior of the cabin, which didn't take more than a few steps. "Where will you put the stove?" she called.

He'd shown her before but went inside. "The stove will go here, so it can warm the whole room. The area closest to the door will be the kitchen and living area. The bedrooms will be on this side. I'll build partitions so we can have privacy."

"What will we do for furnishings?"

"I can make a table and some chairs. Maybe even a rocking chair."

"I wish we had some of Mama's quilts for the bed."

Mandy joined them.

It no longer surprised him to have her appear suddenly and silently.

"I saw some nice fabric at the store," she said. "You could make one for your bed."

Cora's eyes brightened. "That might be fun."

Every nerve in Trace's body fired up with awareness of Mandy in the confines of the cabin. His mind flooded with imaginations. Not for the first time, he thought of her residing here. Sitting in a rocking chair mending something.

He snorted. More likely she'd be out hunting. He tried to dispel the longing that clutched his throat. Because he knew she could cook if she wanted to. He'd seen her mend a tear in her pants with neat tight stitches that even his mother would have praised.

Cora took his sound of disbelief for criticism. "You don't think I can make a quilt?"

"I'm quite certain you can." He wondered how hard to push her. "Question is, will you go to town and select the fabric you like or ask Mandy to do it and settle for what she picks out?"

Mandy's mouth flew open. She stared at him but remained silent.

Cora opened her mouth. Then she touched her cheek and turned away. "I expect we have enough bedding to do us."

Mandy lifted one shoulder in a little shrug.

Trace strode from the house. What right did he have to try and change Cora? He couldn't even change himself.

Mandy followed. "One day she will decide to go to town. She might learn no one cares about her burn half as much as she does. And you." She stalked away before he could point out a differing opinion. In truth, he couldn't find one. Understood the scar on Cora's face was no more disfiguring or difficult to ignore than the hate weighing his heart.

Something landed on his neck. He brushed it away. It happened again. He rubbed at the spot, caught something in his finger, and pulled his hand forward to see a small piece of wood. Like one he'd chopped from a log.

Another hit his neck and then his shoulder. Several hit his head.

If he wasn't mistaken, he heard muffled laughter from around the corner of the cabin.

So Mandy wanted to play, did she?

He brushed at his neck again and complained about the bugs. Then pretended to head toward the tent for something. As soon as he knew he was out of her sight, he changed direction and edged around the walls. He paused at the last corner, listening to her quiet breathing as she listened for him.

He gathered air into his lungs and eased around the corner.

She had her back to him, leaning forward, trying to see where he'd gone.

He tiptoed toward her. When she stiffened, caught some indication of him behind her, he sprang forward and captured her.

She squealed and struggled, but he wouldn't let her escape. She squirmed until she faced him.

"Think it's funny to play tricks on me, do you?" he asked.

A smile wreathed her face and flashed through her eyes as she nodded. Her smile softened as she gave a look so full of promise and longing he thought his heart would burst from his chest. Loving this woman would be such sweet joy. Every day would be full of fun and warmth.

As they considered each other, letting their gazes linger, the air shimmered with hope and possibility.

"Where did you guys go?" Cora called from inside the cabin.

The reality of his life erased the glow of the moment. He let his arms fall to his sides and stepped back. "We're out here."

Mandy reached for him.

He shook his head. "Don't. I can't."

Her hand hung suspended between them, and her face filled with sorrow.

He hated that he was responsible. But he'd tried to replace his hatred with love. But hate poisoned everything.

With a grumble, he ground around and headed for the woods.

How was he to deal with this?

The answers were easy. Forgive and let God exact justice. Trust God's ways. God's ways were higher than man's ways.

But knowing the answers and being able to do them weren't the same thing.

He made no attempt to slip through the woods quietly but crashed past trees, glad of the noise he made, finding relief in bending branches out of his way and hearing them snap back.

He didn't know how long he tromped on in that fashion, but he reached the side of a hill and looked out over the wide valley. The view reminded him of the one he'd seen soon after he'd met Mandy and how he'd called her to share it.

The beauty sucked at his insides.

"Oh God," he yelled, "show me how to forgive." But the words fell into the distance like pebbles dropped in a bottomless pit. Like every desperate prayer he'd uttered over the past days.

Would he never find a way to get rid of the curse of hatred? Would he be forever trapped in this pit? Never able to give his heart in complete, unfettered love to the woman he cared for?

Chapter 13

A dozen days later, Mandy helped Joanna serve the evening meal. Glory was absent, helping Levi with something. Twenty men clustered around the table, eagerly scooping up generous helpings. Talk, as usual, consisted mostly of questions about the gold fields to the north.

Joanna answered as best she could. Mandy said little, her thoughts still back up the hill with Trace and Cora.

She loved Trace and knew he loved her. He'd said so but then said love wasn't possible.

But she wouldn't entertain the word *impossible*. If he couldn't make up his own mind, she'd make it up for him.

In the intervening days she'd prayed as never before. Borrowed Mother's Bible from Joanna and read it, searching for answers. She'd found none that might help Trace, but something had been happening in her own soul. Hope and assurance of God's love filled her, replacing her anger at Pa. She felt blessed. She wanted Trace to find the same thing.

Every day she told him of verses she'd read or how she felt. He always grew hopeful. Hunger filled his eyes. Then he glanced away, often toward the house, or Cora, and she knew the memories had come flooding back. He could not let go of his bitterness.

She could only take a deep breath, swallow her frustration, and continue to pray and love him, hoping at some point both would heal his spirit.

Something in the conversation around the table caught her attention, and she looked at the man who'd spoken. "Who did you say you are looking for?"

"Trace Owens."

That's what she thought. "What's your business with him?"

"It's of a personal nature, but it's imperative I contact him."

"And who might you be?"

Most of the others excused themselves and went outdoors, having no

252

interest in a conversation that didn't have the word *gold* in it. Joanna let Mandy do the talking, but her interest was also focused on this stranger who asked after Trace.

"My name is Austin Collins."

Austin! The man who'd betrayed Trace. . .caused his parents' deaths and Cora's scars. She studied the man. As blond as Trace. As big. And every bit as sad and bitter looking. The way his mouth sagged, she wondered if he had any smile muscles in his face.

Two unhappy men. But she would not tell him where Trace was. Surely it would destroy Trace's very soul to be faced with the man responsible for his pain.

"Sorry, can't say I know anything about this man you seek." She hadn't told a lie. Didn't say she didn't know—just that she couldn't say.

But Joanna's look of disapproval warned Mandy she'd pushed the boundaries of right and wrong.

Austin thanked them for the meal and left the room.

The two sisters grabbed dishes and hurried to the kitchen, where they couldn't be overheard.

"He'll just ask someone else," Joanna warned.

"He won't hear Trace's whereabouts from me." And if she could stop him from searching further, she would. Maybe she could suggest he make inquiries farther north—like the gold fields.

As soon as the dishes were done she hurried outside. Glanced about the cluster of men. Austin went from one to the other, asking questions. If he decided to go up the street. . .

As if he'd read her mind, he left the men and stepped toward the heart of town.

She hurried after him and fell in at his side. "Seems to me the best place to look for someone would be in the gold fields. People only come here on their way north."

"I'll certainly search there, too. I am determined to find him."

"Why is it so important to you?"

He pondered her question for several steps as she tried to edge him away from the houses and businesses up the street, but he continued doggedly on, peering from one side to the other. "I don't see how it's any of your business." He flicked her a glance. "Ma'am."

"What if I make it my business?"

He snorted. "Why would you?"

She considered her response. "Let's say, just for conversation's sake,

253

that if I happened to know this man you're asking about—"

"Trace Owens."

"Or someone like him. Why would I, or anyone, tell a complete stranger about it? You could be one of those lawless men who wander through town looking for easy gold. They don't mind if they find it by panning or by robbing." Did he understand that she cared about his motive in looking for Trace?

"I don't want his gold or anyone's. I just need to talk to Trace." He slowed his steps enough to glance at Mandy. "We grew up together. We were great friends."

"*Humph.* Seems if you were great friends you'd know where he was."

"Something happened."

Yeah. You turned out to be a traitor. Played a part in murdering his parents. "I expect it was something awful enough that this man doesn't want to see you again."

Austin stopped so abruptly that Mandy had to backtrack to his side.

"It was something very awful."

"What did you do?" If she heard the story from his lips, perhaps she would get a clue that would help Trace overcome his pain.

Austin sucked in a long breath, let it out in a shudder. "It's a long story. Not sure you want to hear it."

"Try me." They reached Glory's shop. "Why don't we sit a spell, and you can tell me." She indicated the steps at the front door and almost sagged with relief when he sat down. She sat as well.

"I did something unforgivable."

"Is anything ever that bad?" She wanted to hear how he'd justify his actions.

"Unfortunately, yes." He buried his head in his hands.

Mandy felt no sympathy for him. The man deserved every bit of misery he felt.

"I'm from Missouri, as is Trace. The Bushwhackers are a strong bunch in that state. I once thought I agreed with them enough to join their cause, but I discovered I don't like the way they get their point across. I've left the group."

Mandy brushed dust from one pant leg then leaned back on her elbow, observing the man. It was good to hear he might have regrets.

"I need to find Trace and tell him I left them. But there's more." He stared into space. "I was involved in something that hurt Trace. Hurt his sister and his parents. People I love." Slowly, as if he had to force the words from his lips, he told the story that Mandy had already heard. But Austin's version differed.

"I arranged for Trace to be absent so he wouldn't try to stop them. I thought I was doing him a favor. You know, preventing him from trying to defend his family and maybe getting shot. I thought they only meant to force Mr. Owens to provide them with food and supplies. When I heard what they really intended, I tried to warn the Owenses, but two men held me back. By the time I managed to get free, the house was nothing but a pile of ashes. And Trace was threatening to take justice into his own hands. I think the only reason he didn't was because Cora needed him at her bedside."

The story shocked Mandy to the point she couldn't think.

Austin let out a gust as if his lungs hadn't released air for several minutes. "By the time Cora was able to be left alone, the wheels of justice had determined the fire was an accident. They got away with murder. I left and went north, trying to find a place where I could escape the war and my accusing thoughts." Another deep sigh. "Escaping yourself isn't possible. I did a lot of soul searching. Spent a lot of time on my knees seeking forgiveness. I met a preacher man who assured me God could and would forgive anything. Finally, I found a degree of peace." He rubbed his chest absently.

He'd found the answer to guilt. The same answer must surely apply to hate and unforgiveness. She wanted to grab him and drag him to see Trace this minute. But she still wasn't sure what he wanted.

"So you are wanting to start over again with your friend?"

"I don't know if it's possible. How could he ever forgive me for my part in this? But I need to tell him I'm sorry. I never meant for it to happen. I need to ask his forgiveness." His voice dropped to an agonized whisper. "Even if he's not willing to give it."

Mandy considered her options. Was this an answer to prayer for Trace's healing? If she didn't take the man to see Trace, she faced two possibilities—Austin might find Trace through someone else and go to him, or he might leave on the ferry and Trace would miss this chance to deal with his problem.

She made up her mind. What better person to help Trace than the man who caused his hurt? "I know Trace."

Austin burst to his feet and faced her. "You know him? Where is he?"

"Come on. I'll take you."

As she led the way, he almost ran over her.

Footsteps approached the camp. They weren't taking any pains to be quiet, which meant they either didn't know someone inhabited this part of the hill or they knew and had no interest.

Nevertheless, Trace grabbed his rifle and waited.

Several times men had approached but had quickly departed when they realized Trace wasn't prepared to be welcoming.

Cora didn't head for the tent but pulled on her bonnet as she remained seated on a log. No doubt she expected the men to pass.

Men? He cocked his head. One voice sounded like a woman. In fact, it sounded like Mandy. Was it getting so bad he couldn't hear a woman and not think of her? Yes, it was. If only he could feel free to love her fully.

All his pleading with God for an answer had yielded nothing.

He heard them leave the path and head toward the clearing. He moved forward to meet them.

They stepped away from the trees.

He fell back. Every muscle in his body spasmed with shock. Somehow he found his voice. "Austin. Why are you here?" He half raised his rifle then lowered it. Shooting the man would not ease his anger. "Mandy, why are you with him?"

She signaled the man to hold back and crossed to Trace's side. "He's been looking for you to say he's sorry. You need to hear his side of the story. Hear how God forgave him. He can help you."

Roaring fires of rage seared his veins. "God might forgive him, but I never will. Get out of here. Both of you." He waved the rifle like a club. "I never want to see you again. Either of you."

Austin took a step closer. "Trace, hear me out."

"I'm not interested in anything you have to say. Get out." He drove them away, ignoring Austin's pleading to listen and Mandy's begging eyes. They disappeared through the trees.

"Traitors, both of you," he called after them.

He breathed hard, unable to think beyond the shock of seeing Austin and the horror of knowing Mandy had brought his enemy right to his new home.

He spun around to face the house. All but finished. But he'd find no peace here now. Mandy's presence would haunt him everywhere he turned. Muttering angry words, he grabbed up the saddlebags. "Start packing."

Cora didn't move.

"Did you hear me? We're leaving. Get your stuff together."

"Trace, you aren't being rational. This is our new home." She nodded toward the house. "We can't leave."

"We'll find somewhere else. Maybe we'll find a place where people aren't traitors."

She still didn't move. "People are the same all over. Sometimes they are evil. Sometimes they simply make mistakes." She rose and crossed to face him squarely, her arms across her chest. "And sometimes they actually want to help. But you have to give them a chance."

"I've given all the chances I intend to give. Pack your things. There's at least three hours before dark. We're going to take advantage of it."

"What if I say I'm not going?"

He stopped his furious stuffing of things into bags. "You think you can manage on your own?"

"I could live at the stopping house."

"And let all those men stare at you?" It was cruel but necessary.

Her face crumpled, but she did not cry. "Trace, you have a problem."

"I'm aware of that." The only solution for it was to move on.

Cora packed reluctantly. He saddled the horses and hung their belongings on each. They mounted and headed for the ferry, arriving in time for the last crossing north.

He expected to put a goodly distance between themselves and Bonners Ferry before he'd find a place to camp for the night.

"Where are we going?" Cora asked, a good deal of exasperation lacing her words.

"Might as well go look for gold."

She harrumphed, a sound so much like their ma used to make that Trace stared.

"You will never find enough gold to replace the friendship and love Mandy offered you."

"I intend to try."

"You'll never succeed." She turned her attention to the cat in her arms, dismissing Trace.

As they rode, he relived every minute of the visit from Austin and Mandy. Why had Mandy brought him? Out of malice? He couldn't think so.

Then why?

The answer dawned, slow and certain.

Because she wanted to help him. She thought seeing Austin would serve some good purpose.

He warred with his anger. Only it wasn't fury that caused his stubborn refusal to face the truth. It was pride. He could not let go of his righteous resentment that justice had been denied him. . .that friends had proven false.

He'd prayed for God to help him. Then Mandy said Austin could help him. Had God sent an answer? But why would He choose Austin—his ex-friend and enemy—to carry a message to him? His conscience asked, was he willing to listen to Austin if it meant relief from this burning, unyielding hate and unhappiness?

∞

Mandy rushed past the stopping house. She went on until she reached a grassy hillside overlooking the river where there was no traffic.

She threw herself on the grass and pounded the turf till her fists ached. She lay there crumpled for a while, but the tears wouldn't come. At last she sat up and stared at the water gurgling past.

Trace said he never wanted to see her again. He was determined to remain miserable, rejecting every good gift God offered. Wallowing in his hate like a pig in mud. But she couldn't remain angry. Instead, wave after wave of pain and despair washed over her.

She heard Glory approach but didn't bother to look up.

Glory sank to Mandy's side, their arms brushing. "Joanna told me Trace's old friend showed up asking after him. What happened?"

"I took him to see Trace."

Glory waited without comment.

"The man said he'd changed. Said he regretted any part he'd had in what the Bushwhackers had done. He wanted to ask Trace's forgiveness. I thought it would help Trace to talk to him, so I took him to see Trace."

"I'm guessing it didn't go well."

"Trace chased us away. Said he never wanted to see me again." Her voice broke. Her nose stung, and she sniffed. "I always think I can fix things for people. I should let them sort out their own problems."

Glory wrapped her arm around Mandy. "Sweetie, you only want people to be happy. Nothing wrong with that."

"Then why did it turn out so bad?" She rested her head on Glory's shoulder.

"Because you can't force people to change. They have to decide that on their own."

"Then I guess I don't stand a chance with Trace. He's too pigheaded to give up his anger."

"It's a pretty big thing to give up. After all, his parents were murdered, and no justice was offered. But remember, 'With God all things are possible.'"

"That's what Levi told Trace."

Glory gave a soft laugh. "It's one of his favorite verses."

They sat in contemplative silence for a moment before Mandy spoke again. "What am I supposed to do now? He said to never come back."

"Keep loving him. Keep praying. Don't give up."

It was good advice from a sister who'd kept loving and praying until she and Levi sorted out their problems. "Guess if it worked for you, it can't fail for me."

Glory snorted. "You're saying your problems are nothing compared to mine?"

Mandy tried to laugh but couldn't. "If only it were so."

Glory got to her feet and reached down to pull Mandy up. "I don't imagine any of them are big compared to God's power. Now let's get home before Joanna gets really worried."

∽

The next morning, Mandy rose with a plan in mind. She would return to the clearing and act like nothing had happened. If Trace wanted to get rid of her, he'd soon discover he would require a lot more than angry words.

Three times on the way up the trail she almost changed her mind, remembering the look on Trace's face when he saw Austin and the way he'd driven them away. But she would not let things between them end in such a fashion. Fact was, she didn't intend to let them end at all.

She stepped into the clearing and halted, waiting for Trace's reaction. Silence. Had he seen her coming and ducked away? Taken Cora with him? "Trace, I'm here."

Nothing. Why, he'd even taken down the tent. Why would he do that?

A dreadful suspicion scratched at her brain. She looked for his horses. Gone. Unless he'd moved them out of sight.

She circled the area. The campfire was cold. No pots or dishes lay about. Perhaps they'd moved into the cabin. But she didn't need to go any farther than the door to see the inside was empty.

She darted around the cabin. No tools. Nothing. She went to her twig house and stepped inside. It, too, was empty.

They were gone.

She returned to the middle of the clearing and turned around twice.

Trace had left. Without good-bye. Without telling her. He couldn't be more obvious that he wanted nothing more to do with her.

She collapsed to her knees. "Oh God, why didn't You stop him?" The words rang with a familiar tune. How often had she called out to God the very same thing when Pa left yet again?

"Oh God, bring him back. Please."

Her voice rang out in the silence. "I'll go after him." But she knew the futility of trying to catch up to a man who didn't want to be found. Pa had taught her that lesson well.

She sank into a ball, her palms on the ground, and groaned. She loved Trace, exasperating as he could be, but when had her love ever been enough?

She knew he loved her, too. But his anger and hate quenched it.

For a long time she didn't move. Barely breathed. Didn't want to feel but couldn't stop the pain any more than she could stop the sun from shining.

Glory's words seemed to echo from a distant place. *"With God all things are possible."*

Was their love possible?

Could she trust God to make it so?

"Who else can I trust?" she whispered. But real trust rested in knowing God would fulfill His promises.

She struggled a moment longer. Trace had every reason in the world to be angry, unwilling to forgive. Only God could show him another way. With bowed head she asked for that to be accomplished.

One thing she knew, besides God's faithfulness. Trace loved her. Surely one day, with God's help, his love would conquer all else and he would return.

Maybe not today. Or tomorrow. Or even next week.

But when he did, he would need a house. She pushed to her feet and faced the log cabin. Only a little left to be done on the roof before it was finished.

When he returned, he would find the house ready to live in.

She climbed the ladder to the roof and set to work.

As she hammered, her heart grew calm and steady, knowing God would also be busy doing His work in Trace's heart.

She paused, the hammer suspended midair, and listened. Voices. People were coming. She sank back out of sight on the far side of the roof and waited. Hopefully, the strangers would pass on by, because she was in a precarious, vulnerable position.

The sound of horse hooves stopped. She clung to the roof and waited.

But the riders didn't continue. They turned in and came toward the clearing.

"This is home now."

Cora? That was most certainly Cora's voice. Who did she talk to? Dare she hope?

She rose to her knees and stared down at the pair. "Trace?"

He looked up. Saw her there and stared hard. He blinked and stared again. "Mandy, what are you doing on the roof?"

"Trace. Cora." She scrambled down the ladder and ran toward him. "You've come back." Had Trace come back because he loved her? She paused.

But Trace swung off his horse and ran toward her, caught her in his arms and hugged her to his chest. "I had to come back."

"Why?"

Cora dismounted, gathered Goliath in her arms. "Because my big brother can be very smart at times." She headed for the woods.

Mandy leaned back to study Trace's face, her heart clamoring up her throat at the way his eyes shone, his gaze sought hers and clung. "What did she mean?"

"She thinks I've come to the right decision."

Mandy waited.

He led her to one of the logs they used as a bench and pulled her down beside him, never letting her out of his arms. "Remember how I said hate poisoned love?"

She nodded.

"Well, only if I choose to hold on to hate rather than love." He again searched her face, as if he couldn't get enough of it, had forgotten overnight what she looked like. "I figured it made more sense to let it go and choose love." He traced the line of her jaw with his fingertips, sending delicious bubbles of joy through her veins. "Mandy, I choose love because my heart can hold nothing else when I am with you. Oh, don't get me wrong. I'm not saying I'll never get angry."

"Of course not," she murmured. "I get angry, too. You may have noticed."

He smiled and continued. "Or that I won't chafe at the injustice of my parents' murder."

"Nor should you." She struggled to concentrate on what he said. She watched his lips move and wished he would say where she fit into all this.

"Mandy Hamilton, I love you. I want to spend the rest of my days seeing your smile, laughing at your tricks, growing and learning and being a family with you." His smile reached deep into his eyes and even deeper into her heart.

"Glad you finally found some sense." She took a deep breath. "Trace Owens, I love you. I want to spend my days with you, too. I want to be with you through your bad times and your good. I want you to hold my hand when I go through bad times and share my joy when I go through good."

"Mandy, will you marry me?"

"Just name the day."

He didn't. Instead, he cradled her face in his palms and bent to kiss her, a kiss full of promises for sweet tomorrows.

They leaned against the cabin wall, arms wrapped around each other, and talked about the ways God had taught them to trust His promises. And still later, as the sun began to set and they'd discussed plans with Cora, a visitor approached the yard.

Austin stood before Trace. "I won't leave until you hear what I have to say."

Trace nodded, his eyes wary, and invited Austin to sit on the log bench. His posture remained stiff, but he held his tongue and let Austin explain all that happened.

"I'm truly sorry. I never meant any of this to happen. Will you forgive me?"

Mandy held her breath. All her thoughts and prayers, all of Trace's agonizing, had come to this moment.

Trace paused, his throat working, and gave a curt nod. A decisive nod. "I forgive you."

They shook hands; then Austin gripped Trace's shoulder. "Thank you."

"I only regret those responsible weren't brought to justice."

"Perhaps they were." Austin shrugged. "The three leaders were shot in an ambush a few months after you left. The rest of the gang dispersed.

I'm sure many of them went South to sign up somewhere. But I'm equally certain many of them disappeared, sick of the life they'd lived."

Trace sucked in air. He pressed his hands to his thighs.

Mandy watched him closely. Would he see this as justice or travesty?

His hands relaxed. His shoulders lowered. "It's relief to know they won't kill anyone else and will meet judgment at God's hands."

Mandy gritted her teeth to stifle her whoop of joy. Grinning, she went to Trace's side.

He pulled her close. "It's time to start over. I've found someone to move on with."

Epilogue

M andy looked at herself in the mirror and tugged at the neckline of
her dress, squirmed inside the sleeves, and stuck a loose hairpin
back into place. "I can't imagine what Trace is going to say."

"Probably about the same thing Levi is going to say when he sees me."

Joanna looked from one to the other. "You are both radiant brides.
They'll pinch themselves to see if this is real and wonder how two cowboys like themselves ended up with the prettiest girls anywhere around."

Mandy took one more look at herself then stood tall. "He's never
seen me in a dress."

Joanna chuckled. "The surprise will do him good." She hugged
Mandy, careful not to muss her hair. "You're beautiful." She hugged
Glory and repeated the words. "Your dress looks good on you, too."

Cora peeked out the door at the crowd waiting outside of the
now-completed mission. "Looks like they're ready. Trace and Levi look so
handsome in their black jackets. I can't believe Levi decided against wearing
his vest. I hardly recognize him." She laughed. "They look a little nervous."

She pulled the door shut and faced the Hamilton women. "I'm nervous, too. But Austin assures me my scars are hardly visible."

It was the first time Cora would go out in public without some kind
of bonnet to hide her face.

Mandy hugged the girl who was about to be her sister-in-law. "He's
right, you know. When you smile, no one sees anything but your beauty."

Cora smiled then, proving Mandy's point.

"I expect my business will pick up significantly when people hear I
have a pretty, young assistant," Joanna said, smiling at her new helper,
Cora. "It's time to go."

Cora kissed Mandy's cheek then marched toward her brother.

Mandy held Joanna's elbow on one side, Glory on the other, and they
followed. Joanna released Mandy to Trace, then Glory to Levi. Mandy
knew this was the plan, but all she saw was Trace. . .his blue eyes shining
with love and joy.

Joanna and the Footloose Cowboy

Chapter 1

Bonners Ferry, Idaho
Fall, 1865

S ome thieving scoundrel had picked the wrong day to mess with her. She'd find the guilty party, and when she did—

Well, he'd discover the harsh side of Joanna Hamilton—the twenty-three-year-old woman who baked those pies.

She flung out the kitchen door of Bonners Ferry Stopping House and dashed around the corner to where Cora sat on a stool preparing vegetables for the meal. "Did you see anyone hanging around here? One of my pies is missing. I need them all."

"Joanna, I never thought to see you so worked up about a meal. You serve them every day of the week."

She paused a moment but only to look around, hoping to catch a glimpse of the thief. "I want to make a good impression."

"I'm sure you will." Cora shifted her attention to the hill across the road from the stopping house. "Now that you mention it, I noticed a young boy skulking about. Didn't pay him much mind. I thought he was playing some game. You know, like cowboys and Indians."

"Where did he go?" She didn't like to think of a child stealing, but someone had, and she meant to confront whoever it was. Maybe in time to rescue her pie.

"Scampered up the hill and disappeared into the trees."

Joanna dashed across the road, grateful her progress wasn't impeded by long skirts and frilly petticoats. The split riding skirt she regularly wore allowed her fast-moving feet to keep up with the rolling frustration in her stomach. She hadn't worked all day creating three kinds of pie only to have someone help himself to one.

She climbed the hill and followed a narrow trail into the trees. Not two feet off the path, in a spot cushioned with yellowed and brown leaves, sat a boy of about ten. A mat of black hair tangled around his bent head, his complete concentration on fingering out scoops of apple pie. So intent was he on the food, he didn't notice her. So much for rescuing the pie. Why was this child allowed to roam freely and get into mischief? Seems someone should be supervising his activities. But he had a neglected air about him. . .his soiled trousers torn at the hems, his shirt askew. Seems not only the child needed a scolding.

Joanna sidled up to him. "Looks like good pie," she murmured, keeping her annoyance firmly corralled.

He jumped like a startled rabbit and jerked around to stare at her. Blue eyes. Irish eyes that widened to the size of saucers.

"Good pie?" She kept her voice beguilingly soft.

He nodded.

"Where did you get it?"

Mute.

"Any chance you got it at the stopping house down there?" She nodded over her shoulder.

Still mute.

"I'll assume that's *yes.* Don't suppose you paid for it?"

He scrambled to his feet, his gaze darting toward freedom, but she wasn't about to let him escape.

She caught his arm. "That's my pie. I made it for the men who are going to eat supper at the stopping house. I think we need to talk to your ma and pa about this."

The boy gave her a look fit to cure leather, then his eyes narrowed, and his lips trembled. "My ma's dead." He hung his head in sorrow.

"I'm sorry to hear that." Not that his little act convinced her of any real sorrow. She knew when she was being conned. "Then we'll talk to your pa."

"If you can find him."

She blinked before the change in expression that turned the boy from innocent sadness to full-fledged, flat-out, get-out-of-my-way anger. Her own gut did a similar shift. Her circumstances hadn't been much different growing up. In fact, they weren't a lot different right now. Ma had died when she was fourteen, leaving her in charge of her two younger sisters. And Pa? Well, they'd tried to keep up with him, but he didn't make it easy.

However, that didn't excuse stealing. She would have never tolerated it from her sisters. "Who are you with, then?"

"My uncle."

If she wasn't mistaken, his anger grew hotter.

"Then let's go see your uncle."

The boy didn't budge. "He don't care what I do. He can't wait for my pa to turn up so he can be shed of me."

Her insides twisted. Too often she and her sisters had felt the same way when Pa abandoned them to the unwilling care of others.

Perhaps the boy guessed his words had touched a chord in her. "He never stays in one place longer than he has to. Footloose and fancy-free he calls it."

"Does he now?" She had other words for it. Irresponsible. Neglectful. But it didn't matter to her how this uncle lived his life so long as he looked after the boy properly until he was "shed of him." She crossed her arms. "I think I'd like to speak to your uncle." She urged the boy to the trail and headed away from the fledgling town, assuming said uncle could be found in that direction. She had a few things to say to the man.

The boy dragged his feet every inch. Then he drew to a halt and tipped his head to the left. Joanna looked the direction he indicated and saw a man busy tending to a pile of belongings. No doubt the footloose, fancy-free uncle. From where she stood, silently staring, he appeared to be a big man. He looked clean and tidy. For some reason, that surprised her. He turned to pick up an object, revealing a strong, clean-shaven jaw. A rugged face. She guessed him to be a hard man who would not welcome her demands.

She pushed her shoulders back. She would never let a man make her feel timid. Nor would she admit she suddenly felt small and vulnerable.

Her head said, *Say something.* Her feet refused to budge. Instead, she continued to watch, noting the smooth way he moved. An economy of motion that in a man his size looked graceful. Not that it mattered one way or the other if he was as clumsy as an ox.

Her disadvantage, she informed herself, was she didn't even know his name or the name of the boy at her side. She could easily remedy the last. "What's your name?" she whispered to him.

"Freddy Canfield." A barely discernible mumble.

She chose to ignore the sullen tone in the boy's voice. If she were in charge of this young one, she would insist he say his name proudly and clearly. "Well, Freddy Canfield, I take it that is your uncle."

He nodded, and the look he shot at the unsuspecting man was hot enough to fry bacon. She could almost feel sorry for the uncle.

Freddy still clutched the pie pan with the half-eaten pie.

He'd stolen the pie, Joanna reminded herself. Justice must be served. The boy had to be held responsible.

She pushed forward, half dragging the youngster.

The man heard their approach and straightened to regard them. His gaze widened at Joanna and narrowed significantly at the sight of her hand clutching Freddy's arm. If she wasn't mistaken, he sighed like someone had dropped a huge load on his shoulders.

"Sir, I believe this is your nephew."

"He is."

She guessed he tried mightily to disguise his weariness and almost succeeded. Running the stopping house had given her wagonloads of experience in assessing men in every shape and size and temperament. This one was broad shouldered, well built. She guessed him to be in his thirties. Black hair like his nephew, but brown eyes full of discouragement or wariness. Probably both. His responsibilities seemed to weigh heavily on his shoulders at the moment. Why was he in charge of his nephew? What had occurred to put them at such odds? With a little shake, she brought herself back to the task at hand. "I regret to say he stole a pie from me."

They both looked at the evidence.

"Freddy, is that true?"

Joanna snorted. "What further proof do you need?"

"Don't need proof," he murmured. "Need for the boy to fess up."

Freddy pulled the pie close to his chest. "I done stole it, and I ain't sorry. You want the truth. Well, here it is. I'm sick of your cooking. It's like eating wood bark at the best, and at the worst it's like cow—" He shut his mouth, lips pressed together. He seemed to think better of describing the worst. He turned big, innocent eyes to Joanna. "It's been a long time since I tasted anything half as good as this pie."

Joanna stifled a laugh at his description of his uncle's food and for a moment was almost charmed by the boy's flattery. But not quite. She glimpsed the anger barely hidden in the depths of his gaze. "I feed people every day. It's how I make my living. Having someone steal my food eats into my profits."

The man dug into his pocket and pulled out a handful of coins. "This cover your costs, Miss. . .or is it *Missus*?"

"I'm not married." She considered the money in his palm but hesitated to take it. Her conscience nagged at her. She'd been abrupt—downright unfriendly, in fact. "I'm sorry. I've forgotten my manners. I'm Joanna Hamilton. I own and operate the Bonners Ferry Stopping House." For some unfathomable reason she smoothed her hair back from her face knowing much of it had escaped the leather tie she used to keep it tidy.

"Pleased to meet you, ma'am. Name's Rudy Canfield."

The man had a pleasantly deep voice with a slight drawl. "I've brought this young fella here," he continued, "to turn him over to his father."

The air crackled with tension.

Joanna guessed Mr. Canfield had encountered a few challenges in getting the boy this far. Perhaps a stolen pie was not the worst of them. "Nevertheless. . ." Maybe he didn't need a lecture on how he should take care of the boy. She plucked three coins from his palm. "Thank you. By the way, I serve supper promptly at six. You're more than welcome to sit in." She named the sum for a meal then turned to study the small boy. "Enjoy your pie, Freddy. But I'll abide no more stealing. Hear?"

Freddy's expression seesawed between anger and a desire to convince her of his innocence.

She wouldn't be swayed by any big, blue-eyed gaze nor a slight twinge of sympathy for a confused little boy or a weary uncle. "No stealing. Good-bye, Mr. Canfield." She headed toward town. Her insides were tangled, and she didn't understand why. Ten steps later she ground to a halt, turned around sharply, and returned to the campsite.

Freddy gobbled down the rest of the pie as if afraid she'd come to claim the remains.

Rudy leaned back on his heels, his fingers tucked into the front pockets of his trousers. His casual appearance did not fool her. He tensed, ready to face whatever challenge she meant to hand his way.

"I'm not satisfied with being paid. Seems to me the one who committed the crime should pay the penalty." She held the coins out to Rudy, but he didn't lift his hand to receive them. "Freddy is the culprit. He should pay."

"You want I should horsewhip him?"

She gasped. She shot a look toward Freddy and saw alarm and fear in his eyes. "Is that how you discipline him?"

"Haven't so far, but I'm wondering what you have in mind."

For the space of several silent seconds she didn't respond as she tried to assess the quivering tension between the two. Freddy's eyes wide and watchful. An almost identical expression on Rudy's face.

"I ain't got no money," Freddy said.

Joanna ignored his grammar. "Then best you work off your debt."

Both looked wary.

She sighed. "Like I say, I run the stopping house. There's always chores. Sometimes more than I can keep up with. With your uncle's approval, you can work for me and pay for the pie that way." Again, she held the coins toward Rudy. Finally, after what seemed a very long wait, he pulled his hand from his pocket and let her drop the coins into his palm. "Shall I expect Freddy in about an hour?" That would give her a chance to organize the rest of the meal so she could supervise the boy.

"He'll be there."

"Fine." Not until she was almost back to the stopping house did she realize she'd taken on one more task when she was doing her level best to get out of the work of running the place. If she wanted to make a decent impression, she'd better hustle. She broke into a run.

∞

Across the remnants of their campfire, Rudy studied the boy as he sat on a fallen tree, picking out the last of the stolen pie. Tension in the air marred the pleasantness of the little clearing that was surrounded by trees dressed in yellow leaves. It was plain to see he was Joe's son. The same blue eyes. The same thatch of black hair. Even down to the poor attitude, as if life owed him only kindness and he'd accept nothing less. Too bad life didn't seem to be so inclined most of the time, giving Freddy—like his father—plenty of opportunity to express his displeasure.

He'd had only a passing acquaintance with Freddy until recently, having seen him when Rudy visited his mother, and Freddy's grandmother, twice a year come rain or shine. But he hadn't expected to be stuck with him day in and day out. How had Ma handled this continual resentment? Of course, Freddy might have been happy to be in Ma's care. But Ma was gone. And Freddy had no one but his pa to be bothered with him.

Freddy made no secret of the fact he didn't care an ounce for being in Rudy's care. And to prove it, he got into mischief at every opportunity.

"You know better than to steal. Grandma would turn over in her grave."

Freddy pulled his lips in, practically sucking them out of sight. For one happy moment, Rudy thought the boy would drop his attitude. But then Freddy scowled fit to bring on a thunderstorm. Even mention of the woman who had been largely responsible for raising Freddy brought no softening. Freddy dared the world, and everyone in it, to expect any degree of cooperation from him.

If Rudy expected a turnabout, he could dream in vain.

Although he was thirty-two years old, he'd never had much to do with kids, even this one who had lived with Rudy's ma since Joe's wife, Betty, died.

His heart fisted within him. Betty, who was supposed to have been Rudy's wife. He closed his mind to those memories. A man couldn't ride far glancing over his shoulder to what might have been.

Rudy glared at Freddy. "Miss Joanna could have had you arrested." For a few minutes he'd wondered if she'd had it in mind. He took her for a woman with very high expectations of those around her. No doubt she took him for a neglectful uncle when the truth was he'd done everything in his power—except hog-tie the kid—to keep him out of mischief. Who would have guessed a youngster could get into so much trouble in so little time?

"They don't put ten-year-olds in jail."

"You sure?"

"Well, do they?"

Rudy shrugged. "Beats me. I've gone out of my way to avoid gaining any firsthand knowledge of jails. That's not the point, though."

"I ain't sorry."

Rudy sighed. This was going nowhere. "Let's go see if your father turned up."

Freddy didn't show any sign of moving. Instead, he licked the pie plate as clean as any scrubbing would render it.

"Freddy?"

The boy ignored him.

Rudy strode over to stand over him. "Let's go. Your father should have come by now."

"He never shows up."

A hot feeling raced up Rudy's spine. Yeah, Joe was about ninety-nine percent unreliable, but this time he had no choice. His son didn't have a home. It was time for Joe to cowboy up to his responsibilities instead of shifting them to someone else's lap. "He'll be here." Or Rudy would find him and drag him here.

Freddy shrugged. "No never mind to me if he comes or not."

"Yeah? Well, it matters to me. He's your father, and he'll jolly well look after you." He nudged the boy's boot with his own. "Let's go find him."

With about as much enthusiasm as he'd expect from a rock, Freddy managed to get his feet beneath him. "You really going to make me work for that woman?"

"Miss Joanna? Doesn't seem to me it would be much of a hardship. She appeared kind enough." At least she'd kept her anger simmering beneath the surface. He grinned. She looked like she might have enjoyed nailing Rudy's hide to the nearest tree.

"Did you think she was pretty?"

"Didn't notice." Much. She had shiny brown hair tied at her neck. It rippled when she walked. Soft brown eyes that brought to mind a mother's kiss when her gaze rested on Freddy. But when she looked at Rudy, the feeling was more like a mother's sharp disfavor.

It wouldn't hurt Freddy a bit to have a woman try and straighten him out.

"How come you didn't notice? You blind?"

He chuckled. "She looked like the sort of person you could depend on."

Freddy bounced ahead of Rudy to stare at him. "You can't tell that by looking at someone."

"No, I guess you can't."

Freddy resumed sauntering at Rudy's side. "She makes awfully good pies."

"Wasn't kind of you to say my cooking tasted like wood."

"You're always saying I gotta tell the truth."

"You picked a fine time to remember." They reached the edge of the town—if one could call it that. The ferry crossed the Kootenai River with only one horse and rider aboard. It was usually full going the other direction as men headed for the gold fields to the north. He pulled up to watch, hoping the lone occupant might be Joe. But before the ferry docked, he knew it wasn't. The man was far too big.

"Let's go." He led his nephew down the rutted street toward the businesses.

Half an hour later they'd asked everyone they met if they knew of a man called Joe Canfield. No one did.

"I told ya. He ain't coming."

"He's coming. It's time for you to go to the stopping house."

"This time you better take a good look at Miss Joanna. I think she's pretty."

"Kid. You're ten years old. What do you know about such things?"

Freddy snorted. "I got eyes."

Trouble was, so did Rudy. And they worked perfectly fine.

Joanna stepped out of the stopping house, saw them approaching, and smiled. The woman had a smile that made his heart act all funny, like a fresh-broke horse facing the open road. Or the sensation he got when he got bucked off a stallion. The airless exhilaration of soaring.

Until he hit the ground.

Same lesson he'd learned concerning women. One day you were riding high, thinking everything was fine and dandy. The next you were nursing hurt pride and a whole lot more things that he couldn't explain. Which was why he'd gone out of his way to avoid having anything to do with the fairer sex for the past eleven years.

He wasn't about to change now.

Joanna called a greeting. "Glad to see you made it."

Freddy mumbled something about Rudy making him come, which was so untrue Rudy poked him in the back.

Rudy tipped his head toward Miss Joanna. "I'll wait for him while he does whatever you have for him."

He chose an old stump about ten feet from the door where he had a good view of the ferry coming and going and could see most of the yard surrounding the stopping house. Without turning his head much, he had a pretty good glimpse into the roomy kitchen where Joanna led young Freddy, her hand gentle on his shoulder. The delicious aromas coming from inside turned Rudy's annoyance into hunger.

Freddy glanced back and gave Rudy a self-satisfied smirk. He seemed to think he got a nice deal with being "forced" to work with Joanna.

Rudy grinned. He couldn't argue with the boy on that score.

Chapter 2

Joanna showed Freddy the ash bucket then returned to the door to indicate where to dump it. She felt Rudy's hot gaze practically stinging her cheeks and glanced toward him. His expression was inscrutable, but his eyes impaled her.

She opened her mouth then closed it again. What was there to say? They'd already done the *hello, how are you* bit. And she'd decided against commenting on his responsibility to his young nephew until she learned more about the situation.

He tipped his head in silent greeting. She did likewise and spoke again to Freddy. "After you dump the ashes, bring in wood from the stack. I want the wood box beside the stove full."

"Then what?"

"You can sweep the veranda." She pointed to the broom. "And haul away the vegetable peelings. Come, I'll introduce you to Cora, who also helps me."

Cora was busy preparing the washbasins and hanging towels. She had already filled a washtub with water from the well and set it on the stove. Just before supper she would fill the jugs with hot water so the guests could wash up.

"Cora, this is Freddy, who has come to do some chores." She'd already explained the situation to Cora, who laughed at the idea of Joanna challenging Rudy to deal responsibly with the boy.

Cora turned. One cheek had been burned in a fire, but the scars were now almost invisible.

"Mr. Canfield." Rudy sat close enough that Joanna didn't need to raise her voice. Close enough she felt his watchful interest. "Cora Owens."

Rudy pushed to his feet and lifted his hat. "Ma'am. Pleased to meet you."

Cora swallowed hard. "Likewise."

Freddy saw the black-and-white cat sunning on the edge of the wooden floor and moved away to pet it.

Cora leaned close to Joanna's ear. "You forgot to mention he was as handsome as. . .as. . . Well, he's as good-looking as my brother."

Joanna chuckled. "No one can be better than your brother, can they?"

"Not in my eyes."

"I did, however, mention that he's footloose and fancy-free. The sort of guy to march into your world and pass on through so fast you don't have time to catch your breath."

Joanna returned indoors to check on the meal preparation. The venison roasting in the oven filled the room with a tantalizing aroma. The stove belched out heat that would soon be welcome, as the fall nights tended to get chilly. All the more reason to be gone before winter and its bitter cold.

Cora followed her. "You're taking a lying kid's word on this footloose, fancy-free stuff. Seems to me most men gladly settle down once they find a woman who makes them want to."

"Sure didn't keep my pa from wandering freely."

"Not every man should be branded with the same flaws your pa has."

"I expect that's true." She didn't bother pointing out the truth often came out after the *I dos* when it was too late. Caution seemed the wiser route.

Freddy scurried in, grabbed the ash bucket, and hurried back out.

"Joanna, I sure hate to see you leave this place. Where will I go?"

She hugged the young woman. "I think Austin will take care of that."

Cora blushed clear to her hairline. "He hasn't said anything."

"Give him time."

Freddy rushed in and out again, bringing wood. Cora went to the doorway and watched Rudy for a moment. She looked like she wanted to say something more about the man then shrugged and returned to her tasks.

Joanna, thankful to have the subject abandoned, checked the potatoes. Everything would be done on time and be perfect.

She glanced out the window. Rudy was perched on the stump, and Freddy passed him with an armload of wood. A piece fell to the ground, and Rudy sprang up to retrieve it. He balanced it carefully in Freddy's arms. She couldn't hear what they said but could certainly read their expressions—Freddy's hard and defiant, Rudy's resigned. Perhaps even sorrowful.

Joanna's stomach tightened, and she drew back. Rudy looked as if Freddy's words wounded him. If such was the case, she ached for him.

He smoothed away any expression and returned to the stump, staring into the distance. Obviously hankering to leave this place and resume his wandering.

Perhaps with good reason, if Freddy hurt him over and over.

Before she could think better of it, she poured two cups of coffee and headed outside. He sprang to his feet at her approach.

"I was about to take a break. You care for coffee?"

"Thanks. Don't mind if I do." He took the mug and indicated the stump he'd vacated.

She hesitated. "Don't mean to take your chair."

"I don't mind standing."

But he looked awkward. And she felt uncomfortable. She nodded toward the laundry area. "Grab the little stool by the washstand." He trotted over to get it and plunked down, seemingly intent on studying the coffee steam. "I suppose you spend most of your time on the back of your horse."

He laughed like she'd said the most amusing thing.

She liked the sound of his chuckle and the way deep gouges creased his cheeks. She caught and held his gaze, secretly pleased to have brought this sudden change to his demeanor.

His laughter died, his amusement settling into a grin that maintained the dimples in each cheek.

To her surprise, she realized Cora was right. The man was incredibly handsome. But more than that, he seemed so solid. She mentally shook herself. His size gave that impression. Certainly not anything else.

"I like being on a horse, but I don't live there. I have to get off once in a while to cook some tasteless food."

She laughed, remembering Freddy's insult. Her laughter felt as if it came from deep in her belly. "I'm sure it isn't as bad as Freddy makes out."

"Don't be too certain."

They grinned at each other, their gazes locked together, steady and strong. Joanna decided her foolishness must have something to do with the fact that both her younger sisters had recently married good men and were living their happy ever after. Happy as she was for them, she sometimes, secretly, in the dead of night, wondered if she would end up alone for the rest of her life.

Dismissing such nonsense, she managed to shift her attention to something beyond Rudy's shoulder. "Freddy says you're taking him to his father."

"My brother, Joe. He was supposed to meet us here. He's already two days late."

"I hope you don't mind me asking, but why hasn't he been with his father?" She rushed on before he could answer. "He told me his mother is dead. It just seems. . ." Why did she think everyone else should have what she and her sisters had not? A father who gave them a home.

"My mother has been caring for him, but she passed on recently—"

She touched the back of his hand. "I'm sorry for your loss." She'd only meant to offer condolences as she would to anyone, but her fingers tingled. With a great deal more calm than she felt, she pulled her hand back and clutched her coffee cup.

"Thanks. Joe is all the family Freddy has left, so I sent a letter to him in the gold fields, and he replied that he'd meet us here."

"He's not the only family Freddy has left."

Rudy looked surprised.

"He has you."

He snorted. "Not something he appreciates, I can tell you."

"Why not?" Far as she could tell, he was a nice enough man.

Rudy studied her as if hoping to find the answer to the question in her eyes. Finally, he blinked. "You know, I really can't say. But we're stuck with each other until Joe remembers he's supposed to be here to take his son."

His use of the word *stuck* scratched along her insides. It sounded most unwelcome. No wonder the boy was certain his uncle didn't want him around. She opened her mouth to tell him so but closed it again without speaking. It was none of her concern. They'd be moving on like everyone else in her life. Freddy would soon be with his father, and Rudy would resume his footloose, fancy-free ways.

"Tell me about yourself," Rudy said. "How did you come to be owner and operator of the stopping house?"

Glad to be pulled from her interest in Freddy and his uncle, she smiled, her heart mellow with memories. "My pa has a habit of following the next adventure on the horizon. Myself and my sisters—there are two of them, both younger than me—tried to keep up with him. We were following him to the Kootenais when we saw the opportunity to buy this place and run it. We decided we were grown up enough we didn't need to find our pa to have a home. We could make one here."

"Where are your sisters now?"

"Glory married the preacher man. They have a mission and church up the hill." She pointed to the right. "Mandy married Cora's brother, and they've built a fine log house that direction." She nodded to the left.

"So now you're on your own here."

"Not for long. I'm selling. An interested party is visiting this evening. In fact, I better go tend to the meal preparations. I want everything perfect for his visit." She hurried back to the kitchen.

A little later she wiped her brow with a corner of her apron. "That's about it," she said to herself. Would she ever get used to the empty room? Not that her sisters had hung around all day long, but with them married and living in their own homes, the place seemed vacant. She laughed. She was being sentimental. She was hardly alone. Running a stopping house meant visitors every day. And Cora lived with her.

It wasn't the same, but soon she would be able to pursue her own interests as well.

She pulled the letter from her apron pocket and read it again, even though she knew it by heart. From her friend Sarah, who lived in Sand Point to the south.

California will be perfect. Can you imagine endless sunshine instead of snow and cold? My aunt says we're welcome anytime, so as soon as you sell your stopping house we will be on our way. I can hardly wait.

She folded the pages and put the letter back in her pocket. How long would it take for the man to make up his mind?

☙

From where Rudy sat on the stump, he watched Joanna set the table. She stepped back to assess the arrangement then adjusted the plates and forks. He could see her shoulders heave with a sigh. Seemed this sale was awfully important.

Freddy finished his chores and went to pet the cat, but the cat wandered away. Freddy joined Rudy. "We leaving now?"

"Think we'll eat supper here." The aroma of roasting meat, cinnamon and apple, and a dozen other succulent smells convinced him his food really was as uninviting as Freddy said. Besides, he wanted to see the man who intended to buy Joanna's business. Assess for himself if the prospective buyer was trustworthy. Though why it mattered to him, he was at a loss to say.

"Good. Can you smell the food?"

"I certainly can." His mouth had watered for the past half hour.

Freddy opened his mouth, but Rudy held up his hand. "You don't need to say it. I know I never cooked anything that smelled half so good, though I thought the rabbit I roasted on a spit wasn't too bad."

Freddy made some picturesque gagging sounds.

The ferry crossed to this side again, this time with several men aboard. Rudy straightened and watched them disembark. Freddy stood straight, tension vibrating from him. Rudy ached to drop a hand to the boy's shoulder to steady him but knew from experience it would trigger an angry response. He settled for remaining close, hoping his nearness would communicate that he cared.

The men trooped up the hill toward the stopping house, waiting for the signal to enter. Others drifted down from town. Joanna would have a full house tonight. For a moment he considered changing his mind but couldn't bring himself to do so. And it wasn't solely for Freddy's sake he wanted to stay.

Which of these gathered men wanted to buy the place?

A man wearing a bowler hat stared at Freddy. Rudy shifted to block his view. The stranger jerked his hat off. "Sorry. Didn't mean to be rude. But I'm wondering if you're Rudy Canfield?"

"I am." He moved closer, purposely keeping himself between this man and Freddy. "Who are you, and why do you want to know?"

Joanna stepped to the door at that point and rang the cowbell suspended near the door. "The meal is ready. Come in."

Rudy didn't move as he waited for the man to answer the question.

But the man joined the march toward the door.

Rudy caught his shoulder. "What's your business with me?"

The stranger studied him a moment then let his attention drop to Freddy. "It can wait until after the meal."

Freddy considered the pair. "You ain't gonna change your mind and make me eat rabbit again, are ya?"

Rudy laughed. "No rabbit tonight." He fixed a hard-eyed look at the man. "We'll talk later."

"Indeed we shall."

Rudy dropped the necessary coins into the tin can Joanna held out and favored her with a smile. His heart slammed against his backbone when she smiled back, as if greeting an old friend.

It was a long time since he'd felt welcome anywhere. Even his mother preferred he not spend too much time at her home. Said it stirred up old memories best forgotten. Seems everyone wanted to forget what had happened. None half as much as he did. And Ma was right. Seeing Freddy, knowing the boy should have been his, filled him with anger and regret and so many other things he didn't know how to describe them.

Seems it was a good thing Joanna was moving on, or Rudy might be tempted to plant himself right here in Bonners Ferry and stay just for the privilege of seeing such a smile on a regular basis.

Freddy pushed toward a place on one of the benches surrounding the big table. Right on the end. They crowded in with the others. Rudy glanced around, trying to guess which of these men was the intended buyer. He saw several possibilities but couldn't say for sure.

Joanna took the place at the end of the table just inches away from him.

Freddy fairly gloated, but Rudy couldn't tell if it was for his own sake or Rudy's. Nor did it matter. Yet he felt just a little pleased to be sitting at her right.

Joanna welcomed everyone then stood. "We always say grace before the meal. Would you kindly bow your heads?"

No one demurred.

Rudy least of all. There had been a time in his life when he thought he'd be sitting at the head of his own table saying the same words. Hearing them from Joanna's mouth reminded him gently and sweetly of those dreams.

For the moment, he wouldn't allow them to be marred by how they had been destroyed. How Joe had stolen Betty from him, gotten her with child—Freddy—married her, then left her pretty much to manage on her own.

But the pain of it failed to touch him as he listened to Joanna's words of thanks.

Chapter 3

M r. Tisdale had introduced himself as he entered the dining room. Joanna did a quick assessment. A little older than she'd expected. Probably in his late thirties, early forties. Somewhat effeminate looking with banker's hands and the pale complexion of a man who spent most of his day indoors. But he'd glanced around eagerly enough, and she prayed he liked what he saw.

Nervous tremors owned her hands as she supervised the passing of the food from hand to hand. Twice she caught Rudy watching her. She wondered if he guessed at her state of mind.

"This is excellent," Rudy murmured. "Very impressive."

He meant to encourage her, and her nerves calmed.

The meat and potatoes and vegetables vanished within minutes, as did the three loaves of bread she'd sliced. Then she brought out the pies. There would not be seconds for everyone tonight, thanks to Freddy, but she compensated by slicing generous pieces. She was certain the meal left nothing to be desired. Even the coffee and tea seemed especially flavorful tonight.

She announced the room would be made ready for sleeping in an hour of two. In the meantime, the men were welcome to warm themselves at a fire in the backyard. No one lingered once they were done. Many left without so much as a word of thanks. But not Rudy.

"Much appreciated," he said. "Freddy will help with the evening chores."

"That's not—" She saw his warning glance and stopped her protest. "I'm grateful. Freddy, why don't you see what Cora needs?"

He scampered away.

Rudy waited until he was out of hearing. "He needs something to do besides sit here and wonder why his pa hasn't come."

"Glad to help out."

Mr. Tisdale had left with the others. He stood in the yard talking to a group of men.

Rudy saw her studying Mr. Tisdale and nodded to her. "I'm sure he was suitable impressed. You did a fine job." He patted her shoulder.

She took undue comfort in his assurances. There was nothing more she could do but wait for the man's decision.

She turned to join Cora in the kitchen and help with cleanup, but she paused when a man came to the door. She'd noticed him at the table. A little nervous, but nothing else about him seemed noteworthy.

"Excuse me, miss. I hope you don't mind me stepping inside for a moment. I must talk with Mr. Canfield."

"By all means." She edged away, leaving the men to conduct their business in private. But she didn't have to strain to catch what was said.

"Mr. Canfield, I have the regretful duty of informing you your brother, Joe, is dead."

"What?"

"I'm sorry. There was an accident at the mine. He was crushed."

"Crushed?"

"'Fraid so. We buried him at the town site."

"What am I supposed to do with a kid? He'll just get in the way."

Freddy returned with Cora at his side. His face blanched bone white. The wood he carried fell to the floor.

Joanna sprang forward, calling, "Rudy, come quick."

Rudy was at her side before she reached Freddy.

"He heard," she explained. Thinking the boy needed comfort, she reached for him as did Rudy.

But Freddy pushed them both away. "Leave me alone. I don't need nobody." Joanna drew back, startled by the anger in his face. Rudy's expression showed the same confusion.

Then Freddy turned and fled outside.

Joanna faced Rudy. "I'm sorry." He'd lost his mother recently, and now his brother. Plus he had a hurting ten-year-old to think about.

"What am I going to do? I can't take care of him."

Her sympathy fled like yesterday's sun. "A man has to own up to his responsibilities."

"He's not my kid."

"He is now. And you better do what's right for him. I've had it with men who think they have no obligation to the children in their care."

He studied her with narrowed eyes. "Are we talking about me here?

Or you and your pa?"

She ignored his gibe. "Freddy is a child who needs a home. He deserves someone to care enough for him to provide one."

"Don't we all?"

She had no idea what he meant, but it didn't matter. "You're all that boy has."

"Lady, I'm a cowboy."

"Footloose and fancy-free. I know. Freddy told me."

He scrubbed at his chin. The rasping sound irritated her.

"I can't take him with me while I chase after cows."

"No? Then you better find something else to do, hadn't you?" How many times had she heard excuses from her father, seen the pain in her sisters' faces, and had to push away her own disappointment and resentment in order to comfort them?

He glowered at her. "Like what?" He waved his hand around. "Run this place?"

She snorted. "From what Freddy says of your cooking, you'd run it into the ground." This was getting them nowhere. "You need to figure out something and real soon."

"Yeah. Sure. I'll get right to it."

"First thing you need to do is find Freddy."

"No doubt you got every step of your life figured out, but don't think you can plan mine." He stomped from the room.

No, she didn't have life figured out for her or anyone else. But she intended to make the best of things as she always had. She turned from watching Rudy disappear into the night and hurried to the door. She must talk to Mr. Tisdale. But he wasn't there. She checked the group of men circling the fire. He wasn't among them either. Disappointed, she returned inside and helped Cora wash dishes.

"Where do you suppose Freddy went?" Cora asked, peering into the dusk beyond the window.

"He could disappear completely in the woods if he wanted to."

Cora gasped. "That would be awful. It's cold at nights. He'd be so scared."

"Don't fret. I'm sure his uncle will find him."

"Someone ought to tell him the boy needs some affection."

Joanna laughed, half regret, even less amusement. "They are at odds with each other."

"That's strange."

"I expect there's more going on than we know."

"I don't care. He's only a boy. And now an orphan." Her chin quivered. "If I didn't have a brother to take care of me when my parents died, I don't know what I would have done." Cora touched her cheek unconsciously. The fire that killed her parents had been the cause of her burns. "And I was sixteen. Freddy is only ten."

"I'm sure Mr. Canfield will find him." Only it was already getting dark. "For all we know he has by now, and they've gone back to his camp."

"Sounds cold to me."

Joanna agreed. Plus there was something wrong between the two. They'd have to work it out, seeing as they were destined to be together now.

Unless the man rode away from his responsibilities.

As Pa had a habit of doing. Her insides twisted with the thought.

She must make certain Rudy didn't think he could do the same.

"Rider coming," Cora announced.

Joanna sprang to the window, hoping, praying it was Rudy with Freddy in tow. "It's Glory. Come to see what happened with the sale."

At that moment Mandy clattered in the door. "Well?"

"Wait for Glory and I'll tell you, though there's nothing to tell." Glory burst in and joined her sisters. Joanna really had nothing to report. Mr. Tisdale had not said one way or the other what he thought. Nevertheless, her sisters wanted to hear every detail. She tried to focus on her report, but her mind followed a little boy and his uncle.

Glory eyed her closely. "Something's bothering you. Are you having second thoughts about selling?"

Joanna didn't miss the look Glory and Mandy shared. "Are you two anxious to get rid of me?"

Mandy looked stricken. "Of course not. We don't want you to leave. But it's time you did something for yourself for a change instead of taking care of us."

"Or this stopping house," Glory added.

"I haven't changed my mind, but I don't like hearing you two talk as if I was forced to take care of you. I didn't mind." It clawed at her throat to think they might believe otherwise.

"Of course you didn't," Glory said. "And we were so well behaved. Never once gave you a moment's worry."

Mandy hooted. "Guess we're not counting all the reckless things you did like riding through town like a wild man. Or swinging from the rafters of Mr. McCurdy's barn. Or—"

Glory placed a playful punch on Mandy's shoulder. "What about you? Disappearing for hours and hours into the woods while Joanna fretted that you'd gotten lost or eaten by a wild animal."

"Girls, you were only finding a way to deal with your hurt that Pa left us." She knew that explained Freddy's misbehavior. He felt unwanted.

But what about Rudy? Was it hurt or the search for adventure that drove him? Or both?

She couldn't understand him any more than she'd ever been able to understand Pa. Yes, she comprehended wanting to do something new and different. Like visiting California. She sympathized with Pa, who never got over his sorrow of losing Ma. But shouldn't an adult look past his own hurts and needs to what a child required?

Studying the faces of her sisters, knowing how they'd been hurt over and over by Pa's defection, Joanna vowed she would speak to Rudy again about putting Freddy's needs ahead of his own. He had to understand how it felt to be left behind. Left to cope with needs too bitter and overwhelming for a child. She breathed deeply to dispel the choking memories.

Glory leaned forward as if to share a secret. "Jo, don't look, but I thought I saw a boy peeking in the kitchen window." Glory grabbed her hand.

Joanna forced herself not to turn around. "It must be Freddy," she murmured.

"Freddy who?" Mandy asked the question, but both sisters' expressions demanded an explanation.

"A boy who stole a pie." She told them the whole story in quick, precise statements. "His uncle wants to pursue his life without responsibilities. Poor Freddy has no one."

"This uncle sounds like Pa," Glory said. "Someone ought to straighten him out."

"Exactly what I thought." But first she had to make sure Freddy was safe. "I've got to get the boy."

"We'll prepare the place for the night."

She'd forgotten about making room for men to spread their bedrolls. "Thanks."

Glory stopped her before she made it to the door. "And don't get soft with the man like you always do with Pa."

"I never did."

"She was only trying to be fair about Pa's feelings." Mandy, as always, sprang to her defense. Or was it Pa's defense? She hesitated, wondering if she should explain that she only wanted to protect them from thinking their pa didn't care. She'd learned to bury the thoughts and turn her attention to her sisters' needs.

She didn't have time to deal with it at the moment and slipped outside. "Freddy?" She waited. Nothing. Had she expected he would fling himself into her arms for comfort? This was Freddy, not one of her sisters. "Are you out there?"

To her left she thought she detected a rustle and moved that direction. There he was. Barely visible in the deepening dusk. Sitting on the ground pressed against the corner of the house. "You must be cold. Why don't you come inside?"

Not a sound. Not a movement.

She sat on the edge of the veranda, close enough she could smell the dusty, little-boy scent of him. And feel his fear, laced liberally with anger. "Your uncle is out looking for you. He's worried."

"More'n likely he's hightailing it out of here as fast as he can go."

The possibility had entered her mind as well. And what would happen to Freddy if he did? He'd have to go to Glory and Levi's mission. That's one of the reasons Levi built the big house—to take in waifs, the destitute, and anyone who needed shelter and help. But somehow it didn't seem right to send Freddy there when he had an uncle.

"I don't think he'd ride off not knowing if you are safe or not."

"Why would he care? He's only stuck with me 'cause he's my uncle." Freddy kicked the edge of the house. "I know he doesn't like me. I even know why."

Joanna bit her tongue to keep from asking.

"You wanna know?"

"It's none of my business."

"Well, it sure as guns is mine. Even though I had nothing to do with it." Each word rang with anger and pain. Joanna sensed it because she had gotten good at hearing it in her sisters' angry outbursts.

"It's because of my ma." Freddy seemed determined to tell her. Maybe it would help him deal with the situation if he explained it to her, so she let him talk. Might even help her understand how to approach Rudy, because she fully intended to. She would not stand back and let him abandon this boy.

"Rudy loved my ma. They was supposed to get married. But my pa loved her, too. Guess he loved her most because they got married. Grandma said people get married for reasons apart from love, but I know they loved each other. Then Pa had to leave to go earn enough money for us. So me and Ma moved in with Grandma. Then Ma died. I was only six, so I don't remember much. Then Grandma died, too." He grew sad and thoughtful then seemed to remember he was explaining about Rudy. "So Rudy left 'cause he's a sore loser. Grandma said he wanted nothing more to do with my pa. And that's why he hates me." He was so matter-of-fact he could have been commenting on the weather.

"Oh Freddy, I've seen him with you. He doesn't hate you."

"He's just trying to fool you 'cause you're pretty and you smiled nice at him."

Joanna grinned in the darkness, glad Freddy couldn't see. He might think she was amused at his words, which wasn't the case at all. She found the observation sweet and warming. "I really don't think it matters that much to him what I think." It would probably matter even less when she got through with him. "My sisters are inside. I was just going to serve them tea and cookies. Maybe you'd like to join us."

After a long pause, Freddy said, "Okay."

She waited for him to get his feet under him; then they marched into the stopping house. Mandy and Glory had pushed aside the table in the big room. Already half a dozen men sat on their bedrolls. Others would join them until the space was full.

Freddy perked up. "Maybe I can sleep here."

"It's up to your uncle."

His shoulders slumped.

Glory and Mandy watched from the kitchen doorway. They looked as sad as Freddy.

Time to lighten the atmosphere. "I'm going to make tea. Glory, why don't you get the cookies? Where's Cora?"

"I'm here." She poked her head around the corner.

"Good. I'll leave you all in charge of the place"—she tipped her head toward Freddy to indicate she meant more than the stopping house—"while I go find Freddy's uncle."

Freddy looked eager. "You gonna tell him off?"

"Of course she is," Glory said.

"Of course I'm not," Joanna said at the same time.

Glory rolled her eyes. "If you don't, I will."

Joanna glared at her sister then focused on the matter at hand. "Freddy, have you forgotten you ran away? Who do you think deserves a scolding?"

"Him. He said he didn't want nothin' to do with me."

Near as she could recall those weren't Rudy's exact words, but close enough.

Glory laughed. "You let Joanna take care of him. Now come have cookies and tea."

It was useless to argue with Glory, so Joanna settled for a deep sigh. She slipped on her coat, picked up a lantern, and headed out in search of one Rudy Canfield.

She climbed the hill to where she'd met him earlier—was it just this morning? Lifting the light, she saw his belongings on the ground, his horse and saddle missing. Relief sagged her legs. At least he hadn't abandoned the boy. Yet.

Returning to town, she scurried through the streets, but there was no sign of Rudy. Urgency driving her onward, she took the trail that led toward the mission. She was deep into the woods before she realized how isolated she was. A woman alone, with a circle of lamplight telegraphing her position to any stray miners around. She swallowed and gripped the lantern handle tighter, pausing several times to listen.

Did she hear something off the trail to the right? She strained toward the noise. It didn't sound like someone searching for a child. Indeed, she wondered if a wild animal was thrashing through the woods.

Heart hammering, she drew back and glanced around for something to protect herself with. A broken branch lay at her feet. She turned the lantern low and set it a foot away then bent to pry the length of wood free from the undergrowth. Armed with an inadequate weapon, she held herself as quiet as possible, though the way her heart thundered she wondered how long she could remain undiscovered.

The noise continued. Crash. Crackle. *Arrrggh.*

That sounded decidedly human. She turned her ear toward the sound.

"Why? Why?"

Her lungs released her breath with a whoosh. Not an animal. It was Rudy. She dropped her weapon. Holding the lantern before her, she followed a narrow path through the trees, reached a little clearing, and stopped.

Rudy faced her, startled, a branch hanging from his hand. One glance and she knew he'd been battering the nearby bushes. She stepped closer. Tried to read his expression. He schooled away any emotion, but not before she glimpsed his twisted features.

"What are you doing?" She kept her voice calm.

"Nothing." He tossed the branch aside. "I've looked everywhere and can't find Freddy."

"He's back at the stopping house."

Rudy grabbed her shoulders. "He is? He's okay?"

Her heart hurtled upward at his touch. Did he mean to harm her? She stepped back. "He's fine."

He dropped his hands to his side, the movement seeming to pull his shoulders down with them. "Why does the boy hate me?"

Joanna heard the pain in his voice. Guessed he'd tried to disguise it. All the words she'd rehearsed turned into butterflies and flitted away. "He doesn't hate you. He's hurting, and you say things that aren't kind. He takes them the wrong way."

"What things?" The voice was challenging.

He'd grown all defensive again, but that was to her advantage. Now she could think of the things she'd meant to say instead of feeling sorry for him. "Things like, you're stuck with him. What are you going to do with a kid? What kind of message is that to give a ten-year-old boy with no family apart from you?" She huffed out an exasperated sigh. "Come on, Rudy. Think about it." She meant to be calm and convincing, but her insides churned. "How'd you like for people to say they didn't care to have you around?"

He grew so still and stiff she wondered if she'd gone too far.

"I don't like it at all." He reached for the reins of his horse. "Come on. I've got to see to the boy."

He'd spoken as if he knew what she meant. Did this have anything to do with Freddy's story? But she didn't get a chance to ask. Trying to keep up with Rudy's hurried steps left her breathless. She had to concentrate on the dirt path as they rushed down the hill toward town. Bad enough she had to trot to keep up with him without staring at the back end of the horse the whole time.

But she would not allow him to get ahead of her, just in case he meant to abandon the boy.

Chapter 4

Rudy's insides still ached. Flailing away at the trees hadn't eased the tension at all. Only made him feel foolish and vulnerable when Joanna discovered him. But he was tired of fighting a ten-year-old. He wanted for them to be friends, but if that wasn't possible, he wanted to return to his cowboy life.

Joanna made it clear what she thought of the idea. Easy for her to have the answers. But even if Freddy came around, what was he to do? He didn't have a place for Freddy, and winter would soon be upon them.

As they approached the looming buildings of the main street, Joanna grabbed his elbow and forced him to slow down.

He should have guessed she wasn't prepared to let him deal with this in his own way. No doubt she had the answers all figured out. Not only that, he figured she could freely share them.

"Rudy, maybe Freddy has been taught to hate you."

That brought him to a halt fast enough. "What? Who would do that?"

"I'm not suggesting it was done intentionally."

He turned to face her square on. The lantern she carried hung at her side, throwing sharp angles across her face. He guessed it did the same for him. Likely making him look more forbidding than he felt. "Why would anyone want him to hate me?"

"Freddy told me a story tonight when I found him. He sort of blurted it out. He thinks you hate him. Maybe with good reason seeing as he overheard you on more than one occasion say you didn't know what to do with him, couldn't take care of a boy, and goodness knows what else."

"You've already told me my failings in this regard. I don't see how it has anything to do with you saying he's been taught to hate me."

"I'm getting to it."

"I hope it won't take all night."

"Why? You got an important engagement I'm keeping you from?"

"Yes. My bed."

"Speaking of that. . . Freddy wants to spend the night in the stopping house. I told him he could—"

"You what?"

She sighed. "If it was okay with you."

He swallowed hard. "Huh." He was no closer to getting the facts from her and resigned himself to standing all night on the edge of town in the increasingly cold air.

"Anyway, back to what I was saying."

"Good idea."

"I'll ignore that."

"Sorry." He normally didn't have a comment for anyone, but for some reason he couldn't seem to stop spouting them off with Joanna.

"Freddy said his grandmother told him you and his ma were supposed to be married, but instead she married your brother."

Fire scorched a path through his brain. Not because he hurt any longer over what Betty and Joe had done, but because Joanna sounded all sympathetic. No doubt she would offer condolences. "It's true. So what?"

"So nothing, except it seems you were fortunate to discover how lukewarm her heart was before you actually tied the knot."

He laughed.

"What's so funny?"

"I expected you to be all sorrowful because I got stood up. Instead you tell me it was a good thing." It plumb tickled him, and he chuckled again.

"You don't?"

"Consider myself fortunate?" He'd never given it any thought, but suddenly he realized she was right. "Maybe I am. I've been free to go where I want without hindrance for the past eleven years. Can't complain about that."

"I didn't mean it in that way. But be that as it may, I believe those days are over for you. You are now guardian of a boy."

"Who hates me." He folded his arms. "And I believe you were about to explain why and what my mother has to do with it." He wouldn't listen to ill words spoken of his dead mother. Did she hear the warning note in his voice? And if she did, would she heed it?

"He's taken what his grandmother said and turned it into something else. Apparently she said your brother—"

"Joe."

"Yes, Joe—married his mother, and you wouldn't speak to Joe after that. Freddy figures it's because you hate Joe and, by extension, him."

Rudy made a noise that did little to release his frustration. "I didn't hate Joe, and I certainly don't hate Freddy. Though"—he might as well reveal the whole ugly truth—"I did think Joe charmed Betty just to prove he could take her from me. And"—he held up a hand to stop whatever she meant to say—"I did think he should have stayed around to take care of his responsibilities instead of leaving my mother and Betty to manage on their own."

She nodded. "My opinion exactly." He couldn't see much of Joanna's face in the low light surrounding them, but he understood she didn't simply agree with his opinion about Joe. Likely she thought he should notice the parallel about his responsibility to Freddy. Only difference was, Joe had asked for the responsibility. He hadn't.

"Freddy didn't ask to be left an orphan. Don't you think he's had enough of believing you don't care for him?" Her soft words carried a pleading note.

He scrubbed his chin. "Don't you think I've tried?"

"I expect you have. But now you have to succeed." They headed down the darkened street. The only other lights came from the saloon, and even that business was strangely quiet.

He stayed at her side, his mount at his other hand. "You make it sound so simple. As if it's up to me."

"It is. You're the adult. You win him over." She kept walking.

"How?" He didn't mean to sound so desperate, even though he was. "Tell me how."

She slowed so she could study his face. "You really want help? You really want to make it work?"

He shrugged. Yes, he wanted to make it work. More than she could possibly know. Freddy was all he had left of Betty. Of Joe. Even of his mother. Of course he wanted the boy to like him. He wanted to give the boy love, but at every attempt he'd been kicked in the teeth. "I want to be Freddy's uncle."

She seemed to understand what he meant. "Then I'll help you. . . while I'm still here."

"Mr. Tisdale will soon replace you?"

"He didn't even speak to me tonight."

"Likely feeling things out." She'd only be there a short time, but maybe she could help him before she left.

And why did it twist his gut to think of her leaving? After all, he'd never had trouble leaving any place in his life.

She stood still in the middle of the street, staring into the darkness. "Here's what I suggest. I continue to give Freddy some chores, and you help out around the stopping house, too. I'll do my best to see that you're together. I'll work on Freddy to help him see that you want to be friends. In exchange for your work, I'll feed you and provide you a place to sleep."

He laughed outright at that. "Maybe not having to eat my cooking will make him more willing to like me."

Her low-throated chuckle tickled across his nerves. He was unreasonably pleased with himself. Then he sobered. "You think it will work?"

"I'd say it's worth a try. Add your prayers for God to change his heart."

His jaw tightened. "I don't expect help from God. Haven't in a long time."

They passed a horse pen. The animal neighed. But Joanna was strangely silent.

Blessedly silent. He'd half expected an impassioned sermon after confessing his doubts about God.

"I expect it has something to do with Joe and Betty."

He should have known she wouldn't let it pass. "Maybe," he allowed.

"I was once like that. So many times I prayed our Pa would stay with us. He never did, so I stopped asking. And then I stopped talking to God at all. Stopped reading the Bible. Just stopped thinking about God."

He waited, wondering what had changed. But they passed the last of the businesses, and she offered no more. Sure picked the worst time to decide to keep her mouth shut. "So what happened?"

"To make me think about God again? I was trying to think what it was. I could say it was when Levi—Glory's preacher husband, remember—came to town, but I think it began before that." Her feet slowed to a crawl, and he settled back, content to watch her. "We see a lot of people passing through at the stopping house. I observed them and began to understand many of them are so tied up in their own interests, their own hurts, even their own dreams that they don't realize how their actions and decisions affect others. Slowly I began to accept Pa was like that. Don't expect even God can turn a stubborn man around unless he's willing."

He sorted through her words. Somehow they comforted him, but he couldn't even say why. Maybe Joe and Betty hadn't intentionally hurt him. It was a new thought. Something he'd have to muse on for a while.

They reached the place where he'd have to turn off to return to his camp, and he made up his mind without knowing he had made the decision. "I'll go get our things so Freddy can sleep at the stopping house and be there to do chores in the morning."

"Do you want company?"

Her words slammed into his heart like a giant fist. Did she actually want to spend time with him? He stumbled on a nonexistent lump in the ground and caught himself before Joanna noticed. How many times had he gone from camp to camp, ranch to ranch, even ridden away to nowhere in particular? Always alone. Without anyone offering to accompany him. That's the way it was. The way he wanted it to be. He'd made it clear as springwater, and everyone respected his desire.

But Joanna's offer ripped away scar tissue and revealed a long-unhealed wound of loneliness. Well, guess he wouldn't have to worry about being alone in the future. He had Freddy now.

But it wasn't the boy he wanted to welcome into that lonely place. It was Joanna. He clenched his teeth and pushed aside every bit of weakness.

He'd trusted a woman once. Given her his heart. When she'd turned her back on him, he'd vowed never to trust another female. Ever. Yes, Joanna might show undeserved kindness. Yes, he'd asked her to help him win Freddy's trust. Yes, she made him feel things he hadn't felt in a long time. Things like friendship, companionship, a desire for company. Maybe she even made him want to tell her more about his life. But bottom line, where it really mattered, she was a woman. And he was not about to trust her.

∽

Rudy never said she was welcome to accompany him up the hill. But he hadn't said he didn't want her either, so Joanna traipsed along. The narrow trail forced them to walk almost shoulder to shoulder. It was not an uncomfortable feeling—Rudy at her side, strolling along at a leisurely pace. The horse following on their heels.

She'd offered to help him with Freddy. For the boy's sake. For Rudy's, too, she reluctantly admitted. There was something about his thwarted efforts to befriend the boy that tugged at her emotions. To be rejected hurt. She knew and understood, having felt the same pain with Pa. How often had she begged him to stay, always dreaming he would love her enough to be the parent instead of leaving her with the role? But time and time again he left. Always with instructions for her to take care of her younger sisters. Each time she'd stuff her pain into some distant corner of her heart and put on a cheerful front for the sake of Glory and Mandy. But it hurt. More than words could say.

She couldn't keep the feelings bottled up inside forever, and tonight they burst forth. She told Rudy all of it while they walked through the ghostly shapes of the trees. While they crunched over the dry leaves on the path, she talked. Finally she wound down. "It wasn't until the girls were both happily married to men who would not walk away from them to pursue some distant dream that my pain has begun to heal."

They'd reached the campsite. She looked around, wondering how long they'd been standing under the trees. At some point he'd acquired the lantern. It hung from a nearby branch, throwing long shadows away from its light. She'd never before confessed her feelings to anyone. Her cheeks burned with mortification to the point she expected they glowed in the dark. "I'm sorry. I didn't mean to tell you the whole story." She could barely stammer out the apology.

He gave her a slow nod, his eyes serious. "Didn't mind. Just wish I could do something to take away the hurt your pa has left in you." His gaze held hers.

She found something in his steady look she couldn't explain. Something she'd never felt before. Never expected to feel.

He lifted a hand and touched her cheek, his fingers cool to her skin. "I can see why you're so set on making sure I don't give up on Freddy. You see yourself in the boy."

She nodded, tears welling. She swallowed hard and widened her eyes to keep from letting any escape. Hopefully, the darkness hid her distress.

He flattened his hand against her cheek. His touch, solid and tender, calmed her. And set her heart racing.

She tilted her head slightly into his touch. His palm was rough and warm. "It isn't fair to abandon children." She swallowed again, trying to remove the crab apple–sized lump in her throat.

"If only things could work out in the ideal way you think they should." He withdrew his hand, leaving a cold spot on her jawline. Leaving her feeling as if he'd backed away from something fragile hovering in the air.

Suddenly cold, she hugged her coat closer to her chest and stepped to one side, putting a distance of three feet between them. She wasn't an idealistic child who believed in happy-ever-after. She knew people made mistakes and was willing to take that into account. But mistakes were no excuse for abandoning a child. She lifted her chin and glared at him. "I don't expect things to work out all sunshine and roses, but I'm saying people like you can choose how some things will work out."

"I hear ya. Loud and clear. No need to hammer the subject to death."

"I'm not." So he didn't really understand a thing. She had just told him everything about how it feels to be alone and unwanted, and he didn't even care. The words of protest were hot on her lips. "You're way too much like my pa. Just about the time I think we might be learning to be friends, you jerk back. Surprised you don't throw your things on the back of that horse and ride away." She gave him a look that should have melted him on the spot.

But he laughed.

She stared, trying to decide if she wanted to stomp away or kick dirt at him.

He didn't give her a chance to do either. Instead, he closed the distance between them and caught her shoulders. "Joanna, there seems one thing I can count on with you. You'll never leave me guessing how you feel." He grew serious and looked into her eyes.

She held his gaze without blinking. Try as she might, she couldn't sort her thoughts into neat array. Something about this man slipped past her defenses and made her long for things she had vowed she didn't want.

"It's nice to know I can count on something from someone," he murmured then planted a kiss on her forehead. He jerked back.

She was appalled. Appalled by his behavior, appalled by the way her heart leaped to her throat at his kiss.

"I shouldn't have done that." Avoiding her eyes, he grabbed up a canvas-covered roll and tied it to the saddle.

Bad enough to be kissed in a fatherly way. Worse to have her heart do strange things. But the worst of all was getting an apology. "Don't ever kiss me again and apologize for it." She stalked over to him. "As if I'm a mistake. As if I don't deserve any sign of affection."

He turned to face her. "You are not a mistake. After all, if you weren't here, who would keep nagging me to prove to Freddy that I want to be friends?"

Her eyes burned with a thousand things—disappointments from the past, feeling she could never live up to her pa's expectation. Pa always left with a warning that she was responsible for her sisters. She knew now his leaving and his warning had nothing to do with her or how well she managed. It was only his way of shifting his responsibility to her shoulders. Yet the remnants of uncertainty lingered.

"Joanna, don't push me. I have nothing to offer. I'm a rootless cowboy who is about to see if he can settle down. But I can't make promises. You're right when you say I'm like your pa. Keep that in mind."

She flung away. "Believe me, I'm not about to forget it. Not that it matters one way or the other." Except it did. Or it would if she let it. But she wasn't going to. She'd had enough dealings with men who rode in and out of her life without more than a hasty good-bye. "One man like Pa is more than enough in my life."

He watched her, his expression guarded.

Seeing the resigned look on his face, she wanted to pull her words back. But once spoken, words could not be withdrawn. Maybe she could try and undo the harm they'd wrought. "I'm sorry. I've hurt you, and I have no right to do so. You don't deserve it. I overreacted. I'm sure you aren't the least bit like my pa. Not if you're willing to make an effort to do something for Freddy. I hope you can forgive me for my outburst."

He could have been made out of wood for all the emotion he showed.

"Rudy?" She edged closer. "Are you so angry at me you can't forgive?" She was close enough to see his eyes. In the dim light she thought they appeared wider than normal. Shocked? Had she surprised him with her apology? Or was he so angry he couldn't think? Why had she thought anything she said would make a difference one way or the other? Maybe she was thinking of her pa again. She seemed to have him and Rudy mixed up in her mind. Yes, Rudy reminded her of her pa. But he wasn't the same. She shook her head, trying to clear the confusion. "Rudy, I'm truly sorry."

He shook himself. A thin smile curved his mouth. "No one has ever said they were sorry for hurting me before."

She chuckled. "Does that mean you forgive me?"

"It sure does." His grin widened until it crinkled his eyes. "Lady, it sure does. Now let's get back to your house." He held the lantern high as they navigated the trail.

Happiness bubbled inside Joanna. It felt good to know she'd made peace with Rudy. And yet part of her heart felt tight and anxious. She knew the risks of caring too much. She wasn't about to make that mistake.

Chapter 5

Joanna and Rudy slipped through the kitchen door. He dropped the bedrolls to the floor. The big dining room was dim, the table where they'd eaten had been shoved to one side, the benches pushed beneath it. Only one lamp burned as a man read. A chorus of snores shattered the silence.

Joanna sighed as she led him into the kitchen. The room was warm from the big range on one side and the smells of home cooking and wash water. A set of cupboards filled the better part of two walls. In daylight, a generous window would allow a view of the ferry and travelers. "Sure glad we don't hear that racket in the bedroom." She tipped her head toward the closed door indicating the room she meant. "Will you be able to sleep?"

He brought his thoughts back to her question. "We'll be fine." His gaze shifted to the table where Freddy sat with three young women. Cora, he'd met. The other two must be Joanna's sisters. They eyed him suspiciously.

He went to Freddy. "Glad to see you're okay."

Freddy spared him a glower then gave him a good view of his back.

Rudy pretended it didn't hurt and quirked an eyebrow at Joanna. He hoped she could see he'd tried. Freddy had made his feelings pretty evident.

She lifted one shoulder as if to suggest he would have to be patient. But his patience had about run out.

"Rudy, meet my sisters."

They were cordial enough, but he felt much like a horse about to be sold to the highest bidder. He returned look for look, measuring and assessing every bit as much as they did. All three sisters had the same challenging gaze. All three dressed like women of the West, which, of course, they were. "Took you long enough to find him," Glory said.

Mandy continued her blatant study of him. "Thought you might have had to run him to the ground ten miles down the road."

Joanna laughed. "Found him up the hill toward the mission. Of course, it wasn't the first place I looked. Freddy, he was some worried about you."

Freddy shrugged. "I can take care of myself."

Glory hooted. "I remember being ten. Thought I could do anything. Mostly I tried to."

Freddy perked up. "What'd you do?"

Mandy nudged Glory. "Don't be filling the boy's head with your wild stories." She turned to Freddy. "She thought if she proved to everyone she wasn't afraid of anything, she might convince herself. But she had the same fear the rest of us had."

Rudy gave the youngest sister more careful study. She'd set the bait and reeled it out most wisely. Now she just had to wait for the bite.

And it was almost instant. "What were you afraid of?"

"Being left. Our Pa had a habit of riding away. Most times he made some sort of arrangement for us while he was gone but not always. Once we came home from school and the house was empty. The landlord wouldn't let us stay. We didn't know where to go. I was really worried, but Joanna told me not to fret. She'd find us a place." She gave her older sister a look full of admiration and affection.

A tremendous amount of responsibility had been thrust on Joanna. And from what she'd said, she wouldn't have been more than about fourteen. Small wonder she felt so strongly about men living up to their responsibilities. Somewhere deep inside a conviction rooted itself to bedrock. He would do his best to never let her down.

Freddy seemed to consider Mandy's words.

Joanna sat at Freddy's side. "You have your uncle Rudy to take care of you, so you don't have to worry."

"I'm not worried. I can take care of myself."

Glory leaned back and eyed the boy. "It's a good thing you don't have to. How would you feed yourself? And don't say you'd steal it. Not everyone would be so generous as Joanna."

"He worked for me to pay for it, and I'm satisfied." Joanna lifted her hands to signal the end of the discussion. "Now hadn't you two better be getting home before your husbands come looking for you?"

"Oh, didn't we tell you?" Glory pretended to look surprised. "We told them we were spending the night. In case it's the last time we can all be together here."

Joanna grinned widely. "That's a great idea."

Rudy had sunk to the corner of the bench next to Joanna and now pushed to his feet. "Come along, Freddy, so these ladies can go to bed."

"Aw. I don't want to go."

"You don't have to. I brought our sleeping rolls. We'll sleep here, and in the morning we'll do chores for Miss Joanna and help her out."

The announcement brought a sudden silence to the table. Cora and the two younger sisters stared at Rudy then shifted their gazes to Joanna.

"Yes, I asked if he and Freddy could help. I'll need to leave things shipshape for Mr. Tisdale."

"Good." Freddy swung away from the table. "At least I get good food here."

Rudy knew it was the closest thing to thanks he could expect. But he paused at Joanna's side before he left the room. "Thank you for doing this."

He bade the others good night, and he and Freddy retired to the other room. Freddy curled up on his mat, pulled the covers over his head, and was soon breathing deeply.

Sleep did not come so easily for Rudy as he reviewed the events of the day. He tried to get comfortable, but his thoughts swirled. It was only this morning he met Joanna, and yet he felt as if he'd known her a long time. She likely knew more about him than any of his other acquaintances. He crossed his hands behind his head and studied the darkened ceiling. No one else had ever heard the story of how Joe and Betty hurt him. In fact, he'd not even admitted it to himself. Just rode away without a backward look. If not for Ma, he likely wouldn't have ever returned to the only home he'd ever known. But with Betty living there and Freddy growing from a squalling baby to a toddling two-year-old to a little boy proud for his first day at school, even his brief visits were awkward.

Had Joanna likewise told him more than she'd confessed to others?

He smiled into the darkness. What had come over him to kiss her on the forehead? The feeling was so unfamiliar he didn't even know what to call it.

She made him believe things could be better between him and Freddy. She was prepared to make it happen, even though she had her hands full with getting ready to sell the place. From what he'd seen of her sisters, she managed to help them overcome their fears and likely a degree of anger. Maybe she'd succeed with Freddy equally as well.

She was some kind of woman.

Joanna and Mandy lay side by side in one bed, Cora and Glory in the other. Joanna was tired but knew there would be little sleep tonight. Her sisters seemed set on recounting their many adventures.

Glory reminded them how she and Mandy would hide in the woods and sneak up on each other. "Mandy got to be a lot sneakier than me, though."

Cora laughed. "That's how she caught Trace—sneaking up on him in the woods."

Mandy snorted. "Took a lot more effort than that."

They all laughed.

Glory rolled around, twisting the blankets. Cora complained about her letting in the cold air.

"I have to look at my sister so I can talk to her."

"You can't see her in the dark," Cora protested.

"Which sister?" Mandy and Joanna asked in unison.

"Joanna, what are you doing asking Rudy to work for you? I thought you were going to set him straight about Freddy."

Joanna smiled into the dark, grateful the others couldn't see her face. Little did they know how far her conversation with Rudy had veered from talk of Freddy. Something inside her had shifted. Perhaps because, for the first time ever, she'd told someone exactly how difficult it had been to be the eldest of the sisters, responsible to keep them safe.

"Answer the question," Glory said.

"What better way to make sure he takes responsibility for Freddy than having him where I can keep an eye on him? Besides, I might be able to help him find a way to connect with the boy."

Glory snorted. "You'll end up excusing his behavior just like you always do for Pa."

Joanna wished she could explain. For too many years she'd acted as buffer between her sisters and the hurtfulness of Pa's behavior. She had tried her best to explain him, and she couldn't stop doing it now. "I'm sure Pa was only doing what he thought best."

"For him. But not for us. Never for us." Glory sighed. "But it doesn't bother me the way it used to. Why should it when I have a man like Levi to love me? He'd never walk out on me."

Mandy found Joanna's hand and squeezed it. "Jo, I don't like to think you might be taking on another mothering job with Freddy. You've taken care of us for years. You deserve to follow your own dreams now."

"Thanks, honey. That's exactly what I intend to do. Rudy knows this arrangement is only until I leave. Perhaps by then he and Freddy will be getting along."

"And if they aren't, tell us you're not going to change your mind." Glory wouldn't let it go.

"I'm not going to change my mind." After all, she was not the kind of person who said one thing and did another.

∽

Mr. Tisdale appeared at breakfast and seemed to enjoy the meal. Joanna watched for some signal from him, but he never once met her look. Determined to learn what he'd decided, she waited for him to finish.

He didn't seem to be in a hurry to leave as he engaged in an animated discussion with the man next to him. She caught enough of what was said to know they talked of the gold discovery to the north.

Almost everyone had departed when the pair got to their feet. Joanna rose, too. "Mr. Tisdale, may we talk?"

He nodded and told the other man, "I'll join you shortly."

"I'm wondering what you've decided about my place." She kept her voice calm, though her insides churned. So much depended on his offer. She had a bottom line, but there was still a lot of room to haggle about the price. She wanted enough money to be able to go to California, enjoy herself, and start a new business venture somewhere.

He twisted his cap. "This place is fancier than what I expected. I read some dime novels and thought all I'd need to serve is beans and bannock. I practiced them both until they're passable, but that's all I can cook."

"I'm sure it will be most acceptable. Most of these men only care about getting enough food in their stomachs to get them through the next day."

"It's not what I expected. I hear there is gold for the plucking in the Kootenais. I've decided to head north. I expect I can make a fortune without having to work so hard."

"You've changed your mind?"

"Yes. I'm sorry." He donned his hat and left.

Unable to think, she stared after him. She never considered this possibility. He'd been so eager in their correspondence.

"Joanna?"

Rudy's voice jerked her from her stunned state.

"I couldn't help but overhear. I'm sorry it didn't work out."

For the life of her she couldn't form a word. Barely a thought. She hurried into the kitchen and stared at the stack of dirty dishes Cora scrubbed.

Cora dried her hands and came to Joanna's side. "I heard, too. Are you okay?"

Her brain kicked into gear. "I'll simply have to find another buyer." She took a wet rag and returned to the dining room to scrub the table. Round and round her hands went. She couldn't seem to stop.

Rudy reached out and took the rag from her hands. He gently pushed her to the bench and sat beside her. "You'll find someone else."

She faced him, her eyes burning with emotions she couldn't name. "So he didn't keep his word. Why should I be surprised? You'd think I'd be used to it by now."

He searched her gaze, perhaps seeing more than she intended. The way she'd unburdened her heart to him last night, he likely thought he had the right to see more than she wanted him to. He took her hands and held them between his. "Joanna, there are people you can trust and count on. You have to believe it."

"Do I? Do I have to believe it? Seems to me that's a rather foolish thing to do unless you enjoy having the rug pulled out from under you time and again. I'd think you'd know that as well as I." She clamped her lips in a tight line to control the quaver in her voice.

He didn't blink. Didn't shrink from her anger. Instead, his gaze held steady as if silently promising he would be different.

Pshaw. As if she should believe that. "You're just the same. Can't wait to return to your footloose, fancy-free ways." She managed to get her feet under her and escaped to her bedroom, closing the door tight.

She sat on the edge of the bed, her hands clenched together. Why had she counted so much on Mr. Tisdale's offer? Nothing was for certain until she had his name on a bill of sale and his money in her palm. But he'd been so sure. She'd trusted his words.

How many times did she have to repeat the same lesson?

Was she really so mentally slow?

She stared at her white knuckles and released her clasped hands, smoothing her damp palms on her split skirt. Seeing her mother's Bible, she opened it seeking comfort, guidance. . .sanity.

She found them all as she read familiar passages, hearing her mother's gentle voice in the words. Her fingers turned the pages to Numbers 23:19. "God is not a man, that he should lie; neither the son of man, that he should repent: hath he said, and shall he not do it?"

She knew the verse by heart, but reading it strengthened her resolve. To her sorrow and pain she knew she could not trust man, but she was learning she could depend on God.

Finally she was able to pray. *God, I don't understand.* She had nothing more to say or ask. Except. . . *Help me find another buyer.*

Soon. It would have to be soon. Sarah had warned her they wouldn't be able to cross the mountains once the passes filled with snow.

A few minutes later she left the room with two letters in her hand— one to Sarah explaining what happened and asking if she would mind delaying her trip. *I'll understand if you feel you can't.* The second letter would go to another man who'd expressed interest in buying the stopping house. Originally Joanna had informed him someone else had made an offer. Now she wrote that the place was again on the market if he was interested. The rest was up to God.

Rudy turned from the dishpan, water dripping from his fingers. It crossed her mind that God might have a reason for this delay, for it allowed her time to work with Rudy and Freddy and perhaps help them learn to be friends. And perhaps there was another reason. She recalled Rudy's confession that he didn't think much about God anymore.

God, help me help them.

∞

Rudy turned as the door opened. Joanna stepped out, her expression settled, perhaps even serene. Her shock had fled. Tension had made him aware of each breath, but now Rudy's ribs eased. "Are you okay?"

"I'm fine. Thanks." She glanced around and took in Rudy's shirt- sleeves rolled to his elbows, the water glistening on his hands. Her gaze flicked toward Freddy, who held a bowl he'd been drying. Seems he had forgotten about it as he watched Joanna. Cora had explained to him why Joanna was disappointed.

"Where's Cora?"

"She had an errand. I said we'd take care of the dishes. Freddy is dry- ing. I'm washing."

Freddy, eager to please Joanna, nodded. "We're almost done."

"Thank you. I'll be with you in a bit. First I want to take these letters to be posted." She hurried from the house.

Freddy and Rudy both watched out the window as she rushed along the trail toward the combined mercantile and post office.

Freddy continued to look long after she'd disappeared from sight, his face puckered.

"She'll be back," Rudy said. "We better get the dishes cleaned up before she does."

"Why's she selling this place?"

"She wants to go to California with her friend."

Freddy scowled. "Why does everyone want to leave?"

The question struck a note of misery in Rudy's heart. It echoed Joanna's hurts. But leaving wasn't the same as being unfaithful or untrustworthy. Freddy needed to understand this as much as Joanna did. "Sometimes a person doesn't have any choice. Or there are very good reasons for moving on. If you think about it, this place is the result of someone leaving and moving to a new home."

Freddy glanced around. "I guess." He picked up the next dish to dry it. "But I wish she would keep living here so I could stay with her."

Had he purposely left Rudy out of the picture? Did he expect Rudy would leave him behind? Not that it hadn't crossed his mind. The boy would be better off with someone who could provide a proper home. But he didn't want Freddy to think Rudy's leaving was inevitable. "Seems you and me are going to be together from now on."

Freddy's expression shifted to one far too familiar—angry, defensive, shutting out Rudy. "You can leave if you want. I'll be okay on my own."

A dozen different arguments sprang to Rudy's mind, but he suspected anything he said would be met with increasing anger, so he let it go. "Joanna has asked us to help her for a few days."

"Then what?" The words were spoken as a challenge, but Rudy figured they revealed Freddy's fear. Thanks to Joanna's words last night up on the hill, he was beginning to understand how uncertainty could upset the boy. Freddy needed to know that Rudy would stand by him.

Rudy looked Freddy in the eye. "Then we'll figure out what's next." Would Freddy take comfort in the words?

Freddy perked up, all interest in Rudy gone.

Rudy followed his gaze out the window and grinned. Joanna was on her way back. She swung her arms as she walked, looking happy with her world.

"She's smiling," Freddy announced.

"Yup. She sure is."

"Guess she's not mad."

She stepped into the room, giving them both a beaming smile.

Rudy forgot how to swallow.

Freddy looked like someone had handed him a sweet. "I told you she wasn't mad."

"I figure Joanna never stays mad longer than a minute."

Joanna raised her eyebrows. "You two been talking about me behind my back?"

"Yup." Rudy couldn't contain his grin.

Freddy seemed surprised. "Grandma used to be mad for days."

"I remember that."

Joanna chuckled. "You look like a matching pair. Both smiling while sounding morose and sad. How do you do that?"

"Special skill known only to the Canfield men. Isn't that right, Freddy?"

"Yup." He sounded so much like Rudy that Rudy laughed. As did Joanna. Something warm and sweet seemed to fill the air.

Rudy realized how long he'd been grinning at Joanna and jerked back to the dishpan. But the dishes had all been washed. He went to the door and tossed the water into the nearby trees.

Joanna sprang into action at the same time. "Freddy, would you take these scraps out to the cat?"

Freddy took the container. "What's the cat's name?"

"Cat. That's all."

"How come?"

Joanna kept her attention on something beyond Freddy's shoulder. "Cat doesn't need a name."

Freddy headed outside. "I'm going to name him."

Rudy waited until the door closed behind the boy. "So you don't name cats. Why? Don't want to get too attached to them?"

She made a great show of putting away dishes. "Don't go making something out of nothing."

Except he suspected it was something. "You don't trust cats not to leave either."

She ignored him. So, he had guessed right. He waited and watched.

Finally she stopped all her frantic scurrying about and faced him, her expression revealing nothing. "I guess if I'm to stay a bit longer I'll need some wood split. Maybe you could do that."

"Glad to." He headed for the door. "What are you going to do about the stopping house?"

"I've sent a letter to another man who expressed interest after Mr. Tisdale. This other man has a wife. Maybe it would work better for a married couple."

"So you're still planning to leave?"

"Why?"

"Freddy was hoping you'd stay."

"Why would it matter to Freddy?"

He'd said more than he should. Told himself it was about Freddy, but Freddy couldn't stay if Rudy didn't.

She stared at him so hard her eyes narrowed. "You better not be thinking of riding away and leaving him here."

His heart ached for her. And for him. To her he was simply another man who would likely make promises and then break them. "I was thinking just the opposite, but you will never trust a man, will you?"

"I've never had much reason to."

He crossed his arms. "Maybe it's time to change your mind."

She shook her head, half turned away then spun back to face him. "What do you mean, you were thinking the opposite?"

He'd been thinking he might be wanting to stay, settle down even. But if she couldn't figure that out, he wasn't going to tell her. "You and I are far too much alike." Both so mistrustful of the opposite sex.

Before she could demand an explanation, he left to tackle the woodpile as he'd promised.

He wished he could undo all the disappointments Joanna's pa and likely a dozen other men had dished out to her. He wished he could be what she needed. But he wasn't. He was virtually homeless, which, until now, had been just fine. Now his situation simply made him realize how little he had to offer anyone like Freddy. And if his regrets also brought Joanna to mind. . . Well, what difference did it make? He was the last thing she needed.

Cutting wood proved a good antidote for the regrets burning his veins. But he wondered how it would help Freddy see he didn't hate him.

Chapter 6

Joanna had work to do. Her load wouldn't let up until winter brought an ease to the number of people traveling. Or until she sold. But she couldn't concentrate on her tasks. What did Rudy mean, they were too much alike? She wasn't a wanderer, waiting for a chance to ride off into the sunset, footloose and fancy-free.

But deep down, she knew what he meant.

They both were wary about trusting others, each with their own good reason.

Drawn to the window, she watched him swing the ax, splitting logs one after the other, wood chips scattering around him, chopping more wood in twenty minutes than she would in two hours. It was somehow soothing and reassuring to watch. And enjoyable with the autumn sun shining like it had to get every last ray blasted out before winter. She leaned her hip against the cupboard and enjoyed the sight. Never before had she been so fascinated by work.

Cora clattered in the door, and Joanna jerked away from her guilty contemplation, her cheeks stinging. She had too much work to waste time staring mindlessly out the window. But Cora didn't seem to notice.

"Sorry I had to be away for a bit."

Joanna didn't care. "You're free to come and go whenever you want." She'd never had reason to worry about Cora doing the agreed-upon chores. But Cora's blush caught her interest. "What's Austin up to?"

Cora fluttered her hands. "Why do you mention Austin?"

"Oh, certain little things give me reason to think he's on your mind. Like your rosy cheeks. They aren't pink from cold. And the way your eyes seem lit from inside." She leaned closer. "In fact, you look like someone in love." Not that Joanna was surprised. From the beginning she'd guessed at Austin's feelings. Knew it wouldn't take long for Cora to realize how he felt.

"You're right. I went to see Austin. He's going to be away for a few days."

"Oh?" *Away* could mean anything, but Joanna's caution waved red flags.

"He wants to ride to the gold fields and take photos of the men and what they do."

"Sounds interesting." Austin had a keen interest in taking pictures. But Joanna wondered how far he would ride and when he'd return. She didn't want Cora to wait helplessly day after day like she and her sisters had done most of their lives.

Cora made a tsking sound. "I know you wonder if he'll come back, but I have complete faith in him." She gave Joanna a challenging look. "Someday you are going to learn there are men you can trust." She moved to the cupboard and saw Rudy at the woodpile. "Just be careful to choose the right man."

"You can count on it." She understood Cora's warning about Rudy. Joanna already knew he wasn't the sort of man to build a dream on. He should have *footloose and fancy-free* branded to his forehead.

But she'd promised to help him win Freddy's friendship, so she went in search of the boy. He sat on the edge of the veranda, the cat purring on his lap.

She sat down beside him. "Seems the cat likes you."

"She's lonely and needs a friend."

Don't we all? "Then she's fortunate you came along."

"You think so?"

"I certainly do."

He buried his face in the cat's fur. Freddy was lonely and afraid. She understood that. But he had to stop pushing people away if he wanted things to change.

Something inside her stirred, like an invisible hand using a big spoon on her innards. Did she push people away, too? Was she responsible for her loneliness?

She didn't have time to consider the answers. "Freddy, I have some chores for you. Your uncle is chopping wood that needs to be stacked in the shed."

"Why?"

She assumed he meant, *Why does the wood need to be put in the shed?* "To keep it dry. Come on, I'll show you what to do."

He reluctantly bade the cat good-bye and followed.

Rudy wiped his forehead on his sleeve as he watched them approach. His gaze clung to Joanna, searching.

She tried to guess what he hoped to see. Or was she the one who wanted to see something? Like roots growing from his boots and anchoring to bedrock so he wouldn't be riding off in the blue yonder at first opportunity? She stilled such thoughts. As Cora said, if she meant to start trusting a man, better pick one who wouldn't leave.

Exerting her well-honed self-control, she jerked her gaze away. "Freddy is going to help you stack the wood."

"I could use some help."

She turned to Freddy. "Your uncle will show you what to do."

No missing the stubborn set of Freddy's lips.

She signaled Rudy to join her to one side. When he did, she tried not to think about the warmth coming from his body or the way he stood with his fists on his hips, looking like he owned the world. She put a few more inches between them then found she had to lean closer so Freddy wouldn't overhear her words. "Maybe if you work together stacking the wood. . ."

"Sounds like a plan."

"Okay then." She was done here, but she didn't move. Couldn't seem to remember how. *Joanna, stop being so silly.* "I'll leave you to it." She jerked toward the house.

Later, her wits collected, she began preparations for the meals of the day. She only served breakfast and the evening meal to paying customers, but those who lived and worked at the stopping house needed a noon meal. Cora had a pot of soup simmering, and Joanna mixed up biscuits, chuckling when she recalled Mr. Tisdale's thoughts on a menu. She told Cora about it, and they shared a laugh.

As she worked near the cupboard, she had a good view of the woodpile. But she paid little attention to the wood. Instead, she watched Rudy and Freddy work together. They seemed to have some competition going. First, Rudy would load Freddy's arms as high as he could, and the boy would stagger to the shed to deposit his load. They would be inside for a few minutes. No doubt stacking the wood in neat rows.

Then the pair came out, and Rudy sat on the chopping block while Freddy gathered up wood and stacked Rudy's arms high. And higher until Rudy's face disappeared behind the pile.

Freddy stood back and waited for his uncle to rise.

Rudy eased upward, the wood teetering. He managed to gain his feet and edged toward the shed. He took three steps before pieces began slipping away. He staggered, trying to stop the avalanche. Failed. Most of the wood clattered to the ground, leaving Rudy with only a handful in his arms.

Freddy laughed loudly enough for his voice to reach the kitchen.

Cora joined Joanna at the window. "What are they doing?"

"Who cares? Freddy is enjoying himself."

Across the distance, Rudy's gaze found Joanna's, and they shared a moment of delight in this victory. Her pleasure washed through her insides.

The day had passed pleasantly enough, Rudy decided as he sat at the kitchen table after supper. The dishes had been cleaned up, and he'd helped Cora move the table and benches in the dining room, now ready for men to bed down. Cora informed him Joanna wouldn't let the men inside for a bit. The work done up for the evening, the four of them— Cora, Joanna, Rudy, and Freddy—sat around the smaller table enjoying tea and cookies.

It had been a good day. He enjoyed working around the yard, chopping wood, stacking it, repairing the door on the woodshed, caulking up the cracks to keep the snow and rain out. How many times had he glanced up to watch Joanna hurrying around the yard for one thing or another or working in front of the kitchen window? Several times she'd looked up at the same time, and their gazes had connected. Each time a shot of something strangely like static electricity had raced along his nerves. He'd told himself it meant nothing. Neither of them had plans to stay here. Nor plans to get tied down.

Though Freddy certainly put a knot in those plans for Rudy.

He'd even enjoyed a few moments with Freddy before the boy pulled back and favored him with his familiar scowl. He'd made a game of carrying the wood into the shed. See who could carry the highest load. Then he purposely let his tumble for the sole reason of hearing Freddy laugh.

Yup, it had been a downright decent day. How many more could he expect?

He knew the answer. Not many.

"Tomorrow is Sunday," Joanna announced.

He allowed his gaze to turn toward her, though he'd been fighting the notion since they sat down.

Her smile included them all, but if he wasn't mistaken, it rested a little longer, and perhaps a little warmer, on him.

"We'll go to church up the hill; then we always have a family dinner here."

That would explain the big roast she had waiting in the cool of the icehouse. And the extra pot of potatoes ready to set on the stove.

"Aw." Freddy hung his head and looked around, half discouraged. "Do I have to go?" He looked from Joanna to Rudy as if wondering who had the authority to say he could skip the service.

"I guess if Miss Joanna says we go, then we'll go." Rudy didn't much care for the idea himself but kept his opinion silent. He hadn't darkened the door of a church since—

With a start, he realized the last time he'd attended church was with Betty on his arm. He'd still been expecting her to marry him in two weeks' time. Three days later, she and Joe had made their treacherous announcement. He'd ridden away within the hour.

And left behind so many things.

"I think you might find this preacher to your liking." Joanna spoke to Freddy but darted a look at Rudy. "Levi is married to my sister, Glory. She calls him the rawhide preacher."

Freddy eased forward to perch on the edge of his chair. "How come?"

"Because of the rawhide vest he wears. It has fringes and big silver medallions on the yoke. Glory thought at first he was an outlaw. She said no preacher would wear such a vest." She chuckled, her gaze fully on Rudy now. "It took a bit of work for Levi to convince Glory he was truly a preacher and not some bad guy pulling the wool over everyone's eyes."

"He wasn't a bad guy?" Freddy sat back, so disappointed Joanna laughed.

"No, but he's no sissy. No man who marries one of the buffalo—one of us—could be."

"Buffalo? What were you about to say?"

"Nothing."

He looked at Cora. She grinned. Her eyes sparkled.

"Cora, you best keep it to yourself," Joanna warned.

Cora laughed, her eyes brimming over with fun. "I won't say anything. I promise."

Rudy studied Joanna with a great deal of curiosity. "You weren't buffalo hunters, were you? Somehow I can see the three of you bagging one of those huge creatures and skinning it out."

"I never in my life shot a buffalo." She tried to look disinterested, as if hoping the subject would end.

Cora giggled but kept mum.

Rudy determined he would find out. One way or another. On the same breath he decided he would attend church for the pleasure of accompanying Joanna, if nothing else.

Sunday morning edged with hurry. Hurry and get breakfast served. Hurry and clean up. Then Joanna and Cora slipped to their rooms to prepare for church.

Rudy and Freddy stepped into the small bedroom off the main room, reserved for female travelers. He pulled his best shirt from the bag and examined it. Not too badly wrinkled. A brown shirt worn many times before, but he liked it and saved it for special occasions. Mostly it had been used for Saturday nights to town. He avoided the saloons but often found a literary society offering readings or performances of a play. Sometimes a special singer entertained.

He dug in the bag and found a string tie in the bottom. That ought to dress things up good enough. He slicked back his hair then turned his attention to Freddy.

"A good scrubbing wouldn't hurt you." He'd never thought of the physical needs of the boy, somehow assuming he was old enough to take care of himself. But closer examination revealed certain deficits. "Wait here while I get a washcloth and towel."

"I don't need washing." Freddy looked ready to bolt.

Rudy nailed him to the floor with his don't-mess-with-me look, surprised it had an effect on the boy. "You wait. Besides, you wouldn't want Miss Joanna to be ashamed of us, would you?"

The boy fought an internal battle that played out on his face. Would he continue to defy Rudy simply to prove he didn't like him, or give in for Joanna's sake? At the moment Freddy seemed to care more about Joanna's opinion than proving he hated Rudy. Still, Rudy dashed out and back in record time, getting water to wash the boy before Freddy changed his mind.

Ignoring the muttered complaints, he scrubbed Freddy's neck and removed a shovelful of dirt from his ears. Then he dug through the boy's belongings, surprised at how few things he had and how ragged they were. "Didn't Grandma buy you clothes?"

"Why should she? I wasn't her kid."

Anger as raw as a smoldering forest fire tore through Rudy's insides. Freddy was her grandson. Didn't that count? The son of her favorite child. Was his mother capable of loving only one Canfield male—Joe? "She must have forgotten." Such inadequate words. But if Freddy was half as aware of Ma's indifference as Rudy had been, there were no words to make it right. "Seems like we need to make a trip to the store tomorrow and see what we can find for a boy your size."

Freddy looked interested—for about one second. He shrugged. "Don't matter."

Rudy let the statement pass without comment. He finally found a half-decent shirt and a pair of patched overalls. "At least they're clean. Put them on, then we'll see to your hair."

He tried to tame the thatch of black hair, but it was thick with dirt. And long enough to tie back. Tomorrow might involve finding a barber as well.

They returned to the dining room to wait.

Cora slipped out, fresh and pretty in a pink dress, her fair hair tied back with pink ribbons. A beautiful girl.

Joanna followed on her heels. She wore a newish-looking split skirt. He'd seen her in nothing else. But she wore a blue shirt that made her eyes seem a deeper brown. Her hair had been brushed until it gleamed. She'd tied it back with a bit of leather that held a row of beads. Her cowboy boots were soft suede.

He thought he'd never seen a better-looking woman—a woman ready to face challenges, yet—from the few days he'd known her—with a tender touch and an efficient but kind manner.

"Something wrong?" she asked.

He'd been staring. "No. I like your hair." He slammed his hat on his head and bolted for the door. Now she would wonder if he'd lost his mind. He wondered the same thing.

But outside, he had no place to run, not if he wanted to accompany her to church. And he did. He hadn't spent fifteen minutes greasing down his hair and Freddy's only to change his mind. He ground to a halt and waited for the others.

Cora and Joanna came out arm in arm, with Freddy lagging behind.

Joanna met Rudy's gaze, darted her attention away, then brought it back and gave a fleeting smile.

He'd embarrassed them both. He couldn't explain why he'd complimented her hair when he normally kept his thoughts to himself.

"Let's be on our way," she said, clinging to Cora's arm as they strode through the heart of Bonners Ferry and headed up the hill.

Rudy followed, mentally kicking himself with every step.

They arrived at a large, sun-drenched clearing with a breathtaking view of the river valley. Three buildings gleamed in their newness—a large house he guessed was the mission, a church with a steeple, and beyond, a barn with about a dozen horses in the pen outside.

A handful of people made their way into the church. Joanna led them to join the others gathering for worship.

The interior was surprisingly bright, with a row of windows facing east. They made their way into a wooden pew, the seats and backs polished smooth. Someone had spent hours turning the rough lumber into something worthy of a church.

Cora slipped in first, then Joanna preceded Rudy. He considered shoving Freddy in front of him, but for some inexplicable reason, he shoved him behind and seated himself next to Joanna.

Her arm brushed his as she straightened her skirt, and he felt her stiffen. Wanting to put her at ease, he whispered, "Joanna, I didn't mean to speak out of turn. I'm sorry."

She grew very still. Then she tilted her head close to whisper, "It's not your fault. But I'm not used to compliments, and it surprised me. No apology necessary."

Nor, he guessed, did she want him to retract his statement. She'd likely not heard near enough praise. He could remedy that. He whispered, "I meant it. Your hair is very pretty."

She smiled, keeping her attention on her hands where they lay in her lap. "Thank you."

Then the preacher announced it was time to begin.

"That's Levi," Joanna whispered.

He'd guessed as much when he saw the vest. He wasn't sure what to expect from a rawhide preacher—thunder and damnation probably.

They began with hymns. There were no musical instruments, but the congregation sang in beautiful harmony. Beside him, Joanna's rich alto voice blended perfectly with Cora's sweet soprano. Somewhere nearby, a deep bass joined in.

He'd attended many services growing up, the singing accompanied by a reedy organ and led by a monotone preacher. But never had he heard singing like this. And somewhere deep inside, he felt a warm touch, as if the presence of God hovered near. A bubble of unadulterated joy tickled a corner of his heart, creating a totally unfamiliar and not un-pleasant sensation.

Levi started to preach. Ah, but the man was gentle and persuasive enough to half convince Rudy to throw himself on God's love and mercy.

But preaching didn't reach into the real world. Rudy waited for the feeling to pass. Just like this sense of peace and contentment at Joanna's side would pass, replaced by the reality of life the moment they stepped from this place.

The service ended, and they filed outside where Joanna introduced him to Levi and then Trace, Mandy's husband.

The feeling of something deep and special clung like it meant to set up a homestead.

For the life of him he couldn't decide if he wanted to fight it or see where it went.

Chapter 7

Joanna looked around the table. For the first time there were eight present—the three sisters, husbands of her younger sisters, Cora, and now Rudy and Freddy. She could not explain why she should think it seemed satisfyingly complete, despite Austin's absence.

Levi, as was customary, rose to give the blessing, then they all turned their attention to the food. Joanna paused, the bowl of potatoes in her hand. "I'm going to miss these family dinners."

Levi looked at each of the sisters. "Seems a shame to break up the buffalo gals."

The three girls groaned in unison, and Trace chuckled.

"I suppose it's too much to hope we could get through a meal without this being brought up," Joanna grumbled, not daring to look at Rudy. She could feel his grin.

"The buffalo gals?" His voice rang with amusement. "There has to be a story behind that."

"There certainly is, and it's about time you heard it." Trace filled his plate and tasted his food as he drew the minute out. "Ouch." He jerked his feet away from Mandy and gave her a reproachful look, but other than that paid no mind to the kick she'd delivered. "You see, these girls have followed their pa all over the West. Seems the man has tried everything from work on railroad to gold mining to"—he shot a teasing grin at Mandy—"buffalo hunting."

Trace and Levi laughed heartily.

Joanna hoped her sisters would make their husbands pay when they got home but guessed it wouldn't happen. Their annoyance as they studied their husbands was liberally laced with admiration. Being in love sure took the teeth out of a good disagreement.

"They showed up one day asking after their pa, and someone said, 'You mean the old buffalo hunter?' So they started calling the girls 'the buffalo gals.' Suits them, wouldn't you say?"

Rudy grinned at Joanna, his eyes flashing with amusement and something more, something that slipped right past her hard-learned lessons and plopped all soft and mushy into the bottom of her heart.

"It suits them to a tee."

Was it only her imagination that read admiration and warmth in his voice?

Glory snatched the bowl from Levi's hands. "Who can blame Joanna for wanting to move on when she gets this kind of abuse every time you see her?"

"Abuse?" Levi stared at Glory like she'd appeared out of nowhere. "It's frank admiration of how tough and self-sufficient you gals are. Isn't it, Trace?"

Trace draped an arm over Mandy's shoulders, pulled her close, and kissed her nose. "Very true."

"Yuck," Freddy said.

Glory and Levi chuckled, but Mandy's eyes glowed with love.

Joanna groaned in mock despair. "I fail to see that my little sisters are self-sufficient anymore."

At that, both husbands roared with laughter. It was Levi who finally was able to speak. "They don't need us for anything except"—his eyes filled with warmth—"except love."

"We all need love," Trace said.

Freddy made a rude, disbelieving noise, but Glory and Mandy murmured agreement.

"Seems I'm on my own, then." She lowered her head to study the food on her plate, but she could not stop her gaze from darting to Rudy. She wondered if he, at times, felt the same strange loneliness that crept up unannounced and uninvited to wrap her heart in wintery cold.

Something in his look called to her, asking for something, but she couldn't say what.

"Joanna."

Levi's voice rescued her from her tangled thoughts.

He considered her kindly. "Are you sure you want to sell this place and move?"

"Of course she does." Glory leaned forward to peer around at her husband. "Of course you do. Levi, don't you be trying to persuade her to stay and keep an eye out for us. Joanna, we're all grown up now. You don't need to worry about us anymore. You can do what you want with your life."

"I'm just saying. . ." Levi held out his hands. "Joanna, make sure it's what you want and not what you think everyone expects of you."

"I appreciate your concern, Levi, but I've always done what I wanted."

Both Glory and Mandy spoke at once, voicing protests, each trying to outshout the other.

Trace reached for Mandy's hand to silence her.

Levi laughed, his eyes adoring his wife.

"You have taken care of us as long as I can remember," Mandy said. "Even before Ma died. By then you'd been acting like both Ma and Pa for years. I don't even remember Ma."

"She was sick a lot. I think she got tired of living."

Glory snorted. "More like wore out from following Pa around. Some men just aren't made for staying. Thankfully, I found one who is."

"Me, too," Mandy said.

Again Joanna felt cold and alone and dared not look toward Rudy. He'd made no secret of the fact he wasn't the sort made for staying. Footloose and fancy-free. And she would do well to remember it. But what difference did it make? Her plans didn't include staying either.

Thankfully, the conversation turned to other things, and the rest of the meal passed pleasantly enough. Yes, she would miss these Sunday afternoon family gatherings. But there had to be something more out there for her.

Had she inherited her pa's wanderlust? Heaven forbid.

Everyone moved at a leisurely pace on Sunday, so it was much later before the meal was over and the dishes done. Levi and Glory were the first to leave, saying they must check on the folks at the mission.

As Trace and Mandy prepared to depart, Joanna noticed a longing look in Cora's eyes. "You go with them. You haven't had a visit in a while. I'll manage supper on my own."

"I'll help her," Rudy offered.

"Me, too," Freddy added.

With those two offers, Joanna didn't feel quite so alone.

Cora accepted with a grin and left with her brother and new sister-in-law.

Rudy and Freddy ducked into the far bedroom and changed out of their Sunday clothes; then Freddy hurried to take the ashes out. Rudy followed, whistling under his breath. Through the window Joanna watched him set out the washbasins. Every few minutes he would glance toward her, mouth some words, and chuckle.

She could read his lips. Buffalo gals. So he thought that was funny? Let him laugh. Everyone deserved to enjoy a bit of humor.

After he did this the fourth time, she no longer felt so charitable and marched from the kitchen. He saw her coming, leaned back on his heels, and grinned.

His smile welcomed and teased at the same time. Something wrenched within her, a sensation both sweet and painful. She didn't waste time trying to figure out what it meant but steamed forward, not pausing until she was practically toe-to-toe with him. "You think being called the buffalo gals is funny?"

"Sure do, ma'am. Funniest thing I've heard since—well, never mind. It's plumb sweet, that's what it is."

Sweet? She crossed her arms. "You stop to think we might not like it?"

He sobered. "Can't see why you wouldn't. I think the Buffalo Gals of Bonners Ferry are going to put this place on the map."

"It's already on the map."

"Then you're going to make it famous."

"I'm not staying to see if your prediction comes true or not."

Every remnant of his smile fled, and his eyes grew hard as stone. "Nope. You'll be leaving on the first train out of here."

She snorted. "There's no train, and I'm not leaving until I sell this place." Why was she always insisting she would soon be gone? To Levi, to her sisters, and now to Rudy. They already knew it, and yet over and over she repeated it.

"Guess there's nothing to make you want to stay." It wasn't a question but an acknowledgment of the facts. No reason she should take objection to it, but she did.

"My sisters are here."

"Obviously not enough."

"You're talking in riddles." Then it hit her what he likely meant. "You saying I'm like my pa?"

"I expect you have your reasons for wanting to leave. We all have our reasons."

She couldn't think. Couldn't speak. She wasn't like Pa. She kept telling herself that. She didn't want to leave to get away from painful memories or to avoid responsibility. "Sometimes we need a reason to stay."

Freddy sauntered into sight, carrying the cat over his shoulder. The animal seemed completely comfortable though Joanna couldn't see how it was possible.

"You have a reason to stay someplace now." Rudy nodded toward Freddy. "Him."

Her confusion and anger dissipated like early-morning fog. "He seems almost happy at times."

"Still hates me a good percentage of the day."

She'd promised to help them and instead had got all twisted up with her own feelings. She wouldn't let it happen again. "I have a suggestion. Why don't you two make something together?"

"Like what?"

"I don't know. Surely you can think of something."

"Maybe."

The customers began to congregate, and Joanna hurried away to finish supper preparations.

∞

Rudy stared after her. She certainly swung from prickly to helpful with the speed of a raging fire. But her suggestion was perfect, and he knew exactly what he'd make. . .a cart that functioned like a wheelbarrow so she could move firewood and other loads with little effort.

But now he needed to help her with the meal as he'd promised. "Freddy, Joanna needs our help."

Freddy lowered the cat to a stool and took his time about saying good-bye to her. Rudy studied the pair. Seems he'd need to consider getting Freddy a pet when they settled someplace. A pet seemed to bring out a gentle side in the boy. "Wash up. Joanna wouldn't want you handling the food with dirty hands."

Freddy spared him a scowl. "I was gonna wash without you telling me."

"Sorry. No offense meant."

Freddy headed for the washstand without acknowledging Rudy's apology. Rudy scrubbed good, too, then they went into the kitchen.

"How can we help?"

"The table needs to be set." She glanced out the window. "Not many here tonight. Set it for twelve."

Rudy counted out the tin plates and handed them to Freddy then grabbed handfuls of cutlery and followed. The next few minutes were busy with preparing the table. By the time they finished, Joanna was ready to let the men in. She glanced at Freddy and seemed to make up her mind on something.

"Freddy, why don't you collect the money? All you have to do is stand at the door. Everyone drops in the same amount. Here." She handed him the can.

Freddy's chest expanded enough to threaten the seams on his shirt, and he favored Joanna with a wide smile as he took the can. But the look he sent Rudy's direction did not include a smile. The boy couldn't have been plainer about what he meant by the set of his mouth. He wanted Rudy to know he liked doing things for Miss Joanna. He wouldn't willingly, eagerly, do them for Rudy.

The knowledge cut through Rudy's thoughts, leaving a jagged wound. Why should he care so much? They were stuck together and had to make the best of it. No reason to expect more. He didn't need the boy's affection. Didn't need approval from anyone.

Joanna touched his arm.

The brush of her fingers soothed his troubled feelings.

"He's afraid and thinks if he can stay angry at you, he can't be hurt if you leave."

"I'm not leaving him."

"Does he know that?"

"He should."

"Sometimes a person needs to hear it said."

"I don't believe words mean anything. Actions are what matters." He'd tried to make it clear, but Freddy didn't believe him.

Her low laughter was musical and sweet. "Both matter."

The men began to file in, and there was no more time for discussion. Rudy was grateful. Or so he told himself. But inside him a longing, full of dark emptiness, made itself felt. Words. Only one person had ever given him words of affection and commitment. . .Betty. They meant nothing. So why did an empty spot in his heart practically beg for words?

He snorted at his foolish thinking and headed for the kitchen, where he took a big bowl of potatoes and carried them to the table. As he returned to get another bowl of food, Joanna headed for the dining room with a pitcher of gravy. They met in the doorway and as they passed, their shoulders brushed.

"Sorry," he murmured. He should have waited for her to go first.

"Not a problem."

Their gazes caught and held, and that empty spot opened its hungry mouth. She smiled, and a frisson of light entered the darkness.

"No need to be nervous around me," she said, her voice singing through his thoughts. "I'm not going to bite you."

He chuckled more out of confusion than amusement and hurried to take the platter of meat from the warming oven.

No, she might not bite, but she was going to leave. Why did it matter one way or the other if she seemed anxious to be on her way? It didn't. Except. . . Well, except he wondered if she really wanted to go. Or was she driven by the same spirit her wandering father had?

She said a person needed a reason to stay.

What would be enough reason for her?

He dismissed the question and forced himself to focus on the meal.

Joanna certainly knew how to prepare an abundance of tasty food. He'd never heard a word of complaint from any of those sitting around the table, and tonight was no exception. The stopping house wouldn't be the same without her. Especially if someone bought it with the idea of serving beans and bannock every meal. He ducked his head to hide a smile.

Seems a shame for the eldest buffalo gal to abandon Bonners Ferry.

But it was none of his concern, and he'd do well to remember it.

Monday afternoon, when it looked like Joanna had a few minutes to spare, Rudy appealed to her. "Freddy needs new clothes. The ones he has are either too small or practically worn out." Mostly they were both. "I've never purchased things for anyone but myself. Would you come with us to help?"

"I've never bought things for a boy."

"You still know more about it than I do. After all, you raised two younger sisters." He refrained from referring to them as the buffalo gals, but it tickled him to think of them as such.

She laughed. "Seems you should remember being a little boy better than I would."

He let himself drink from her smile.

"You were a small boy once, were you not?"

Her words forced him back to that time, and his heart clenched as if someone squeezed it with a giant, cruel fist. "I prefer not to recall those days."

Her eyes narrowed, and she studied him.

He would not allow himself to turn from her gaze but did his best to keep his face void of emotion. He failed miserably. The memories flooded his insides as if a dam of contaminated water had broken free.

The concern in her eyes said he hadn't disguised his feelings.

"Rudy." She touched his arm, and her touch warred with the raging pain until he feared his insides would explode. "What happened?"

He knew she meant what happened in his childhood to create a maelstrom of emotions that he couldn't hide. He clamped his teeth together. He would not spill the truth. It belonged in the past. But the words erupted unbidden, uncensored. "I wasn't wanted. Joe was a year older, and my mother's world revolved around him. I was only an added inconvenience." *Stop. Stop. Stop.*

But the words continued to pour forth. "She had words for me, all right. Every day she spoke them. 'Get out of my sight.' 'Don't hurt your brother.' 'Don't bother me.' 'I wish you were never born.'"

Joanna's eyes glistened. "Rudy, how awful."

Finally, mercifully, the words stopped. But the pain boiled within him. He should have never lifted the lid.

Joanna led him to the table, and he bent wooden knees to sit on a chair.

"Rudy, no wonder you run."

"I don't run."

"You leave. It's the same thing. But you can't outrun your pain. Maybe you need to stop trying."

"This from a woman who can't wait to get out of here." His voice sounded bitter even to his own ears, but how could she offer advice when she was leaving on the first train? So what if there wasn't a train? She had other means of transportation to choose from.

"I'm not leaving to run away from my feelings. I'm going to look for another business."

"I suppose if you tell yourself that often enough, you believe it."

She pursed her mouth. But he pressed on.

"You're leaving because your sisters no longer need you, and without them you don't know what to do with yourself. You don't know how to be Joanna without being the big sister." He couldn't explain where the words came from, but once spoken, he knew them to be true.

She pushed to her feet. "How do we end up arguing like this? I only wanted to express my sympathy and sorrow."

Rudy's mouth dropped open. Why should she care how he felt?

She must have read the disbelief in his face. "Yes, sorrow. It hurts me to think of you as a little boy feeling unloved. Worse, being told you were unwanted."

Her anger fled, and her eyes again filled with a softness that made him want to yell. Fill the air with curses at the way he'd been treated. Let his pain erupt into dark and angry words.

"Rudy, someone needs to love the hurting away." She blinked and lowered her gaze as if she'd said more than she meant.

And his heart leaped like a deer in fresh green pasture.

"Or maybe you need to love someone else to heal it." She jerked toward the window. "There's a little boy who seems as hurt by his upbringing as you were. The difference being you can change it. You can love him and prevent him from growing up to feel like you do."

Had she suspected what he'd seen? That his mother treated Freddy much as she'd treated Rudy. Could he undo the damage?

His heart went out to the youngster who had no one but him—a man who didn't know how to love.

Could he learn how?

Or was it too late?

Such thoughts were too confusing. Too troubling. Time to get back to normal. "Will you come shopping with us?"

"Certainly. When?"

"No time like the present."

She nodded and went to get a purse of coins and a basket. "I'll pick up a few things, too."

They went outside and called Freddy, who ran to join them. "Where we going?"

"Shopping for something for you to wear," Rudy said. But if he thought Freddy would show a little interest, he would wait in vain.

Together they trooped toward the mercantile. Rudy and Joanna walked side by side while Freddy ran ahead, dashing back and forth. And despite his best resolution to do otherwise, Rudy let himself think how nice it would be if Joanna stayed. If he stayed. And if they saw each other often. Maybe daily. And shopping trips like this became a regular activity.

He shook his head. When had a trip to the store ever seemed like a big event? He must be sickening with something to be so muddle brained.

Chapter 8

Joanna tried to retain her anger at Rudy for suggesting she didn't know how to manage on her own. She wasn't running away from her life because she didn't think she was needed anymore. What nonsense.

She quickened her pace toward the mercantile, but she struggled to dredge up any remnant of her anger. How could she be upset, knowing that Rudy's mother had told him he was unwanted? How dreadful. What kind of mother would say such cruel things? No wonder Rudy did his best to act like he had no feelings for anyone.

She glanced sideways at him. Right now he seemed cheerful. But she'd seen how Freddy's bad attitude wounded him, and she knew underneath the surface of the footloose, fancy-free man lay a hurting, needy heart.

Her arms ached to hold and comfort him. . .which she refused to admit. However, he and Freddy must find a way to love each other. Two hurting people from the same home. She almost cried aloud at the thought that Freddy had been treated the same way as Rudy. She vowed she would help them any way she could. With God's help. This must be why the sale of the stopping house had fallen through. . .to give her a chance to show these two how to love each other.

They reached the store. Rudy held the door open for her, and she couldn't avoid brushing his chest as she squeezed through. A zing of something resembling joy raced through her heart. It would be fun, satisfying, to see Rudy and Freddy get past their hurt.

The scent of lemon oil, old cheese, and jute rope greeted them. She paused to allow her eyes to adjust to the dimmer interior of the building. Rudy hovered behind her, so close she could feel the warmth from his body and smell a heart-stirring mixture of leather and hay.

Freddy made a beeline for the ready-made wear. "I'm getting new clothes," he announced to the storekeeper.

"Well, well, that's good news for both of us." Rubbing his hands together, the man hurried to Freddy's side. He eyed the boy up and down. "You'll be wanting trousers and shirts and new boots, too, I'd say." He glanced at the two adults. "Good morning, Miss Joanna. Are you with this boy?"

Joanna finally found the ability to step forward. She introduced Rudy. "Freddy's uncle."

The storekeeper shook hands then began to sort through the stack of clothes. "I don't carry a lot of children's items, but I can certainly order anything you need, and it will come from Sand Point in two days' time. But here is a pair of trousers that should fit the young man." He held them up to Freddy's waist.

Rudy turned a questioning look toward Joanna, and she nodded.

"They look fine," he said. "Any shirts?"

There was a dark gray one that fit.

"That should be serviceable," Joanna said. "Won't show the dirt too quickly."

Rudy chuckled. "I hadn't thought of that, but no doubt it's something I need to keep in mind. Now what else does he need?"

The storekeeper leaned forward, eager to offer suggestions, but Rudy waited for Joanna to answer. So she and Rudy and Freddy had a little conference. She listed what she thought was essential—underwear, socks, boots—

"He'll soon need a decent winter coat."

Freddy rocked from foot to foot, his attention glued to the glass-fronted display case toward the front of the store.

Joanna nudged Rudy. "Seems Freddy has his eye on something. Wonder what it is?" She turned sideways and leaned close to Rudy to whisper, "You might consider getting him something besides clothing." In her attempt to keep as much distance between them as possible, she leaned too far forward. She lost her balance and grabbed Rudy's arm.

He caught her by the shoulders to right her.

She looked into his face. At the yearning expression in his eyes, her heart rattled against her ribs. The moment lingered as they studied each other. She wondered if her gaze was as revealing as his, because for certain she felt something. A loneliness that made no sense yet called out to be relieved. A longing that wouldn't be satisfied by food or drink.

Someone needs to love the hurting away. She's spoken the words to

Rudy, but they echoed in her heart. He wasn't the only one who needed to love the hurt away. Wasn't that what she'd done for her sisters? Why then hadn't it done its work in her heart?

"It's the best knife I ever saw." Freddy's voice brought her back to reality. She smiled her thanks to Rudy for his help then turned her attention to Freddy, who had his nose pressed to the glass of the display case.

Rudy knelt beside him. "It is a pretty special knife. Is that a hand-carved handle?"

The storekeeper didn't waste a minute pulling it from the case and extolling its virtues. "Finest steel. This knife will hold an edge better than any of those others."

Rudy examined the blade then handed it to Freddy to inspect. "What do you think?"

Freddy looked around ready to bust from his skin. "It's a fine knife."

"You think a boy your age would have any use for it?"

"Oh yeah. I could do lots of things with a knife. I could shave off kindling for Miss Joanna. I could chop meat from the old soup bones for the kitty. Why, I bet I could carve something really useful."

Rudy's grin said it all. Freddy's eagerness with him was something new, and Rudy fairly glowed.

Joanna stood back and watched the two of them, praying the moment would be the first of many.

Rudy nodded, suddenly all serious as if this was the most important decision of the day. But Joanna saw the gleam that lingered in his eyes. "Sure sounds like you need a knife real bad," he said to Freddy. "Maybe we should buy this one, seeing as it's such a fine knife."

Freddy grew still, his gaze shifting from the knife to his uncle in a mixture of hope and fear.

Joanna's heart thudded in her chest. Rudy and Freddy were more alike than either of them knew—afraid of love, yet wanting it so much it hurt. And at the same time fearing rejection so badly they couldn't let anyone know their desires.

Freddy swallowed noticeably. "Maybe we should buy it." His words squeaked from his throat.

"It's your decision." Rudy handed him the knife again. "You must choose if this is the knife for you."

"Oh, it is. I'm certain."

"Then we'll take it."

Freddy's eyes never left the knife as the storekeeper took it and returned it reverently to the leather sheath meant for a man's belt.

"Guess he'll need a belt, too," Rudy said.

A few minutes later they left the store, a belt through the loops of Freddy's new trousers and the knife hanging from the belt. Rudy had placed an order with the storekeeper for a wardrobe that would see the boy through the winter.

At the post office Joanna had received a letter from Sarah. She would wait until she was alone to read it; in case Sarah announced she'd found another travel companion, Joanna would rather deal with any disappointment in private.

She and Rudy walked side by side, and Freddy marched ahead, as proud as any boy she'd ever seen. "You've made him happy."

"He likes me at the moment for the knife."

"It's as good a place to start as any." Did Freddy realize how generous Rudy had been?

At that moment Freddy stopped marching forward and slowly turned to retrace his steps until he was only a few feet away. He obviously wanted to say something but rocked from side to side as if unable to find the words.

Rudy and Joanna waited.

Freddy looked at his uncle then away. He patted his knife as if to make sure it still hung from his belt. "Uncle Rudy, thank you for the knife. It's the best thing I ever got in my whole life." The words came out like bullets shot from a gun. Freddy turned and fled down the street, not pausing until he was twenty feet away.

"He thanked me." Rudy sounded surprised.

"Of course he did."

"And he didn't look angry. He even called me 'uncle.'"

Joanna chuckled and tucked her hand into the crook of his arm. "Love works miracles."

"I bought him a knife. What's that got to do with love?"

"There's more than one way to show love." Words might come later when they were both ready to believe them.

∞

Back at the stopping house, Rudy gave Freddy a few safety tips on using his knife—point the blade away from yourself when cutting, never rush when working with your knife, keep your fingers above where you are cutting, always store it safely. Freddy listened and observed carefully as

Rudy talked then allowed Rudy to supervise his first few attempts at using the knife.

Rudy could not stop something foreign and pleasant from bubbling inside him. "You'll do just fine." He swallowed his caution and squeezed Freddy's shoulder. When the boy didn't jerk away or voice a complaint, Rudy's smile grew so wide he wondered it didn't pop his ears off.

He hung around the yard. He didn't have any pressing business keeping him there except the pleasure of watching Freddy enjoy his knife. He'd planned on continuing north after turning Freddy over to his pa. He figured he'd find a job on some ranch, but helping out at the stopping house suited him fine at the moment. In exchange for their work, Joanna provided room and board. Under that arrangement, he had enough money to keep them going for several months.

The boy knelt in the dirt by the chopping block and worked away on a piece of wood, learning to cut shavings from it. Most of them wouldn't be much good as kindling or anything else, but that didn't matter. Nothing mattered half so much as seeing Freddy enjoy something Rudy had given him.

Wanting to share the moment, he turned toward the window. Joanna was there and smiled. He mouthed the words *thank you.*

She lifted her hands to signify she didn't know what he meant.

He pointed toward Freddy then shook his head. What was he thinking? She'd done nothing except. . .be there. Encourage him. Let him realize Freddy might be hurting. But he wouldn't know where to begin to try to explain. One thing he knew and understood was somehow she'd had a part in this moment.

Suddenly feeling as if his insides lay exposed, he turned from the window and got real interested in examining a loose board on the side of the storage shed. What had come over him to confess his mother had never wanted him? A man didn't complain about his mother. It was downright weak. Worse. A man should honor his mother.

He went into the shed, found a hammer, and drove several nails into the errant board. With each blow he drove the past back into place and used huge spikes to secure the invisible, interior door shut.

He returned the hammer to the shed and had a look around, remembering he meant to make a cart for Joanna. No time like the present to start the project. Finding some bits of lumber, he assessed them for possibilities then went outside. "Freddy, wanna help me make something?"

Freddy carefully sheathed his knife before he joined Rudy. "Whatcha making?"

He explained his plan. "I thought we should work inside the shed so it will be a surprise for Miss Joanna. What do you think?"

Freddy nodded solemnly. "I think she'd like it."

Together they measured and cut. The boy was pleasant company when he was in a mellow mood, but Rudy couldn't help wondering how long it would last.

For the next few days, they spent every spare moment in the shed working on the cart. Rudy had discovered that so long as they concentrated on this project, Freddy was docile enough. But all he had to do was ask the boy to help carry water or suggest he should wash up for the meal, and he earned himself a scowl fit to cure leather.

What did he have to do to persuade Freddy to be friends?

Rudy asked him to leave the cat and tend to his chores. Freddy again favored him with one of his scorching looks. Rudy sighed. He hated to admit how much it hurt.

Joanna slipped to his side, her presence soothing his pain. "Don't let it discourage you. You're making great progress."

"Sometimes I wonder. Seems I should be past letting things like this hurt me." Now where had that come from? Why was it every time Joanna got within speaking distance he said something weak-kneed? He couldn't imagine what she thought of him acting like a down-in-the-mouth sissy.

"I'd say it's a good thing you aren't. It would only show you had no feelings. No ability to love. Makes me glad to see that's not true."

Made her glad, did it? Huh. Well, that made him feel good. . .made him want to do something special for her. "We should celebrate progress." A slap alongside his head seemed about the wisest thing at the moment.

"What a great idea. Let's go on a picnic. I know just the spot. Tomorrow?"

"Let me check my schedule." He made a show of tapping his chin and thinking deeply on the subject, but she knew as well as he that his schedule included nothing of pressing importance. He only wanted the time to settle his runaway thoughts into a slow canter. She actually sounded like she wanted to go somewhere with him. "Yup. I can work it in tomorrow."

She chuckled. "Great."

He echoed the word inside his head.

Joanna slipped away to visit Mandy. She'd been wanting to tell someone the contents of her letter from Sarah, and now she needed to enlist Mandy's help.

"Rudy and I are taking Freddy on a picnic tomorrow. If you and Trace could help Cora manage supper, then we wouldn't have to hurry back. Would you mind?"

Mandy studied her with knowing eyes. "We'd love to help. You know, Joanna, it's about time you did something fun for a change."

Why were her sisters so insistent she have fun, do something for herself? It got to be annoying after a bit. "You make it sound like I've lived my life as a reluctant martyr. I haven't, you know. No one forced me to live my life as I have."

Mandy quirked an eyebrow.

"Okay, in a way Pa did. But I did it gladly. After all, we're family, and I love you two."

Mandy hugged her. "I know. But still I worry that you've always had so much responsibility."

Joanna shook her head. "I was also blessed. Do you stop to consider that?"

"Blessed? How?"

She squeezed her sister's hands. "By love. We've always loved each other and always will. We shouldn't take that for granted. Rudy told me how his mother withheld love from him, and I have a notion she's done the same with Freddy." She didn't want to give any more details. After all, it was Rudy's story. "It makes me realize how fortunate we've been. Yes, our ma died, and our pa doesn't hang around, but we've always had each other."

"You're right. And looking at what we don't have serves no purpose."

They shifted the conversation to other things. Mandy showed the latest developments on the log house. Trace was working on adding another room. "Where is he now?"

"Out hunting. He says he wants a good supply of meat before winter hits."

They moved outside and sat in the autumn sun. "Any news from your other prospective buyer?" Mandy asked.

"No, but I had a letter from Sarah. She says there is another woman who has expressed an interest in accompanying her to California, but she prefers me as a traveling companion and will wait to see if I can sell the place. She says we have a few more weeks before we must leave."

"Then I hope and pray the sale happens quickly."

Joanna left a short time later. Usually a visit with either of her sisters made her feel settled, but not this time. She kept thinking of Sarah's letter. Every time she did, she saw Freddy and Rudy riding away. Why the idea should give her pause didn't make sense. Rudy had never planned to stay. He only did so to work things out with Freddy, and he was making progress on that front. So why did she feel wrung out and hung to dry in a cold wind when she thought of Sarah's letter? And even worse, tattered and torn when she realized Rudy and Freddy would soon be moving on.

They had no reason to stay.

Would anything make Rudy change his mind and settle down?

Chapter 9

"A picnic?" Emotions chased each other across Freddy's face. Surprise then a flash of excitement quickly wiped away with fear then settling into indifference.

Rudy understood his confusion. Likely he'd never gone on a picnic or anything just for the fun of it. Rudy certainly couldn't remember doing so as a child. Sure, he'd eaten outdoors lots of times, especially since he'd taken to a cowboy sort of life. But just for fun? Just to share time with others?

Or was he reading too much into the situation? Expecting something always resulted in disappointment. He ought to know that well enough. "Miss Joanna says she wants to show us a nice place."

Freddy nodded. "Can I bring my knife?"

"Don't see why not." Rudy wished he could take something along to guard himself against hoping for things beyond his reach. But all he had at his disposal was the good sense to be cautious.

Joanna set a picnic basket on the veranda where he and Freddy waited. "I'll just grab a wrap, and then I'm ready to go."

Rudy picked up the basket. She sure must have packed a lot of food. But hauling the thing gave him something to pin his thoughts to besides admiring Joanna and wishing things could be different.

He might as well wish for the stars to land in his pocket. A man couldn't undo the past or change who he was or how he felt.

Joanna pointed to the trail leading up the hill, and Freddy scampered ahead, exploring every root and cluster of trees along the path.

"It's a glorious day, isn't it?" Joanna lifted her arms heavenward as if embracing the world.

"I haven't paid much attention, but it is." One of those golden autumn days when the light had a warm glow to it, the wind was gentle and kind, the leaves flashed like coins caught on the branches, and the air practically burst with a scent peculiar to fall and crispy foliage. And beside him, a woman whose brown eyes were even warmer than the sunshine and who carried an inner source of light that shone through her.

"Days like this remind me how much God loves me."

He couldn't say he agreed. Nothing much made him think God loved him. After all, if his mother couldn't love him, who could? Betty had answered that question for him in an unmistakable way. Seemed no one could. But he wasn't about to introduce any note of discord.

They drew near a clearing with a log house.

"This is where Trace and Mandy live."

"Nice house."

"That's the one Trace built." She directed his attention to a crude shed. "That's the one Mandy built." Then she told an amusing story of a race between Mandy and Trace. The agreement was, whoever got their house built first got the land. "Trace called it a twig house."

"So who won?"

"I guess Trace, though Mandy would say she did. But she abandoned her house to help Trace with his, and now they share it as man and wife."

He chuckled. "Your sisters are quite a pair."

"You wouldn't consider them tame in any way, that's for sure."

"Yet it doesn't seem to bother either Levi or Trace."

"Love sees beyond the surface."

They studied each other, something fragile hanging between them. Did she see beneath his exterior? And if she did, what would she see? He didn't like what lay inside—loneliness and uncertainty that clawed at his heart.

He cleared his throat and looked away. "Where are you taking us?"

A teasing flash filled her eyes. "To a special spot, if you're up to a bit of a climb."

"I have to say I've walked more the past few days than I have since I was a boy. Mostly I ride my horse."

"Think you'll manage?"

"I'll manage." Even if his heels developed huge blisters and his toes cramped, he would make it. In fact, he could think of nothing that would keep him from enjoying this afternoon, including his fears and concerns. He shoved them firmly into the background.

They turned onto a narrower trail that required they walk single file. Joanna led the way with Freddy at her heels. Rudy brought up the rear. The trail grew steeper and rocky. Aspen trees crowded close enough to form a canopy overhead.

Freddy slipped, but Rudy steadied him. Freddy hurried onward without saying a thing, still uncomfortable with Rudy touching him.

Finally, about the time Rudy thought his feet might not take much more, Joanna reached a level area and waited for them. Rudy climbed to her side and looked around.

"We're almost on top of the world," he said. Below lay the wide river valley, ripe with autumn colors and dotted with dark spruce and pine. Beyond it, fluffy clouds topped the blue mountains.

Joanna took her time admiring the view.

"Can I play in the trees?" Freddy asked.

"Don't go far. Wouldn't want a bear finding you."

Freddy hesitated then slipped into the trees, darting from trunk to trunk.

"Do you come here often?" Rudy asked Joanna.

"This is only the second time I've been here. Mandy brought Glory and me to this spot before their weddings. The two of them chose the same day to be married," she added. "Mandy wanted us to have a special occasion before our family broke up."

He sensed again how lost she felt without her sisters. But he didn't say anything this time. "A special occasion, you say?"

She laughed, understanding his disbelief. "What would you expect from the buffalo gals? Certainly not a tea party." Her gaze drifted toward the distance. "We spent a lot of time here talking about the past and looking toward the future."

"I suppose the three of you have many good memories."

She gave a long sigh. "We seldom talked about the past. Glory always got so angry, and Mandy had this dream that Pa would come back and we'd be an ideal family. But that day I realized we hadn't been an ideal family for a long time. I could remember Ma being strong and taking care of us. The other two can't."

"How much older are you?" She talked like she was a decade older, but she seemed so young.

"I'm twenty-three—three years older than Glory and four years older than Mandy."

"Still so young."

She slanted a look at him, her eyes brimming with curiosity and teasing. "How about you? How old are you?"

"I'm positively ancient." Much too old to be wishing this moment with her could last forever.

"Ancient would be old and bent. You're certainly not that, so maybe you can be a little more specific."

Did he detect a hint of rosy color in her cheeks? He decided he liked knowing she might blush around him. "I'm thirty-two."

"Phew. Barely older than me."

"Old enough to be wise?"

"I don't know. Are you?"

"I doubt it." Now that he gave it a moment's consideration, he felt as if he'd spent the last eleven years avoiding everything but survival.

She squinted up at the bright sky and the fluffy clouds drifting across the blue canvas. "I tried to help the girls remember times when we'd been a real family. But you know, as we talked, I realized we were an unconventional family. Still are." She didn't give him a chance to say the words. "And it didn't matter."

He chuckled.

"We learned at an early age to amuse ourselves. I suppose we ran wild. We played cops and robbers and thought nothing of chasing through people's yards. The best was when we were out of town and could run and play without anyone to complain."

"It sounds like fun."

"It was. But I think we'd gotten into the habit of remembering only the bad parts."

He wasn't keen on the way she eyed him as if she wanted him to examine his memories. "I have no wish to look at my past. I don't look into the future either. I just take each day and do what it requires."

"So you pretend you have no past, no future, and practically no present?"

He could find no argument, though he wanted to. Her words were too close to the truth.

She took his silence for agreement. "Should you let the past have that much control over your life?"

"It has no part in my life one way or the other."

Her gaze was both sad and challenging. "From what you've said, I guess it has a powerful hold on you. But never mind that. I have no wish to start an argument."

"Good to know." He did his best to keep the annoyance out of his voice but failed. She lifted one corner of her mouth in a half smile.

"So you talked about the future, too? Is this when you decided you want to go to California?"

"I suppose it is. The girls wanted to know what I would do with them both moving out."

"So rather than have them feel sorry for you or perhaps worry about you, you came up with this plan."

"I decided it's time for me to move on. Find out what I want to do."

He tipped his head as he considered her. Had she realized what she'd said?

She recognized his unspoken question. "I mean do what I want to do."

He nodded, knowing full well she'd been closer to the truth the first time.

She shifted her attention to the picnic basket at his feet. "The best thing about our day here was we talked about how much we love each other. Saying the words made our love so real."

"You are most fortunate that you've had each other."

"I know it. But now. . ." Her voice grew dreamy. "You have Freddy. You have someone to love and to love you in return." Bending, she lifted the lid of the basket and pulled out a gray woolen blanket. Mouthwatering aromas of fresh bread and something spicy caught his senses.

"Neither of us knows the first thing about loving." His mouth had done it again. Said things without checking with his brain first.

Joanna flicked the blanket to the ground. "Let's sit." She sat down and patted a spot beside her. "You know, Rudy, my sisters and I weren't always loving and kind to each other. We went through a few years when we couldn't believe in love."

"What happened?" He adjusted himself on the blanket, keeping his feet on the grass.

"I suppose we realized we only had each other so we might as well make the best of it."

Her words were the same ones he considered when he thought of he and Freddy thrust together.

She continued. "But one of the biggest things was, Levi came and started preaching about God's love. That's when I found my ma's old Bible, and we began to read it. We read it together each night, but we also would find time to read it alone. Knowing and believing God loves me healed my heart. It was His love that loved my hurting away."

"If only it was that easy for everyone."

She pressed her hand to his. "I believe it's as easy or as hard as you make it."

The warmth of her hand spread throughout his body like a summer wind reminding him of pleasant days and peaceful evenings. "I find it impossible to believe God loves me when my own mother didn't. I know I should honor her and not speak badly of her. But it's the truth. She didn't love me."

"You aren't dishonoring her to speak the truth. And by facing the past, perhaps you are finding a way to bring healing to your heart."

He turned his hand and held hers, hoping his grip didn't reveal how desperately he needed her to keep talking. Was it possible for the wound he tried so hard to ignore to be healed?

"I have a favorite Bible verse." She held his eyes in an urgent look. Knowing she cared opened his heart a fraction more. "It's Numbers 23:19. 'God is not a man, that he should lie; neither the son of man, that he should repent: hath he said, and shall he not do it?' To me that means God's love isn't like man's love. We can trust it. If He says He loves us, He does."

Hope, raw and naked, showed in her eyes. She really cared whether or not he believed it. It made him ache to say he did. But between the wanting to and the being able to was a valley as deep and wide as the one that lay before them, only it was dark and empty.

He did not know how to cross to the other side.

She sighed. "I know it's hard to accept, but why don't you read your Bible and see for yourself what God says? He does not speak empty words."

"I might do that." First he'd have to get the storekeeper to order a Bible, because he didn't own one. Never had.

"Rudy, you never mention your father. What happened to him?"

"He died when we were babies. My mother raised us alone. My father left her well enough provided for that we didn't lack for anything."

"Except love."

"Only I lacked that. Joe had plenty of it."

"But not, I think, Freddy."

A zephyr of a breeze caught the corner of the blanket, and he pinned the cloth down with his heel. "That surprises me. After all, he's Joe's son. I'd think that would earn him favor." He shrugged. "No explaining it, I guess."

"Rudy." She squeezed his hand tight and leaned closer. "Please remember that God isn't like your mother or even my father. He says He loves us, and He does. He says He'll never leave us, and He doesn't."

He let himself swim in her concern. The sun caught in her eyes, filling them with warmth and something more. It was as if she spoke silent hope and faith. She believed so completely. "Is it easy to believe?" His voice sounded distant.

"It's easy enough once you decide. It sometimes takes a while to let yourself accept the truth and rest in it."

"Rest in it. You make it sound so appealing."

"Rudy." She leaned so close he felt her breath on his cheeks. "I wish for you to find the same love and healing I have found in God's love."

"Do you really care that much?"

She nodded, her eyes brimming with. . .

He wouldn't let himself try to name the look in her eyes. He drank from her gaze, let his eyes drift across her sun-kissed cheeks and come to rest on her lips—parted with eagerness. She said she cared. Her words caught at heavy corners of his heart and lifted it skyward, light and airy as a bird on the wing. She cared. For the moment he would not consider what it meant, how it threatened his boundaries. "Joanna." He whispered her name.

She leaned closer.

Dare he kiss her? Would it send her running into the woods? Would it end this fragile sense of friendship and caring between them?

He sat up straight and forced his attention to the view, though he saw none of it. He was not about to risk losing her friendship for the sake of a kiss.

∞

Joanna pulled her hand to her lap. What had she been thinking to practically kiss Rudy? Poor unsuspecting man. Of course he wasn't interested in that sort of relationship between them.

Nor was she.

Though she did care about him. Him and Freddy. She sensed the longing emptiness within Rudy. His need for love. She silently prayed that he might find healing in God's love.

She longed for more. But she couldn't explain what it was. She squeezed her hands together to keep from reaching for Rudy again.

"There's lots of hiding places in the trees," Freddy called, his voice hopeful.

She wondered if anyone had ever played with him. Surely he'd had playmates at school. But his words gave her an idea. She scrambled to her feet. "Let's play a game."

"Okay." Freddy stood before them, bouncing on the balls of his feet.

"It will take all three of us." She tilted her head to signal Rudy to get up and join them.

"I'm too old for games," he muttered without moving.

"You're certainly not too old. In fact, it might be just the thing. Come on, get up." She couldn't say what she meant, and he, thankfully, did not ask.

Sending her a look of pure martyrdom, he pushed to his feet. "What's the game?"

"Doesn't have a name, but my sisters and I used to play it by the hour." It was a combination of hide-and-seek and cops and robbers. "One of us is the bad guy, and we have to try and catch him." She set out the perimeters so none of them could go too far away.

"Can I be the bad guy?" Freddy asked.

"I could get a little worried about how eager you are for that role." She gave him a mock-stern look. "So long as you remember it's only a game."

He nodded vigorously.

"Okay, you're the bad guy. We'll give you a head start; then you have to hide or slip away from us so we can't catch you. Your turn is over when we capture you."

Freddy raced into the trees and disappeared from sight.

She turned to Rudy. "The trick is for us to work as a team so he can't slip past us once we find him."

"Let's go capture the bad guy." He grinned in a way that made Jo-anna giggle.

He signaled for her to go to the right while he went left. After a moment the woods grew quiet. She couldn't hear either of the others, but it hadn't been so long since she'd played the game that she'd lost her skill. She edged forward silently, slowly, pausing often to listen. There. A snap to her left. She eased toward it. Freddy, moving forward, glancing often over his shoulder.

She stayed out of sight and knew he hadn't spotted her.

Now to find Rudy. She moved with the stealth of years of playing this game with her sisters. Freddy's passage wasn't silent, so she tracked him with her ear. But she didn't hear Rudy anywhere. She eased forward, searching the shadows. Where had he gone?

Creeping forward slowly, she crisscrossed the area, each time listening for a sound, seeking for a visual. But he'd disappeared. Seems he knew how to move in the trees as quietly as Mandy, who vowed she was so silent she could sneak up on a deer at a watering hole.

Something caught her arm. She stifled a scream and turned terror-filled eyes to—

"Rudy," she whispered. She took a deep breath while her hammering heart slowed. "Are you trying to scare me to death?"

He pulled her into the hollow of some bushes. The space was too small for the two of them, and she was crushed to his chest. "Sure was fun watching you sneak around." His mouth was at her ear, his breath warm on her cheek.

"How long have you been spying on me?"

"Not long enough." He seemed breathless.

She wondered at his meaning. "What are we doing?"

"Waiting for Freddy to come by. Then we'll scare him just like I did you."

"Oh." So they would stay like this until Freddy came looking for them? Kind of a backward way to play the game, but somehow she didn't mind. She was comfortable enough cradled against his chest. In fact, it was downright pleasant. She could surely allow herself to enjoy this for a moment or two. Then they'd go back to their same old cautious, guarded way around each other.

"Shh. Here he comes."

So soon? Why, she was just getting to like this.

"Get ready." He pushed her forward, but his hands remained on her upper arms, steadying her.

A very comforting feeling, she decided.

"Now." He leaped forward, taking her before him. They yelled loudly.

Freddy shrieked and tried to run away, but she grabbed his arm and prevented his escape.

"We got the bad guy." Rudy swept the boy into the air and swung him around.

Freddy shouted with laughter. The sound triggered something in Joanna, and she began to giggle.

Rudy set Freddy on his feet, but he collapsed to the ground, shaking with laughter. Joanna tried to get serious, but one look at the confusion in Rudy's face and she couldn't stop laughing either.

Rudy planted his hands on his hips and stared from Joanna to Freddy. "Is this a new game we're playing?"

But his expression was of enjoyment. Pure, simple, sweet enjoyment.

Joanna had never seen him look so happy. An answering joy and pleasure filled her heart.

Chapter 10

Rudy's insides felt light and sweet. He'd made Freddy laugh. He'd enjoyed holding Joanna close and noted she hadn't objected. Having her resting against his chest, feeling the silky strands of hair across his face, breathing in her scent—home cooking and sunshine—had filled him with a desire to keep her there...or at least be near her...for the rest of his life.

Was this love? He couldn't think so, because he didn't trust love. He didn't even know what it was. He'd only known Joanna a few days. How could he even think his feelings were love?

Maybe it was gratitude for the things she said to him. Sometimes hard things, but spoken out of concern for him.

Or was it just the moment, the setting?

He simply didn't know.

But a question battered the inside of his head. Was it possible for him to leave his past behind and look to the future? Or even enjoy the present without fear and restrictions?

He wanted to know.

And if he discovered it was indeed possible, did he have the boldness to believe and accept the change?

Joanna finally stopped laughing and sighed deeply. "It's time to eat."

They trooped back to the clearing where they'd left the picnic basket. They sat on the blanket and shared thick sandwiches with generous slabs of meat, followed by delicious oatmeal cookies with a hint of cinnamon. It had recently become his favorite fragrance, making him think of Joanna.

Rudy lounged on one elbow, his feet aiming for the trees, and enjoyed himself. The smell of fine food, the gentle breeze laden with hints of pine and poplar trees, the warm woolen blanket scratching at his skin, and his two most favorite people in the world. What could be better?

When had he enjoyed anything but work? Not in a long time. Maybe never. Part of his brain—a distant part—suggested he should be careful. A larger, friendlier part said to enjoy the moment.

Freddy finished and moved away to find something to dig at with his knife.

Neither Joanna nor Rudy left the comfort of their picnic area. Finally Joanna yawned and stretched. "I suppose we better head back before dark."

He'd been watching the shadows grow long and gray and wondered how late they could stay before darkness hid the trail down. "It's time." He slowly got to his feet, reluctant to end the day. Something had happened here, and he wasn't sure what it was or where it led.

Or if he even wanted to find out.

The next few days passed swiftly. He'd ordered the Bible. It took only three days to arrive from Sand Point. He started to read it, searching for something, even though he wasn't sure what it was until he found Jeremiah 31:3. *"I have loved thee with an everlasting love: therefore with lovingkindness have I drawn thee."* The words grabbed his heart and would not let go. He read them over and over. Loved. Loved by God. Everlasting love.

Was it possible?

Throughout the following days he helped around the stopping house thus earning meals for himself and Freddy. When his chores were done, he continued to work on the cart for Joanna. But always the words of scripture followed him, with Joanna's on their heels. She cared about him.

They attended church again, and Levi's gentle conviction reinforced the truth that beckoned.

Rudy felt as if he hovered on the brink of something new that was as frightening as it was tantalizing.

Freddy and Rudy often accompanied Joanna to the store or to run errands. She enjoyed their company more than made sense. Today they had gone to the mercantile to check for mail. Joanna looked at the long-awaited letter in her hand.

"Aren't you gonna open it?" Freddy asked.

I need to keep things in perspective. She said the words on a daily basis but couldn't decide what perspective she should choose. Should she guard her heart against caring, knowing that Rudy, by his own confession, was not the staying kind? Or should she listen to her heart's reminder of the times they sat and talked after the others in the house had settled down? The questions he asked about his Bible reading. The way his gaze searched hers, probing deep, past her caution to an emptiness that welcomed him.

This letter might make it all clear.

And she couldn't bring herself to open it. "I'll wait until I get home." She tucked it into her pocket.

"Why?" Freddy demanded.

She wasn't about to admit her heart thundered against her ribs with an emotion she couldn't identify, but it felt a lot like fear. Which didn't make sense. Shouldn't it be excitement? Freddy watched her curiously. She smiled at him and started walking back home.

Rudy fell in at her side. Although he was far too polite to pry, she felt his curiosity.

They drew abreast of Glory's old shop.

Rudy slowed his steps and looked at the FOR SALE OR RENT sign.

"That's Glory's building. She used to run a farrier business here. For a little while Levi lived in the back room with some children he'd rescued."

Freddy heard her and asked, "What happened to the children?"

"Their parents were both dead, but they had grandparents who came and got them."

"Oh." It plainly wasn't good news in his opinion.

"They were very nice people. The children are most happy with them."

"Yeah?" Not convinced.

Rudy peered through a window. "Does she still do the farriering business?"

"She works up at the mission now."

Rudy tried the door. "Maybe I'll ask her to have a look."

Joanna swallowed so hard she figured both Rudy and Freddy heard.

Rudy continued to look in the windows. Freddy opened the gate at the side of the building and peered into the small pen where Glory had kept her horses.

"You want to see inside? I know where she hides the key." Her lungs felt impossibly tight.

At Rudy's eager look she walked to the corner of the building, felt for the key behind a loose board in the clapboard siding, and opened the creaky front door.

Rudy stepped inside, seemingly unmindful of the dust motes disturbed by their entrance, and just stood there, a considering look on his face.

Freddy examined every corner, touched the horseshoes Glory had nailed to the wall, picked up a handful of nails from a can and dropped them back. The clatter echoed in the empty room.

Rudy strode across the room and opened the door to the small living quarters. "Freddy, what do you think? Could the two of us manage in here?"

"Seen better. Seen worse."

Joanna choked back a laugh and saw from the gleam in Rudy's eyes that he, too, was amused. Dare she hope. . . ? She tried to swallow again, but her mouth was dry. "Are you thinking of staying?" Her thoughts went to the letter in her pocket. Did she want to leave if Rudy stayed?

He shrugged. "Just a thought." He stepped back into the sunshine.

As she locked up, she tried to assess what he meant. Was this only a passing idea? What would it take for him to settle down? She wished she could be the reason. But she couldn't say so. Nor could she let herself think any further on the topic. Asking a man to stay when his feet told him to leave simply did not work.

They made their way back to the stopping house. Cora and Mandy had supper prepared.

"Care for coffee?" she asked Rudy. He accepted and sat across from her at the kitchen table.

She took out the letter and opened it. Perhaps if the man was no longer interested, Rudy might consider it enough reason to stay.

Aware of his attention, she silently read the letter.

"Bad news?" he asked. "He's changed his mind?"

"No." She folded the page and returned it to the envelope. "He's still keenly interested and will be here the day after tomorrow."

"This is what you want. Right?"

She nodded. It's what she wanted, so why was she disappointed? "I suppose I'm afraid to get too excited in case it falls through again." She looked around. "If I want to make a good impression, I'll have to give the place a good cleaning before he gets here."

Rudy had forgotten she planned to leave. Let himself begin to plan a future here that included seeing her daily, spending evenings talking with her. And in some quiet, hidden place, he'd hoped she might share the same idea.

Instead, she was still planning to sell the place and head to California with a friend.

He hurried from the kitchen, his mind twisting with disappointment. Where did that leave him? And Freddy?

On their own. The open road to follow. Nothing had changed. Why had he thought different?

His feet dragged across the yard. He and Freddy would finish the cart before the man came. They'd give it to Joanna, knowing she would leave it when she headed west.

"Freddy?" No sign of the boy.

He looked around. Freddy sat on the edge of the veranda, holding the black-and-white, ever-patient cat to his chest so hard he wondered the cat didn't squirm away. Freddy looked at Rudy with dark, angry eyes.

Rudy sighed. He had hoped they were done with the scowls and all that accompanied them. Knowing he couldn't walk away from the boy's anger, he crossed the yard and sat beside Freddy. "Thought we should finish the cart for Joanna."

"Why? She's leaving."

He'd overheard the conversation. Rudy understood the anger. Felt a twist of it himself. Along with a long emptiness he should have grown comfortable with by now. But he wasn't. "We've known from the start she planned to leave."

Freddy pushed the cat from his lap. "It don't matter to me." He stomped toward the trail, and when he thought he was out of sight, he broke into a run.

Rudy reached for the cat and pulled it to his lap. "Nothing is ever what we want it to be," he murmured. The ball of fur rewarded him with a sympathetic purr. Then a fluttering leaf caught its attention, and it leaped from his lap. "Can't even count on cats."

He headed for the shed, but his heart wasn't in building a cart. He veered in the direction of the woodpile. Driving the ax over and over through a log was the only way he could think of dealing with the way his insides raged.

The next two days were busy. Cora and Joanna scrubbed every surface in the house. Rudy and Freddy—when he could find the boy—hauled in wood and water and carried out ashes and the used water.

But the activity did nothing to ease the tension building inside Rudy. He felt awkward and unable to say anything to Joanna beyond, "Here's the water. Do you need anything more?"

The expected visitor arrived midafternoon of the second day. Rudy leaned against the corner of the woodshed and took a good look. Mr. Avery and his wife were younger than he'd expected. Probably close to his age. They looked around with interest before Joanna opened the door and invited them inside.

Her gaze found Rudy, and he straightened. But he could not pull away. Why did he feel as if she accused him? He could think of nothing he'd done or left undone that would make her look at him so. Then she turned to the Averys and closed the door behind them.

Rudy pushed away from the woodshed and headed up the trail, feeling a little like Freddy. He wanted to break into a run as soon as he was out of sight.

The Averys were present for supper, and their eager expressions said it all. They liked this place.

Rudy kept part of his attention on his food and the rest on Freddy, who muttered under his breath at everything the Averys said. Thankfully, they didn't seem to notice. But Rudy wondered if he would have to drag the boy from the table.

He avoided looking at Joanna, not knowing if he could bear to see excitement and joy in her face. But he must know for sure. He stole a glance her way.

His gaze collided with hers. And his mouthful of food stalled halfway down his throat. Her brown eyes were steady and full of determination. As if she had decided so she would follow through.

Is this what she really wanted?

He forced his attention back to his plate and worked at getting his food down.

Obviously she wanted to sell, or she wouldn't do it. Joanna knew what she wanted and how to get it. Look at how she'd taken care of her sisters.

What was there about looking after her sisters that scratched at the back of his mind? He failed to find it.

Later that night, the Averys took the small bedroom off the dining room. The other guests bedded down in the dining room, some staying up to read by lantern light.

Freddy brought in the last of the firewood to fill the box for morning, and Rudy emptied out the last of the wash water.

"Cora and I were about to have tea. Will you join us?" Joanna said.

It was their customary bedtime routine. Often the two of them would sit and visit long after Cora and Freddy had gone to bed.

He clenched his jaw muscles tight. He should have never accepted the first invitation. Nor allowed himself to anticipate those evening hours. If he'd never enjoyed them, he wouldn't know how much it would hurt to lose them.

"I'm going to bed." Freddy hurried from the room without a backward look.

Rudy watched him leave. He should follow. But he couldn't deny himself this pleasure any sooner than he had to. He sat while Cora poured tea.

Joanna waited for her to sit. "The Averys are very interested in taking over the stopping house. They want to do so immediately, and of course, the sooner Sarah and I leave for California, the better."

Rudy nodded as misery touched every corner of his heart. "You'll be able to follow your dream." Though for the life of him he couldn't remember her ever mentioning California as a place she longed to visit. Of course, he didn't pretend to know everything about her.

"Cora," she continued. "They would like you to stay on and help them learn how things are done." Her smile touched her eyes as she studied Cora. "Though I don't expect you'll be wanting to stay too long."

Cora blushed prettily.

Joanna chuckled. "I think when Austin comes back you will be making other plans."

"Maybe." Cora's smile lit her face. "I hope so."

Rudy managed to say something he hoped sounded happy for them both.

A few minutes later, Cora excused herself. Rudy stared at his empty cup. He should go, too, but somehow couldn't make either his feet or his mouth work.

"I'm going to miss our evening visits," Joanna said.

Then don't go. But the words would not leave his mouth. How could he ask her to give up her dreams? How could he expect her to have any lasting feelings toward him? "You'll be enjoying your time with your friend." It was Rudy who would have a huge hole in his heart that Joanna had filled. Freddy, too, would feel the loss.

He couldn't remain any longer, silently bemoaning the fact she was about to do exactly what she'd planned from the beginning. He stumbled to his feet. "Good night."

He fled to the other room and arranged himself on his bedroll. He knew Freddy was still awake from the way he stiffened.

There'd likely be little sleep for either of them tonight.

But he drifted off sooner than he anticipated into a nightmare in which he heard Joanna calling. Desperate. Pleading. But a thick fog blinded him, and he couldn't find her because of the murkiness.

He struggled against the haze.

He fought his way through his sleep, knowing if he woke up he could escape the fear.

He wakened with a jolt and sat straight up.

The room was dark except for a flickering light under the kitchen door. Had someone left on a lantern? He had to put it out. He pulled on his trousers and headed for the room, gasping as he sucked in acrid smoke.

"Fire!" he yelled. "Fire!" He raced through the kitchen and banged on the bedroom door where Joanna and Cora slept. "Wake up! There's a fire."

Chapter 11

M en began to waken. "Organize a bucket brigade," he yelled as he continued to bang on Joanna's door.

She emerged, her split skirt pulled on over a baggy faded shirt of some sort. Boots on her feet. Her hair hung in a thick braid. He saw it all in an instant.

She looked at him with startled eyes then past him to the flames licking at the corner of the kitchen. She grabbed his arms. "The place is on fire."

He gripped her shoulders for a moment to assure himself she was real and solid and this wasn't a continuation of his nightmare. "Make sure everyone is up." He allowed himself one second to see if she understood then raced away.

Two pails of water stood on the cupboard, ready for breakfast preparations. He tossed the contents into the fire. The flames sizzled and fell back but only for as long as it took for the buckets to empty. The fire centered in the corner near the door. Something glowed—the shell of another bucket? But the flames licked up the wall and headed for the ceiling before he could get a good look. He headed outside and called to the men. "Hurry with the water."

He joined the line already forming, making sure he was closest to the fire, treading lightly in his bare feet. He saw Joanna leave the house, Cora at her side.

"Everyone is out safely," she assured him.

Then he forgot everything but tossing bucket after bucket of water on the flames. He barely registered the line of men passing buckets from hand to hand or the man working the pump handle furiously. Smoke stung his eyes and burned his lungs. His eyes watered, but he fought onward. They would save the stopping house if he had to beat the fire out with his bare hands.

Bit by bit they reduced the flames until nothing remained but a blackened, drenched skeleton of a wall.

"It's out." He held a bucket of water ready in his hands in case something rekindled. But the wall was sodden. Unlikely to burn. Nevertheless, he wasn't about to take a chance. "Line up buckets of water in case it flares up someplace."

Only then did he take stock.

His clothes were soaked through. His feet hurt. He realized he stood barefoot in the yard and glanced at the others. The men were in various stages of dress, and a few of them were also barefoot.

"You all need to wash. I'll make coffee." Joanna hustled about, organizing a fire where it belonged—in the fire pit to the back of the lot. Then she hurried inside.

Rudy followed and heard her cry out. He rushed into the kitchen.

"It's ruined," she moaned. "Everything is ruined."

Morning threw pale light into the sky, illuminating the mess. One wall blackened and still dripping, water dripping off the top of the stove and from the cupboard, the floor a muddy mess of soot and ashes.

He stood at her side. "It's fixable."

"I can't run a place like this. Or sell it." Her voice quivered as she stood in gray muck in the middle of the kitchen.

His insides turned to jelly at her distress, and he draped an arm over her shoulders to comfort her.

"You're all wet," she murmured. But she didn't edge away.

"It's just water."

She tried to smile. "I guess that's good to know."

He wondered if she was going to break down, but she sighed. "It could be worse." They stared at the mess for a moment then she pulled herself straight. "I better see to my guests."

Someone had put a pot of water to heat over the fire outside. Men traipsed in and out, collecting their things. Some washed up. Others simply left, most of them murmuring words of sympathy to Joanna. Everyone knew her business was in shambles.

Mr. and Mrs. Avery retired to their bedroom and emerged after the others left. "I'm sorry," Mr. Avery said. "This was an ideal situation for us. But now. . . Well, now it's badly damaged. I'm afraid we'll have to withdraw my offer."

"I understand," Joanna said.

Rudy again moved to her side. When she turned toward him, he pulled her to his chest and held her close. "You've still got the building. It only needs a few repairs."

"The smoke damage is everywhere. Everything will have to be scrubbed. Every wall, the ceiling, the bedding." Her voice grew weaker with each word, and she leaned into him as if he was all that held her up.

He kind of liked the feeling.

Cora came out of the house where she'd gone to inspect the damage. "It's a mess." She sat on the edge of the veranda. "I hate fires."

Joanna broke from Rudy's grasp and ran to Cora. She sat at her side and wrapped her arms around the girl. "It must bring back awful memories."

Cora closed her eyes and clung to Joanna. Then she sighed deeply. "I'm going to see if there's anything left for our breakfast."

Rudy joined Joanna on the veranda.

"Cora's parents died in a fire, and that's how she got the scar on her face."

"I didn't know. And yet she stayed and helped. A brave girl."

They sat in exhausted silence.

"I wonder how the fire started," she said.

"It started here." He led the way to the corner and kicked at the slush. A circle of black metal came free. He squatted down and examined it. "I'd say this used to be an ash pail."

"I don't understand. I am always so careful with hot ashes."

He'd noticed Freddy whittling off curls of wood last night. Thought the boy was making some kindling. But why had he sat here? Why was the ash pail here? The explanation that sprang to mind made him shudder. No. Freddy wouldn't do such a thing.

But he couldn't meet Joanna's eyes. He straightened and moved toward the door. He'd ask Freddy before he allowed himself any more suspicions.

He scanned the circle of men around the fire. Freddy wasn't with them. He walked around the yard, checked both the woodshed and the storage shed in case the boy had taken shelter there. But there was no sign of the boy. Nothing.

Finally he returned to the house, where Joanna and Cora were dumping the buckets of water on the floor and mucking out the gray mess. "Have either of you seen Freddy?"

They spun around to face him. Both looked startled, but he focused on Joanna.

"I haven't seen him," she said.

"Me either," Cora echoed.

Joanna set aside the filthy broom and came to Rudy's side. "Isn't he outside?"

"I've looked. I can't find him anywhere."

"He'd be frightened by the fire. Likely he's hiding."

Rudy sighed and scrubbed at his neck. "Maybe for good reason."

"What are you saying?"

He explained his suspicions. "It's Freddy's job to empty the ashes. He's been taught how to handle them. Knows better than to leave a bucket of hot ashes against a wooden wall."

"Are you saying he did this deliberately?"

"I hope I'm wrong." He wouldn't know for certain until he talked to Freddy, but he knew. He simply knew Freddy was responsible. He wished he didn't. How could he ever make it up to Joanna for ruining her plans? She'd likely never speak to either Freddy or him again.

"But why? Why would he do this to me?"

Rudy understood the why. Just not the method. "He didn't want you to leave."

Joanna retreated to the table and sat on a chair, not seeming to notice it was wet and dirty. "Why didn't he say something?"

Rudy shrugged. "Probably didn't see how it would make a difference." Any more than he did. But now—a traitorous thought filled his mind—perhaps he would have time to show her how they could all stay and work together. He hated that he hoped to benefit from her disaster.

"I don't understand." Joanna slapped her palms on her thighs. "But it doesn't matter now. We need to find him."

"And when we do?" He wondered what she had in mind.

Her eyes narrowed. "If you recall our first meeting. . ."

He grinned. "Yup. I sure do. You were all upset and fiery because he'd stolen a pie."

"And if you recall, I said the culprit should pay the price. I still believe that. When we find him, he is going to have to come back here and help clean up the mess and repair the damage."

He nodded, hoping he looked appropriately stern. But he failed to see how Freddy would construe the work as a punishment and not a reward. "Freddy and I will see that it's cleaned up and repaired." He kept his anticipation to himself.

"I'm going to look around," Joanna said.

He followed her outside and waited as she entered each building.

Finally she accepted the obvious and stood in the middle of the yard. "He's not here."

"I know."

"Where would he go?"

"Your guess is as good as mine. I'm going to look for him."

"I'm coming with you."

He'd hoped she would.

They searched through town, stopping often to provide details on the fire. Without exception, people voiced their sympathy and offered to help any way they could. She thanked them then asked if they'd seen Freddy. No one had.

They hurried on. They walked as far as Levi and Glory's mission and explained what had happened.

"I'll check all the buildings and see if he's hiding here," Levi offered. Glory insisted they have breakfast.

"I'll go help Cora as soon as I'm done here," she said.

Rudy began to wonder if he'd get a chance to do any work at all or if all the kind family and neighbors would do it for him.

Levi came back from searching the buildings and grounds. "No sign of Freddy. I'll help you look for him."

They returned to Bonners Ferry and decided to split up, Levi searching up the hill overlooking the ferry while Rudy and Joanna went to the trail that led away from town into the woods. An hour later, they returned to the stopping house, but Cora still hadn't seen him. They headed up the trail toward Trace and Mandy's, stopping often to listen for any sign of Freddy. The woods were strangely silent.

At the log cabin they relayed news of the fire and Freddy's disappearance. "We'll go down and help clean up," Trace said. "Unless you want us to help you find Freddy?"

Rudy considered their offer. "I don't think he could have gone far." Though with every passing moment he could get farther and farther away. Unless he found a place to hide. Suddenly Rudy remembered a perfect hiding place with a beautiful view. "I think I know where he might be. You go down and help Cora while we find him."

Trace and Mandy began to gather together cleaning supplies while Rudy and Joanna returned to the trail. "Let's look where we had the picnic."

She nodded. "Why didn't I think of that?"

For a bit they walked side by side. He took her hand, wanting to offer comfort and support and so much more. She squeezed his hand and smiled at him. The trail narrowed, and she let him lead the way.

They arrived at the spot. Memories of the fun they'd had momentarily eased his worry. He wondered if she felt the same way as she again squeezed his hand.

"Freddy," they called in unison.

Nothing but the flutter of bird wings.

"Maybe he's hiding," Joanna said.

Rudy squatted down to examine the ground. Joanna placed her hand on his shoulder, and he almost forgot about Freddy. He'd felt close to Joanna in this spot. He'd considered whether it was safe to believe in love. He still wondered, but now was not the time. He shifted to study the rest of the clearing. "I don't see any sign of him being here, but I might have missed it."

They searched the woods, knowing Freddy might refuse to answer their calls. An hour later, they returned to the clearing without him.

"I can't believe he isn't here," he said. "I don't mind saying I'm getting a little worried."

"Me, too. After all, despite his big, brave talk, he is only ten years old."

"Could he have fallen?"

"Broke a leg maybe. Or someone kidnapped him."

Rudy laughed at the idea. "They'd soon be bringing him back."

Joanna chuckled. "I suppose they would. But don't worry, we'll find him."

He allowed himself to drink hope from her gaze. "We better go down to the stopping house. Maybe Levi has him."

Hand in hand, as if it were the most natural thing in the world—and Rudy admitted it sort of felt that way—they hurried back to town, pausing often to call Freddy's name and searching any likely bushes and trees along the path.

They burst into the stopping house, where half a dozen people used mops and rags to sop up the mess of the fire. A tarp had been tacked over the burned wall. Maybe they'd leave the rebuilding for him.

Levi was there. "I didn't find him. Thought you would have."

"Not a sign."

"We need to enlist a bit more help." Levi turned to the cleaning crew. "Glory, Mandy, could you come here?"

"If anyone can find him, these two can." Levi outlined a search grid. "First, we'll pray for success." Levi prayed aloud.

For the first time that Rudy could remember, he wanted to believe God could help him and would choose to do so. Maybe not for his sake or even Freddy's, but because of Levi's steadfast faith.

This time four more headed out to search for his missing nephew—Joanna's sisters and their husbands. But Joanna and Rudy stayed together. They were to search toward the ferry and ask the ferryman if he'd seen anything. He scoured the area for any sign of a boy but saw none. However, it was impossible to say if he'd been on the trail. The men leaving the stopping house had scuffed the path.

The ferryman said he knew Freddy. "He often comes to watch me load and unload. But nope, can't say I've seen anything of him since yesterday."

Rudy could no longer deny the burn of worry in the pit of his stomach. He rubbed his neck. "Where could he be?"

Joanna squeezed his arm. "He's got to be somewhere."

"But where?"

"Rudy, God sees. God will help us find him."

"I can't believe He cares about me enough to help me find Freddy."

Joanna pulled him around to look squarely into his eyes. "He loves you as much as He loves me or Levi or anyone else in the world."

He ached to believe it. "How do you know?"

"You told me you read the verse that says He loves you with an everlasting love."

"But I wasn't born when that was written. How can it mean me?"

"Doesn't everlasting mean from beginning of time to the end of time?"

"Maybe."

"Seems that would have to include the day you were born."

"I want to think so, but. . ." How could he voice all his fears and hurts and disappointments without sounding like a whiner?

"We mustn't make the mistake of equating God's love with that of people who failed to love us as they should."

"That makes sense."

Still he found it difficult to believe. But four hours later when they again assembled in the stopping house, he realized he had nothing to lose but Freddy. He sat on a still-damp chair and stared at the plate of food Cora set before him. She placed one before Joanna as well. Joanna's sisters and husbands had returned and eaten earlier and stood by, obviously wishing they could offer some sort of help.

Rudy guessed they'd all run out of ideas. He forked the food to his mouth more out of need to have something to do than out of hunger. But he quickly forgot the food and put his fork down.

"How can he simply have disappeared?" He saw a guarded look between Levi and Trace.

"You think he's met with harm, don't you?"

Levi rocked his head back and forth. "We've searched high and low. There isn't a rock within miles that hasn't been turned over in an effort to find him."

Rudy's shoulders slumped. "There's a lot of trees and mountains surrounding this place." Was Freddy lost out there? Fallen into the river? Or fallen off a cliff?

Joanna pressed her hand to his. "We'll find him. We must."

But one look in her face and he saw the same desperation and fear that gripped his insides until every breath pained him.

"Where is he?" He was past caring if everyone thought he was weak. "I can't give up on him. I can't lose him." He held Joanna's hand in a deadly vise. It was the only thing that anchored him to hope.

She answered his desperate plea with a reassuring look. "We haven't looked across the river."

"The ferryman said he hadn't been on the ferry."

Joanna's smile barely lifted the corners of her mouth. "We're talking about Freddy. You don't think it's possible he sneaked on without being noticed?"

He was willing to believe anything at this point. "He could if he put his mind to it." He pushed back from the table and pulled Joanna to her feet. "We're going to look for him over there." Darkness would soon be upon them. They must find him soon.

The others stood, too, their words of reassurance overlapping. "We'll be praying." "We'll continue to look around here." "Let us know if you need help."

"We'll ride." He decided. Before he finished, Glory headed for the door.

"I'll saddle your horses," she said.

Cora tossed bread and cheese into a sack. "He'll be hungry."

He could have hugged her for believing he would find Freddy.

A few minutes later they were on the ferry with the horses. He and Joanna stood side by side watching the water slip by.

"What happens if I don't find him?" The thought crawled into his brain and refused to budge.

Joanna took his arm and tugged him around to face her. Her eyes were steady and demanded his full attention. "We'll find him. We must."

"You've said that over and over, and yet we still haven't. What happens if we don't?" He had to know how he was supposed to manage if the hours turned into days and they never found Freddy.

"If—and I'm only saying this for sake of answering your question—if we don't find him, I will be here to help you through each day."

His gaze locked on hers. He couldn't have turned away for anything. Did she realize the sort of promise she'd just given? Or was she only trying to give him strength? He suspected it was the latter. He knew he should guard his heart and mind against believing it was more, but right now he lacked the will. He needed her at his side.

"Thank you," he whispered, pulling her into his arms. Her head pressed into the hollow of his shoulder. Her arms wrapped around him and held him tight.

They stood holding each other until the ferry pulled to the other side of the river; then they swung up into saddles and headed down the trail.

There was no need or opportunity for conversation as they paused often to study the trail, to search the bushes, to call Freddy's name and listen for an answer. But her presence was like a warm bit of sunshine.

They rode for an hour. Then he pulled to a halt, dismounted, and helped Joanna down. "Do we keep going? I mean, how far would he go?" He glanced at the sun heading for the western horizon and tried not to think how dark and cold it would soon be. Already he could smell the damp evening air rising from the ground.

Joanna pressed her lips tight. Her eyes glistened. Tears pooled at the corners of her eyes.

He gently thumbed away the moisture, wishing he could say something to comfort her, but words were empty in light of a missing boy.

"I was so certain we'd find him." Her voice quivered, and she leaned into his arms.

They held each other. The long ache that wove through his insides did not have the power to destroy him. Not while Joanna held him tight.

She eased back but stayed within his arms. "I suppose we might as well go on a bit longer." She looked so sad, so weary, that he cupped her chin and lifted her face so he could study her more fully.

"I'm sorry to bring all this trouble on you."

She smiled despite her tears. "Trouble shared is trouble halved."

He didn't know if she meant his trouble or hers. Or if it mattered one way or the other. But her words renewed his hope. He still held her chin, still looked deep into her dark brown eyes. Before he could think better of it, he lowered his head and kissed her lightly on the lips. He immediately pulled back. "I probably shouldn't have done that, but I'm just so grateful for your help."

"You don't hear me objecting, do you?"

They caught up the horses' reins and walked farther down the path. He mulled over her words. She hadn't objected. He'd seen her handle unwanted attention at the stopping house, and she left little doubt when it wasn't welcome. He managed to moderate the smile on his face.

Something at the side of the trail caught his attention. . .raw marks on a tree. He stopped to examine it. Someone had slashed at the bark. Little jabs below his waist level.

Joanna studied the marks as well. "Do you think. . . ?"

"Looks like Freddy's work." He examined the surroundings more closely. A bent twig, but nothing more. He stood and bellowed, "Freddy, are you here?"

Both he and Joanna strained for any sound. Nothing.

His insides soured. He had no proof this slashing was Freddy's work. Nothing to make him think the boy had been here but hope and desperation. Absolutely nothing.

"Freddy," he roared again.

Joanna touched his elbow, pressed her fingers to her lips. "Listen."

Chapter 12

J oanna clung to Rudy's arm, hardly daring to hope she heard a faint cry. She stared into Rudy's face, finding sweet comfort in his steady gaze. Enjoying the masculine scent of him. He'd kissed her, perhaps as much to reassure her as anything. But something had changed in her heart, though she was at a loss to say what it was. Nor was this the time to consider it.

The sound came again—it didn't seem like a coyote or dog.

"Could it be?" she asked, hardly daring to believe it could be a human voice. She tipped her head against the wind that had grown steadily cooler as the shadows lengthened.

"Freddy," they called in unison.

Another cry. It was certainly someone calling. Joanna's heart beat a frantic tattoo. She gripped the reins. "Over there," she shouted, pointing into the trees at the side of the trail.

They dashed forward, leading the horses and pausing to call again then followed the muted cry up a rugged hill scattered with rocks. They slowed their pace to allow the horses to pick their way and to avoid stumbling on the rough ground. It wouldn't do for one of them to end up injured.

They reached the crest. "Freddy."

The answering shout was closer. They pushed onward.

Joanna saw him first, curled up into a ball next to a cold-looking boulder. The ground beneath him looked equally cold and uncomfortable—only a few tufts of grass on bare soil.

She grabbed Rudy's hand, and they hurried to Freddy's side. Rudy knelt and cupped his head. Joanna couldn't see clearly for the moisture in her eyes, but it looked like Rudy's eyes glistened with unshed tears as well.

"Are you hurt?" he asked the boy.

Freddy pointed at his ankle. Blood dried on a gash. "I can't walk."

Rudy sat in the dirt beside Freddy and pulled the boy into his arms. "I was so worried. I looked everywhere and couldn't find you. I thought maybe you were gone." He squeezed his eyes shut as he held the boy close.

"You don't want to see me again," Freddy mumbled. "Not after what I did. You hate me for sure."

Joanna clamped her mouth shut against the moan of protest. She'd hoped Rudy's suspicions were wrong, but Freddy hadn't wasted any time admitting he had started the fire. However, the damage seemed inconsequential in comparison to her relief at finding the boy.

"You did wrong. But that doesn't mean I don't want to see you. And I certainly don't hate you." He gulped. "I love you."

Joanna's throat thickened until she couldn't swallow. She sat on Freddy's other side.

Rudy lifted his arm and pulled her in close to the boy.

Freddy sobbed. "Miss Joanna, I'm sorry. I didn't think a little fire would do so much damage."

"Shh. I know you didn't. But Freddy, if you wanted to tell me something it would be better for us all if you said the words."

Freddy's sobs quieted. "It's too late." He rubbed his eyes.

"It's never too late."

He stared at the ground, still wrapped in Rudy's arms. "I want to stay in Bonners Ferry. I want us all to stay."

Joanna realized she wanted it, too, but she couldn't give a promise that included Rudy. Only he could give that. "Well, Freddy, I'll be staying awhile, seeing as the Averys don't want to buy the stopping house now."

"I'm sorry," he mumbled, his tears flowing again.

She wasn't. Not if it gave her a chance to spend more time with Rudy. And Freddy. But she couldn't say so. Not with Rudy looking flummoxed. A gentle smile began in the pit of her stomach and climbed to her heart then spread across her lips. He'd told Freddy he loved him. Seems he no longer thought he couldn't love or receive love.

He hugged Freddy again. "Now let's have a look at the ankle."

The cut wasn't deep enough to be serious, but his ankle was swollen.

"Good thing we brought horses," Rudy said. He carried the boy to where they'd left the animals, lifted him to the saddle, and swung up behind him.

Joanna couldn't stop smiling at the way Rudy held the boy. And the fact that Freddy let him. She'd guess Rudy wasn't going to allow Freddy out of his sight for a good long while. She got into her own saddle, and they made their way carefully back to the trail and returned to the ferry.

The ferryman blinked several times when he saw Freddy. "How did you get across without me seeing you, you young scamp?"

Freddy pointed to a crate of goods. "Hid behind a box like that."

"I'll be checking for stowaways more carefully, won't I?" He reached out to shake Rudy's hand. "Glad to see the young fella is okay."

Mandy stood at the shore, shading her eyes. She saw them coming and yelled, "It's Rudy and Joanna. Freddy is with them!"

Half a dozen people trooped down to the ferry, shouting a welcome.

Freddy rode the horse across though both Rudy and Joanna had dismounted. When they reached the other side, Rudy lifted Freddy down. He reached for Joanna, keeping her at his side as they climbed the hill to the stopping house with a crowd escorting them. Inside, Freddy was enthroned on a chair, examined, and asked a hundred questions. As soon as everyone was satisfied he would live and stepped away, the cat jumped to his lap and curled up, as glad to see the boy as the rest of them.

"Don't go making him into a hero," Rudy warned. "His mischief has done a lot of damage." He shifted so Freddy could see the burned skeleton of a wall.

The place had been cleaned up, so Joanna could almost think there hadn't been a fire except for the stark evidence of the blackened frame where the wall once stood and the overwhelming stench of smoke and carbolic soap. But she couldn't find it in her to be upset at the moment. "Freddy is safely home. That's all that matters right now." And Rudy stood close, holding her hand like they belonged together.

Cora brought warm water to wash Freddy's streaked face and dirty hands then turned her attention to the swollen ankle. "Guess you better keep this up for a few days."

Rudy snagged a chair and dragged it close so Freddy could prop his foot on it.

"Both of you sit," Glory ordered.

"I don't—" Joanna began.

"No arguing." Both sisters faced her.

"You've been out scouring the area for Freddy while we took care of things here," Mandy said.

"Now you're going to let us take care of you for a change." Glory nodded her head once, ending any objections.

Joanna nodded meekly and pulled up a chair to sit beside Freddy. Rudy pulled a second chair to the other side, and they smiled at each other over the boy's head.

The others swung into action, setting the kitchen table and serving a nice meal. A sign had been posted to the outside of the building, informing one and all that the stopping house would not be serving supper.

"It's almost like our Sunday meals," Mandy said.

Joanna looked around the table. "This is nice." Did she really want to leave here? Her gaze slipped toward Rudy, and she knew he'd been watching her. For a moment, she let herself hold his look, wondering if he read the wishes of her heart. She'd be content to live here if he decided to stay. Otherwise, the place was only a building.

Before the meal ended, Freddy's head drooped over his plate. Rudy pushed away from the table. "I hope you all will understand if I take this boy to bed and get him settled."

Joanna sprang to her feet. "You two take the bedroom. He'll be more comfortable there."

He nodded. "Thank you." His gaze lingered a moment. "For everything." Then he scooped Freddy into his arms and strode from the room.

Everyone was quiet until they heard the door close, then Glory edged forward. "Thank you for everything?"

Joanna fixed her with her best big-sister stare. "He means because I helped find Freddy."

Glory purposely ignored Joanna and turned to Mandy. "Did you see the way he looked at her? And how he held her hand?"

"Sure did. I'd say there's something special going on."

Joanna sighed. "There's nothing." Though she hoped she was wrong. He hadn't said anything but thanks, she reminded herself. Yes, he'd kissed her, but was she reading more into it than he meant? After all, they were both worried and finding comfort in their friendship.

Yet, she guessed he didn't give out kisses lightly any more than he often spoke the words *I love you* to anyone.

"Girls," Levi murmured. "Joanna's tired. Maybe you can wait until morning before you begin harassing her."

Both sisters turned their attention to Levi, informing him they were doing no such thing.

Joanna guessed Levi expected that's exactly how they would respond, and she flashed him a smile of gratitude.

They wouldn't allow her to help clean up. Weary clear through, she wondered if she would have been any help.

She expected them to leave once they were done, but Mandy announced they were all staying, seeing as the dining room was empty of guests. Joanna's tears of exhaustion were close to the surface, and she could only nod agreement before she staggered to bed. Even the smoky smell of her pillow didn't make it less welcoming.

Just before fatigue claimed her thoughts she allowed herself to remember the closeness she'd felt with Rudy throughout the day. Surely he'd felt it, too. Didn't his kiss prove so?

Maybe tomorrow he would speak of his feelings.

But the next day he carried Freddy from the bedroom and settled him on a chair. "As soon as breakfast is over, Freddy and I are going to start repairing the wall."

She wondered how much help Freddy would be.

As she assisted Cora to serve the meal, she stole glances at Rudy, wondering if he would let her know his feelings in some subtle way. But his smile lacked the warmth she sought.

She pulled her own emotions under control. She was reading too much into Rudy's behavior. Did she mean yesterday or today? She couldn't say and grabbed a rag to attack the smoke-smudged cupboard with gusto.

∞

Rudy would not allow himself to think past the work of fixing the damaged wall. He'd seen how powerful his feelings could be if he let them loose. They made him want to hug everyone, shout with joy to the heavens, kiss Joanna, and say "I love you" over and over again.

They frightened him.

Made him feel naked and vulnerable.

Loving and the longing for it had never led to anything but searing pain.

Yes, he'd admitted he loved Freddy. Practically his own flesh and blood. He probably wouldn't say it again unless the boy disappeared another time. Which he hoped wouldn't happen.

Tangled along with his feelings was his confusion about God.

Was it possible God loved him? And even if he thought so, could he rest in that love?

Too many questions and doubts.

The best thing he could do was keep his mind on the task of repairs.

Unfortunately, they required he spend much time in the kitchen, which meant he had the pleasure and confusion of seeing Joanna almost every minute of every waking hour. How was he to maintain a calm distance, keep his feelings bolted down, when every time he glanced her way his heart did a strange little dance against his ribs?

The best he could hope for was to do the work as fast as possible. But he wanted Freddy to have a part in it, which slowed him down considerably.

The first day, he asked Freddy to hold things for him as he sat with his swollen leg propped up on a chair. The second day, he got him to sit at a sawhorse and help measure pieces of wood. The third day, Freddy insisted on hobbling about, so Rudy taught him how to hammer in a nail. After a few lessons, he managed to get a nail in without bending it to a useless twist. The boy's company provided a buffer against his feelings toward Joanna. He welcomed it, though the work would have been ten times faster on his own.

Freddy paused from tackling another nail. "Guess Miss Joanna is going to be staying now."

"Guess so." He pounded in a nail. "Nobody wants to buy a building like this."

"But Miss Cora is still leaving to marry that Austin man?"

"Not for a little while, but yes, she'll eventually leave." It was nice to have Freddy want to chat peaceably with him.

"Well." Freddy let the hammer hang from his hand and turned to consider Rudy seriously. "Seems to me she's gonna need someone to help her then."

"Suppose that might be so." He stepped back to eyeball what they'd accomplished. On his own, it might take a week to do this job properly. With Freddy's help, it might take two.

He frowned, his emotions warring within him at the prospect. More time to see Joanna and fill his senses with her presence. More time to fight the feelings he couldn't allow himself to have.

"Well, Uncle Rudy, here's what I think."

"Yeah."

"I think we should stay and help her."

Freddy stood a good three feet away, but Rudy felt like the boy had taken the hammer and slammed it into his belly. Stay? It was a thought he'd been trying to outrun for days. Freddy had pulled it out in the open so Rudy couldn't avoid it.

He couldn't stay. Because. . .

He couldn't think of the reasons, but he knew he had them.

Something to do with not believing in love. Except he realized he did. Freddy was watching him.

Rudy schooled his thoughts into submission.

"Don't you think that's a good idea?" the boy persisted.

An excellent idea. Except it scared him half to death. "We don't know if she's got other plans." He ignored the way Freddy's mouth drew into a stubborn line.

Rudy turned his attention to the wall and pounded in a nail that didn't need to be pounded in.

"You're planning to leave. Just like you always do. Footloose and fancy-free." Freddy's words dripped with disapproval.

"I'm not leaving you." It was the most he could promise. He turned to stare out the window, hoping for some peace. Joanna walked toward the pump, carrying a bucket of water in each hand. She and Cora, with Joanna's sisters helping, had washed the walls and ceiling again. They'd scrubbed a whole lot of bedding and hung it in the cool breeze to dry. He smelled the freshness of it just looking at her. Though he couldn't miss the lingering smoke smell inside, which grew fainter every day.

His turmoil increased by leaps and bounds. "Hang on," he called to her. Without waiting for a response, he trotted out and reached for the pails.

His hands brushed hers as he took them. Against his orders, his gaze jerked toward her, and he couldn't look away.

She smiled. Her eyes were soft and full of. . .welcome? "Thanks."

He realized what he truly wanted. To stay. But more. To share life with Joanna.

His heart threatened to explode from his chest.

His fears cried out a protest.

He jerked back, spilling water on his boots, and hurried into the house. Rather than return to work, he made some half-intelligible excuse about taking care of the horses and hurried away, knowing he was running as he'd never run before.

Only trouble was, he couldn't ride away until he'd finished what he set out to do.

∞

Joanna excused herself, ducked into the bedroom, and sank to the edge of the bed. No tears. No crying. Nothing but a long ache down a familiar path. Why had she let herself care for a man so much like her pa? It served her right for feeling torn up inside.

Rudy had called himself footloose and fancy-free. He'd admitted he didn't know how to love or be loved. He couldn't have been much plainer.

Oh, why couldn't the men she loved love her back?

She sat up, a hard knot in her throat. She'd waste no more time wishing for things she couldn't have. Pulling her writing things close, she began a letter to Sarah. She'd put it off long enough, waiting for different news. Yes, she'd hoped in a secret corner of her heart—a secret corner she pretended didn't exist—that she'd be writing to say she now had a reason to stay in Bonners Ferry. . .a reason that included love.

But she was staying anyway because she had no choice. The stopping house hadn't sold. She couldn't walk away from it.

She finished the letter and took it to be posted, lingering at the mercantile long after she'd completed her task. She didn't know if she could face Rudy without her feelings spilling out on her face. A new shipment of yarn had arrived, and it gave her an idea. She'd make both Rudy and Freddy mittens for the winter so when they left, they would take something of her with them.

A tiny bit of her love.

Chapter 13

"M iss Joanna, would you read the Bible to me?" Freddy asked as they sat for their bedtime cup of tea.

Rudy slanted a look at the boy. He read a few verses to him every night. Why was he asking Joanna to do the same?

Freddy's gaze rested on Joanna, as adoring as the cat lapping up Freddy's affection.

Rudy relaxed. Seems the boy only wanted some of Joanna's attention. And he could hardly blame him for that.

"Why, certainly." Joanna went to her bedroom to get her Bible. "Anything in particular?"

"Uncle Rudy says God loves me. I like hearing that from the Bible."

Rudy chuckled. "You saying you don't believe me?"

Freddy's eyes rounded with innocence. "Just want to make sure."

Joanna's smile touched them both with approval. And Rudy wondered if his chest swelled as noticeably as Freddy's. "You can believe your uncle, because he's telling you what God says. God never lies. Never changes His mind." She turned the pages slowly. "I think you'll like these verses from John, chapter three. Here it is. Verse sixteen. 'For God so loved the world. . .'" She read a few moments then looked up, such peace in her expression that Rudy couldn't look away.

"Did those verses help?" she asked Freddy.

He nodded. "I liked them. Thank you." He yawned and stretched. "Guess I'll go to bed."

Rudy made to push to his feet.

Freddy waved him back. "You stay and enjoy another cup of tea. I'll get myself to bed." And he sauntered away, leaving Rudy staring at him in surprise.

Was Freddy purposely being a matchmaker? He silently thanked him for allowing them this time to visit. Cora had gone out with Austin, so he was alone with Joanna.

"It's nice to know you're helping Freddy learn of God's love." Joanna's gentle words warmed his heart. He realized he'd been trying so hard not to feel anything that he'd grown cold inside.

"I've been reading the Bible to him most nights."

"Like I used to do with Glory and Mandy."

"You were fortunate to have each other."

"We realize it. And now you and Freddy have each other."

Did she mean it to be a warning that he couldn't expect more?

"When was the last time you heard from your pa?"

"About a year ago. He'd been in Wyoming, working on a ranch. We caught up with him there, and three days later he heard about the gold rush in the Kootenais. The three of us argued about whether or not to follow him, but there was nothing to keep us in Wyoming. When we got here, we found the stopping house." She gave a contented chuckle. "I guess God led us here."

"Led you?" That was a new concept. Thinking God loved him was almost more than he could get his head around. "You really think God cares what you decide to do or where you decide to live?"

"I do." She told him of verses that made her think that way.

He shook his head. "This is hard to believe. If God leads people, then why does He allow people to do bad things?"

"Like how your mother treated you?"

The pain surfaced, stinging his eyes. "And how your pa treats you."

"It's like I said before. Neither of us can measure God's love and care by how people act."

"It's easy to say that. But feelings don't simply disappear in a flash."

"I don't mean to suggest otherwise." She studied her hands, folded in her lap. "For years I've struggled with feeling I don't deserve love."

Why did she swallow so hard and shift her gaze away? It was all he could do to keep from reaching for her and assuring her she deserved love like no other. But could he, of all people, offer it to her?

"I tried to be mother and father to my sisters, and yet all Pa ever said to me was take care of them. And when they got into mischief as they often did, if he heard about it, he held me responsible."

"That wasn't fair."

She sighed. "No, it wasn't. But that's just the point. People aren't always what we want them to be. Often they fail to give us love when that's what we want most of all." Her gaze drilled him.

"Joanna." He wanted to say how much he loved her. But she was worth a hundred times better man than he would ever be, and he choked back the words. "You make me want to believe without any lingering doubts."

"I pray you will."

At the way she sighed, he wondered if he'd disappointed her by admitting he still had doubts. But he couldn't pretend he didn't.

∽

Two mornings later, Freddy hustled into his clothes. "Hurry up, Uncle Rudy. I got something to do, and you need to help me."

"I do?" Hungry for the kind of assurance Joanna had, Rudy spent time reading his Bible. "What are we going to do that's so important?"

"Come on. Hurry." He practically dragged Rudy from the bedroom and across the dining room.

Joanna came to the kitchen doorway. "Are you going somewhere?"

Rudy lifted his free hand. "Freddy is, and I'm apparently going along."

Joanna shifted her gaze to the boy. "Where are you going?"

"It's a secret." He pushed Rudy out the door, closed it behind him, then continued his hurried trip across the yard to the toolshed. "We have to finish the cart."

"I plumb forgot. You're right. We'll work on it together. But why is it so urgent?"

"It's not why I was in such a hurry." He climbed into the half-finished cart and pulled back a board. "I got this for Joanna." It was a beautiful, soft piece of white rabbit fur.

"Where did you get this?"

Freddy stroked the fur and avoided Rudy's gaze.

Rudy knew it was worth more money than the boy could possibly get his hands on honestly. "Freddy, tell me where you got this."

"A man came over on the ferry yesterday. He had a bunch of furs. Said he planned to sell them. So I bought one." He rushed on before Rudy could demand to know how. "I thought Joanna would like one. Feel it. It's so nice and soft. I bet she would like to make a pillow out of it or one of those muff things ladies use to keep their hands warm."

"Yes, I'm sure she'll like it very much, but where did you get the money to buy it?"

Freddy jumped to the ground and came round to face Rudy. "Please don't be mad, but I traded my knife."

Freddy could have knocked Rudy over with his little finger. "Why would you do that?"

"Because I want her to know how much I love her." Freddy's face grew red. He looked down, suddenly intent on kicking a rock loose from the dirt.

"You could have just told her."

He glanced at Rudy then back at the scuffed toe of his shoe. "I'm scared to. She might think I'm silly."

This boy was certainly closely related to Rudy. But he showed his feelings better. "It was your knife to do with as you choose."

"You're not mad?"

"No. Now let's go eat breakfast before Joanna comes looking for us."

"Wait. I want to give it to her for a special reason. Like her birthday or something. But I don't know when it is."

"Why don't you ask Glory or Mandy?"

His face lit up. "Okay. I can do that. But what if her birthday is a long ways away? Then what?"

Rudy laughed. "Then I guess we'll have to make up a special occasion."

Freddy nodded, all smiles. "That would be good."

Rudy agreed. Maybe he could dream up something suitable for a special occasion himself. But what? All he could think at the moment was how much he loved her. But he was afraid to say it. Was there some occasion that would enable him to speak the words?

Usually Mandy or Glory—often both of them—visited every day, but the afternoon trudged onward without either of them appearing.

Freddy abandoned all pretense of work. "I gotta find out about her birthday. Let me go to the mission."

Rudy shook his head. "It can wait until tomorrow. It's Sunday. Everyone will be here."

Joanna entered the kitchen at that moment. "The wall looks good. I can't thank you enough for doing the repairs."

Rudy and Freddy exchanged guilty looks. He supposed Freddy was remembering his foolishness, while Rudy's insides flooded with heat that she should think he deserved thanks. The repairs had given him an opportunity to continue enjoying her presence.

She busied herself in the kitchen. "I'll soon open for business again, though I don't expect many customers once winter sets in." She'd already let a handful of people sit at the dining room table and spend the night. None of them complained about the faint odor of smoke, mostly covered by the smell of roast venison or apple pie. "Glory and Levi have a full house up at the mission, what with those who were almost drowned in that accident last week. Glory says two of the children are very ill with pneumonia."

Freddy and Rudy stopped cutting a board and listened as Joanna talked.

"Is everyone going to be okay?" Rudy asked.

"They're all improving." She ducked into the depths of a cupboard and emerged with a rolling pin in hand. "Goodness! Things have been rearranged, and I have a hard time locating them."

Freddy steadied the board in place. Rudy placed a nail but he didn't hammer it. Not while Joanna chattered on.

"Glory and Levi have a lot of responsibility. It will be nice for them to sit down and enjoy dinner here tomorrow."

Rudy smiled. Joanna liked knowing she could do something for her sister. He pounded in a nail.

"I expect Cora will be marrying soon. Austin won't want to wait long."

Freddy jerked around. "Who's going to help you then?"

Joanna stopped measuring flour. "Why, I don't know, Freddy." She looked out the window with a faraway gaze in her eyes.

She must surely be thinking of California and regretting she wasn't on her way. Rudy shot Freddy a warning look. Thankfully, he did not pursue the subject.

Rudy turned away from her distant expression and drove three more nails into place then he put his hammer away. He could not stay and endure his disappointment.

"Freddy, you can clean up while I run a few errands." He strode from the house before he could make a fool of himself and suggest she might like to stay and let him help her run the place.

⬭

Joanna watched him scurry from the kitchen as if he couldn't get away fast enough. How many times had he hurried away in the past couple of weeks? Too many. He obviously regretted opening his arms to her and kissing her. And yet she continued to hope he'd open his heart in welcome.

She sighed and continued measuring flour for pies. She'd given him every opportunity to say something about his feelings. Why, she'd practically told him she loved him, leaving him plenty of time to respond. Instead, he ran. Would he always run? She'd had a glimpse of the depth and power of his love, and she longed to have it for herself.

Freddy tidied up the area where he and Rudy had been working then came to sit at the table. He watched as Joanna rolled out pie dough. "You make good pies."

She chuckled, remembering how he'd stolen a whole pie and eaten it all. "And you would know, wouldn't you?"

"I was hungry."

"And angry, too, I think."

"I guess. My insides got all upset when I thought no one wanted me."

"But now you know your uncle Rudy does."

He nodded but looked thoughtful.

At least she'd accomplished that, though she'd done nothing but say a few words and give the pair a chance to get to know and trust each other. That should have been enough to satisfy her, but it was only a drop in the empty barrel of what she wanted.

"I told Uncle Rudy we should stay here and help you."

A shot of surprise jolted through her. "You did? What did he say?"

"I don't remember. Except he didn't say we could."

Her eyes welled, and she blinked back the tears. What had she expected? "I guess he has other plans." Did Freddy know what they were? She wouldn't ask, and he didn't say.

He rested his arms on the table and propped his chin as he continued to watch her. Then his eyes brightened. "When's your birthday?"

"What an odd question. Why do you ask?"

He lifted one shoulder. "Just wondering."

"It's in April. April the fifth."

"Oh. That's a long time from now."

"I suppose so."

"Will you do something special?"

Why the concern about birthdays? Did Freddy have one coming soon? Perhaps he was afraid it would be overlooked. "My sisters and

I have always had a little party. Usually just the three of us. But now I guess it will include their husbands." He looked so interested, she continued. "We make a cake and put on rose flowers made of icing."

"You can make flowers out of icing?"

She nodded. "We lived with a lady one winter who taught us cake decorating. She made wedding cakes that were very pretty."

He sank back. "I guess that's just girlie stuff."

Laughing, she continued. "When we were younger, we never had any spending money for gifts, and our pa never remembered our birthdays. So we always found some little thing we thought the birthday girl would like."

"What kind of thing?"

"Once Mandy and I made a horsehair rope for Glory. I expect she still has it."

"What did you get?"

She smiled at the fond memory. "I'll just put these into the oven; then I have something to show you." She slipped the pies in to bake then went to the bedroom and got a card her sisters had made her a couple of years ago. They could now afford to buy little things if they chose, but the things they found or made each other remained the most precious.

She returned to the kitchen. "They gave me this card. See the tiny little flowers covering the front and how they scalloped the edges?" Neither of the girls liked doing what they called "prissy" work, so it was all the more special. She opened it. The poem inside, copied from a schoolbook, was all the more sweet because of the imperfect penmanship.

Freddy leaned close to read it, and she sat beside him. "Why all this talk about birthdays? Do you have one coming up?"

He bolted to his feet. "No." And rushed outdoors.

She sighed. Why did she have this effect on both Freddy and his uncle? There were times when, apart from her sisters, she wondered if anyone made sense.

Rudy and Freddy returned in time for supper, and both were unusually quiet throughout the meal. In fact, Cora did most of the talking, telling them about the pictures Austin had taken in the gold fields.

When Rudy followed on Freddy's heels to the bedroom, Joanna admitted her disappointment to herself. She had hoped for another evening visit.

Sunday brought a welcome change as they made their way to the mission for church. Austin joined them in town, claiming Cora's attention and leaving Joanna and Rudy to walk side by side as Freddy ran on ahead.

They drew abreast of the place where she'd found him beating the trees in frustration, and she swallowed back a sigh. Seems they hadn't progressed from that moment.

But she could not continue to feel sad as they sang hymns and listened to Levi's encouraging sermon then gathered round the table at the stopping house for dinner. Nine of them, with Austin at Cora's side.

Conversation was easy as they discussed the events of the week. As soon as the dishes were done, Austin showed his photographs. Mandy took extra care examining the pictures with people in them.

Joanna and Glory exchanged glances. Joanna tried to signal her not to mention it.

But Glory only rolled her eyes before turning to Mandy. "You won't see Pa in them."

Mandy didn't even look up. "How do you know?"

"What difference would it make if you do? You going to track him down and bring him back? Maybe get him to settle here and be a real father?"

"Oh, Glory. You're always so angry at him." Mandy bent over another picture. "I don't expect him to start a home for us. None of us need it anymore." She jerked her attention toward Joanna, her eyes wide as if she'd just realized something. "Unless Joanna wants him to make a home with her."

Joanna snorted. "I think I can manage on my own."

Mandy already had her attention back on the pictures. She picked up one and turned it toward the light from the window. "That's him right there."

"Let me see." Glory held out her hand.

The two of them leaned over the picture. Glory sat back. "I don't see how you can say so."

Mandy handed the picture to Joanna. "What do you think?" She pointed to a man bundled up in a shapeless coat, a battered hat upon his head.

Joanna could barely make out his profile other than to see a mat of dark whiskers. "I don't know if it's him or not." What difference did it make? He couldn't undo the past. But she refrained from saying so. After all, she seemed the only one unable to shed the hurt and move on.

She watched Rudy from beneath her lashes as he looked at the pictures. It wasn't that she didn't know how to love. It was more a matter of loving unwisely.

Austin gathered up the pictures amid a flurry of thank-yous. "I'm glad you enjoyed them."

Trace went to the door to retrieve a parcel. He set it on the table. "I brought a game to play." He spread out a game board. "The Mansion of Happiness."

Joanna chuckled. "So this is how you get there. I've always wondered." Everyone laughed, and she met Rudy's eyes. Something sweet flickered between them, as if he promised they wanted the same thing and hoped they would find it.

She looked away and shook her head. How silly to think they'd find what they wanted by playing a game.

A spinner indicated how many moves they should make. If one of them landed on a vice, they had to miss a turn. If they landed on a virtue, they got to move six places.

Joanna took her turn. She landed on "passion."

Glory read the rules. " 'Whoever gets into a passion must be taken to the water and have a ducking to cool him.' "

Joanna was forced to return to the beginning.

Twice more the same thing happened. "I think someone is trying to tell me something," she complained. "I guess it's folly for me to allow deep feelings."

Mandy reached across the table and squeezed her hands. "I think it surely refers to passions that run so high we are tempted to do immoral things."

Joanna nodded, afraid she'd revealed too much. This game made her feel like she was being warned against love.

It was again her turn. "I'm going to get out of the water for good this time." She flicked the spinner, and everyone groaned. The same number. The same destination. She didn't even bother counting it out.

"There's something wrong with this game," Levi said.

Everyone turned to him, demanding an explanation.

" 'Love.' You should land there and go directly to the Mansion of Happiness." He pulled Glory close and kissed her forehead.

Joanna groaned. "So you're saying if you fall in love you're there, but the rest of us have to work for it?"

"In your case, I think you need to avoid passion all together."

She laughed along with the rest of them, but it wasn't funny. Was she destined to live a life without love?

Chapter 14

H er birthday isn't until April." Freddy's voice was heavy with disappointment.

Rudy rubbed the boy's head. "Then we'll find some other special reason."

"What? It's too early for Christmas. What else is there?"

The tarp had been taken down. They were repairing the outside of the wall now and would soon be finished, which gave him an idea. "We could have a celebration when the wall is finished. That would be a special occasion, wouldn't it?"

"Oh yes." The boy jumped around. "I can hardly wait."

"Slow down. We want to do a good job." Plus, he wanted a reason to stay.

The game on Sunday had set him to thinking. Or rather, Levi's words had. Was love the way to happiness? Even if it was, how did one know it was real? Or that it could be trusted? He fought an internal war day after day, wanting on one hand to simply believe in the power of love—his love for Joanna—but fearing on the other hand that she didn't return his feelings.

If he revealed his love and she said she didn't love him, he would lose all hope. He wasn't sure he could survive such a disaster.

He purposely shifted his mind to other things. Freddy had come up with a nice gift for Joanna. Rudy would have to do the same if they meant to have a celebration, and seeing the pictures Austin had taken gave him an idea. He would go find Austin and discuss it with him.

Austin was most agreeable.

The next few days, Rudy worked steadily on the repairs. Although the days grew shorter and the nights colder, he knew he could finish before winter set in. As he hammered he continued to think of the "Mansion of Happiness." Perhaps happiness was a journey of many steps as the board game suggested, rather than one step away, as Levi said. Maybe he could slowly reveal his love for Joanna. One step at a time. It felt doable. Less risk. At any point he could pull back and protect his heart.

This celebration and his gift to her would be the first step.

Four days later, he was done.

"Can we celebrate tonight?" Freddy asked.

"Do you want to say something to Joanna about it?"

Freddy shook his head hard. "No. I want it to be a surprise."

"Okay. Then tonight after supper. Does that work?"

"Yup. Can I have some paper to wrap my present in?"

"I have to go to the store. I'll bring some back. Now help me put away all the tools; then you can sweep up while I take care of a few errands."

He helped Freddy for a few minutes then headed for the business district of Bonners Ferry, stopping at the store first. Then at Austin's.

"It's perfect," Rudy said. He'd come by Austin's studio several times to work on the finished product. Now he wrapped his surprise in brown store paper. "I'll give it to her tonight."

Austin grinned. "I'll take Cora out for a walk so you can be alone."

Freddy would be there, but Rudy would be as alone as he needed to be. This was only the first step.

He secreted his gift in his room while Joanna worked in the kitchen. He found Freddy and helped him wrap the fur and tie the parcel shut. Freddy hurried inside and stowed it in the bedroom. Since Freddy's accident, the two of them had stayed there every night.

That evening, he and Freddy washed up extra well and put on clean shirts for supper. Four guests had come to the stopping house for supper, so if Joanna wondered at their attire, she didn't comment.

After supper, he and Freddy helped with dishes. He pushed the table back and prepared the room for the guests and any others who might show up.

Austin dropped by to take Cora out and winked at Rudy in passing.

Suddenly Rudy wondered if he was doing the right thing. Too much, too soon? But he'd promised Freddy, who looked about ready to explode with anticipation.

Joanna let the guests in early because of the cold. They settled down gratefully in the dining room. Then she, Rudy, and Freddy retired to the kitchen.

Alone. Finally.

"The wall is repaired," Rudy noted.

"Just in time for winter." She smiled her approval. "Thanks."

"It's good and solid. I thought I might hang your washtubs inside for the winter." *Washtubs?* Why was he talking about washtubs? This wasn't what he'd planned. He knew Freddy wasn't impressed.

Rudy tried again. "We thought we should have a little party to celebrate the finished repairs."

Joanna's eyes sparkled. "What a good idea. I'll make hot chocolate, and we'll eat the rest of the cake."

Freddy's eyes gleamed. Rudy guessed he looked equally pleased. He lifted an eyebrow to ask Freddy if now was the time for presents.

Freddy shook his head. Apparently there was a right and a wrong way to do these things. Who knew?

"Business will likely be much slower now," Joanna said as they enjoyed the hot drink and thick slices of chocolate cake.

Rudy got the feeling she couldn't think of anything else to say.

Freddy finished his cake and nudged Rudy under the table. "Now?"

Freddy nodded.

Rudy pushed to his feet. "Excuse us a moment. We'll be right back." They hurried to the bedroom, picked up their packages, then returned to the kitchen.

Freddy went to her. "This is for you. It's a present."

Joanna paused, her forkful of cake in midair. "A present? What for?"

"Because we couldn't wait for your birthday," Freddy explained.

Joanna lifted a puzzled gaze to Rudy.

He wanted to say, "Because we love you." But his tongue wouldn't let him. He cleared his throat. "We just wanted to say how much we've appreciated your kindness."

There. That was the first step.

She studied him a moment longer, searching his gaze.

One step at a time, he cautioned, as words of love filled his heart. He shuffled forward enough to put his gift on the corner of the table.

She turned her attention to the package Freddy had handed her and carefully untied the strings and folded back the paper. "Ohh." She lifted the fur and pressed it to her cheek.

Rudy swallowed hard at the look of pleasure in her face.

"This is lovely, Freddy. Thank you."

Freddy practically turned inside out. "You can make a pillow or a muff."

"I certainly shall." She hugged Freddy and planted a kiss on his forehead.

The boy's smile could light a room.

Rudy dropped to the chair across the table. Of course she wouldn't hug him and kiss him. He shouldn't expect it. He shoved his parcel closer.

Smiling, she untied the strings, folded back the paper, and stared.

He tried to explain why he'd chosen this, but his mouth was so dry his tongue felt wooden.

She lifted it. "A picture of you and Freddy on horseback. It's beautiful."

"The stopping house behind us." He had insisted on it. He'd even made a frame so she could hang it. Suddenly it seemed crude. "Austin took the picture." At least she couldn't fault the photographer.

She held it at arm's length while Freddy peered over her shoulder. "It's absolutely perfect. Thank you."

Was it his imagination that her eyes seemed awash?

"I didn't know we were having a party with gifts, but I do have something for you." She set the picture on the table next to the fur and stepped out of the room.

Rudy stared at the gifts. Why had he thought this was a good idea?

Joanna returned. "I didn't have time to wrap them, but I made you these." She handed them each a pair of gray knitted mittens. "You'll need them once winter comes."

Freddy put on his and grinned. "Thank you. I really, really like them."

"Me, too," Rudy said, wondering if his voice sounded as thick as it felt. The mittens were nothing special. Made of heavy wool. Practical. But no one had ever made something especially for him. Did it mean she cared more than just friendship? Or was she just doing for them as she did for everyone—her sisters and the guests who came every day. She seemed to like taking care of people. "When did you have time?"

"A person can find a way if they want to."

The way she looked at him he wondered if she meant the mittens or something else.

Freddy yawned. "Guess I'll go to bed."

Rudy should go, too, but he couldn't make his feet move.

Joanna didn't speak until the door closed behind Freddy. "I can't believe you both did this." She ran her finger across the picture then smoothed the fur. "How did Freddy get the rabbit fur?"

"He ran into a man at the ferry selling furs."

"Selling?"

"I had the same thought. He traded his knife for it."

She gasped. "His knife. He loved that knife. Why would he do that?"

"He wanted you to know how much he cares for you." Would she realize his gift carried the same message?

"I'll cherish them both." Her voice seemed a little shaky. He wondered if she could feel his love.

She studied the picture again, tracing the frame with her finger. "The footloose cowboy and his nephew."

"Maybe not so footloose anymore." Maybe he'd found a reason to stay. "Joanna." He tried to think how to say he cared without blurting out words that would likely scare her into retreat. "You're a special woman."

She chuckled. "I'm not going to ask you to elaborate."

Good thing she didn't, but his brain did so anyway. She knew how to touch a person to make him feel valued. She made a person feel happy inside. "For one thing, you make the best pies."

"You sound like Freddy." Her smile seemed a little strained. She didn't look at him.

Maybe she didn't like thinking the only thing he appreciated was her cooking. "Course that's only one little thing."

She tilted her head.

He must stop there. "I suppose it's time for bed." He rose and swung from the chair while she got up and stepped away from the table. They arrived at the same spot in the kitchen at the same time and stopped inches from each other.

He couldn't stop himself from drowning in her gaze. *I love you.* Could she see it in his eyes, his expression? It was too soon to tell her. He must stick to his plan.

"It was a lovely evening. Thank you again for the picture." She stood on tiptoe and planted a kiss on his jaw.

The touch of her lips was like being struck by lightning. The kiss jolted through his veins and sent a blast of overheated air through his brain, practically frying it. The heat seared his tongue. He caught her arms, aching to kiss her. *Not yet.* It was too soon. He'd gone too far, too fast, last time, when Freddy was lost. They'd been awkward and ill at ease for days afterward.

He dropped his arms to his side and backed away. "Glad you like it. Thanks for the mittens." He fled from the room and lay fully clothed on the bed, waiting for his heartbeat to slow to a gallop.

It would be hours before his mind settled enough for him to fall asleep.

How was he going to measure out his journey to love—the Mansion of Happiness—one step at a time? But he would. He knew he could never take the fast route Levi talked about.

Because he was too uncertain. Too afraid.

He was a coward, but better a live coward than a dead hero. He didn't mean his body but his heart.

No, he'd take his time. Step two would be to suggest a partnership in running the stopping house.

Joanna stared after him. With a deep sigh she returned to the table to study the gifts. The picture of Rudy and Freddy was wonderful. She traced her finger over Rudy's face. Was this his way of saying good-bye? She stroked the silky fur Freddy had given her, her heart wooden within her chest. Were they about to move on?

But what had Rudy meant about not being so footloose anymore? He'd explained that Freddy meant his gift to say how much he cared.

Did Rudy's gift carry the same message?

A slow smile engulfed her face. Did he care about her but was afraid to say the words? She would let herself think so.

Tomorrow she would hang the picture on the new wall, where she could see it while she worked.

And she'd let herself dream that more was possible. That the footloose cowboy was considering hanging up his spurs.

She watched Rudy closely the next few days. He and Freddy chopped wood and then disappeared into the toolshed. She'd glanced in a few days ago and saw they were making a cart.

He'd said nothing about his feelings, but on the other hand, he'd not saddled his horse and ridden away.

She took that as a good sign.

Supper was almost ready. A trickle of men continued to pass through. Men determined to get in on the gold rush. She set the table and opened the door to welcome the guests.

Three filed by and dropped in their coins.

A fourth stopped in front of her. She glanced up to see what the man wanted and gasped. "Pa."

"Yup. Your old pappy's back." He nodded as if it was the best news in the world.

"Hi, Pa. No need for you to pay. You're my father." She waved him in. Rudy heard her, and his gaze drifted from Pa back to her, watchful.

She smiled. Rudy looked about ready to tell Pa it was time to start acting like a father. She lifted one shoulder. She'd long since given up expecting anything fatherly from him.

As she took care of her guests, she studied Pa. A big man with a hearty laugh. Black whiskers with a touch of gray along the edges. He was no longer a young man. It kind of surprised her to realize it.

The others finished and left the room. Pa lingered.

"You stay and visit." Rudy carried away the dishes to the kitchen, and he and Freddy started washing them.

"Jo, girl, I done got your letter saying your sisters got married. I take it they live nearby."

Funny how he seemed to get a letter from her, but they never got one from him. "They do." She told him about Glory and Levi's mission and the log house Trace and Mandy had built.

"Good to hear. Good to know you're close by to keep an eye out for them."

Joanna bristled. "They don't need me to watch over them anymore."

"Girl, as the oldest, you're responsible for them."

"You came all the way here just to tell me that?"

"Nope. In fact, I kind of figure now they have husbands maybe you can move on."

She kind of figured the same thing.

"You were always a good one to run a house. I figure you and me could join up. You can come with me and run my house now."

If she ever wondered whether she had her father's wanderlust, his offer convinced her otherwise. "Pa, I plan to settle down someplace."

"That a fact?"

"You're welcome to stay as long as you like. There's plenty of room here. I'll send a message to the others, and they'll come and visit tomorrow."

Her pa looked around. "Nice place you got here. I just might light awhile."

"You're always welcome." She wondered how long *awhile* would be this time.

Pa pushed away. "I'll join the others outside."

She waited until he left to release her pent-up emotion in a loud whoosh.

Rudy stood in the kitchen doorway, a towel around his waist. "Everything okay?"

She hesitated, not sure how to respond. "Everything is as usual."

He chuckled. "You mean he's here today, gone tomorrow?"

"I don't expect him to stay. If I had to guess, he's outside right now listening to tales of excitement and adventure. Having a family could never compete with that."

"Most men would disagree."

She crossed the room and stood close enough to wonder if she saw a flash of longing in his eyes. "Do you wish you had a family?" A wife?

"I have Freddy. That's the most family I've ever really had."

Their gazes held, searching past what was to what might have been. What might still be.

"Life is full of opportunities," she whispered. "If a person is willing to reach out for them."

He brushed her cheek with his knuckles. "Are you thinking about joining up with your pa?"

He'd misunderstood her meaning.

"Not at all." She pushed past him before she could demand to know why he was so blind to her love. She would put it in words but feared if she did it would scare him away.

She could only pray Pa wouldn't entice Rudy to join him in seeking adventure.

The next morning, Rudy took the message of their pa's visit to both of the sisters. They showed up at the stopping house a short time later, escorted by their husbands. Both men gave the older man accusing looks. They'd seen how his defection had hurt their wives. They wouldn't be letting him hurt them again.

Rudy felt the same way toward Joanna. If only he could prevent the man from saying or doing something to hurt her again.

Mandy was cautiously eager. "Hi, Pa. I knew you'd come back."

"Always do," the man said.

"Just about long enough to upset our lives, and then you're gone again." Glory wasn't the least bit welcoming.

At the way she flashed defiant looks at Levi, Rudy wondered if he'd dragged her down the hill.

They stayed and visited all afternoon, listening to their pa's stories of adventure and gold finds.

"I notice he doesn't seem to be offering any of his gold to the girls," Trace murmured as he went to the stove to pour himself a cup of coffee.

"I doubt he has any gold." Rudy had seen no evidence.

"Any idea how long he plans to stay?"

"Joanna says not long. He asked her to go with him."

Trace drew back and stared at Rudy. "She's not going, is she?"

"Told him she had other plans."

"Right. California."

"It's getting a little late in the season for that, isn't it?"

"I'd say she has a few days yet before she'll have to postpone the trip until spring."

Rudy lifted the stove lid and stirred the fire. He'd thought she wouldn't be leaving. . .that those plans had fallen through because of the fire. Surely she wouldn't leave while her pa was here.

Might be a good thing if the man hung around a bit.

Chapter 15

Five days later, Mr. Hamilton was still there. In fact, he'd settled in like he meant to put down roots.

Rudy had given up the bedroom for the man, even though the older man said he didn't mind sleeping on the floor. Rudy kind of hoped a comfortable bed would make him linger. . .just long enough to make travel west too risky.

He needed time to carry out his plans.

Maybe tonight he'd get an opportunity to talk to Joanna. Having her pa around served a purpose but made it harder and harder for Rudy to be alone with her. And oh, how he missed it.

The cart was finished. He thought he'd take her to the shed and show her what they'd made. That way he could more likely have a bit of time alone with her. He counted the hours.

The dining room door opened, letting in a draft of cold air. Winter edged closer every night.

"Hello, Joanna. Are you there?" A woman's voice filled the air.

Rudy looked up from the bench he was constructing along the new wall. It would give her a sturdy place to set the laundry tubs.

"Sarah." Joanna squealed and dashed for the door. "What are you doing here?" She dragged a very pretty young woman into the kitchen. A black coat covered most of what she wore, allowing only a glimpse of a white blouse and dark skirt with a plain vest to match. An inadequate number of pins corralled her mass of blond hair so that much of it tumbled to her shoulders and beyond. Her blue eyes flashed with interest while she looked around. Her gaze lit on Rudy as he hunkered down, securing the bench to the wall.

"Hello. You must be Rudy. Joanna mentioned you in her letters. I'm her friend Sarah. I've come to convince her to join me in traveling to California."

Rudy rose slowly, wiped his hand on his pants, and decided against shaking. Instead, he nodded. "Pleased to meet you." Though *pleased* was not the right word. He didn't want someone pulling Joanna away.

"Sit down and tell me everything." Joanna filled the kettle and sliced a piece of cake for her guest.

"You go first." Sarah took in the new wall. "Is that where the fire was?" Her gaze rested forcefully on Rudy, and she measured him.

He drew himself tall, somehow knowing he must pass inspection.

"Rudy's done a good job of rebuilding it."

"It looks finished." Sarah's words rang with conviction. "No reason to stay in Bonners Ferry."

"Unfortunately, the sale fell through."

"So you said." Sarah again measured Rudy. What was she scheming?

"I haven't had time to write and let you know Pa showed up."

That got Sarah's attention. "Here? How long is he staying?"

"He doesn't say, but even if he did, I wouldn't expect him to settle anywhere. But you know, he's getting older."

"Maybe he prefers a nice warm house for the winter."

"Maybe."

"So let's talk about this California trip."

"Sarah, I thought you'd be gone by now. If you delay too long, you'll have to wait until spring."

"I have no intention of spending a snowy, cold winter here when I could enjoy sunshine and warm ocean breezes."

"I'm sorry I've caused you so much wasted time."

"That's why I'm here. To get you to reconsider. It seems to me, there's a way you can arrange your affairs so you can leave. With your pa here, there's no reason you can't leave him in charge until another buyer comes along."

Rudy stared at Sarah. He shifted to meet Joanna's gaze. Her eyes were wide. Did this mean she welcomed Sarah's suggestion?

That blond woman had no right to come and put a wrench in his plans.

Rudy grabbed the hammer and jerked open the outside door. He would not stay and listen to them. He stomped to the shed, put the hammer away, and stared at the finished cart. So much for a moment alone with Joanna tonight. So much for taking one step at a time toward the Mansion of Happiness.

Freddy was down at the ferry, one of his favorite places, talking to the ferryman.

The place closed in around Rudy. He saddled his horse and rode away as fast as he could.

He rode south, retracing the journey that brought him here weeks ago. He'd come looking for his brother, Joe, intent on turning Freddy over to him then riding back to his own life.

He now realized his rootless life was his way of running from his emotions. He realized a number of things had changed for him. He no longer looked at his past with the same amount of pain. He loved Freddy as if he were his own.

He reached a spot that allowed him to stare into the distance and reined up to contemplate.

Freddy was now part of his life.

Joanna owned a large portion of his heart.

She'd convinced him to read the Bible. One verse clung to his thoughts. *"I have loved thee with an everlasting love."*

He knew it was true because God said it, and God wasn't like men to say one thing but mean another. He thought of something Levi said in one of his sermons. *"We must know in order to believe. Then we must believe in order to know."* He'd gone on to explain how we might puzzle about the truths in the Bible, but to claim them for ourselves we have to make a choice to believe as well.

Rudy knew God meant it when He said He loved him.

All there was left to do was believe it. *God, I believe You love me.*

Light seemed to fill his heart. Yes, God loved him. Had loved him all the years he'd spent running. What a waste.

Exactly.

He wasn't about to waste another day. He headed back to Bonners Ferry.

∽

"I can't go," Joanna insisted again as Sarah continued to try her persuasive arguments. Yes, it was possible she could leave the stopping house in Pa's care or even ask Austin and Cora to run the place until it sold.

But if she left, how could she ever hope her love for Rudy would have a chance? So often she saw something in his eyes that gave her hope. On more than one occasion she'd been certain he was about to say something. Each time he jerked back. Afraid.

She understood his fear. Shared it to some degree.

Loving required a willingness to take a risk. Both of them had been hurt by unrequited love, and it had made them cautious.

She was willing to allow him all the time he needed.

But when he rode out of the yard in a hot hurry, her heart clambered up the back of her throat and stuck there. She'd only been able to breathe normally when she saw Freddy down at the ferry. Rudy wouldn't go without him.

She listened to Sarah's excited plans and answered questions, but a good portion of her mind waited for Rudy to return. Would she always live with this fear that he'd ride out without a backward look?

Not until she heard him ride into the yard and enter the dining room did her lungs relax.

Sarah tapped Joanna's elbow. "I said, my aunt says there are plenty of opportunities. There's a position for a housekeeper in one of the fancy hotels, if you're interested."

Joanna managed to bring a portion of her thoughts back to the conversation. "I can't go."

Sarah sighed impatiently. "What's holding you back?"

Joanna shook her head. She wasn't about to confess she loved a footloose cowboy and hoped he returned her love.

She heard Rudy moving around the dining room; then his footsteps headed for the door. He opened and closed it. His boots thudded on the porch. Then his horse whinnied.

Joanna sprang to the window. Rudy sat in the saddle, his bags in his hand. He reined around and rode from the yard.

She fell back into her chair. What was holding her back? Nothing. But her throat closed off so she couldn't answer Sarah.

Glory clattered into the kitchen at that moment. "Hi, Sarah. Come to say good-bye to Jo?"

"No. I've come to convince her to go with me. After all, what's to keep her here?"

"You mean besides her lovely sisters, the stopping house, and a man who adores her?"

"What are you talking about?" Sarah's eyes narrowed as if she meant to take care of such a man.

"She's talking nonsense," Joanna managed to squeak out.

"Oh, come on. I've seen the way Rudy looks at you."

"Yes, well, he just packed his bags and rode out. He's leaving." Just like Pa always did.

"He's moving into my shop." Glory crossed her arms, a satisfied look on her face.

Joanna's mouth fell open. She couldn't speak. But a question hammered at the inside of her head, and she forced her tongue to work. "Why?"

Glory snorted. "Seems that's a question you should ask him yourself." She planted her face a few inches from Joanna's. "Unless you're too afraid."

"I'm not afraid." But she was.

"Of course you are. Love is risky. But let me tell you, it's worth it. And not everyone is as careless about our feelings as Pa. Now, I can't promise you that Rudy won't want to move on at some point. But so what if he does? Marry him and go with him. You know moving on isn't so hard. We've done it dozens of times. So stop running from what's in your heart. Go to him. Ask him what he thinks, how he feels." She waited. "Go."

Joanna hesitated.

Glory pulled her to her feet. "Now."

Joanna managed to make her legs move toward the door. What if she told Rudy she cared, and he laughed? But then, what did she have to lose except the possibility of love?

"Sarah, I'll be back. Wait for me." She stepped from the landing, her feet already moving at a good clip. By the time she reached Glory's shop she was at full gallop. Not even bothering to knock, she burst in and skidded to a halt, panting for air.

Rudy stood next to a row of freshly dusted shelves, his hat on his head. "I was just about to step out."

"Oh." That didn't sound very welcoming. Maybe this little visit wasn't a good idea.

"Yup. Going to find you and tell you I'm staying."

Joanna started breathing again. "You could continue to stay at the stopping house."

"Could, I guess. But seems if I'm going to court you properly, I shouldn't be under the same roof."

"Court?" Her hopes raced for the sky. "You're going to court me?"

His expression grew guarded. "If you'll let me."

She chuckled. "Rudy Canfield, I think it's time we stopped tiptoeing around what we feel. Or at least, what I know I feel and what I think you feel." She swallowed. "It's hard to put our hearts on the line when we've been hurt so many times. But some things are worth the risk. Rudy, I love you." There. She'd said it. She met his gaze boldly, waiting his reply.

An array of emotions chased across his face. Surprise widened his eyes. Uncertainty drew worry lines across his forehead. Hope smoothed them away then belief brought joy to his face and lifted the corners of his mouth. "You love me?" He let out a whoop that made her jump; then he grabbed her shoulders. "Joanna, I love you. With my whole heart. I never want to leave you. Ever."

Her heart took flight like a happy meadowlark. Her eyes filled with tears of joy. And her smile claimed a large portion of her face. "How long have you known?"

"I fought it for a long time because I didn't believe anyone could love me."

She smoothed her hands over his stubbly cheeks. "Loving you isn't hard."

He turned his mouth to her palm and kissed it. "I think I started to love you the day you stomped into my campsite and demanded justice for a stolen pie." He grabbed her hands and pressed them to his chest. "When did you start loving me?"

"I loved you from the start. In fact, I think I've been loving you long before we met."

He blinked his confusion.

"I needed a man who knew how to love me past the hurts. That was you. I have waited for you most of my life."

"Joanna, I love you. Can I court you?"

"You could do better than that. You could marry me."

Both of them laughed and sealed their love with a kiss.

A month later

P a, you look just fine." Joanna admired her father. He'd shaved and donned new clothes for the wedding.

"You remind me of your mother in that dress." His eyes shone with tears. "She was one good woman."

"Yes, she was." It no longer hurt to think of how Pa had worn their mother out, dragging her from place to place. Her mother did it out of love. She'd do the same for Rudy though, for now, he wanted to stay and run the stopping house.

She smiled at her sisters, who both wore dresses for the occasion.

"I hope this is the last time," Glory said. "These skirts and petticoats tangle around my ankles and about trip me up."

Mandy laughed. "They don't look right on you either." Then before Glory could start a ruckus, she turned to Joanna. "But you look radiant in that dress."

Joanna went to the mirror. She'd gone shopping in Sand Point with Sarah. All the wedding dresses were too fancy for her. She couldn't imagine wearing one. When she saw this gown of blue sprigged lawn, called a summer dress, she decided she could be comfortable in it for an afternoon and even wear it again, should the occasion arise.

Rudy had assured her he would be happy to marry her in a split skirt. "I love you as you are."

"Thank you, but I think my mother would be pleased to think I wore a dress for my wedding." She said the same to her sisters, and both agreed. In fact, they both said they would wear dresses for the same reason.

This was for Mother.

Glory and Mandy sauntered up the aisle.

Joanna took Pa's arm and stepped into the church.

Rudy stood at the front, Freddy at his side. Rudy wore a white shirt and black jacket that he'd borrowed from Levi. He looked extremely handsome, but it was the look in his eyes that held her attention. Love—pure, simple, and enduring.

She didn't recall walking the length of the aisle, nor could she say who sat in the pews. But she would never forget the moment her arm rested on Rudy's, and they exchanged their vows.

Levi pronounced them man and wife.

Rudy kissed her gently, reverently, then they faced their friends and family.

"I have waited all my life for this kind of love," Rudy whispered. "I will never stop thanking God for it."

She smiled up at him. She would never grow weary of hearing how much he loved her. Nor would she ever stop telling him.

Both of them had found the love they wanted and needed.

To God be the glory.

Linda Ford draws on her own experiences living in the Canadian prairie and Rockies to paint wonderful adventures in romance and faith. She lives in Alberta, Canada, with her family, and she writes as much as her full-time job of taking care of a paraplegic and four kids, who are still at home, will allow. Linda says, "I thank God that He has given me a full, productive life and that I'm not bored. I thank Him for placing a little bit of the creative energy revealed in His creation into me, and I pray I might use my writing for His honor and glory."